SHE WAS THERE TO BE MADE LOVE TO

Here in this tropical haven.

Buck pulled Cory down to sit on the warm dry sand, and his strong hand slid around to encircle the back of her neck. His lips sought hers, assured and demanding, and desire flamed in her as she strained against him.

His hands began to slide her dress from her shoulders. "Take it off," he coaxed.

Cory stood up and the dress fell to the ground. Her dark half-slip gleamed in the reflected light from the water. Fantasy turned it into a grass skirt. The crushed but still fragrant plumeria blossoms around her neck half covered, half revealed the rise and fall of her bare breasts.

"Beautiful," Buck whispered as he stepped toward her, his arms outstretched.

D1311125

Books by Lucy Lee

SUPERROMANCES

10—HEART'S FURY
44—THE RITE OF LOVE
93—HEART'S PARADISE

These books may be available at your local bookseller.

For a free catalog listing all titles currently available,
send your name and address to:

Harlequin Reader Service
P.O. Box 52040, Phoenix, AZ 85072-9988
Canadian address: Stratford, Ontario N5A 6W2

LUCY LEE

HEART'S PARADISE

A SUPERROMANCE FROM
WORLDWIDE

TORONTO · NEW YORK · LONDON · PARIS
AMSTERDAM · STOCKHOLM · HAMBURG
ATHENS · MILAN · TOKYO · SYDNEY

Published December 1983

First printing October 1983

ISBN 0-373-70093-8

CHAPTER ONE

CORINNE WELLS WAS JUGGLING a bag of groceries and taking her apartment key from her purse when she heard the shrill ringing of her phone. Hurriedly she fought to open the door and rushed to pick up the receiver.

"Hello?" she said breathlessly.

"Cory! Thank heavens you've come home!" Her friend Ann's voice sounded in Cory's ear. "What made you so late?"

"I stopped to buy food," Cory said calmly. "What's wrong?"

"Oh, the most terrible thing!" Ann exclaimed. "I just got a letter from my aunt!"

"Your aunt in Hawaii? Is...is she sick?"

"She's broken her hip! She wants me to come out there and stay with her till she can walk again!" Ann's voice ended in a wail.

"That doesn't seem too terrible," Cory ventured.

"It is!" The wail increased in volume. "I can't leave my job now! I've been promised a promotion! I can't disappear for two months. Not to mention the fact that things are going rather well between Dave and me," she added with a certain smugness that sent a twinge of envy along Cory's spine.

"I see what you mean," she agreed thoughtfully.

"But what can I do?" Ann cried. "I can't *not* go. She's the only relative I have. Oh, why did this have to happen *now*?"

"Take Dave with you," Cory suggested jokingly. "Maybe you can turn it into a honeymoon."

"I may be able to take Dave, but I can't take my job!" Ann was indignant. "The worst of it is, in my last letter I told Aunt Hazel I was considering quitting. I never thought the promotion would come through. She says that's why she didn't hesitate to ask me. And, of course, it is Hawaii, and most people would jump at the chance."

"I know I would!" Cory agreed.

"You would?" Ann's voice sounded suddenly alert.

"Two months in Hawaii. . . away from the miserable cold and rain of northern New Jersey in November and December. Who wouldn't?"

"Hey, then, you go! In my place!"

"You're kidding!"

"I'm not! I'm deadly serious."

"But I was just talking in general." Even as she said the words Cory was conscious of a stirring of excitement. How marvelous to go someplace far away, leaving all her heartbreak behind—if that was possible.

"*I'm* not talking in general! I'm talking about you!" Ann cut into Cory's thoughts. "You've never had a real vacation since I've known you. You didn't go away after your mother died because you met that swine—"

"But your aunt doesn't want *me*," Cory protested. "Besides, what about my job?"

"Oh, to heck with your job! Ask for a leave of absence. That's what I'd have to do. My aunt won't care whether it's you or me. She needs someone to help her. Period. Cory, it wouldn't cost you a thing! She'll pay the plane fare and the grocery bills. And she has a spare bedroom."

Trying to ignore the excitement beginning to rise in her, Cory asked cautiously, "What kind of help does she need?"

"Just do a little shopping and maybe get a couple of meals a day. That's all. Errands...that sort of thing. She says—wait a minute, I'll read it to you.... Oh, Cory, this is suddenly exciting! It would be perfect for you!"

"It would certainly be something not to run into Paul and his new girl friend every time I go anywhere," Cory agreed bitterly. "I just saw them at the supermarket, of all places. I wanted to die."

"Exactly," Ann agreed. "Here—" She began reading: "'Miki, who does my cleaning, can't drive, and there will be other errands—bank, post office, etc.' When she wrote this she was still in the hospital, but she's getting out October 31—Halloween. That's only one week! Oh, Cory, what am I going to do? If I leave now, they'll say—" her voice dropped pontifically "—'That's what happens when we hire a frivolous female instead of a steady man.'"

"I guess there isn't really any reason why I

couldn't go," Cory said slowly, "if your aunt would want me—"

"Really?" Ann squeaked. "Of course she'll want you! You're a much better driver than I am. A much better companion, for that matter. Responsible. And calm. And you're used to caring for an invalid—"

Cory made a wry face at the receiver and then felt guilty, though she had no reason. She'd done the best she could while her mother was alive. Now her mother was gone, and she could think of no reason why she couldn't go to Hawaii. Paul had made it perfectly clear that he didn't want her.

Her boss at the bank would object. She smiled at the thought of his consternation. Maybe, by the time she returned, he'd appreciate the work she did as supervisor of the credit department. If not, there were other banks.

"Do you really mean it, Cory?" Ann was beginning to doubt the easy solution to her problem. "Will you consider it?"

"I'll think about it while I get my dinner. I'll call you later."

"Great!" Ann suddenly sounded on top of the world. "I'll be thinking about how to put it to Aunt Hazel."

While she worked in the kitchen Cory tried to bring to mind reasons why she could not suddenly take off for Hawaii for two months, or even three. The basics would be paid for, so she could afford to continue to pay the rent on her apartment, the telephone and the utilities out of her savings. Was her life really so empty that she could pull up stakes at a moment's notice? Apparently it was. Now, anyway. Of course, all the time her mother was crippled and in a wheel-chair, she hadn't been able to go anywhere, except to work. And then, shortly after her mother's death she had met Paul, and she hadn't wanted to go anywhere away from him.... Resolutely she brought her thoughts back to the present. Why shouldn't she go? She would have to arrange to do something with her car.

A cold rain had begun to fall. She could hear it splattering against the living-room windows. She went to look, then stood watching wet leaves drop glistening onto wet pavement. In Hawaii— Dare she think what it would be like there? Ann's Aunt Hazel would undoubtedly say no to having anyone but her niece. Cory stood with her forehead pressed against the window. She was a slim young woman of medium height, her long ash-blond hair pale in the unlighted room. Her eyes, large, brown and trusting, made her look younger than her twenty-four years. They seemed to say that her life was calm and dutiful. During the five years since her mother's accident she had become adept at hiding any wild and rebellious wishes. All wide-eyed and innocent she had met Paul. After that experience she was determined to be cool and calculating. Underneath the smooth surface, anger seethed. Hell could freeze over before she trusted a man again.

She turned back to the kitchen. Such opportunities to escape didn't happen in real life. Nevertheless, while she ate her solitary meal she brought the atlas to the table and allowed herself to study the Hawaiian islands.

What people on the East Coast knew about the fiftieth state was shockingly little. Honolulu, of course, was the capital, and Waikiki was a favourite tourist destination. She wondered which of the seven inhabited islands Aunt Hazel lived on. They had such exotic names—Hawaii, Maui, Oahu, Kauai, Molokai, Lanai, Niihau. The thought of going there changed from crazy to enticing.

While she was asking herself dreamily which suitcase she would take, the phone rang. Picking it up, she heard Ann's urgent voice. "Are you still thinking of going?"

Cory laughed a little wildly. "I guess so. I haven't thought of any reason why I can't go—if she wants me. Have you thought of what to say to her?"

"I've thought, and I've said it!" Ann's voice rang triumphantly. "I've just finished talking to her. She wants you to come. She's wiring money for your fare."

Cory gulped. "You—you telephoned her?"

"I phoned her at the hospital."

"What excuse did you give for not going?"

"I told her the boss is beginning to take me seriously. She understood perfectly. Guess what time it is out there?"

"The middle of the night?" Cory felt as though she were in the middle of a dream.

"No, silly, it's the other way. It's three in the afternoon. Aunt Hazel wants to know how soon you can come. I promised to call her back.

AT THE HONOLULU AIRPORT, a still-dazed Cory transferred from the big jet to the prop plane that took small contingents of passengers to the island of Kauai.

In the past nine days she had learned something about her hostess and her destination. Hazel McNab was Ann's father's much older sister, a librarian nearing retirement. Kauai was pronounced "cow-why." The farthest to the northwest of the major islands, it was called the Garden Isle, and the movie *South Pacific* had been filmed there.

Cory had left Newark airport early that morning, but despite long hours of flying, the time in Honolulu was early afternoon. She was being met on Kauai by two of Hazel's friends. They would deliver her and her luggage to Aunt Hazel's condominium.

At the end of the half-hour flight the plane banked in a turn. Suddenly the expanse of rippled water below ended and lines of white surf rolled toward sandy beaches. Green fields were backed by small green mountains—a lush lovely landscape on a small gentle scale. Cory felt a choke in her throat. The sight was beautiful, and unexpectedly welcoming.

Leaving the plane she followed the other passengers to the baggage pickup area, a roofed-over slab with benches. While she waited for her suitcase to be unloaded, she looked eagerly around. Fields of sugarcane surrounded the airport. White puffy clouds hovered over the jagged green mountains. She could see the ocean across the airfield. It made her very aware that she had landed on an island. In the shade the temperature was that of a perfect summer's day.

All around her people were being met, climbing into cars and driving away. She eyed the remaining bystanders curiously. Could any of them be Aunt Hazel's friends?

She didn't mind waiting. Just looking around was exhilarating, breathing the clean air, feeling the soft breeze caress her face. Her body, confined too long in one position, seemed to demand both rest and exercise. Watching the baggage being unloaded, she was struck by the quiet—no shouts, no raised voices.

I like it here already, she thought with surprise.

She reclaimed her single large suitcase and was removing her suit jacket when a big dark green car pulled up and two tanned, gray-haired ladies emerged, wearing slacks and looking very much at ease. Aunt Hazel's friends, without doubt. They came smilingly toward her.

"You must be Hazel's niece," the taller one said.

"Her niece's friend," the other corrected. "Corinne. Is that right?" She was carrying a long loop of creamy-white flowers.

"Yes, Corinne Wells." Cory smiled back.

The woman raised the loop of flowers and put it over Cory's head to hang around her neck. "Welcome to Hawaii, my dear." She kissed Cory on both cheeks.

"Thank you," Cory whispered, touched by the unexpected gesture.

The lady patted her hand. "I'm Mae Bower and this is my sister, Irene."

Irene was the slimmer, younger and livelier of the two. After an exchange of hellos she picked up Cory's heavy suitcase before Cory could protest, and carried it to the trunk of the car.

"Are you exhausted?" Mae asked. "We're driving you straight to Hazel's. I'm sure all you want to do is take a bath and go to bed. How many hours ago did you leave New Jersey?"

"Early this morning. I've lost track somewhere. And yes, I am tired," she admitted.

They put her in the front seat. Irene got behind the wheel and they set out. Cory sank back with relief, fingering the waxy white blossoms of the lei. The perfume from the flowers' golden centers filled the car. "These smell heavenly," she said.

"Plumeria," Irene told her.

"What a beautiful way to welcome people."

"Well, it's a pleasure for us to welcome you," Mae Bower assured her from the back seat. "We're so glad you could come to Hazel."

"You won't have a bit of trouble getting along with her," Irene promised, maneuvering the car onto the highway. "She wants you to enjoy yourself while you're here and not be tied down to waiting on her."

"And if there's anything we can do to help, you must call us," Mae added.

"This is Kauai's main road," Irene said of the two-lane highway they were driving on. "It goes most of the way around the island, except for the

Na Pali Coast. That's a stretch of green sea cliffs and valleys that's inaccessible by car.''

"I read a little about Kauai in one of the guidebooks," Cory offered.

"Good! Then you know the basics," Irene approved.

"I think so. The book said almost everyone lives around the island's rim and the interior is given over to sugarcane and wild pigs and goats?"

"True enough," Mae agreed.

The road ran within sight of the shore, and Cory caught glimpses of dark blue water. Between the succession of villages, fields of tall, grasslike plants prompted her to ask, "Is that sugarcane?"

"Indeed it is," Irene said.

They passed a red dirt road leading off at a right angle.

"Those side roads are what we call haul cane roads," Irene added. "They're private roads between fields for the use of sugar plantation trucks and machinery."

Cory stole a glance at her watch. Four o'clock! She wouldn't be able to go to bed for hours yet.

Somewhat belatedly she asked, "How is Miss McNab feeling?" She turned in her seat to address both sisters.

Mae answered. "Coming along as well as you could expect. She'll be walking in a few weeks. I broke my hip two years ago. It was a nuisance, but I recovered."

They drove in silence, Cory too tired to make conversation. Their route left the highway and entered a tunnel of trees.

"How beautiful!" Cory gasped.

The road emerged from the trees to become a street with single-story shops scattered along one side.

"This is Hala's main street," Irene said. "Hazel lives in one of the new condominiums."

Cory glimpsed wooden houses and tree-filled yards. Then the car entered what looked like the grounds of an estate, and pulled into a parking space beneath a long low building. Flowering bushes instead of walls screened the parked cars from view.

"Here we are." Irene insisted on carrying Cory's suitcase. Cory carried her tote bag, purse and jacket.

"Hazel's condo is on the second floor," Mae explained, leading the way.

"She'll have to learn to manage stairs again," Irene added.

They pressed a buzzer and a small Oriental woman flung the door wide.

"Hello, Miki," the sisters greeted her. "Here we are."

"Come in, come in. Miss McNab waiting," the woman said, wresting the heavy suitcase from Irene.

Mae performed introductions, and Cory and Miki smiled at each other.

Inside Miki set aside the suitcase and reached for Cory's tote bag and jacket, saying, "Go meet. I put everything in your room."

From the corner of her eye Cory was surprised to see both Irene and Mae kick off their expensive leather sandals and pad barefoot into the living room. Cory trod hesitantly across thick white wall-to-wall carpeting.

A cheerful-looking woman with short iron-gray hair was seated on a red couch.

"Here she is, Hazel," Irene was saying.

Sharp gray eyes inspected Cory as Hazel McNab extended her hand. "I'm so grateful to you for coming all this way. Pardon me for not getting up, but you understand why I can't."

"I'm grateful to you, Miss McNab, for letting me come." Cory found herself smiling naturally.

"Good! Then we shall both be grateful to each other and get along just fine." She laughed and Cory recognized a family likeness to Ann. "Sit down a moment and then Miki will show you your room and you can take a nap or a bath, or both, if you like. Ah, I see someone welcomed you with a lei! I should have thought of that!"

"Mae's the thoughtful one, as you know," Irene said. "However—" she turned to Cory "—we're all delighted you could come. Mae, doesn't she remind you of Emma Lassiter? Not her features, exactly, but the color of her hair and something about the shape of her face.... She's about her size, too, as I remember."

Cory tried not to look self-conscious.

"I thought so as soon as I saw her," Mae agreed. "Hazel, you remember who we're talking about?"

"Oh, yes." From her serious tone the memory was something she didn't want to be associated with.

Irene sensed the change of atmosphere and rose. "Hazel, I think we should leave so you two can get acquainted. Let us know if we can do anything."

"We will," Hazel McNab promised. She looked at Cory. "I'm sure you'd rather rest than anything else."

"I think I would," Cory agreed.

The room to which Miki led Cory made her breath catch. The first thing she saw was sliding glass doors, outside of which lay a wide stretch of lawn ending in a hedge of some tropical plant. Just beyond, blue water sparkled.

"Is that the beach?" Cory gasped.

"Yes, very handy!" Miki laughed. "This your bathroom." She opened a door. "Miss McNab have her own. You like tea?"

Cory chose instead a long, hot bath, at the end of which drowsiness overcame her. In her underwear she stretched luxuriously on the double bed and fell asleep. When she woke, the sky outside was pale gray and gold. Sunset! Hastily pulling shorts and a T-shirt from her suitcase, she dressed and padded barefoot to the living room.

Hazel McNab was reading by lamplight. She was wearing a full sleeveless dress in a gay red-and-white print. Beneath the long skirt her feet were bare. Rimless glasses glinted as she looked up.

"Feeling better?"

"Much better. But I didn't mean to go to sleep."

"I'm sure you needed it. I thought we'd make everything simple this evening and have TV dinners.

Do you mind? I had Miki buy two with fried chicken.''

"Sounds wonderful," Cory agreed, glad, since she still felt groggy, that she didn't have to grope her way around a strange kitchen.

"Drink first? You'll find liquor on the sideboard and white wine in the refrigerator. I'll have Scotch over ice, if you don't mind getting it, please.''

Leaving the frozen dinners to heat in the oven, Cory poured the drinks, selecting sherry for herself, then joined her hostess.

"Now tell me all about Ann," Miss McNab directed, "and by the way, you must call me Hazel. Everyone uses first names here, even business people. What do you think of this new boyfriend? Have you met him?''

Cory was happy to be able to give a good report, both of Dave and of the wonderful prospects of Ann's job as a city planning engineer.

As they finished eating, Hazel said, "Now you mustn't take your duties too seriously. All I need tomorrow is some books from the library, and we'll need some things from the supermarket. Then maybe you'd like to try out the beach.''

Cory's brown eyes sparkled. "I can't believe I'm really here!''

Hazel nodded understandingly, and a moment later when Cory stifled a yawn, she added, "Do go to bed whenever you like. It would be after midnight in New Jersey. You'll want to leave the door to the lanai open for air. Back home we'd call it a balcony, but here it's a lanai.''

Cory disposed of the frozen dinner trays and went gratefully to her bedroom. She slipped into the summery nightgown that Ann had given her as a going-away present. In the seconds before she fell asleep she was struck by the silence. Except for the sound of waves striking the beach, all was quiet. No hum of traffic, no horns or shouts, no barking dogs or radios. Only crickets. Perhaps she had left her heartache behind, too. She hadn't thought of Paul all day.

CORY WOKE WITH a feeling of excitement. Beyond the sliding screen door the sky was still dark. The clock on the bedside table said 5:00 A.M. Feeling perfectly rested, she sprang out of bed and began unpacking. She hadn't brought a lot of clothes, partly because most of her summer things had suddenly looked shabby. In addition, she'd had trouble believing that warm weather wear was all she'd need, so she had come prepared to add to her wardrobe here.

She hung some of her things in the empty closet and put the rest into drawers. At the last minute she had included a small sketchbook along with an artist's pen and a selection of pencils. She had always enjoyed making small delicately detailed drawings of interesting landscapes, and now the opportunity to draw graceful coconut palms and other new kinds of foliage excited her.

Finally she put on the shorts and T-shirt she had donned yesterday, and crept out to the kitchen to make coffee and familiarize herself with the contents of the cupboards.

By the time Hazel emerged from her bedroom with the aid of an aluminum walker, Cory had the table set and bacon and eggs ready to cook.

Over breakfast Hazel said, "You mustn't think you have to fix three meals a day for me. I'll get my own breakfast and lunch; I need the exercise. If you fix our dinner and shop for groceries, the rest of the time will be your own. After supper is a good time to run the dishwasher. If you'll fetch the wooden box on my dresser, I'll give you a set of keys for the car and the door and the mailbox. And there's a map of Kauai on the coffee table." She smiled. "Not that you could get lost. I should mention, though, that drivers here don't use their horns except in emergencies."

"No wonder it's so blessedly quiet!" Cory exclaimed.

"You won't see billboards, either, anywhere in Hawaii. Most people here respect the natural scenery."

"How marvelous!" In retrospect Cory realized she hadn't seen any ugly signs.

With directions and shopping list she went downstairs to find Hazel's car, a bright blue compact. Cautiously she set out.

The morning was still fresh, the air unexpectedly clear for so warm a day. White clouds hovered above the sharp mountains. Everywhere she looked she saw flowers in unexpected places—red hibiscus on hedges, white blossoms on trees, and then a twiggy tree ablaze with orange clusters. She started to laugh. "I can hardly believe it, but I'm really, really here!" she said aloud.

She pulled into the library's parking lot and looked appreciatively at the flowering bushes. Inside at the desk the girl was wearing a long dress similar to Hazel's. Real Hawaiian muumuus, apparently, were floor-length. Cory noted the sandals the girl was wearing. Back east they were called rubber thongs or shower shoes.

Before leaving the condominium Cory had mentioned changing into slacks.

"Don't bother," Hazel had said. "People wear shorts everywhere here. With legs like yours, it's downright selfish to cover them up."

On the way to the library Cory had seen a delivery truck driver, two high-school youths and an elderly man all with bare legs. But their legs were so brown! She glanced at her own pale limbs. She wouldn't be long in remedying that, she thought, and was thankful that she could take her time and acquire a tan instead of a sunburn.

She drove slowly back to Hazel's and carried in the books and groceries.

"Any trouble with the car?" Hazel asked.

"It drives like a dream," Cory pronounced.

She took her sketch pad when she went to the beach, mainly to have something to give her attention to so she wouldn't feel self-conscious sitting alone. When she had donned her one-piece suit and was ready to set out, Hazel made sure Cory had a good sunscreen lotion and told her to take a mat to sit on—one of the woven tatami mats that stood rolled in a basket on the lanai.

"I can't believe that all I have to do to go to the

beach is walk across the lawn!'' Cory exulted.

"That's all," Hazel said. "However, you might want to walk down the beach to the hotel where there are more people, and a lifeguard. You can see the surfers better from there, too. Don't stay out too long. Remember, this is your first day."

Cory crossed the grass and stepped through the double row of head-high plantings and onto the sand. She thrilled at the sight of the curve of beach, the coconut palms leaning against the sky and the white foam of breaking surf far out on the blue water. She stood still, absorbing the beauty of the scene and savoring the surprising luck that had brought her here.

An unwelcome thought intruded: *If Paul hadn't dumped me, I wouldn't be here.* She sighed. Paul had been the most wonderful thing that had ever happened to her. But she couldn't have him, so Hawaii was going to be a wonderful second best. Determinedly she put him out of her mind and set off along the water's edge toward a sprinkling of people stretched on the sand at the head of the crescent-shaped cove.

A row of trees along the edge of the hotel lawn cast protective shade over a long strip of sand.

Cory spread her mat near a dark-haired young woman who already had a perfect tan, dropped her bag and towel on the mat, and moved bravely toward the water.

Drawing a breath, she stepped in and nearly laughed aloud. The water was warm! Hardly cooler than the air!

She plunged in, swam for a bit and then floated on her back, looking up at the pale blue sky dotted with white clouds. Turning her head slightly she caught sight of the coconut palms rising above all the other greenery. What perfect symbols they were of tropical islands!

I'd like to stay here forever.

The thought came out of nowhere—perhaps from the depths of her subconscious, because consciously she hadn't been there long enough to make such a decision. Yet how long did it take to fall in love with a place—an island? She felt the tug at her heart when the plane came in to land. The thought of New Jersey was bitter.

She swam vigorously for several minutes, enjoying the use of muscles that demanded to be stretched. More than once the taste of saltwater surprised her. Warm water seemed to mean a swimming pool.

What a pleasure it was to realize she didn't have to overdo swimming today. The beach and the warm weather would be here tomorrow and the next day. She walked dripping to her mat and enjoyed the touch of the rough dry towel on her arms and legs. She twisted her long pale hair into a thick roll out of her way. Hiding her brown eyes behind dark lenses, she stretched out on her mat to begin her tan and observe the people around her.

How quiet and relaxed everyone was! Just a flick of the imagination was needed to turn all these pink-skinned people into happy Polynesians; the clean beach and warm blue water part of their heritage.

Mine, too, if I lived here, she thought involuntarily.

The next few days flew by between running errands, cooking dinner and spending mornings at the beach. Nevertheless, Cory found time to look at ads for employment and was shocked by their scarcity.

"What if I wanted to stay here?" she asked one night at dinner.

After a moment's silence Hazel said carefully, "Jobs aren't easy to find."

"I wouldn't have to work in a bank," Cory ventured.

"It wouldn't hurt to look," Hazel said with a slight shrug. "I don't know what the job market is now, but most employers choose kamaainas over newcomers. They feel people who live here should have first chance. You don't mean right away, do you? You have your hands pretty full looking after me."

"I'm still wound up to East Coast time." Cory's smile was twisted. "Back home I did a full day's work, cooked dinner, and shopped in the evening."

"I'm afraid your evenings here aren't very exciting—" Hazel sounded troubled.

"I didn't mean that!" Cory exclaimed hurriedly. "It's just—well, I know it's too soon to decide I want to stay here, but—"

"But still you feel that way." Hazel was smiling. "I understand. That was my reaction twenty years ago."

"It was?" Cory's spirits soared. "Did you feel—" she sought for words "—as though this was where you were *meant* to be? As though you should have been born here, but some mistake happened?" She would not have been surprised if the older woman had dismissed her fanciful words with an amused laugh, but Hazel's voice was serious when she nodded.

"A gut reaction, as the current phrase is?"

"I suppose so." Cory wrinkled her nose.

"Or, somewhat more elegantly: 'The boat had no sooner docked than my heart recognized its paradise,'" she quoted.

"That's nice. Who said it?"

"I've forgotten. One of the first visitors to the islands."

Thoughtfully Cory repeated the phrase: "'My heart recognized its paradise.' That's exactly the way I feel!"

"Then the best thing for you is to start looking for work. What would you do about your possessions back in New Jersey?"

"I don't know!" Cory broke into a laugh. "You must think I'm crazy!"

"Not at all. You have to make the decision to change your life before you can work out the details. Knowing what you want comes first."

BY THE WEEKEND Cory had learned her way around the village of Hala and made several acquaintances among the tourists staying at the hotel. She had completed two sketches, and when she took a shower she could see the line where her bathing suit ended and her tan began.

On Saturday morning she strolled to her usual spot and was surprised to see the beach more crowded. With a laugh at how quickly one could forget the nine-to-five grind, she realized that many of the people on the beach today were kamaainas—that enviable term meaning longtime Hawaii residents—and they undoubtedly had jobs during the week.

She watched three teenage boys arrive with surfboards. They knelt to attach them to their ankles by a leash before lying flat on them to paddle out beyond the big rollers. They should enjoy themselves. The surf was high today—six to eight feet—the morning paper had reported.

She could see the bobbing heads of surfers already out there. A brown youth with a shock of sun-bleached hair stood up on his board as the sea heaved beneath him. He rode the curl for the space of two breaths before the board shot flashing into the sun and he plunged beneath the wall of crashing white water. On the next wave a girl in a red suit defied gravity, riding her surfboard for what seemed a long time before the white foam swallowed her. Apparently the surfers dove easily beneath the tons of crashing water.

When the next wave arrived, the stalwart figure of a man rose to catch it. Cory held her breath as he swooped across the beautifully curling blue water, white surf breaking at his heels. She could tell by the way he shifted stance that he had his watery steed well under control. He looked a veritable god of the sea. When the power of the wave diminished, instead of falling in head over heels, he plunged into the water smoothly, with intent.

Cory released her breath in a sigh of satisfaction. Suddenly she longed for binoculars. The surfers were a long way out and one had to squint to see them in the flashing water. She shaded her eyes and waited for the man to appear again. He was dark haired and brown skinned, wearing black trunks. His surfboard was red. There he was! He rose on the board and rode the wave again. Her heart beat faster at the exciting beauty of the figure in motion, at the perfection of her surroundings: the perfect soft breeze, the warm sun, the dark blue of the water. She drew deep breaths of sheer contentment.

During the intervals between the man's performances she watched the other surfers and began making lightning sketches. Nothing she'd want to show anybody, but they were fun to do—quick stick figures that conveyed the meaning of motion. She hadn't seen her star performer take his turn for some time. He had quit or was taking a long rest. That made her realize she'd spent more time in the sun than she'd intended. She tucked her sketch pad into her basket, stood up, and began rolling up her mat.

Her back to the water, she didn't see the man and the girl come wading out, surfboards under their arms. Cory was tying the strings around the rolled mat when she heard footsteps and conversation.

A girl's admiring voice said, ''Aside from the pointers you gave me, I learned a lot just watching you.''

A man's voice replied laughingly, "I was showing off for you."

Cory heard a trill of amusement in the girl's voice. "Be serious! I know good surfing when I see it. I feel terribly lucky you're willing to help me."

"Lucky you come Hawaii, eh?"

The girl giggled and they were about to pass Cory when the man said in a tone of unbelieving surprise, "Emma?"

Since she wasn't aware of anyone else in the vicinity, Cory swung around to see whom he was talking to. To her shock she met his eyes and saw the light of joyous recognition fade to chagrin.

Almost before she understood that he was speaking to her, he said in a brisk tone designed to cover his disappointment, "You're not Emma, are you?"

"No." Cory smiled gently, but the man continued to stand there, looking her up and down, and Cory, staring back at him, almost forgot to breathe. His physique was as beautiful as any she'd ever seen. Muscles bulged beneath his tanned, wet skin. Droplets flew as he shook the water from his hair, and his black locks sprang into thick curls like those adorning a Greek sculpture. His face was as handsome as his build. His cleft chin was square, his nose straight and handsome, his thick wet lashes forming little points above eyes of startling blue.

The smile that his wide mouth returned was wistful.

The girl tittered and they pressed on toward the hotel.

Cory stared after them. What stunning creatures

they were! Like beings in a television commercial.
The girl looked like a tourist. She wasn't very
brown, but he— She watched them separate to
enter the dressing rooms. He called something to
the girl that sounded like, "See you da kine ba!"

Enlightenment flashed in Cory's brain. He was
talking pidgin! And he was the one who had been
performing so magnificently on the surfboard! He
must be a present-day beachcomber, one of those
reputedly carefree souls who followed the sun and
combed the beaches for tourists, teaching surfing
by day and good-naturedly hustling free drinks,
meals and friendships after dark. Emma was probably last year's customer—or last month's.

*I'm getting a little tired of being told I look like
other people,* Cory thought. *Who was that person
the Bower sisters compared me to?*

She found herself wondering idly what it would
cost to take surfing lessons, a ridiculous fantasy
because she couldn't even swim terribly well. And
hiring an instructor was out of the question.

She sighed again and wished she were bolder. Oh,
well, the girl was a tourist, and the man, whatever
he was, must live on the island. She would see him
again, and he would notice her if she looked like
Emma. There was no risk in watching for him simply to appreciate his looks and the way he rode a
surfboard, no more risk than admiring coco palms
against the sunset. She wouldn't be thinking of him
in any personal way, she explained to herself, as the
hot anger she felt over Paul's desertion surged back
in warning.

CHAPTER TWO

CORY WALKED UP THE BEACH to the shade and unrolled her mat again. Maybe he would come back. She could still see the swing of his shoulders, the way the black trunks clung to his agile hips. She guessed he must be in his early thirties. She wondered how long he had been on the island.

Thinking it over, she decided his final words to the girl had meant he'd meet her in the hotel bar. Cory wished she had the nerve to go to the bar and have another look at him, but such action savored of a schoolgirl crush.

She went back to drawing the young surfers with swift strokes until a shadow was thrown across the paper. She looked up to see a bikini-clad figure standing above her.

The young woman gave a friendly grin. ''I hope you don't mind my looking. You've very good.''

''Thank you.'' Cory returned her smile.

''Mind if I join you? My name's Sondra.''

''Please do.'' Cory introduced herself and sized up Sondra as she spread her mat and sat down. Well tanned, she wore her bikini as though she were someone who'd spent her whole life on beaches. She appeared to be about Cory's age.

"Staying at the hotel?" Sondra asked.

"No. Are you?"

Sondra shook her head. Her shoulder-length frizzy hair looked sun-bleached and dry. "I live here in Hala."

"So do I." Cory explained the circumstances.

"Where are you from on the mainland?" Sondra questioned.

"New Jersey. And you?"

"Southern California. I've been here more than two years, though. I've seen you on the beach a few other mornings. Are you an artist?"

"I wish!" Cory laughed. "I just fool around."

"May I see the rest?"

Cory handed over the sketchbook.

Sondra glanced quickly through it. "Very nice," she pronounced. "Do you ever do buildings? Old houses, stores—that sort of thing?"

"I have done. Why?"

Sondra gave her a friendly smile. "I've seen artists earn a few bucks by making a bunch of sketches of local landmarks and having them made into notepaper. They sell pretty well." She squinted at Cory. "I run a gift shop. That's how I know."

"What fun!" Cory exclaimed. "Is it easy, selling to tourists?"

"Well, frankly, business isn't too good." Sondra began rubbing oil on her smooth tan.

"I take it you have some help or you wouldn't be at the beach," Cory suggested.

Sondra stretched out on her back and positioned sunglasses over her eyes. "I don't open till afternoon. My boyfriend works nights, so I spend my mornings with him...usually." She turned onto her stomach and appeared to go to sleep.

Cory lay back, covering her eyes with one arm. Sondra had the right idea. Instead of trying to find a job, start a business of one's own. She glanced at the other woman, wanting to ask how she got started, but Sondra's closed eyes didn't encourage further conversation.

She thought about working up a set of sketches suitable for notepaper. Turning out a group of drawings that looked professional would at least give her something to do. She laughed to herself. *Spinning my wheels again,* she thought. *How long does it take to slow down?*

She didn't mention the beachcomber when she returned to the condo. If she was going to have a crush, the least she could do was keep it secret. Thanks to him the dull ache caused by Paul had ceased for a time. However, she did tell Hazel about meeting Sondra.

"I know the shop," Hazel said. "She can't make much of a living. She isn't open half the time."

Cory smiled. "She's a laid-back southern Californian, I gathered. She said, though, that business isn't too good."

"There are apartments behind some of those shops," Hazel said. "She probably makes enough money to pay the rent and buy food. That's really all she needs."

"Hazel...." Cory remembered the question she wanted to ask. "What was the name of that girl Mae Bower said I looked like?"

"Emma Lassiter." Hazel eyed Cory questioningly.

"Someone on the beach took me for her!" Cory exclaimed. "He came up behind me and said 'Emma!'" Into her memory flashed the picture of the beachcomber standing there, his look of joyful recognition fading. She wished she had been Emma.

"I'm not surprised," Hazel said sourly. "You do look like her, but I hope it won't bother you. She was too well-known, if you see my point."

"A—a prostitute?"

"Heavens, nothing like that! But she was wild to a fault. She and her husband were Canadian. She finally got cut up in a car wreck, with another man. Her husband took her back to the mainland so she could have plastic surgery. That was the last anybody heard of her. Mae and Irene remember her because their nephew was running around with her, too. Anyhow, don't let the resemblance bother you. Everyone thought she was quite pretty. You're quieter, of course."

"I hope so, from what you tell me!" Cory laughed and went off to shower and dress.

The next morning she arrived at the beach with the hope of seeing the beachcomber again.

"Why shouldn't I watch him?" she said aloud. "He's a terrific surfer—poetry in motion." But she wasn't fooling herself. She wanted to see him close up, too, hear him talk and watch him stalk barefooted across the sand.

I must be hopelessly juvenile, she thought. *Maybe that's what Paul found wrong with me.*

She'd been over that road a hundred times. She'd lost all her confidence thinking of the faults that might have made Paul leave. Was she too quiet, un-exciting, inexperienced, naive...the doubts went on and on. Damn him!

The beachcomber didn't appear. Nor did Sondra. Cory made up her mind to ask Sondra about him the next time she saw her. Very casually, of course. Perhaps Sondra knew him; this was a small community.

Or maybe he hung out on some other part of the island, she thought as she walked back to the condo. He might have come to the beach because the girl he was with was staying at the hotel.

She spent the afternoon making a fourth at bridge with Hazel, Irene and Mae.

Next morning she had barely arrived at her favorite spot on the sand when she saw Sondra coming toward her. She hailed the other woman with the feeling of having made a friend. Sondra was wearing a faded red bikini that had seen many hours of sun.

"I looked for you yesterday morning," Cory said brightly while Sondra was settling herself on the sand.

Sondra's smile was crooked. "Johnny and I were out so late Saturday night I couldn't make it out of bed yesterday. He's a bartender at the hotel, so he doesn't get off until after midnight. Did you have an exciting day?"

"I played bridge," Cory stated.

Sondra grinned. "Do people still do that?"

"It's a good way to entertain Hazel," Cory replied defensively. "She can't go downstairs yet."

"Yeah. I forgot about that."

"So how was business Saturday?" Cory asked eagerly.

Sondra shrugged. "Okay. Not what it ought to be, but okay."

"Where is your shop? What's it called?"

"Treasure-Trove. It's in the mall beyond the hotel."

"I like that name! I've been planning to check out that mall."

"You should." Sondra cast a faintly critical glance at Cory's swimsuit. "It's a tourist shopping center, but the prices aren't out of line."

"I've been waiting to get a better idea of what I want," Cory responded.

"I'll go with you if you'd like," Sondra offered. "I love to shop."

The beachcomber didn't appear, nor did the girl he'd been with. Sondra chattered away about herself while Cory concentrated on drawing the curved beach and graceful palms, with the foliage-softened mountains in the background.

"I like your idea of doing sketches for note-paper," Cory broke into Sondra's reminiscences. "How many should I have?"

"Half a dozen, maybe." Sondra turned over and sank into semioblivion.

Cory decided to visit Sondra's shop and see for herself what it was like. Playing cards wasn't a very satisfactory way to spend one's time if you were young and energetic. Even Sondra worked half a day.

THE FOLLOWING AFTERNOON Cory was surprised to see how charming and uncommercial the mall looked. There were plants and shade trees everywhere and a minimum of cement. Wooden storefronts and wide wooden awnings gave the area a relaxed, old-time air. Among the pools and patios huge iron cogwheels and other machinery had been painted soft colors and set up as sculpture. A plaque beside one such piece said Parts From the Old Sugar Mill at Kahuku.

She loitered before the window displays of beachwear. It seemed as though she needed everything. The few pieces of suitable clothing she'd brought were either shabby or uninteresting. Watching the hotel visitors for the better part of a week, she had begun to wish her clothes showed more imagination. She already felt like a different person from the depressed woman who had left New Jersey.

She found herself in front of a window displaying jewelry and brass objects, paper knives that said Kauai and Hawaii, and paperweights in the shapes of shells and whales. Tinkling pottery wind chimes hung in the doorway. Inside on the white walls, three oil paintings depicting Hawaiian scenes drew Cory's attention. In their childlike simplicity she glimpsed sophisticated humor. Then she saw Sondra behind the counter in a muumuu and dangling earrings. She was waiting on customers, but she waved a greeting as Cory walked in.

Cory watched with interest. The couple paid for their purchases and hesitantly asked Sondra to recommend a good restaurant. Sondra named one. "Best on the island," she said.

After the couple left, Sondra perched herself on the stool behind the cash register. "That was probably my rush of business for the day," she said. "What do you think of the place?"

"I haven't had time to look around, but it seems charming. This mall is quite something. . .so. . .so relaxed and pleasant. In fact, there doesn't seem to be anything unpleasant about all of Kauai."

Sondra grinned. "You haven't been here long."

"You only have to be some places for a minute and unpleasantness hits you."

"Listen—" Sondra slid off the stool. "Would you keep an eye on things for a minute while I unpack some boxes of new stock? Look around. If someone wants to buy something, call me. I'll be right in here—" She disappeared through a narrow doorway.

Cory drew a dismayed breath and then laughed. She'd wanted to know what running a gift shop was like, and here she was, doing it. She began at one end, looking at items and reading prices.

No customers came in. Cory had examined everything the shop contained and was admiring the oil paintings at close range when Sondra reappeared, her arms full of stolid-faced wooden statuettes.

Cory helped her place them on an empty shelf. "What are these supposed to be?" she inquired.

"Some Polynesian god."

Examining one of the figures more closely, Cory was surprised to see a small sticker on its base that said Made in the Philippines.

"Shouldn't I remove this?" she suggested mildly.

"I think it's illegal." Sondra looked embarrassed. "It's junk, but it sells."

While she worked, Cory looked around the scantily stocked shelves. There really wasn't much of a selection. *If this were mine, I'd have only real Hawaiian crafts,* she thought. *This shopping mall looks so nice, I'd want to sell classy things to go with it.*

"Your shop's very attractive," she said, referring in her own mind to its location and storefront, the layout of the rooms and shelves.

"But the merchandise is a bunch of junk," Sondra responded, unconsciously echoing Cory's thoughts. "I never get enough money ahead to stock more expensive items. I'm surprised Tim lets me show his paintings with this lot."

"You know the painter then?" Cory asked with interest.

"He's the high school art teacher. Want to meet him? He's unattached."

Cory hesitated and then said steadily, "I don't have to meet him. I just think his work's awfully good."

"Stick around and you can tell him. He'll love to hear it. I sold one for him yesterday. He's coming in to collect."

Cory looked at her watch.

"Do stay," Sondra urged. "It's good for business. People see you here and think they'll be safe from having their arms twisted or something."

"Do the paintings sell for a lot?"

"Five hundred dollars."

"Have you sold many?"

"Two, so far."

Cory was surprised that the unknown painter didn't mind having his work associated with souvenirs. Just then a smiling, brown-skinned, black-haired man in his early thirties lounged into the shop wearing shorts, zoris and a red-and-white aloha shirt. He kissed Sondra with mocking possessiveness and eyed Cory laughingly as though he would like to kiss her, too.

Giggling, Sondra introduced him: "My boyfriend, Johnny Komo."

"With a *K*," Johnny stipulated. "Hawaiian, not Italian."

"Where have you been?" Sondra asked him.

"Fishing. I sold everything to the chef at the hotel."

"Johnny fishes with a net, like his ancestors have done for centuries."

"From the reef," he added. "You fish?"

"No, but I'd certainly like to watch sometime."

"We take her, eh?" Johnny squeezed Sondra again, making her smile. Cory wondered fleetingly what it would be like to have such a warmly affectionate and obviously masculine boyfriend.

A customer wandered in and then another. Johnny disappeared into the back room.

Cory was about to say she'd meet the painter another day when Sondra said, "Here he comes."

The slim, blond young man who came through the open door was dressed like Johnny in shorts, zoris and a Hawaiian-print shirt. He was carrying a clumsily wrapped framed painting.

"You brought another one!" Sondra greeted him.

"Is that okay?"

"Of course! And I want you to meet someone who's been admiring your work." Sondra performed the introductions.

The painter's name was Tim Cooper. He gazed at Cory with guileless gray eyes.

"This is my latest. He stripped away the newspaper wrappings and moved behind the counter to hang the painting on an empty nail. Stepping back, he tilted his head to appraise it. It showed a row of weathered wooden shacks built on a seawall above lightly running surf, the buildings half-hidden by tropical greenery. In the background rose blue green mountains. But it was more than a rendition of the scene. It seemed to illustrate a way of life— simple, leisurely, evoking a sweetly sad nostalgic longing.

"That's not here," Sondra said.

"I did it last week on Maui. It's Lahaina."

Cory turned from the painting to find Tim looking at her.

"I met Cory sketching on the beach," Sondra said, taking some bills from the bottom of the cash register and handing them to Tim. "I thought right away that you two should meet each other. She's going to do a bunch of pencil sketches for notepaper."

"I haven't seen you around, so you must be new here," Tim said, as though he would certainly have noticed her. "Are you here on vacation?"

Cory explained to him that she was caring for a friend's aunt.

"You'll be here a few months then. Want to go sketching some time?"

"What a come-on!" Sondra laughed.

Tim's smile was open. "I like her. She likes my work!"

Pleased, Cory said, "I'd like to go sketching."

"When?"

"When's a good time for you? Sondra says you teach school."

"Not on weekends." He glanced at his watch. "I have to make the bank before it closes. Thanks a lot, Sondra." He kissed her cheek and smiled at Cory. "I'll be in touch."

Her eyes followed him out the door. "He doesn't know where I'm staying!" she exclaimed disappointedly. It would have been nice to have someone to go sketching with. Sondra's spare time obviously was taken up with Johnny.

"He probably knows your librarian friend," Sondra said. "How big do you think this place is?"

A group of tourists flocked in, nearly filling the shop.

"See you on the beach!" Cory waved and made her way to the door. Walking to Hazel's car, another surge of happiness filled her. Here she was, in the midst of split-leaved philodendrons and all the most cherished houseplants back home. The temperature was again phenomenally perfect, and the air was sparkling despite the bright sunshine. She felt for the first time a sense of belonging and pride. She wondered if Tim had a girl friend—not that she was looking for that kind of relationship.

Then for some crazy reason she thought of the beachcomber.

Over dinner she described to Hazel her visit to Sondra's shop and the two men she had met there.

"I know Tim Cooper," Hazel said. "We showed his paintings at the library last year. He's quite talented."

"He invited me to go sketching," Cory said. "What's he like?"

"Hard to say." Hazel frowned. "Pleasant, but...." She shrugged. "I heard his girl friend got a teaching job in Honolulu, so maybe he's just unhappy."

It occurred to Cory that Ann might have told Hazel about Cory's broken romance. She cringed, as usual, at the thought of Paul, but this time she replaced him with the memory of Tim's open admiration.

The following Saturday morning the sun had barely risen when Cory leapt out of bed. Drinking a hasty glass of orange juice, she left a note in case Tim telephoned, then set off to explore the beach in the direction away from the hotel. Hazel, she had learned, preferred to breakfast alone.

The tide was out and she went only a short distance before she discovered the interesting pools the coral formed at low water. Small bright fish swam around in them, darting from one to another through gaps like miniature caverns. Tiny crabs moved around, unaware that Cory was spying on them.

She found a higher knob of coral and sat on it,

using her beach towel for a cushion. Her rubber-soled zoris soaked up water like sponges, but she kept them on, having been warned that coral inflicted nasty, festering wounds.

She became absorbed in the life of the tidal pool, and then by the whole view. Reaching for her sketchbook, she began to draw—the pools and coral in the foreground, the stretch of smooth water beyond, and on the horizon the curve of the beach, the palm trees and clouds.

The sun warmed her skin, and she was thinking about a cooling dip when she found herself regarded intently by a thin, dark-haired boy, about fourteen. He was holding a surfboard under one brown arm. A snorkeling mask dangled from his free hand. He smiled, showing a chipped front tooth.

"Would you mind watching this mask while I go surfing?" he asked politely.

Cory hesitated. "I was thinking of swimming myself."

"You could still watch my stuff. You won't go out beyond the reef, will you?"

"Hardly!" Cory laughed.

The boy grinned back. "Want to use my snorkel? There are lots of nice fish here."

"I don't know how."

"It's easy. Just put on this mask and stick the tube up through the strap like this—" He demonstrated. "Put the end in your mouth and breathe through it and float. You'll see all kinds of fish right out there." He pointed to where she planned to swim.

"All right, I'll keep an eye on it anyway," Cory agreed.

"Use it if you want to," he offered again. "My name's Paco."

"I'm Cory." She smiled.

Seeming in no hurry to join the boys sitting astride their surfboards out in the deep water he dug one toe into the sand.

"Can I see what you're drawing?"

Cory held out the sketchbook. Paco accepted it, dropping the mask and leaning the surfboard against his thigh.

"That's nice," he said, handing it back after a swift appraisal. "Okay! See you in about half an hour!" He leashed the surfboard to his ankle and carried it into the water. He belly flopped onto the board and paddled toward the line of white that swept so breathtakingly across the dark blue.

Cory chose one of the larger pools where the coral gave way to sand and clear water. Leaving towel, mat, basket and drawing pad on the sand, she took the mask with her and stepped into the water. As on every other day, the temperature seemed ideal. She held the mask to her face and pulled the rubber strap over her head. Kneeling on the sandy bottom, she put her face into the water. Her vision of the sand cleared, then became perfect.

She caught a flash of movement where the water was deeper. Drawn to explore, she pushed off from the sand and floated face down across the pool. She was gazing almost eye level with a school of pretty yellow fish, small pancake-shaped creatures with black-edged fins. Suddenly she ran out of breath and stood up, gasping. She was back in the world of air again. Her glimpse of underwater beauty might never have been.

"Oh, I have to do this!" she exclaimed aloud. She waded out to get the fins and breathing tube. Sliding her feet into the black rubber fins and laughing a little, she backed self-consciously into the water the way she had seen people do. She slid the mask over her wet hair and rather distastefully put the end of the tube in her mouth, but when she thought about the mysterious world she was about to enter she accepted the unfamiliar equipment as necessary. Taking a deep breath she launched herself.

With three kicks of the flippers she was floating over a universe belonging to her alone. A school of pink-and-yellow-striped fish with blue lavender backs swam across her vision like bits from a rainbow.

She drew an excited breath and inhaled saltwater. She choked, gasped and choked again. At once she felt trapped, afraid to breathe, yet her lungs demanded air. Her head seemed to be held by a vice. She was strapped into a glass-and-rubber mask that was smothering her, and she was unable to stand up so she could tear it off. Her feet were encased in black contraptions meant for swimming, not standing. Coughing, spluttering and attempting to tear the mask away from her nose, she fought to get her body upright. Her feet sought the sandy bottom and encountered—nothing. Panic swept her.

She drew another breath and gulped more sea-
water. Her arms flailed the surface and she fought
the mask. This was what it was like to drown. The
mask had sealed her into a watery glass casket.

Then, as reason clicked off and she knew with
sheer terror that if she could not find her footing
she was going to drown, an arm, warm and human,
circled her chest and lifted her a few inches higher in
the water.

A man's voice in her ear said, "Catch your
breath. I'm holding you."

Gasping, coughing, she wrenched the mask from
her head and rolled her eyes to see who had rescued
her.

The beachcomber! As her lungs cried for air, her
brain took in his handsome tanned features and sea-
blue eyes. His dark wet eyelashes registered on her
mind the instant before the blessed air rushed into
her heaving lungs and saltwater burned her wind-
pipe.

"Relax," he ordered. "Trust me."

His brown, brawny arm beneath her breasts was
holding her high enough that her panic subsided.
How wonderful, how reassuring that arm felt! With
his body beneath hers, supporting her on one hip,
he swam with strong backstrokes of his free arm. In
seconds he brought them both into shallow water.

"Now you can stand up," he said loudly, finding
his feet in the chest-high swell.

Speechless with gratitude and forgetting the flippers, Cory put her feet down, promptly lost her
balance and fell against him. His hard-muscled arm

caught her around the shoulders. For one blissful second she was held close to a wet bare chest covered with fine dark hair, her face against his collarbone. She was alarmed at the sensation of pleasure that ran through her—and astonished that at such a time she could fleetingly compare him with Paul. This man was bigger, stronger—a lifesaver.

Ordering her to keep her balance by holding onto him, he bent to remove the offending flippers. She raised one foot and then the other.

"Now," he said, "let's get you out." Carrying the flippers in one hand, he slipped his arm around her waist and helped her walk out onto the warm, dry sand.

Her throat and nasal passages felt raw, and her embarrassment was acute. What a fool he must think her!

"Thank you," she managed to whisper.

"Feeling better?" he asked, his blue eyes concerned.

She met his gaze and managed to nod before her eyes skittered away.

He strode up the sloping sand to where her mat and towel lay. He unrolled the mat and spread the thick colorful towel upon it. Then he waved her to a seat.

"Take it easy for a bit and then try again."

Cory stared at him in such astonishment that he grinned.

"It's like falling off a horse; if you don't do it now, you'll lose your nerve. You can do it again. You don't have to go so far out. Wade in about waist-deep and practice breathing with the mask on. But you should do it before you leave.''

He went on standing above her, his blue-and-white jogging shorts dripping water. He had retrieved a towel from where he'd thrown it and had slung it around his neck. He must have been taking an early-morning run. She stole a glance at the bronzed thighs so near her eye level.

"How did you happen to see me?" she asked, wishing he would stop standing over her. What if he made her go in again? She quailed at the thought.

He smoothed back his wet hair. "I was running on the beach and saw you flailing around."

Cory lowered her eyes to his bare feet. They were well formed and strongly arched. He wasn't wearing running shoes. She wondered if he had ever worn regular shoes. There was something wonderfully primitive about tanned bare feet on the clean sand.

"I felt trapped," she explained, "and I hadn't realized the water was over my head."

"You'd have made it back all right," he assured her, "but you might have been turned off snorkeling forever."

"You think I'm not down on it now?" She looked askance at the mask and flippers.

"That was nothing!" He grinned and began backing away. "I have a lot of miles to run. Try it again before you leave today. You'll be glad you did."

Instead of going, he was looking her over with an interest that kept her heart beating madly.

"You're not Emma's sister, are you?"

Cory met his eyes and felt a different kind of drowning. His blue irises reflected the deep aquamarine of the sea, and the dark lashes fringing his friendly glance seemed incredibly thick. He was breathtakingly handsome, yet he was acting and talking as though he were an ordinary mortal and expected a normal reply. Cory still wasn't sure she wasn't dreaming.

"No," she said. One word was all she could manage.

"See you around the hotel!" He broke into an easy, long-legged stride that appeared effortless. Cory's eyes followed him, enjoying the graceful strength of his shoulders, the way his back tapered to taut buttocks. At last a curve of the beach hid his figure from sight.

Had it really happened? Had that gorgeously masculine creature actually stopped what he was doing to come to her rescue? She lay on her towel and let her mind dwell on every single moment. The snorkeling experience hadn't been all bad. Maybe she'd try to take his advice and put the mask on again if the boy didn't come for it first.... A little spasm of pleasurable excitement traveled over her body as she remembered the feel of his arms around her.

How had she looked to him? She glanced down at the one-piece suit that she'd had since she was eighteen. Despite the urging of therapists, her mother had liked neither beaches nor swimming pools, and Cory had seldom felt right about going off and leaving her.

But now— All the other young women on the beach wore bikinis. She squirmed at the thought that the beachcomber had seen her looking less than her best. She knew her slender, delicately boned body was attractive.

I'll shop for one this afternoon, she promised herself, and the mere decision made her feel better

CHAPTER THREE

CORY DROWSED FOR A BIT, but at length she sat up. Paco had been gone a long time. She eyed the mask. If she was going to try snorkeling again, she'd better do it now. The beachcomber would be sure to ask, if she ever met him again.

Doggedly she plunged into the water, found solid footing, and adjusted the mask. She put her face in the water, consciously breathing through her mouth into the tube. She was rewarded with the sight of a black fish with glowing orange, yellow and blue markings—a fish the size of her hand. Before it swam out of the area made visible by the mask, an electric blue fish with yellow fins sailed across her view. She watched with awe. Five disc-shaped creatures with fins and black vertical stripes swam past her legs as though flesh-colored columns were part of their world. How tame they were! And how marvelously strange and beautiful!

She was inhaling too deeply and too quickly. She straightened, left the underwater world, and breathed normally. There! She'd followed the beachcomber's advice and could call it quits.

She saw Paco beyond the reef paddling shoreward. She waded out of the water and met him on the beach.

"Have a good time?" she asked.

"Okay." He shrugged. "Did you see me?"

"You were too far out. I couldn't tell which was you."

"Did you try snorkeling?"

"I sure did!" She decided not to mention her demoralizing failure. "I had no idea such beautiful fish were so close."

The boy nodded. "I draw some," he confided. "I like drawing people. Want me to do a sketch of you?"

"If I can lie on my mat."

"Sure, that would be good."

They returned to where she had been lying. The boy drew with assurance, using Cory's sketchbook and pencils.

"I'll hold this pose for fifteen minutes, okay?" she stressed.

"Okay," he agreed, concentrating on the work.

Lying on her stomach, chin propped on elbows, she presented a picture anyone would be pleased to capture on paper or film. Her small waist swelled into feminine curves. Her legs, bent at the knee, raised unconsciously saucy calves that diminished to trim ankles. Her light brown eyes were arresting, paired as they were with flaxen hair that was becoming streaked under the island sun. Her features were pretty, if not devastating. Her thoughtful gaze and her calm self-possession were alluring and somehow mysterious. She seemed to be thinking of a life several centuries removed.

While Paco drew silently Cory was wishing

dreamily that the bronzed stranger would reappear. The surf wasn't high today. Did that explain why he wasn't riding the waves like a sea god?

She thought of her snorkeling experience. It took only a small effort to bring the fish swimming back across her vision. Unaware of her as they were, she felt a vague fondness for them, as though, because she had discovered them, they were her own creations.

After fifteen minutes she said, "I'm beginning to fry."

"I'm finished." His final stroke was a flourish. "Want to see it?" he questioned, suddenly shy.

"Sure do." She took the pad, prepared to praise him whatever the sketch looked like. Involuntarily she exclaimed, "That's good! Why, Paco, that's really good!"

"Thanks," he said. "You can have it."

Engrossed in studying the sketch, they didn't notice the man who came through an opening in the hedge until a male voice said, "I'll take it if she doesn't want it."

Cory looked up to see the artist, Tim, and was conscious of disappointment. Whom had she expected? Of course she was glad to see him! He was wearing swim trunks and zoris. He squatted beside them and Cory couldn't help noticing his lean brown legs covered with golden hair.

"Paco's good at talking pretty women into posing for him," Tim teased.

The boy grinned.

"Paco's my most promising student," Tim told

Cory, throwing an arm around the boy's neck and pulling him off balance. Affectionately he ruffled Paco's hair.

Paco looked embarrassed but his eyes shone with admiration. "Tim's a really good artist," he mumbled.

Tim was carrying a towel and a large sketch pad. He looked boyish compared to the picture in Cory's mind of a certain well-muscled surfer.

"What are you dressed for?" Paco asked.

"Sketching. . . swimming—"

"We've already sketched and swum," Paco said.

"Let's see the sketch." Tim reached for the pad and studied it.

"I think it's good," Cory affirmed.

"How could he miss?" Tim said gallantly. "Yes, Paco, you're getting good. Mind if I look at your sketches, Cory?"

"Go ahead."

"Not bad at all," he murmured approvingly as he studied the drawings of beach and surfers. "Sondra's right. You could work up some views to sell. Why don't we all go someplace and sketch, someplace in the shade."

"I don't have a pad," Paco objected.

"I have an extra in the car," Tim told him. "I'll lend you a pencil, too. Cory? Are you free?"

"I think so," Cory said. "How did you know I was here?"

"Easy. I phoned Hazel."

It was indeed a small community.

"Where are we going?" Paco questioned as they

walked to Tim's car, a nearly new pickup truck with outsize tires.

"Hanapepe? I bet Cory would like those old buildings."

Paco made a face.

"How about you doing that backyard of chicken coops you can see from the swinging bridge?" Tim suggested. "It'll be good practice for perspective."

Paco looked unconvinced.

"Face it, nothing will look good compared to your model." He grinned at Cory in such a straightforward manner that she felt no uneasiness.

"We'll pick up some lunch on the way," he told them when they were in the car. "I told Hazel I wanted to take you sketching, and she said to tell you to go ahead."

They spent a pleasant afternoon, first picnicking on the grassy riverbank, the only sound the repeated crowing of roosters. The weather was perfect, the surroundings lush, tropical. As always, white clouds hovered over the mountains.

I could stay here the rest of my life, Cory thought.

She made one very satisfactory drawing of a small green wooden building that housed the barbershop. Red-and-white-striped barber poles were painted on either side of the doorway. It would have been fun to do in pastels.

They drove back in the late afternoon, tired but full of a sense of accomplishment. Paco got out at the hotel, where he stored his surfboard.

"I'd like to do this again next Saturday," Tim said diffidently. "Would you care to, Cory?"

"I'd love to."

"Paco?" Tim prompted.

"Sure."

"And next time, bring your own pad," Tim ordered jokingly, handing Paco his finished sketches.

They arranged to meet on the beach the following Saturday at an early hour.

Tim said, "In the meantime, Paco, you can help me think of places Cory might like to draw."

When he let her out in the parking lot of the condo, he kissed her lightly on the cheek.

He seems safe enough, she thought as she made salad for dinner that evening. He could never rouse her emotions the way Paul had done, so he wasn't dangerous.

ON SUNDAY CORY SCANNED the paper for job openings. She found one, a bank in the island's largest town advertising for a secretary.

"Perfect," she told Hazel. "I'm sure I'm well qualified."

When she arrived for her interview, however, three young Oriental women were waiting, too. The one Cory talked to had been born on Kauai.

When Cory's turn came, her prospective employer shook his head. "We can't consider newcomers to Kauai, no matter how much they want to stay. We feel obliged to hire people who live here. I'm sure you understand."

Depressed, she bought a bowl of *saimin* for lunch, the local noodle soup that was strictly Hawaiian despite its Eastern-sounding name. Then she went to Treasure-Trove and poured her tale of disappointment into Sondra's ear.

"I know what you need," Sondra consoled. "Let's go buy you some new clothes tomorrow morning."

"I hate to shop," Cory grumbled. "I'm not good at it, either."

"I like shopping because I have a flair for it," Sondra bragged. "Make a list of what you need, and we'll have fun, I promise. Want to do something to help me out now?"

"Sure."

"Help dust. The whole place has to be gone over every day. Now that's something I do hate."

She handed Cory a feather duster, which was something Cory wouldn't have used if the store were hers. She'd use a damp cloth and do it right.

When she finished, she still felt disgruntled. She returned home and reported her lack of success.

"Go for a swim," Hazel advised. "Enjoy yourself. You'll be taking care of me for weeks yet."

"You don't let me do much." Cory smiled wryly.

"It seems that way because you're still running in high gear," Hazel told her, "but you can't do any more today toward getting a job, can you?"

Cory admitted she couldn't, and sure enough, once she was floating in the warm water watching the palm fronds sway in the breeze from the trade wind, nothing seemed to matter beyond the fact that tomorrow she was going to get some new clothes. She even reminded herself that if Paul hadn't dumped her, she wouldn't be here. She had Hawaii instead of Paul, but her heart still ached when she thought of him.

The next morning, however, she set off with Sondra in high spirits. She had taken her friend's advice and made a list.

Sondra read it over. "You don't have anything here to wear job hunting," she pointed out.

"That's it—'dress.'"

"At the bottom of the list! And 'bikini' at the top!" Sondra laughed. "You're catching the aloha spirit."

"I do seem to have more use for a swimsuit," Cory admitted, "just about every day."

In the mall Cory looked at the prices in the shop window and sighed. "I don't see how working people manage out here."

"We don't buy winter clothes, for one thing. Are you short of money?"

"No, I'm just not used to spending it on clothes."

Sondra laughed with a tinge of exasperation. "This is the best time of your life to get used to it, then."

Cory needed only a little urging to buy two bikinis—a black one that set off her slight tan to perfection, and a flowered one with splashes of hot pink and yellow that made her pale hair glow like silver. After that she bought white slacks and a coral-colored T-shirt gathered at the neck and piped in white to wear with the slacks.

Sondra then announced that Cory must have a

long-sleeved white lace shirt to wear over the bikini, en route to the beach and back. It could go with the slacks on occasion, too.

Cory also let herself be convinced she needed two new pairs of shorts. When she tried them on, she looked trimmer than she had thought possible. Her thighs emerged smooth and tanned from the pale blue shorts, and the waistband nipped in to fit perfectly above her hips. She pictured herself meeting the surfer. How confident she would be!

"Okay, now we'll shop for the muumuus," Sondra directed. "Or are you exhausted?"

Cory shook her head, her brown eyes sparkling. She liked the way she looked in the clothes Sondra had helped choose.

"You certainly know what you're doing," she said appreciatively.

Sondra accepted the praise as her due. She guided Cory to a shop where muumuus filled the racks like colorful flowers.

"You'll want two at least," Sondra said. "One for dress up, one for daytime."

Some had high necks and short sleeves, and others had low necks and elbow-length sleeves, but all fell straight to the floor in full gathers from round or V-necked yokes.

"The hem should be just off the ground," Sondra announced, "so it's good that you're wearing high-heeled sandals."

While Cory tried on an attractive daytime muumuu printed with tiny blue forget-me-nots and trimmed with narrow blue ribbon, Sondra said, "You know how these became the fashion here? They're based on the old Mother Hubbard gowns the missionaries' wives introduced when they found the Hawaiian women naked, or as good as naked.''

A saleslady hovered solicitously and Cory felt like a princess. No wonder the style had survived. It was so loose and comfortable, being waistless, yet it was regal, too. Where else could one walk down the street in daytime with a long skirt swishing around one's bare ankles?

Cory eyed herself in the mirror and thought she would look like a princess, too, if she let her hair hang. Today, for ease, she had pinned it into a bun on the crown of her head.

"She looks lovely in that blue, doesn't she?" the saleslady said to Sondra.

"Yes, she does. You'll knock Tim dead," Sondra promised.

"I don't want to do that," Cory denied. Nevertheless she bought the dress.

"Now for a really dressy one," Sondra said gleefully.

They chose a dark green print of tiny flowers with dots of lavender and a white lace yoke. The high-necked round yoke extended down over Cory's shoulders to little puffed sleeves. An insert of lavender ribbon edged the lace, and a band of lace and lavender ribbon topped the generous flounce.

"Perfect! Sondra exclaimed when Cory emerged from the dressing room wearing it. "With your blond hair up like that, you look like a Victorian heroine."

Cory couldn't resist feeling pleased with herself, with the dress, with the compliments—with everything except the price, which was quite shocking.

"I'm exhausted," she said when they left the store. "Let's go have lunch."

"What about a dress to wear to job interviews?"

Cory shook her head. "I don't have any scheduled. Besides, it must be nearly time to open your shop."

Sondra made a face.

"I'd love it," Cory exclaimed. "Having my own business. I think it would be wonderful."

"I'm not really knocking it." Sondra smiled. "And it does give me a place to live."

In the mall's outdoor café they lunched on avocado-and-tomato sandwiches topped with alfalfa sprouts and shredded lettuce. Cory loved to watch the tiny barred doves walking tamely among the tables picking up crumbs. Overhead a widespreading tree shaded their table. Around the perimeters of the tables the tropic greenery grew lushly. Cory sat back in her chair with a blissful sigh.

"Everything's so *clean* here."

They finished eating and parted. On the way to the car Cory shook her head at herself, smiling at the same time. She couldn't believe she had spent so much.

When shown the clothes, Hazel agreed that Cory's purchases were all quite necessary.

"Even two bikinis," Hazel said with a twinkle. "It's terrible to climb into a wet bathing suit."

"There's not much of these to climb into," Cory

felt compelled to point out. "The fact is, I just wanted them both."

"Then you should have them," Hazel pronounced.

Over the next few days Cory went to the beach at various times of the day, but she caught no glimpses of the surfer. She came close to mentioning him to Sondra, but in the end she said nothing.

Then she saw him under totally different circumstances. She had driven to one of the sugar mill towns to sketch the old cottages.

"There aren't many left," Hazel had said. "Nothing wooden survives here very long because of termites, but you can still find a few. They're very picturesque and typical of Hawaii. I wish I could show you the ones I mean, but I'm not ready to go down those stairs yet."

Cory followed Hazel's directions to a row of tumbledown houses, single-storied and square and built high off the ground, with rusty corrugated iron roofs. They were surrounded by lush tropical plantings—mangoes, bananas, breadfruit. In the front yards crotons glowed red and yellow, and a vine with orange-and-lavender flowers trailed along a fence.

Living in them might not be so picturesque, Cory reflected, but it was impossible to associate poverty with Hawaii. No one lucky enough to live here the year around could be considered deprived.

She parked the car, sat in a shady spot, and began to draw. After a time an elderly woman in a muumuu emerged onto one of the porches and threw scraps to three bantamlike chickens. A few cars passed along the unpaved street, but Cory hardly noticed until her sketch was nearly finished. She was glancing critically from it to the house when a red sports car came down the street, moving slowly but still bouncing into every other pothole. Cory was caught by the contrast between car and shacks.

Then her eyes widened. The car's sole occupant was the surfer! He was wearing black sunglasses, but there was no mistaking him. As he passed she glimpsed a black long-sleeved knit shirt.

He was too busy avoiding potholes to see Cory sitting by the roadside. She was left with a glow of excitement; thrilled simply at seeing him.

She shook her head at herself, but continued to think about him. Business must be good if he drove a car like that. Maybe he did have a regular job besides teaching surfing. She'd seen him only on weekends, after all. Maybe he worked all week, but the idea seemed ludicrous. She couldn't imagine him in an office. Actually, she had trouble believing anybody in Hawaii worked. She glanced at her watch. Eleven-thirty, and she was growing hungry. The sketch was finished. She decided to pack up and drive a little way in the direction he had come from.

The potholed road led to condominiums built along the shore, but they were approachable more directly by a graveled road. Cory turned onto it, no wiser than before. At least no one knew of her foolishness.

She arrived home to find Irene and Mae Bower

drinking coffee with Hazel. Cory showed them her drawing.

"Oh, yes," Irene said, "one of the old dwellings for cane workers. They are picturesque, aren't they? But hopelessly falling down."

Mae sighed and looked from the drawing to Cory. "These were part of the Hawaii of our childhood. It was lovely here then—"

"But it's gone, and we must make the best of it," Irene interposed. She turned to Hazel. "The builder keeps promising Buchanan to finish the last of the new housing. Buchanan's our nephew—grand-nephew really," she told Cory. "Thank goodness the people in the old houses aren't pushing for the move. Nobody likes change, I suppose."

"One thing that hasn't changed is your Thanksgiving invitation," Hazel said. "Cory, you're invited to the Bowers', too."

Cory could hardly believe it was time for Thanksgiving. She thanked the sisters for the invitation.

When they had gone, she said exultantly, "I can wear my new muumuu!"

"Most appropriate," Hazel agreed.

Cory wished wistfully that her first social gathering on Kauai were going to include some people her own age, but at least she had tomorrow's sketching party to look forward to. She would wear her new shorts, and this afternoon she could wear one of her new bikinis to the beach. What a life!

On Saturday morning, before the appointed time for meeting Tim and Paco, Cory went for a swim. She held a half-formed hope that she might see the surfer—only so she could tell him she'd tried to use the mask again.

She didn't see him. Paco and Tim arrived and decided to take Cory to sketch an unusual carving in a local cemetery—a Buddha holding a child in his arms. Later they drove to the remains of the Old Russian Fort, of which only a half-acre of stones were left. It had been built in 1817 by the czar's soldiers, ostensibly for Kaumualii, the King of Kauai, though it flew a Russian flag.

By the time Tim, Cory and Paco made sketches and read the fort's complicated history it was lunchtime. They ate the sandwiches they had brought and decided to call it a day. Back at the beach, Paco said he had plans for the afternoon and disappeared in the direction of the hotel, probably to get his surfboard. Tim asked what Cory was doing that evening. She was glad she could tell him that Hazel had suggested teaching her to play mah-jongg, and she felt she should comply. After all, she was Hazel's guest.

"Mah-jongg on Saturday night?" Tim scoffed. "How old are you—eighty?"

"Why? What exciting offer were you going to make?"

Tim raised his eyebrows suggestively and leered.

"No, thank you," Cory replied breezily. With a wave of her hand she turned away and headed up the beach to the condominium.

CHAPTER FOUR

ON THANKSGIVING MORNING Cory crossed the beach and plunged into the wonderfully warm water with a tingle of excitement. Today was going to be different. She and Hazel were scheduled to arrive at the Bower home around two o'clock for an afternoon of mah-jongg before dinner.

As always, the water was perfect. In New Jersey cold rain was probably falling, bringing down the last bedraggled leaves. She lay floating on her back. She could glimpse the palms against the blueness overhead, the clouds peeping over the green mountains. What beauty! What peace! How dare the thought intrude that a Thanksgiving at the Bowers' wasn't very exciting! The family still lived in the old plantation house. Cory smiled. "Old" in Hawaii meant it was built sixty years ago. She should count herself privileged to be invited. The ordinary tourist would never get to see such a place.

Hazel said the Bowers were an old kamaaina family. They owned the Bower Sugar Company with its acres of cane fields and the mill that turned the cane into raw sugar. The family also owned the hotel down the beach. Their brother Lester still managed it.

Leaving the water, Cory looked hopefully up and down the strand. No sign of the man whose image she couldn't forget. Perhaps today he was sleeping late somewhere, his dark head resting against a while pillow, while on the adjoining pillow.... Her imagination inserted her own sun-streaked silver blond hair, fanning out alluringly. She brought her body to a sudden halt before stepping through the hedge. How dare her mind present such crazy pictures. No one knew better than she the pain an over-active imagination could cause. Her sun-reddened lips twisted with bitter memory. She had imagined Paul loved her.

The thing to do now was to wash the salt from her hair and get ready for dinner at the Bowers'.

When her hair was dry and shining and she came out of her room wearing the long graceful dress, Hazel exclaimed, "Corinne, you look lovely! That muumuu is very becoming, and your tan makes your hair look silvery."

Cory flushed. Hazel was sweet to try to make her feel confident of her appearance, but Cory felt embarrassed. She hoped she hadn't given Hazel the impression that she was moping, or worse yet, that she lacked confidence. She didn't really—or at least only temporarily. She was simply determined not to give any man a chance to tear her emotions to shreds again.

She said firmly, "Your muumuu is becoming, too." It was a print of pinks and reds that set off Hazel's gray hair and gave her a distinguished look.

When it was time to go, Hazel descended the

stairs easily. "I still have to get back up them," she muttered, but she didn't appear unduly worried.

"Too bad about the Bowers," Hazel mused as they drove. "The family has been here four or five generations. That's a long time in Hawaii. They were top of the heap, you might say. Now they're down to one heir, and he isn't married. Irene and Mae's eldest brother ran the sugar plantation. His son had one child before he was killed in Korea. After the old man died, they tried hiring managers for a while, but it didn't work out. Their nephew— great-nephew, actually—manages it now. He lives at the house with the rest of them but I don't suppose he'll be there today. He has his own social life, according to local gossip." Hazel's voice was faintly disapproving. "Of that whole family, Buchanan is the last Bower. See that row of trees ahead? That's the road that leads up to the house."

For the last few miles Cory had been seeing small neat signs at the edge of the fields that read: Bower Sugar Company, Ltd. She turned onto a red dirt road that ran between the row of tall feathery ironwoods and another cane field. The road rose gently with the lay of the land. The cane field and the line of ironwoods ended, and two brick gateposts marked the beginning of a smooth driveway between double rows of straight gray-barked palms.

"Those are royal palms," Hazel said. "In the past royal palms were planted to mark the abode of the great—" her tone was light "—like Iolani Palace in Honolulu, and plantation managers' houses like this one."

The house was a two-story white colonial with a red tile roof, set on a terrace. Cory hardly spared it a glance, so taken was she by the huge tree in the center of the circular driveway.

"What kind is it?" she gasped.

"A banyan. They trim the hanging shoots to keep it from spreading."

They left Hazel's car dwarfed by the huge tree trunk and climbed the steps to a cement walk tastefully tinted the same red as Kauai's red earth and the tiled roof. A long porch shaded six floor-to-ceiling windows, bespeaking the graciousness of another era. While they waited for the door to be opened Cory looked back at the view. Another tremendous banyan tree on the wide terrace almost dwarfed the big house. Everything here was on a magnificent scale. Beyond the circular driveway a wide sweep of lawn ended at a low hedge. Beyond that the cane field blocked all sight and sound of the highway, and past the cane stretched the broad blue expanse of the Pacific Ocean.

Mae opened the door and greeted them exuberantly. They stepped into a huge, gracefully proportioned living room, which was sparsely furnished and at once gave an impression of cool airiness with its white walls and woodwork. The floor, however, was carpeted, and though Mae said they needn't remove their shoes, Cory had grown so accustomed to going barefoot that her new high-heeled sandals seemed unnecessarily confining, and she slipped out of them with alacrity.

Aside from scattered occasional tables, the fur-

niture consisted of three couches placed in a U
before a large fireplace, and a rattan coffee table.
An elderly man rose from one of the couches. Mae
introduced him to Cory as her brother Lester.

Irene came from the lanai wearing shorts. Lester
was attired in a subdued Hawaiian-print sport shirt
that had obviously come from the best shop in
town. Irene greeted them and suggested they all
move out to the lanai while she went to the kitchen
to fetch ice tea.

She stopped at the bottom of a graceful flight of
stairs to call, "Patrick! Our guests are here!"

Cory felt a spurt of excitement. Was that the
grandnephew? She heard the patter of bare feet, but
the person who appeared at the head of the stairs
was a boy. He bounded downstairs so fast that he
reached the bottom and stood in front of her before
she recognized him.

"Paco!" she exclaimed, surprised and delighted.

"Hi." He tossed back his hair. "I knew you were
coming." His T-shirt said I'd Rather be Surfing.
Cory thought it probably expressed his exact senti-
ments.

"Well, I didn't know you'd be here," she laughed,
"or that your name is Patrick, either."

"It isn't really." Paco made a face. "But the
aunts said I had to be called something civilized.
Want me to show you around the place?"

"Let's go out to the lanai first. Your aunt's
bringing ice tea."

They arrived on the lanai at the same time that
Irene emerged from the kitchen.

"I'm going to show Cory around," Paco announced.

"Let her sit down a minute first," Irene directed.

Cory gave Paco a friendly grin and sat beside Lester. He and Hazel appeared to be on good terms. They're the right age for each other, too, Cory thought, wanting to find a romance for someone.

The floor of the lanai was brick. In the corners and along the walls a dazzling array of flowers bloomed in pots. Comfortable outdoor furniture made the area an attractive place to relax. Cory noted that the mah-jongg set awaited them. She hoped she could remember the rules.

The talk turned to the past, and Cory was glad when Paco set down his glass and stood up.

"Let's go," he said.

They walked through the house to the front door so Cory could slip into her shoes, and then made their way around the front and across the back driveway. Steps led to a second terrace, a walkway and vine-covered cottages. Near them was a fenced pool and tennis court.

"Guest cottages," Paco said.

"Hmm!" Cory raised her eyebrows to indicate she was impressed.

"Nobody uses them now, but in the old days people came to Kauai by boat and the roads weren't very good. Aunt Irene says this house was like a hotel. Any visitors or people who came about the sugar business had to put up here. When the aunts and Lester were growing up, they had gardeners

who grew all the food. And dog kennels there—''
Paco pointed, but Cory saw only vines sprawling
over structures of some sort.

"What were the dogs for?"

"Hunting wild pigs."

Cory and Paco inspected the garden beds and the
plantings of fruit trees—papaya and mangoes and a
grove of bananas. He showed her some stone-
walled beds.

"These used to be fish ponds. They even raised
their own fish, but now they're just flower beds."

"Who does the gardening now?" Cory asked.
The beds seemed to go on and on. "Your aunts?"

"No—" The idea made Paco laugh. "We still
have two gardeners—one for flowers and the lawn
and stuff. The other one raises vegetables and fruit."

Even today it was a glimpse of another way of
life, Cory reflected. She wondered how it appeared
to Paco. Did he take it for granted? Had he ever
been away from Kauai? And where did he fit in?
Hazel had said the grandnephew was the last of the
line. An illegitimate son? She studied Paco's
features. He didn't look like the Bowers she'd met.
His black hair was straight, his eyes dark brown,
and of course he was deeply tanned. She wondered
what Buchanan Bower looked like.

"We'd better go back," she said reluctantly.
"They want to play mah-jongg this afternoon, and
I promised to play."

"Me, too," Paco said without enthusiasm.
"Would you rather go swimming in the pool?" he
asked hopefully. "They don't really need us to
play."

"I didn't bring a suit."

His face fell, then brightened. "Want to play tennis?"

Cory had to admit she didn't know how. She had never in her life known anyone who owned a tennis court, or belonged to a tennis club, for that matter.

The long afternoon passed pleasantly enough, although a couple of times Cory asked herself if she was awake or dreaming. It was hard to believe people were seriously celebrating Thanksgiving. Thanksgiving came when the leaves were off the trees and the air had a nip in it. Someone should be bustling in the kitchen, slamming oven doors. Paco and Lester should be watching a football game. The ocean should be gray and ominous, not blue and sparkling in the sun.

Of course, someone was working in the kitchen—the Bowers' cook. Would there be pumpkin pie, she wondered.

She concentrated on her game and tried to smother the nagging thought that life was passing her by. She looked across at Paco. He didn't seem to mind spending the holiday afternoon this way.

At five o'clock they quit playing. Lester mixed drinks at a liquor trolley and Irene brought out two trays of exquisitely prepared *pupus*, the Hawaiian version of hors d'oeuvres, consisting of strips of ham rolled around fresh pineapple chunks, squares of papaya on toothpicks, cheese and a bowl of macadamia nuts.

Irene picked up her drink and glanced at her watch. "I do hope Buchanan will get home in time for dinner," she said to Hazel.

"Where is he?" Hazel asked.

"Working at the mill! Didn't Mae tell you? Something important broke."

Mae said, "He's taking his responsibility seriously at last."

"It's quite amazing," Irene added. "He leaves the house at daybreak and doesn't come home till after dark. He seems quite obsessed. Who'd have ever thought he'd take to it so well and settle down?"

"He's old enough!" Lester reminded them.

"Yes, but there were times when we despaired. Perhaps that's best forgotten."

"He gets more like Gerald every day," said Mae. She shook her head. "They used to say Gerald worked harder than any of the people under him. Gerald was our brother," she explained to Cory.

Irene said, "Well, I told him what time dinner would be—"

"We wanted him to settle down and take over the sugar business for years," Mae told Cory mournfully. "Hazel knows how we hoped he'd give up the sea and come home, but we didn't want him to work himself to death, either."

A sort of choking snort from Paco drew everyone's attention.

"Sorry," he apologized. "The soda went down wrong."

Irene studied him. "Patrick, why don't you show Cory your paintings? She draws, too, you know."

"I'd love to see them!" Cory jumped up.

"Take your drink," Irene directed.

Cory liked her the better of the two sisters. Mae was sweetly sentimental, but Irene was understanding. She had guessed that Cory was longing to get up and move around.

On the way to Paco's room they passed a number of doors that opened onto spacious rooms. Cory caught glimpses of dark wood and plain curtains and an absence of frills, and one room that was frothy with lace and filmy curtains. She wasn't surprised to find that Paco's room was huge, his narrow bed lost in one corner. What did surprise her was the easel and the paintings hung on the walls.

"You *are* serious!" she exclaimed.

"Yeah, I guess I am." Suddenly he flopped back on his bed and burst into wild giggles. His irrepressible laughter drew a smile to Cory's lips.

"What is it?" she begged.

He sat up, holding his sides. "I'm sorry," he gasped. "I couldn't hold back anymore, listening to all that yak about *poor Buchanan*. 'Buchanan works so hard!' " he mimicked. " 'Buchanan's so *serious*. He spends all his time at the mill,' and now they're afraid Buchanan will work himself to death!" His boyish laughter made Cory smile.

"It's possible to become a workaholic," she suggested.

"You know where he is right now?" Paco jumped up and stared out the window at the water. "He's out on his boat with some girl! Or he's surfing, over on the other side of the island where he hopes no one will see him."

"What makes you think so?"

"Cause he wouldn't take me! No, I have to stay and entertain the guests." Paco's tone was resentful. "I could have gone to the mill and still got back before you arrived. It's just a mile away on the other side of the highway. That's how I know he wasn't going there."

"Well, I wouldn't tell the aunts," Cory said mildly. "It would be a shame to destroy their illusions."

"Oh, he works hard," Paco conceded. "But he's not working today. He's sailing. He just didn't want to stay here entertaining Hazel and her friend. I didn't tell him you were young and pretty," Paco grinned mischievously.

"That's just as well," Cory said briskly. "If he has a sailboat he probably has lots of girl friends."

"Yeah," Paco said unconcernedly.

So much for Buchanan Bower, Cory thought.

"Hadn't we better go back?" she suggested. "We're missing all the *pupus*."

Out on the lanai Cory noted that Irene had changed her shorts for a sophisticated long dress that looked more Parisian than Hawaiian. She refilled Cory's glass and urged her to try a square of *aku-aku*, a raw fish the Japanese consider a great delicacy.

"My dear, I've been wanting to tell you all afternoon how lovely you look in your new muumuu," she said. "It's too bad Buchanan isn't here," she added.

Cory decided she liked the fish and murmured her thanks for the compliment.

"Are you making some friends your own age?" Irene asked.

Cory told her about Sondra and Tim, Paco's art teacher. "Paco—Patrick—has a lot of talent, hasn't he?"

Irene nodded. "We're very pleased that he's interested in something besides surfing."

"Surfing looks very healthy."

"Oh, yes, but so many of those boys have no ambition beyond catching the next wave. They finish school and can't earn a living. And then they take to growing marijuana to earn money, or worse yet, stealing someone else's crop, and the first thing you know everybody's after them and they're in all kinds of trouble."

Trouble? In paradise? Cory wanted to close her ears. How could anybody get in trouble riding the beautiful blue curling waves? She wondered if the bronzed surfer had earned his sporty red car by growing marijuana. Or had some rich woman given it to him? One thing was sure, she'd never know.

The meal was an unexpected combination of hot weather food and traditional Thanksgiving fare: a handsome roast turkey surrounded by dishes of potato salad and cranberry salad, sliced avocado and melon balls. The maid took away the extra place setting.

When she left the room, Mae exclaimed, "Hazel! Guess what Lester heard at the club? Julia Vagos is coming home!"

"Coming to stay?" Hazel looked at Lester.

"Very likely. She's left her husband, I hear."

Lester was spare and precise despite his flamboyant clothes.

"Who's she?" Paco looked up from his plate.

"Vagos Sugar," Irene said briefly.

"Old man Vagos's daughter?" Paco squinted suspiciously around the table. "Would she be about Buck's age?"

"Yes, she is, and don't you say a word!" Irene ordered with mock menace.

Who is Buck, Cory wondered.

"We've never pushed it," Mae told Hazel. "And, of course, when she got married we thought no more about it. But now, if she's left her husband. . . with sugar in such a precarious state. . . a merger of Bower and Vagos would be the best thing for everybody."

Lester pursed his lips. "It certainly would."

"I wonder what Julia looks like now," Irene mused. "She used to be such a skinny little thing. I don't know why you're getting your hopes up. Buchanan never looked twice at her. The only woman he ever seemed serious about was that Emma Lassiter."

"How could he be serious about her? She was married!" Mae snapped.

"Thank heaven! I was sorry for what happened to her, but I was glad for Buchanan's sake. He must have seen then what she was."

The woman had been in a car wreck with another man, Cory recalled. She looked up to find Lester regarding her thoughtfully from his place at the end of the table. She remembered that she had been taken to be Emma's sister.

His eyes shifted. "Yes, well, I think we'd better leave Buchanan to make his own choice."

"You would say that!" Irene exclaimed with a shrug, but she changed the conversation.

Cory, like Paco, concentrated on the food, enjoying a meal she hadn't cooked.

Paco informed her that dessert would be papaya sherbet and coconut cake. The deft maid was removing the plates when the sound of a car broke the secluded quiet outside.

"There's Buchanan," Irene said with assurance.

Cory felt a ripple of excitement. At least she was going to meet the heir to all this.

The maid put his place setting back on the table. Cory heard leisurely footsteps cross the lanai and enter the kitchen. A man's voice spoke a friendly greeting to the cook. Cory noticed that the middle-aged maid was looking as expectant as she herself felt.

No wonder! The man who entered was the golden surfer!

Cory's breath caught in her throat. Her first thought was that there was some mistake, but everyone was greeting him quite naturally.

He was wearing a crisp white knitted shirt and superbly tailored khaki shorts. They hung so handsomely on his hips that Cory had difficulty removing her gaze.

When she did raise her eyes, she found him staring at her like someone in a trance.

"Corinne, this is our grandnephew, Buchanan." Irene was watching him closely.

He seemed to come to as well. "We've already met," he said abruptly. "But I didn't expect to find her here." He sounded almost accusing.

She tried to speak and found herself breathless. She felt her face grow warm from embarrassment, and her voice came out in a squeak.

"We met on the beach," she explained quickly, hoping he'd leave it at that.

He took the seat across from her, beside Paco.

"I met her before today, too," Paco said. "On the beach. She knows my art teacher."

"Tim Cooper?" Buchanan asked narrowly. "Is he a friend of yours?"

What business was it of his? Cory almost bristled, but she made herself say politely, "I haven't been here long enough to make friends. Why?" she forced herself to add.

"Just nosy." His sudden smile dazzled her, taking her mind from his strange question.

"Tim's a great guy," Paco assured them.

While Buchanan ate his sherbet and answered his aunt's questions about his day's work, he continued to stare at Cory. Each time she accidentally met his blue eyes she suffered a shock wave.

What was going on with her, she asked herself furiously. She had been surprised to meet him, yes. Did she have to start every time he caught her eye? At last she focused her attention on her sherbet and tried to readjust her memories of him. Thinking was difficult. Blood was pounding in her veins as though she was standing at the top of one of Kauai's clifflike mountains.

She forced her memory to play back her former impressions. She had seen him surfing near the hotel—the Bower family's hotel—with an alluring girl, no doubt a hotel guest. She had seen him running on the beach—near the hotel. She had seen him in his car—a car she could now picture as entirely fitting to his circumstances.

How wise she had been not to talk about her crush on a mysterious stranger! Sondra would have laughed. Perhaps Cory would even tell her the next time she saw her—make a good story of it. Her brown eyes sparkled with amusement. Forgetting the danger, she raised them for another look at Buchanan Bower, to see him as he was—rich, eligible, a busy executive, as far out of her social circle as he had been before.

His looks were perfection. If she had tried to imagine the ideal male to fit into this background, she would have imagined someone like him. Yet her best imaginings could never have conjured up Buchanan. He was so alive, so vital, yet he moved with lazy, careless grace—relaxed, perfectly at home every place she'd seen him. But he *was* at home! She allowed herself to smile.

"What's funny, Cory?" Paco asked.

"Oh! Nothing!" she exclaimed quickly.

Buchanan was talking to his uncle but he turned at Paco's words and again smiled dazzlingly across the table at her.

"Did you try it again?" he asked, as she had known he would sometime.

"Yes," she said briefly.

"Try what?" Paco asked.

"Snorkeling," Cory said. Again there was silence around the table. It was unnerving. At least they couldn't accuse her of playing up to their wonderful Buchanan.

She glanced at Hazel, who smiled encouragingly and said, "Buchanan, Cory's never seen a sugar mill. Can't you arrange for her to see something of it?"

"The mill's shut down," Mae objected.

"All the better. She won't be in anyone's way," Hazel insisted. "You've seen her drawings, Mae. I think a sketch of one of the sugar mills would go well in the series. She's going to have them printed as notepaper," Hazel explained to Buchanan.

"Sure." He looked at Cory with lazy, half-closed lids, but she caught a blue sparkle hidden beneath his thick black lashes. "What day would suit you?"

"You don't have to pin her down now," Mae interposed.

Cory replied vaguely, "Any day—"

"How about tomorrow then? Around one?"

A weird hollow sensation filled Cory's chest, as though an elevator had suddenly descended, leaving her heart in her throat.

"Uh—" She looked questioningly at Hazel, her eyes skimming past Mae's frown.

"I don't need you for anything tomorrow," Hazel said.

"All right," Cory told Buchanan, trying to sound businesslike. That's all the invitation was, anyhow, a polite response to Hazel's request, but the shiver of excitement that tightened her grip on her spoon warned her that she was flirting with trouble.

Lester drew Buchanan into a business discussion, Paco went to the kitchen for more sherbet, and Cory was left to her thoughts. She was appalled at how thrilled she was by the simple invitation. Did his prompt response mean he was eager to see her, or was it that the day after a holiday was simply a slow day?

When they rose from the table and Hazel indicated it was time to leave, no one pressed them to stay.

Cory said her goodbyes. Hazel kissed the sisters and turned to Buchanan. Before she could kiss him, he slid his arm through hers, saying, "I'll help you to the car, Aunt Hazel."

A fuss was made that the car should have been brought around to the back so Hazel wouldn't have to descend the terrace steps. Buchanan held out his hand to Cory. It was square and masterful. A wayward flash of memory recalled that that hand had touched her, had held her wet body against his.

"Give me the keys," he instructed. "I'll drive the car around."

As Cory gave them to him, their fingers touched. A lightninglike flash ran up her arm, leaving her trembling. She gripped her purse and offered her arm to help Hazel through the house and across the lanai.

Buchanan pulled Hazel's car in beside a row of azaleas in terra-cotta pots the color of the driveway.

His red sports car was there, too, clashing defiantly with the terra-cotta. It indicated the character of its owner. He did as he pleased, despite the maneuvering of his aunts.

As Cory got into the car, she heard him say, "Thanks a lot, Aunt Hazel."

"For what?" Hazel's voice sounded particularly innocent as she settled awkwardly into the passenger seat.

"For being my best friend," he said laughingly and closed her door.

Cory drove away from the estate with relief. Buchanan's mere presence strained her nerves. She never felt able to take a deep breath when he was near.

"Well, what did you think of Buck?" Hazel demanded as soon as they were on the highway.

"You mean Buchanan?" Cory stalled.

"Oh, nobody calls him Buchanan out of his aunts' hearing."

"He's very good-looking." Cory thought she could safely state the obvious. "I gather he's reserved for—what was her name—Julia Vagos?"

From the corner of her eye Cory saw Hazel shake her head. "Irene and Mae and I have been friends since I came here thirty years ago, and they didn't used to be at all snobbish, but now they're worried. Buck doesn't seem the least interested in getting married, and sugar is in trouble. They see the family business and the Bower name dying out together. But they're wasting their time trying to push Buck into anything." She gave a ladylike snort. "He used to come into the library when he was a little boy and march straight to the adult shelves. He knew what he wanted then, and I daresay he's worse now. Apparently he doesn't want to get married."

"Where does Paco come in?" Cory asked to stop herself from imagining Buchanan—Buck—as a small, adorable boy.

"He's no relation, although naturally people have gossiped." Cory felt Hazel give her a shrewd glance. "He's a kid that Buck picked up in some port when he was in the merchant marine. There's another instance of Buck doing his own thing. As soon as he graduated from Harvard, he got mate's papers and went to sea. He may be qualified as a captain by now. He wouldn't have anything to do with the sugar business till several years after his grandfather died. It's well he was independent. Can you imagine what would have happened to a compliant boy raised by three doting old relatives?"

Cory smiled, her eyes on the road.

"I ate too much," Hazel said regretfully. "One always does at Thanksgiving. Why do we keep having these huge meals when everyone is too fat already? Did you have a good time?"

"Yes." Cory realized her voice held reservations and added sincerely, "What a beautiful home they have!"

"You look very fetching in your muumuu, too," Hazel said. "I expect Buck was sorry he hadn't come home earlier."

Cory laughed. "Paco said he wasn't working, he was probably sailing."

"I don't doubt it. He wouldn't get any men to come in on Thanksgiving."

"But if the machinery's broken down, they must be in a hurry to fix it."

"It's not broken down; the mills *shut* down for repairs during the winter rainy season. The trucks and tractors can't cope with the mud."

Back at the condo Hazel climbed the stairs without much difficulty.

"I'm glad to be home," she exclaimed, sinking into her favorite chair.

Cory was glad, too. She wanted to slip into her room and daydream about the beachcomber. She caught herself up short. He was no longer a beachcomber—an imaginary man around whom she had built a desert island fantasy. He was Buchanan Bower, a real person, with a nickname, Buck. Tomorrow she had an appointment to meet him and be shown the sugar mill. She wished Hazel hadn't suggested it. She wished she hadn't found out who he was. She was going to miss her romantic beachcomber.

Besides, a real man threatened the cocoon of safety in which she had tried to wrap her emotions. Just seeing him on the beach seemed to raise her blood pressure. To become acquainted, to spend time with him, spelled danger.

She promised herself to be very, very cautious.

CHAPTER FIVE

CORY GOT THE DIRECTIONS from Hazel and drove to the mill the next afternoon. The day was beautiful, as always.

Hazel, when consulted, had told her she must certainly wear shorts. Cory had chosen the white ones, flaring and cuffed, and paired them with a feminine-looking white eyelet top. She couldn't decide how to wear her hair. She caught herself wondering how the rich Julia Vagos would dress, which was ridiculous.

At last she gave up. She wasn't going there to captivate him. She wasn't interested in captivating men. She put her hair into a single braid and hoped for the best.

"You know how to get there, don't you?" Hazel had asked. "You go the way we did yesterday, but instead of turning off the highway toward the mountains, turn toward the ocean. The mill office is at the end of the street."

Driving along the highway, Cory asked herself why she had gone along with this visit. Oh, well, he would show her through the mill, she would make her sketch and depart. He might even assign someone else to take her around. Nevertheless, her stomach was churning.

She turned off the highway onto the road to the mill office and found herself on a street laid out like a New England village. The branches of the thick trees met in a canopy overhead, and the houses that squatted behind the wide lawns were painted white. But the houses weren't saltboxes and the effect remained tantalizingly tropical.

The buildings ahead that looked like a collection of airplane hangars must be the mill. She pulled into the office parking lot and studied the juxtaposition of roofs and windowless walls, rust-colored conveyors and chutes. Her lunch lay in her stomach like lead. What was wrong with her, she scolded herself. Buck Bower was just an ordinary human being.

But when she stepped into the building, her hands were ice-cold, and she felt numb.

The office interior was painted institutional green, and the floors were bare wood. It was clearly the clerical part of an agricultural business. No money had been spent on frills.

She was ushered into Buck's office by a smiling woman who seemed to know why she was there.

Buck was standing just inside the door, which threw Cory into confusion. She hadn't expected to find him towering over her in this sudden way. No hint of the beachcomber hung around him this morning. He was wearing no-nonsense, unpolished riding boots, sharply creased brown riding pants and a short-sleeved yellow shirt with a button-down collar.

She stammered hello.

"Ready to go?"

The secretary retreated, leaving the door open. Buck smiled down at Cory with a pleased expression.

"Yes," she replied. Her face felt frozen. Her heart was thudding in her ears and she was short of breath.

He motioned her through the outer office and turned toward his car.

"We'll drive over," he announced, glancing down at her sandals. "No sense in walking you through the mud."

She sat stiffly beside him while he drove the short distance to the open door of one of the huge sheds. The red dirt before the shed was muddy. Rusty water filled the ruts.

"Sit still, I'll let you out," he said and went around to open her door.

When she stepped out, he took her arm. Again the touch of his fingers on her bare skin sent a tingle up her shoulder and across her neck. Her heart leapt, and she had to bite her lips to keep from trembling when his shirt brushed her and she caught a whiff of his after-shave lotion. She seemed to feel the rise and fall of his chest, so close to her arm beneath the starched cotton.

He guided her over puddles while she tried her utmost to keep her mind on what was actually happening and not let her thoughts go skipping off. She was thrilled with the excitement of being with him, having his attention, being the object of his blue-eyed regard.

"You understand the mill isn't working right now," he said as they crossed the rough ground.

"Yes." Was that the only word she knew? Couldn't she come up with a more intelligent response?

Buck didn't seem to notice. They stepped inside the garagelike doorway and Buck greeted one of the men working there.

"This is Miss Wells. She wants to see how a sugar mill works."

Cory and the man smiled at each other, and Buck proceeded to explain what was going on.

"This is the machine shop where we make our repairs. See these rollers?" He pointed to two huge cylinders studded with formidable-looking teeth. "These crush the cane. They start with coarse rollers and get finer and finer. The way cane is harvested nowadays, with bulldozers and cranes, a lot of trash also gets carried to the mill, and the rollers take quite a beating. These two have already been remachined. Here's one that hasn't been worked on yet."

Did he have to touch her shoulder like that to make her turn? The two-inch-thick steel teeth were gouged and broken, but Cory saw them through glazed eyes. Was he aware of the way she was reacting to him—as if her bones were turning to syrup?

One of the workers turned on a huge grinder and stood by while it ground slowly along a roller's length. Sparks flew. The screech was earsplitting.

Buck touched her arm, and again a tantalizing tremor like a charge of electricity ran through her.

He bent his head to speak in her ear, his breath warm and intimate. She felt a powerful longing to lean against his chest. Delighted at the excuse to stare at his mouth, she watched his lips move, but when he finished speaking, she had to shake her head. The outlandish screech drowned his words.

Gripping her arm, he moved purposefully away from the noise toward the next, bigger building, which opened off the one they were in. Looking up, she saw overhead walkways and flights of metal steps.

"This is the main part of the mill," he told her. "The stalks of cane come in through the loading chute. The leaves have already been burnt off in the field. I guess you know about that?"

Cory wanted to say yes, but she couldn't lie to him, no matter how ignorant he thought her. "Not really," she said, realizing again the difference in their backgrounds. Julia Vagos would know all about cane.

Buck seemed pleased to explain, however. "Special crews set fire to the fields with bottled gas torches. They keep the fire controlled, and the flames strip away the leaves. The blaze flashes through too fast to burn the green stalks. Once here, the stalks are washed to get rid of the mud and boulders, and all the debris is combed out. The stalks are shredded, and then they start through the mill."

He took her up one of the flights of iron stairs and onto a catwalk. "See, the rollers fit in along here. By the time the juices are squeezed out, the cane looks like sawdust."

"Where does the power come from to run all this?" Cory asked.

Buck smiled with satisfaction. "From the cane itself! What remains after the juice is extracted is called bagasse. Bagasse fuels our steam generator and also generates electricity to run the conveyors and pumps. This year we even sold electricity to the local power company."

He led her to another part of the building.

"This is the boiling house. I could explain the whole series of condensers and centrifugals the juice goes through, but it's better to see it. You'll have to come back when the mill's operating. Anyhow, it comes out as syrup, and is piped into tanks where it crystalizes into raw sugar. After that it goes to the refinery."

"Tell me something." Cory made herself ask. "Do you buy sugar like the rest of us?"

Buck laughed. "We don't own the refinery. They send us packages at Christmas of all the products they make—cubes, powdered sugar, et cetera—but the rest of the year we buy it, same as everybody else." He hesitated. "Well, that's about it." He sounded regretful. "I could show you more, but you wouldn't find it very interesting—not when everything's shut down."

He turned back the way they had come and Cory followed. No one was watching and she dared to let her gaze linger on the tall, well-formed figure ahead of her. He moved with the easy grace of an athlete, and he spoke to the men with the assurance of someone born to command. His boots were marked with the red mud of the cane fields. She wondered if his style of dress was a carry-over from his grandfather's era when managers rode around the plantation on horses or mules. His thick dark hair curled above the yellow shirt collar, and the material stretched tautly across his broad shoulders. She loved seeing him here in the midst of his strange, unknown kingdom, its unfamiliarity adding to his mystery. Yet he was as much at home here as he was at the beach.

At the doorway he waited and ushered her through the machine shop. "Do you still want to draw the place?" he asked doubtfully. "It doesn't look very scenic to me."

"Not scenic," she said steadily, "but the shapes and masses are interesting. A lot depends on the artist's interpretation."

"I'll be interested to see what you make of it." He helped her into the car and looked at his watch. "What angle are you going to draw it from?"

"I liked the view from the parking lot," she told him, "but I may walk around a bit."

He slid behind the wheel. Before she could think of anything further to say he was pulling into the space marked Bower.

"I have some work to do—" he began.

"Oh, I won't take up any more of your time," she interrupted.

"I was going to say, I don't know how long your drawing will take, but later this afternoon I could drive you through some of the cane roads. They're not public, you know."

Was he saying he wanted more of her company?

"The drawing will take more than an afternoon," she said gravely. "I thought I'd just do some sketches today...and see how it goes," she added lamely. At the moment her hands were shaking so badly she didn't think she could hold a pencil. She longed for him to go so she could calm down. What was *wrong* with her, anyway?

His eyes met and held hers. "A couple of hours...will that give you enough time?"

Time to calm down? Perhaps he knew how devastating he was.

"Fine!" she said hurriedly, and went to get her sketch pad from Hazel's car. When she turned, he was behind her.

She looked up and their eyes met. Without warning he reached for her. None too gently his hands closed around her shoulders.

With a flurried gasp she took a step backward and bumped against the car.

At her expression of surprise he gave his head a shake and dropped his hands to his side. "Sorry," he muttered. "See you in an hour or two." He strode out of the parking lot.

Cory gazed after him in confusion. The expression on his face had been like that of a sleepwalker. What had come over him? It was as though he suddenly saw her differently, or thought she was someone else. Emma?

What would happen if she drove with him out into the back roads of the cane fields? Nothing, of course! He merely meant to make a good job of showing her a sugar plantation to please his "Aunt" Hazel.

The parking lot afforded the only possible view of the mill. Fields of cane pressed close to the conglomeration of buildings on three sides, leaving clear only the working space in front where the trucks pulled in to unload cane and load up raw sugar.

Self-consciously Cory spread her mat on a patch of grass and rested her back against a tree trunk. For a while her fingers trembled so nervously she could hardly draw a straight line, but she forced herself to concentrate. She became involved in drawing and gradually grew calmer. For a while she escaped her feelings and worked well.

She had plenty of warning when he returned. He came out of the office whistling, and Cory looked up to see him striding toward her. Despite all her resolutions to be cool, she dropped her pencil. She groped for it in the grass, feeling ridiculously inadequate. Must she get turned upside down the minute she saw this man?

He squatted beside her and tilted her drawing with one capable brown hand so he could study it. He was so close she could see the smooth-shaven jaw, the individual hairs growing at his temples, the tender curve of his ear. Again he smelled freshly of after-shave. Had he used it just now for her appreciation? The idea made her feel slightly heady.

If he turned and looked into her eyes instead of at her drawing, she wouldn't be able to bear it. She froze against the tree trunk.

Sure enough, he did turn his head and stare straight into her eyes.

"You look so much like someone I used to know," he said tenderly.

Her frozen posture found its way into her voice. "I know," she said coldly. "Someone named Emma Lassiter."

"Oh! You've heard about her," he remarked with a tinge of bitterness.

"Some" Cory admitted.

He stood up and offered Cory his hand. "Ready to go?"

Obviously she'd said the wrong thing and annoyed him. Good! She hated the idea of being compared with someone else. She was herself—unique.

"Emma was a very beautiful girl," he said on the way to his car.

Mollified, she slid into the seat. He gave her a smiling glance as he got in. She did her best to look relaxed.

"I can't seem to keep from staring at you," he marveled.

Cory sought wildly for a clever reply. All she came up with was, "Hazel doesn't think I look much like her."

"You don't, in a way," he decided. Before she knew what he meant to do, he took her chin in his hand. She wasn't surprised. He was probably the type who couldn't keep his hands off women.

"Face to face, you don't," he said. "Her eyes were blue, for one thing. But your profile, and from the back— I could've sworn you were she. Like I said, she was very beautiful. And generous." He watched for Cory's reaction.

"Don't count on that!" she replied smartly.

He laughed. "You knew what I meant! You can't be as innocent as you look."

"Of course I can!" she snapped. It was none of his business how innocent she was.

To her relief he took his fingers from her face and started the car. His touch had been quite devoid of intimacy. Nevertheless, she had felt it to her toes, and her moment of ease was gone.

Driving up the tree-lined street, he said wonderingly, "Seeing you has turned my head around. I have a lot of preconceived ideas of what you're like. You're probably not like Emma at all."

"Well, I certainly wouldn't run around with other men if I were married," she blurted.

"She was unhappy here. So was I at the time," he said bleakly.

"You?" Cory was astounded.

"I wasn't crazy about settling down and taking on the responsibility of all this. I'd been a sailor for ten years. Once I got involved, of course, it was different. This life suits me now."

From the highway he turned onto a red dirt road running straight and smooth between the pale green fields. A sign at the turn-off said Keep Off-Private-Haul Cane Road.

Cory had noticed such signs at the entrance to roads all over the island. At first thought it seemed very selfish to bar the inhabitants from using these back roads, but perhaps the signs were only there for tourists.

"Do those signs really mean what they say?" she asked.

"They sure do!" Buck all but growled. "We harvest these fields with bulldozers and tractors, and load the cane into trailer trucks. It's no place for cars to be driving through. Cranes pick up the cane in ten-ton bites. You can imagine what that would do to a Volkswagen."

The cane growing on one side of the wide road was taller than on the other. The straight road seemed endless, undulating and rising, heading toward the mountains. They passed crossroads dividing the wide-reaching fields.

"That's what we call tasseling." Buck gestured toward the field on his side of the road where feathery seed heads caught the slanting sun. "Notice how all these fields are in different stages of growth? It takes two years for cane to mature. Planting and harvesting is carefully planned to keep the mill running. My grandfather was good at that. He knew these fields like the palm of his hand. In his day they had Hawaiian names. Now they have numbers."

A white bird with long legs and a long neck flapped up from the side of the road.

"Hey, old fellow, getting hungry?" Buck called to it.

"What type of bird was that?" Cory asked. The island didn't seem to have many birds.

Buck's face had taken on a more cheerful expression. "That was a cattle egret. They were brought here to control cattle insects, but once they discovered the cane fields they left the cattle. As soon as harvesting starts they arrive. They dine on whatever the bulldozers turn up: insects, flies, spiders, lizards—even mice. They're completely at ease. When the bulldozer backs up, the egrets walk out of the way. We call them the ground crew. When we're not harvesting, like now, they go back and hang around the cattle."

"It's a beautiful bird," Cory remarked. What a striking accent it made in the vast stretch of red earth and green cane!

Unexpectedly Buck halted the car in the middle of the road and turned to Cory.

"I want to talk to you about Emma," he stated.

Cory's stomach jolted. All she found to say was, "Shouldn't you pull off the road?"

"We're not harvesting cane now." He turned in his seat to face her, his arm draped on the steering wheel.

"Go ahead," she said, steeling herself not to mind. If Emma was the only subject they had in common, so be it.

Buck gave a half laugh. "I don't know what I want to say. It's just that you look so damn much like her I haven't been able to get her out of my head the last couple of days."

"Tell me about her," Cory directed, making an effort to sound interested.

He sat back in the bucket seat and gazed at the

wide, smooth road disappearing over the slight rise ahead. Fleecy, moving clouds filled the sky.

"It's been two years," he mused. "She was about your age. Twenty-four, twenty-five?" He looked at her for confirmation.

"Twenty-four."

"I thought I'd found the ideal woman. Except that she was married. I guess I was as mixed up as she was, maybe more. Half of me wanted to be here, half of me wanted to keep roving. In a way, she did me a favor: when I found out I wasn't the only man she was running around with, I lived, slept and breathed cane for a year. Maybe I put my feelings for her into running the plantation, because I finally accepted this life. I was born and bred to it, and now I know I love it."

I love this life, too, Cory wanted to say.

"Well!" He slapped the steering wheel with open hands. "I don't know why I'm telling you all this, except to explain, maybe, why I kept staring at you yesterday."

"Maybe you're still in love with her," Cory forced herself to say. It would be better for her—for him, she meant—to face the truth now.

"I don't know." His smile was wistful. "Her husband took her back to the mainland, which was what she wanted all along. For all I know she has a couple of kids by now, or she may be driving some other sucker crazy."

Her own hurt still fresh in her heart, Cory heard the harshness in Buck's voice with understanding. Obviously Emma still mattered.

He reached across Cory to open the glove compartment. She let her gaze dwell on his bare brown arm dusted with fine dark hair. The yellow shirtsleeve stretched to reveal tanned biceps as he groped in the opening and brought out a large jackknife.

"Ever chew sugarcane?" he asked, raising dark brows.

"Never," she confessed, her mood immediately lightened by his change of subject.

He slid out of the car and came around to open her door.

"Come out," he coaxes, "I'll cut you some."

He chose a stalk and chopped. With another stroke he slashed away the top, ending with a pipe of cane about two feet long.

"Look—" he pointed to the joints. "Roots will sprout from any of these. All you have to do is lay it in the ground—or on the ground." Dexterously he cut out a section and split it into chewable sticks. He handed Cory one. She put it in her mouth and chewed.

"It tastes just like sugar!" she exclaimed, and then laughed at the simplicity of her words. "I mean— I guess I thought only sugar out of a sugar bowl tasted like that. It's amazing."

"So are you," he said and reached for her. "Did anyone ever tell you you have the most delightful shoulders? So sturdy and little, and yet round and feminine. Just begging to be hugged, squeezed." His hands curved to fit her shoulders. Before Cory could find her breath his thumbs coursed along her collarbone and then his hands were sliding tantalizingly up the sides of her neck. For a moment his thumbs caressed the soft skin beneath her chin. Then with the slightest pressure he raised her face. Her eyes focused on his mouth, its masculine shape relaxed and sensuous as it approached her own.

He was holding only her face, as he might grasp a flower in order to inhale its perfume. She could have backed away, easily twisted out of his light grasp and escaped, but she did not. She stood her ground, trembling, wanting his kiss even while she sensed it wasn't for her. He was kissing a woman named Emma. But his mouth was warm, tender, reassuring. Her lips moved under his and she felt—or heard—him draw a great breath: a breath of satisfaction, a breath of desire. She knew she should resist, not respond as though all he had to do was make the first move and she would fall into his arms. But she seemed to have lost her will when she entered the cane fields. It was as if she had entered a different world. She willed the kiss to go on and on.

At last he raised his head and looked deep into her eyes.

"I've been wanting to do that from the moment I saw you on the beach. I came close last week when I hauled you out of the water, but you'd had enough of a shock for one day." He smiled. "I thought you were a tourist, here for a couple of weeks, and you're not the kind of girl to get involved for two weeks, are you?"

"No," she shot back.

He merely grinned. "Want to go for a swim? We'll stop at Hazel's and get your suit. There's a beautiful beach at the end of the highway that I'll bet you haven't seen.''

He was still holding her face. He hadn't kissed her, but the woman she looked like. Disappointed, she twisted away.

''I have to get dinner for Hazel,'' she told him steadily.

''Oh, yeah, I forgot about her.'' He cupped her chin with one bronzed hand and brushed her lips lightly. ''I'll give you a rain check,'' he added as though he were doing her a favor.

''Thanks,'' she mocked and headed back to the car. He opened her door with a flourish.

''All right, you know about my past,'' he said, slipping into his seat. ''Tell me about yours.''

''There's nothing to tell,'' Cory said resentfully as he started the engine. She wasn't going to entertain him with the story of her heartbreak. She gave him a few sentences about her job in New Jersey and her mother.

''I can see you're a loyal person,'' he remarked.

He turned a corner onto another field road.

''Well, you can go back and tell Hazel I've shown you all there is to see,'' he said into the silence.

''I hope it wasn't too much trouble.''

''No trouble at all,'' he said gallantly. ''When are you coming back to finish your sketch?''

''Monday, maybe,'' she said vaguely. She wasn't going to bother him again.

''If you do—''

His words were cut short. They were approaching a blind corner where two field roads crossed. The tasseled cane made it impossible for Buck to see the pickup truck rolling out of the side road until the two vehicles came within inches of colliding. Buck slammed on his brakes, shooting out a strong arm to keep Cory from hitting the windshield. The air whooshed from her chest as she was flung against it.

The pickup had been moving slowly, but as it braked a body seemed to come hurtling out of the air. With arms flailing, the man crashed onto the hood and slid to the ground to sprawl in front of the two vehicles.

Buck swore violently. "Stay in here!" he commanded and leapt from the car.

Frightened by his tone, Cory did as she was told. The man on the ground was already sitting up, shaking his head as if to clear it. To her astonishment she saw it was Johnny Komo. And the driver emerging from the pickup was Tim.

Buck was standing over Johnny, hands on hips. He didn't appear to be repentant or concerned, yet the near accident had been his fault. He was the one who had been driving fast.

Where had Johnny been riding? He couldn't have been flung from the cab! He must have been outside, riding on the hood. But why? He was picking himself up. Forgetting that Buck had ordered her to stay in the car, she sprang out, crying, "Johnny! Are you all right?"

He looked dazed and was rubbing his hip.

At the sight of Cory, Tim's face reddened, whether from embarrassment or anger she had no way of telling. He didn't speak to her. He put a hand under Johnny's arm and helped him toward the passenger door. Over his shoulder he said with a trace of reproach, "We were just taking a short-cut."

"Sure you were!"

"We were! We were up in the hills hunting for a *heiau*—the base of a temple Johnny's grandmother told us about—but we got off on the wrong road. Johnny was standing on the hood trying to see where we were."

"Get in your truck and get out. If I or any of my men catch you in here again, I'll have you up for trespassing. That's a promise!" He watched belligerently while Tim hurried around to the driver's seat.

Tim threw Cory a helpless look and did as he was ordered.

Without sparing her a glance, Buck said, "I thought I told you to stay in the car."

Cory was boiling with indignation, but she resumed her seat. How dare he behave in such an arrogant, overbearing way, just because somebody took a shortcut through his precious fields? Local people, too. They knew the company wasn't harvesting cane.

Tim started the engine and turned the pickup toward the highway. Buck slid behind the wheel and swung his car in a half circle.

"I'll have to follow them to make sure they go," he muttered.

"Why wouldn't they go?" she demanded angrily.

"You think they want to stay in the cane?" She turned to look at him. He was still scowling.

He didn't answer her. The thought swept through her mind that he must have made a tough first mate. A scene from some Hollywood sea epic flashed before her eyes...a sailing ship...*Mutiny on the Bounty*, or *Moby Dick*. Buck might even be a descendant of those early seafarers who came to Hawaii with the whaling ships.

In front of them the pickup reached the highway, gathered speed and shot away.

Buck drove in the other direction, toward the mill. A heavy silence filled the car until he turned onto the tree-lined street. Cory was thinking that she wanted nothing more to do with such an uncompromising, possessive, hardhearted man, no matter how handsome he was.

"So you know that character, Johnny Komo?" He scowled in her direction as though she were at fault.

"Yes, I do!" she exploded. "He happens to be the boyfriend of a friend of mine. I've met him, and he's nice. I can't understand why you should object to their driving on your precious roads when you're not harvesting. Why shouldn't they take a shortcut?"

He looked at her curiously as he swung into the parking lot. "Is that what you think they were doing—taking a shortcut? From where?"

"From the mountains, they said. What else is back there? What did you think they were doing?"

He slid out of the car with swift, angry motions

and came to open her door. "How long have you been on Kauai—a month?"

"Three weeks. But—"

"Then isn't it possible that you don't know everything yet? Look, whatever your friends were up to, those roads are private property. The signs say, Keep Out; they *mean* keep out." His jaw jutted forward. "I don't have to give a reason."

To her surprise he walked with her to her car and reached for the door handle. Instead of opening the door, he paused. His hand came up to clasp her shoulder.

"Listen, I'm sorry I lost my temper. I'm certainly not mad at you! Before that encounter I was about to ask you to have dinner with me. Hazel can spare you one night. Tomorrow's Saturday—"

For a moment Cory forgot to breathe. Did she want this?

As she hesitated, he said, "How about the Coco Palms? Have you seen the torchlighting?"

She managed to shake her head.

"Good! I'll pick you up about six. Okay?" He opened the door and she got behind the wheel. His high-handedness swept away any possible refusal.

"Okay," she gulped.

He stood back and watched her leave the parking lot.

She drove home in a trance.

CHAPTER SIX

WHAT SHALL I WEAR? was Cory's first thought when she came out of her daze. She parked the car, scarcely aware that she was doing so, and ascended the stairs to the condominium. Hazel would expect a description of her afternoon at the mill. She must decide quickly how much she wanted to tell.

She unbuckled her sandals at the door, glancing with fondness instead of dismay at the red mud clinging to them. She had not only been through the sugar mill, she reminded herself, she had been out in the fields with Buck. She had actually spent much of her afternoon with—and been kissed by—the plantation's decidedly attractive owner.

Hazel wasn't in the living room. In barefoot silence Cory went to her bedroom and flung herself on the bed. Looking up at the ceiling, hands behind her head, she allowed herself to relive every moment of the afternoon. She recognized the danger, though. Buck Bower was the type of man any woman would fall in love with, but he was also the type of man who would break a woman's heart. The pain she still suffered over Paul ought to make her reluctant to have anything to do with him. Yet here she was, thinking about him, remembering his kiss. He had kissed her because she looked like his old girl friend. Why had she let him kiss her? Well, because she didn't want him to think she was some kind of prude who would make something over a simple kiss. But why hadn't she told him firmly that she wouldn't...*couldn't*...go out to dinner with him? She sighed.

Oh, a simple dinner date ought to be safe enough. The man was still in love with someone else, and so was she. And furious, too. Damn Paul! She owed it to herself to go out and have a good time. She'd be a fool to sit home brooding when someone else found her attractive—even though she reminded him of a former lover. She sighed again. They could console each other, she thought wryly. The next time he wanted to talk about his past, she would certainly tell him about Paul, make it clear right away that she wasn't looking for romance.

Cory suddenly recalled the stunning appearance of the woman she'd first seen Buck with. He wasn't exactly playing the hermit, was he? And Paco had admitted Buck had lots of girl friends.

Cory got up from the bed. It was time to think about dinner. Hazel would soon emerge from her room. Shoving the possible problems aside, Cory admitted that the fact that she had a date made her feel better. It was one in the eye for Paul, even though he'd never know—or care.

Cory reported to Hazel only what she herself had done. She had been shown through the mill, had begun her drawing, and had gone for a ride on some of the haul cane roads.

Hazel was delighted when Cory told her that Buck had invited her to dine at the Coco Palms.

"That's lovely!" she exclaimed. "You'll have a charming evening, and the Coco Palms is one of the places you *must* see."

It's not me he's taking, Cory almost said aloud. *It's Emma.*

"Of course, you must wear your fancy muumuu," Hazel went on, "even though you wore it yesterday. He won't expect you to have a closetful of clothes. Do you want to offer him a drink here before you set out?"

Cory liked that idea. Hazel would enjoy a half hour of socializing before being left to have dinner alone.

In bed that night Cory lay thinking about Buck, half pleased, half apprehensive at the thought that he might slip beneath her determined defenses. She mustn't let this date go to her head. He might even be taking her out to please Hazel, of whom he was fond.

Nevertheless, she foolishly allowed herself to replay every incident of the day, remembering every look he had given her, doing her best to recall everything he said. In the parking lot, when he had taken her by the shoulders, she had thought he was going to kiss her, even though it was broad daylight and they were in front of his office. Instead, she'd received that strange look that had sent a shiver all over her. And then, later, he had kissed her. Twice.

The beachcomber image had slipped away. It was Buck Bower who had rescued her from her folly with the snorkel. Buck Bower had mistaken her for his old love. Buck Bower had driven past in his red Ferrari. She slid her hands down the silken sides of her nightdress. How had her body felt to him that day?

She was amazed she could be this excited about someone besides Paul.

SHE DECIDED TO change her appearance a bit for Saturday night, so after her shower she swept her hair up into a swirl atop her head and pinned it there. Immediately she felt insecure and wished it back down around her shoulders. The fact was, she admitted, she was going to feel insecure tonight no matter how she dressed. She could only do her best and put on a brave show.

With a return of self-confidence she slipped the beautiful lace-topped muumuu over her head and zipped it up. She was wearing her mother's opal earrings. They might have been designed with lace in mind, they looked so old-fashioned and fragile. She put on her makeup with unusual care, knowing she'd need every shred of confidence it might give her. She used green eye shadow to match the dress's basic color. Mascara darkened her lashes and brown eyeliner emphasized her wide-eyed gaze.

She was using a new tube of brighter, lighter lipstick than she had used back in gray old New Jersey. She filled in her lips and sat back to appraise the result.

She looked fine. A painful voice in her head whispered that she was quite pretty...and what good had it done?

She made a face at herself in the mirror and sprayed white ginger cologne on her wrists.

When she rose from the dressing table, her polished toes peeped from beneath the folds of the muumuu's hem. She slipped into high-heeled sandals, picked up her straw purse and went to the living room, confident of Hazel's approval.

"Lovely!" Hazel exclaimed. "I must say, I'm delighted to have a guest attractive enough to catch Buck Bower's attention."

"I hope it won't cause trouble," Cory offered hesitantly. "His aunts seem to be counting on Julia Vagos to revive the family fortunes."

Hazel laughed. "That's Mae's idea. I think Irene would be glad if he'd marry anyone. Anyhow, marriage is beside the point. I'm just happy you've found someone to take you around."

"He thinks I look like that woman, too—the one who was in the car wreck," Cory muttered. "I think he was in love with her."

Hazel snorted. "You don't look that much like her."

"He thinks I do," Cory opposed quietly.

Hazel shook her head. "Buck's not such a romantic! He can't possibly imagine you're like that woman. She was wild!"

But exciting, Cory thought resentfully. Men may think they admire loyal women, but they lose their hearts...or their heads...to flighty ones who give them a breathless chase. Was that what Paul's new girl friend had done? What was exciting about floundering underwater in a snorkeling mask?

Her meditations were interrupted by the door chime. She sprang to her feet. "There he is!"

"All right, let him in. And remember, you look *very* lovely, and not like anyone else in the world."

Hazel was sweet, Cory thought as she sped to the door. She smiled when she realized that with all the cogitation about what she was going to wear, she hadn't thought at all about how Buck would look. He wouldn't wear a suit. Nobody wore suits here.

Before she could venture a guess she was opening the door. The impact of his good looks made her head spin.

"Come in!" she invited in a sparkling voice that didn't sound like hers.

"Hello," he said, and his eyes registered appreciation. He was holding a lei of white flowers. He put it over Cory's head and looked at her intently, leaving her with the sensation of falling. She went rigid as he bent his head to give her the required kisses.

Flustered by her awkward reception of the simple ceremony, she stammered, "Come in." The lei sent up its heady fragrance of real white ginger and overpowered her cologne.

"Buchanan!" Hazel called from the couch. "I want you to have a drink here with us before you carry Cory off."

"Sure." He slipped easily out of the leather zoris he was wearing and paced barefoot across the rug to salute Hazel on the cheek, too. He sank into one of the living-room chairs.

"I'll have bourbon," he told Cory, looking her over again from head to foot.

While she fixed the drinks she had time to examine him in her mind's eye. He was wearing black pants and a black polo shirt with a white collar and white bands on the short sleeves. Beneath the knitted cotton his chest muscles bulged in flat slabs. He certainly looked like an islander with his black hair and deep tan. The only unexpected color was the flash of his blue eyes.

Cory poured sherry for herself and carried the tray to the coffee table.

Buck smiled at her and took his drink. Cory was interested to see that his charm affected Hazel, too. She was talking animatedly, and it was obvious she liked him.

Sipping her sherry, Cory felt surprisingly relaxed.

Buck and Hazel were talking about the growing of *pakalolo*—marijuana. The local authorities had passed a new law making it illegal for helicopters to make unregistered landings. The purpose of the law was to stop the helicopters from being used to bring bales of marijuana out of inaccessible valleys. Hazel scoffed at the idea that the law would accomplish anything. Buck was explaining what the authorities hoped to accomplish. It had to do with local politics. Cory was always forgetting what a small community the whole island was.

Buck finished his drink and set his glass on the coffee table.

"Cory hasn't said a word," he commented. "She hasn't learned yet what a hot issue this is."

Hazel seized the chance to press her point. "You agree that the authorities aren't controlling it. They can't! All they do is make periodic raids that hit the small growers. The big ones go free."

"How do you know the big growers don't get caught, too, from time to time?"

"It's never in the papers if they do."

"That's because they keep their operations looking small." Buck rose to his feet. "Ready to go, Cory?"

"I'm sure you know," Hazel said shrewdly. "After all, you grew up on this island. You probably have a good idea who the big operators are."

Buck grinned at her. "Don't forget, I was away from here for more than ten years. A lot of people moved in during that time. Come on, Cory, we've bored you long enough."

"I wasn't bored," Cory said truthfully. She had enjoyed listening to Buck's deep authoritative voice and watching the play of expression across his face and the way he unself-consciously propped one bare foot on the other knee.

This really was a different country, she told herself. Here she was, going to dinner at a famous restaurant with a barefoot beau.

She had focused her gaze on Buck's muscular forearm with its sprinkling of black hair. There was pleasure in studying the way his hand grasped his glass, the masculine squareness of his wrist. She couldn't remember admiring Paul's wrists, or even noticing them.

One overall look at the man sitting at ease on Hazel's upholstered rattan furniture brought Cory a clear truth. This man was good-looking and well built to his fingertips. Everything about him was attractive.

They slipped into their shoes, wished Hazel goodnight and went down to Buck's car. Cory's ease evaporated the moment they stepped outside. The more she tried to think of something to say, the more blank her mind became.

Buck broke the silence by asking, "Are you hungry?"

Cory managed to say yes. What was the point of taking a woman to dinner if she wasn't hungry?

"I made a reservation," Buck said. "The first time you go there, you have to have a table along the rail so you can see the ceremony."

A hard, brief shower had fallen while they sat in Hazel's livingroom. Dark clouds still hovered, but by the time they arrived at the hotel the setting sun was casting a last triumphant glow through the coconut grove. The moist air held a touch of coolness.

Buck parked the car and led Cory along palmstudded paths and across a causeway to a roofed dining terrace overlooking the lagoon. A waiter was leaning over the terrace rail feeding enormous red and gold carp for the amusement of the early diners. He was wearing an aloha shirt, as the flowery Hawaiian-print sport shirts were called here.

The weird orange glow of sunset under overhead clouds had faded by the time they were shown to their table by the railing. Buck seated Cory where she could look across the water. He pointed out the flambeaux that would be lighted during the ceremony. In the lingering dusk she could discern figures moving among the palms and what looked like a palm-thatched shelter.

"That's one of the Kings' or Queens' cottages," Buck said. "They cost over a hundred dollars a night now."

So much for palm-thatched huts! Cory laughed and relaxed. This evening was going to be fun as well as memorable. Now that it was dark and only candlelight lit his handsome features, Buck didn't look so intimidating. Their drinks came, and the glow of candles on each table brought the huge space down to a dimly lit intimacy.

From across the lagoon sounded the deep-throated call of a conch shell. Cory's blood tingled. A voice, projected by loudspeaker but seeming to come from the darkness itself, told the legendary story of how in old Hawaii the conch shell had summoned the nobility from the valley to feasts in this very grove. Then a man wearing only a cloth around his loins dashed through the trees carrying a blazing torch, pausing to fire the tall iron holders scattered along the paths. Light flickered on brown skin. In his wake the torches blazed orange amid black, curving tree trunks. A second youth kindled a torch at the central fire and sped to set ablaze the fire pits along the opposite bank of the lagoon. A drum continued to summon the long-dead nobles, the *alii*.

The smoking lights flickering on the water and the twisted tree trunks gave a dreamlike quality to the scene. Cory could easily imagine tall, well-fed rulers arriving in red-and-yellow feather cloaks. When the scattered lights had chased away the gloom of night, the drum ceased. The torches flared and smoked in the breeze.

Cory sighed and sipped her drink. "That was wonderful!"

Buck had ordered mai tais, saying, "I'm out to show you the sights, so let's do it right. This is the classic Hawaiian drink."

"What's in it?" Cory asked.

"Light and dark rum, orange curaçao and lime juice. And sugar." He tasted his. "Like it?"

"It's great!" She took a long pull at her straw. The alcohol would help her relax, and with dinner coming she needn't worry about losing her head.

It did help. The rum warmed her blood, and she pretended that she came often to this elegant setting with this handsome man.

"I wonder how Kauai looks to someone like you who's seeing it for the first time," Buck said meditatively.

Cory talked easily about her impressions of life on the island, and Buck appeared fascinated by everything she said.

For their meal he ordered broiled steaks of *mahimahi*. "That's dolphinfish," he explained. "Not porpoises, heaven forbid. They cook fish excellently here."

It was served with a salad and lightly cooked rounds of zucchini.

"Delicious!" Cory pronounced. "Is this a Hawaiian classic, too?"

"Definitely. I'm surprised you haven't tried it already."

She reminded him that she hadn't eaten out.

"Of course!" He waved his fork. "I keep forgetting you're not a tourist."

Their conversation seemed to be laboring and Cory fell silent. Why make an effort to be entertaining when he couldn't even remember who she was or what she was doing on Kauai.

"Do you remember who I am at all?" she burst out after a moment's quiet.

That startled him. He stared at her without speaking and she stared back belligerently.

"Do you classify all the women you meet by the length of time they're going to be here?" she gibed.

"Just about," he said provocatively. His voice held a hint of lazy laughter that suddenly infuriated her.

"No wonder you can't remember who you're with," she said acidly, and then she couldn't remember what he had said to make her so furious.

He didn't answer her question. He twisted his wineglass and smiled into it. "You don't act at all like Emma when you're mad," he said infuriatingly. "She used to raise holy hell when she'd had a couple of drinks and I said something she didn't like." He grinned wickedly, as though hoping Cory might do the same.

"I'm certainly not going to put on a performance to satisfy you," she said coldly.

"Good. What are you going to choose for dessert?" His tone was amused.

He called the waitress. Cory made her choice and subsided into silence.

"Sulking?" he asked after a bit.

Stunned by her own uncharacteristic behavior, she apologized lamely. "I don't know what came over me," she finished, shocked at her sudden spurt of temper.

"Mai tais can do that to a beginner," he said forgivingly. She felt her anger rise again at his lofty tolerance.

Luckily dessert arrived just then. Cory pretended to concentrate on it though her head still buzzed with annoyance. The coconut pudding she had chosen came as an individual mold topped by an orange sauce and ringed with slices of fresh papaya, pineapple and orange.

"Like it?" Buck inquired.

"It's—different." She ate slowly, pretending to savor the mild, melony taste of papaya, the sharp sweetness of fresh pineapple. Actually, the food might have been sawdust. How could she have ruined the slim chance she had to make him glad he'd asked her out? He was being polite and bored now.

"I like your hair like that," he said in the middle of her meditation. So he had noticed it was pinned atop her head.

Is that the way Emma wore hers, she wanted to

ask. She managed, instead, to thank him, but her words sounded forced.

"Do you feel all right?" he asked solicitously. "I should never have ordered you a mai tai. I forgot you had two sherries at Hazel's."

His remark seemed to be the final insult. She finished her dessert and laid her spoon carefully on the table. "Thank you very much for a delightful meal," she said with great formality, and tried to rise. The room swirled and she dropped back on her chair with a thud.

"What did you say was in that drink?" she gasped.

"Never mind," he soothed. "I've ordered some coffee and the show's about to start. You'll feel all right by the time it's over. They do make the drinks pretty strong here."

He looked so concerned that if she had been sitting beisde him instead of across the table, she would have laid her head on his shoulder. The next moment she realized that would be a foolish thing to do.

The coffee arrived. She took a hasty sip and burned her tongue.

A group of singers filed onto the stage, the women in muumuus, the men in aloha shirts.

"These are local people," Buck said. "They perform a lot at church luaus."

They sang, accompanying themselves on guitars and ukuleles. Three older women did a graceful hula, then three of the younger women danced. It was so beautiful that tears came to Cory's eyes, though the outlines of the performers were a little vague.

Next the stage lights dimmed and a spotlight streamed onto the causeway. A man and woman stepped into the light and proceeded to sing the hauntingly beautiful "Hawaiian Wedding Song." The flickering flambeaux were reflected in the dark water.

How could I have spoken so unguardedly, Cory inwardly lamented. The sight of Buck's brown hand resting on the white tablecloth made her doubly regretful. Her fingers stole out to cover his.

He clasped her hand in a warm, strong grasp. His smile assured her that she was forgiven. She subsided into a blissful daze and let the music sweep over her.

The song ended and Cory withdrew her hand to join in the applause. The group sang another number and filed off the stage.

"Ready to go?" Buck asked.

Cory felt she could have stayed forever, but the evening had to end.

As she stood up she swayed and clutched the table. Buck inserted a competent hand beneath her arm.

"Thank you," she said blithely. "I don't know what came over me." She gave him a perky smile.

He didn't buy her nonchalance. "Go ahead," he said. "I'll be right behind you." As she threaded her way among the tables she felt his hand resting lightly on her shoulder. She overcame a wild urge to fall back against his chest. Then he slipped his arm through hers and steered her toward the entrance.

"What's it like living here all your life?" Cory asked.

"I had to go away and find out what the rest of the world was like before I appreciated it."

Cory drew a deep breath. The darkness was filled with perfume. "It's the most beautiful place I've ever seen," she marveled.

Buck squeezed her arm. "The whole world looks rosy after two mai tais."

At the car Buck gave her a thoughtful look. "How about a walk on the beach?"

Cory shook her head. "I'd rather go home." She wanted the evening to end before she lost her head and threw caution to the winds.

"I'm not taking you home in this state!" Buck exclaimed with a laugh. "Hazel would have my ears."

"What state?" Cory demanded. "I'm not in any state! I'm perfectly sober."

"Of course you are," Buck soothed. "Now, how about a walk?"

"Lovely," Cory said regally.

She settled back in her seat to watch the roadside spin away from Buck's headlights. With no high-powered streetlights to repel the darkness, the night seemed very black. Much of Kauai was definitely country. Few lights shone from the buildings dotting the road, and not many cars passed going the other way.

He turned onto a bumpy road, drove down it to

where Cory could see water glinting, and shut off the engine.

"This is a good spot," he said. He got out and opened her door and held out his hand. "Come on. By the time we've walked to the end of this beach and back, you'll be sober."

She let him help her out and promptly lost her balance as her sandals sank into the dry sand.

"Leave your shoes in the car," he said.

They strolled a long way without speaking. Eventually Buck broke the silence.

"How long do you think you'll be staying?" he required.

"Till sometime in January," she told him. She wasn't going to bore him by raving about how she wanted to stay for good.

"We'll have to do some exciting things before you leave."

"Like what?" Cory asked warily. She would have to decide very soon whether she wanted this acquaintance to go further.

"You mean, what's exciting here?" he was saying. "It depends...I find you exciting, for instance."

Something inside Cory that had been rather relaxed, clamped shut. She was cold sober now. Here she was, miles from anywhere, alone with this man she couldn't begin to handle. He was clever and sophisticated and experienced. Women probably threw themselves at him.

"Do you like sailing?" he asked.

"I don't know," she said stoutly. "I've never

been sailing." The sooner they ended this farce that she was his type of playgirl, the better.

"Some people don't like Kauai because they say there isn't enough happening. Do you find it dull?"

A remembered sentence clicked in Cory's mind. Buck's married girl friend had found it dull here. Presumably that's why she ran wild.

"No, I don't," Cory said honestly. "But I haven't had a very breathtaking life."

They walked in silence until they came to a tumble of rocks jutting into the sea, then turned back. The half-moon had risen out of the ocean.

It gives a lot of light even though it isn't full," Cory remarked.

"You should see it from the deck of a sailboat when it's full," Buck said, taking her hand.

"It sounds nice," she said carefully, knowing he'd never take her sailing. She had been impossibly awkward this evening. One part of her wanted desperately to make a good impression. The other part kept saying, *don't try, he's dangerous.*

He dropped her hand and slid his arm around her waist.

"You don't seem to know how very attractive you are," he said, coming to a halt. He pulled her around to face him and looked quizzically into her eyes. "I can't believe it's not an act," he said musingly.

"I don't know what you mean by 'an act,' " she returned seriously. "I used to think I knew all the answers, but then I got the wind taken out of my sails—"

"Too bad," he said offhandedly. "Or maybe I mean *good*, if it's kept you from being supersophisticated like most of the women who come out here alone. They're usually on their own for the first time after a divorce." He shook his head. "They're all planning to get married again as soon as possible, to a more exciting man. How'd I get off on that? That has nothing to do with us."

All right, so he liked her tonight, but that didn't mean anything. Tomorrow he might change. Hadn't she learned that men were fickle? She made a move to slide out of his arms. His embrace tightened.

"What's the matter? Did I hit the nail on the head? Did you make a bad marriage? Are you hoping to meet a more exciting man?"

"No!" She wrenched away from him. "I haven't been married and I'm not hoping to meet a more exciting man!" His words made her realize that the affair with Paul could have been worse. At least she was free of legal entanglements.

He recaptured her easily, pinning her arms against her body.

"Let me go," she insisted.

"Why?"

Because it's better to make the move myself than to have you release me, she thought, but she couldn't say that. She wriggled again.

He loosed her, remarking with tolerant satisfaction, "What a child you are!"

It was impossible, she found, to stalk rapidly over dry sand. After only a few steps her leg muscles were crying for mercy and she was growing short of breath.

"What's your hurry?" he asked, amusement in his voice. He was keeping up with her easily, and she felt he was toying with her.

"It's late."

"It's barely eleven o'clock." He caught her hand and brought her to a halt facing him. He raised one solid capable hand to cradle her face. His thumb pressed her chin up. When he bent his head to touch her lips with his, he did it lightly, teasingly. She stood motionless, her arms at her sides, the long skirt of her muumuu covering her bare feet. The moon was a bright patch over Buck's shoulder, the waves lapped the sand.

I'm not actually here, she thought when he lifted his head. *This is a mad wild dream.* She refused to let herself feel anything.

"Are you really such a cool little thing?" he asked. "You're a real challenge to a man."

"I don't want to be a challenge!" she exclaimed.

"Then you shouldn't look the way you do. They must all be blind in—where is it you come from—New Jersey."

Despite her intentions to keep in mind that this evening was as insubstantial as a dream, unexpected warmth licked over her. She tried to remember why it was so important to hold this man off, and failed. The effects of the mai tais had worn off. She didn't feel belligerent now. Still, she wasn't going to provide the kind of diversion Buck appeared to expect. She turned her face away.

He put his hands on her shoulders and gave her a little shake. "What are you thinking about?"

"Nothing—"

"Is something going on between you and Tim Cooper?" Buck's amorous mood seemed to have passed, and he began walking again, pulling her along by his grip on her arm. "Paco tells me the three of you are going sketching tomorrow."

"Does that mean something has to be going on?"

"I suppose not," he growled. "But watch him. I've warned Paco and I'm warning you— Don't let him get you involved in any trouble."

"What kind of trouble could we possibly get involved in?"

Buck gave an exasperated laugh. "I can see I'm going to start feeling responsible for you."

"You needn't." His remark gave her a queer jolt.

"You look—" He dropped her arm to make a helpless gesture with both hands.

"I know, I look like someone else!"

He halted, taking her again by both shoulders and holding her at arm's length.

"That isn't what I was going to say at all! You look like you've been packed in tissue paper and just taken out of the box." He studied her face in the moonlight.

Cory laughed. "I assure you, I haven't."

"You think this island is paradise, but you forget the people here are the same as anywhere else." He slid one arm around her shoulders and started walking again. "Come on, I'd better get you home before my car turns into a pumpkin."

Cory was silent on the ride home. Did she really look as inexperienced as he said? How could she, when Paul had given her such a taste of life's bitterness?

They slid their feet into shoes again. They were only minutes away from Hazel's condominium.

Buck helped her out of the car and tucked his arms around her.

"Cory," he murmured before his lips, masterful, sensuous, descended on hers.

Her heart fluttered. His strong forearm across her back pulled her close against his chest, crushing her lei. She felt his heart thudding against her breast.

He was holding her on tiptoe against him and she moved to regain her balance. He lifted his head, looked at her and smiled.

"You're just as sweet to kiss as you look," he said, and bent his head for more.

Something was happening to Cory. Paul had never kissed her like this. Buck was kissing her as if he enjoyed it, not as though it were a necessary preliminary to getting a woman into bed. Cory felt like a lump of brown sugar, crumbling, melting into syrup.

"Kiss me back," Buck urged, squeezing her shoulder.

Against her better judgment she began to do so. His breathing grew faster.

Still holding her close against him with one arm, Buck ran his other hand caressingly, exploringly up her side to cover her breast. She drew a sharp breath compounded of pleasure and fear. Through the fabric her breast responded to the touch of his palm. She would have drawn away from him but his arm refused to let her go. He took his mouth from her lips to spot sweet kisses over her face. With her eyes closed she couldn't guess where the next one would fall. She grew short of breath and tried to pull away. Buck ran a trail of fiery kisses down the side of her neck to the high lace collar of her muumuu and muttered an imprecation.

"Those missionaries knew what they were doing when they designed these things!" Nevertheless, she felt his warm lips through the lace, on her collarbone, on her cleavage.

He loosed her and stepped back a pace. "Let me see where *you* are under this thing," he said, reaching out his hands to span her waist. "Ah, there! Mmm...very nice. I remember your body when I hauled you out of the water."

"Do you often get acquainted with tourists that way?"

"Only the pretty ones. I let the rest drown."

She drew a sharp breath, but he only laughed and slid his hands up her ribs to cup both her breasts.

She hadn't bargained for the effect his hands— warm, big, capable—would have on her. Suddenly she longed for his touch all over her body. She didn't try to resist the desire to lean against him, to have him hold her once more before she went upstairs.

However, he kept one large hand clasped over her

fast-beating heart, and this time when he kissed her she felt the thrill to her toes.

"You're the most exciting thing on this island," he murmured. His lips against the corner of her mouth gave her the delirious feeling that she was somehow in control of the situation, and in control of him. She felt expansive and allowed her hands to move across his back, exploring with her fingertips the muscles there, the shape of his shoulder blades.

"Let's go over to my place at the hotel," he whispered.

She froze instantly. Had she not guessed that he had some setup there where he took the divorcées he picked up at the bar or at the beach?

"Certainly not!" She drew back. "I'm not one of your two-week tourists!"

"You're a two-month one," he joked, but Cory didn't find the remark funny. She had known from the start that this night wasn't going to turn out well, and here was the end. If only her heart weren't beating so hard. If only one part of her didn't long to do as he suggested! How could that be? Wasn't she still crushed over Paul? Yet she was perfectly ready to be hurt all over again. And she knew with terrible clarity that a broken love affair with Buck Bower would hurt more than she could ever imagine.

"No!" She turned and stalked upstairs.

He didn't try to follow. She took a hasty glance over the iron railings of the upstairs walkway. He was standing where she had left him, waiting for her to unlock the door and slip safely inside.

I didn't thank him! she remembered. Turning back she gave him a flippant wave. He gestured in return.

Inside the door she carefully removed her lei and listened to him start his car and drive away. *So much for that,* she thought sadly.

CHAPTER SEVEN

HAZEL, OF COURSE, wanted to know the next morning how Cory's date went. Cory had opened her eyes to see the lei Buck had given her, now no more than a strand of drooping petals hanging limply over the doorknob. It symbolized the evening. Better to discard it and forget the evening had ever happened.

She reported her date the same way she had reported her trip through the sugar mill. She told Hazel how memorable the torchlighting was, how she had enjoyed the entertainment, and how much she liked dolphinfish. She almost managed to keep from mentioning Buck at all, but he was what Hazel wanted to talk about.

"Did Buck behave himself?" she questioned.

They were in the kitchen. Cory poured herself coffee while she deliberated over her answer.

After a pause she said, "He wanted me to go over to his place at the hotel, his...love nest, I suppose you'd call it."

Hazel laughed. "I'm not surprised. He has a bit of a reputation. The suite isn't a love nest, however. It's where they entertain people on sugar mill business."

"Like the guest cottages they used to use at the house? Paco showed me those."

"Exactly."

Cory's brow cleared. "Anyhow, I didn't go. He wasn't inviting me there for mill business."

"I shouldn't think so!" Hazel laughed. "But you mustn't think he keeps a playroom, because he doesn't. I expect it was good for him to be turned down. He's too used to being a boss."

Cory was annoyed at the way her spirits rose. She began to feel quite cheerful. Maybe, just maybe, he wasn't quite the playboy she had thought he was. That beachcomber image still got in the way.

"Tim and Paco and I are going sketching this morning," she said, "but I'll have a swim first."

Half an hour later she returned from the beach in good humor. She was looking forward to an uncomplicated day.

She donned dark green shorts and the white eyelet top she had worn to the mill, and put her hair into a single braid. Some day she would have to go back and finish drawing the mill, but it could wait.

She met Tim and Paco and they set off in Tim's fancy pickup. Cory expected him to mention the near collision in the cane fields, but he didn't bring it up. Maybe he didn't want to talk about it in front of Paco.

Tim was wearing the only clothes Cory had seen him in—shorts, zoris and aloha shirt. She wondered what he wore to class. His light brown hair was newly cut. Despite his shorts, he looked very much the schoolteacher on his day off.

Paco's T-shirt message this day was in Chinese.

"It says Happy New Year," he told Cory. "Buck got it for me last year in Honolulu."

They set out, Cory sitting in the middle.

Tim said, "Paco and I thought you might like to make some rubbings of petroglyphs. We heard about this stone up in the hills. It might make a good sketch, too. We haven't seen it."

"Wait a minute!" Cory laughed. "Am I supposed to know what petroglyphs are?"

"They're primitive carvings scratched on rocks," Paco explained. "They might mean something special, or they might be just doodles. Nobody knows."

"And what are we going to do with them?"

"Make rubbings," Paco said. "You tape rice paper on the stone and then you rub the paper with a crayon. You get the outline of the carving. They're just lines."

"Like rubbings of gravestons?" Cory asked.

"Same thing," Tim said.

"Petroglyphs look like this." Paco drew stick figures on the back of his drawing pad.

"I bet nobody thought to bring food and drink! That's what I get for running around with artists." Tim braked and pulled into a drive-in food stand.

They bought boxes of fried chicken and continued on their way.

"We have to cut through the Bower plantation to get there," he announced.

"On haul cane roads?" Cory exclaimed. "But— You're joking!"

"No problem." Tim threw her a warning look. "Paco's with us."

"You mean Paco's part of the establishment?" Cory questioned with a laugh, hoping to recover her slip.

Tim grinned. "That's right. No Trespassing signs don't apply to him. Why do you think I brought him along?"

Paco grinned. "Hey, can I see that map Johnny drew you?"

"Look in the glove compartment." Tim swung off onto a haul cane road identical to the others Cory had seen, but he seemed to know where he was going.

Cory held her breath, hoping they wouldn't encounter Buck. What would happen if they did—another scene? Surely not with Paco along. Tim obviously didn't expect any unpleasantness.

The sharp steep mountains loomed closer. The cane fields ended and the wide red road became a track closed in on either side by a thick hedge of trees. They were driving into an ever narrowing valley. Behind the roadside thicket Cory could see green bushy walls rising almost perpendicular, but the porous lava rock welcomed the seeds and roots of any plant determined enough to elbow its way in.

"Where is this stone?" she asked suspiciously. "Don't tell me it's up on one of those ridges! I didn't come dressed for mountain climbing."

"It's supposed to be along this road," Tim said. "Actually, it should be along this streambed that the road follows."

"Yeah, the rock was here before the road," Paco reminded them.

"There!" Tim braked and gestured.

A simple cement span crossed the dry streambed at that point. On the bank, safely above any sudden onslaught of water, sat a round black boulder the size of a large office desk.

"I believe that's it," Tim amended. "Let's go look." He parked the pickup and he and Paco clambered along the rough bank to look closely at the stone. Cory surveyed the scene from the bridge. A koa tree with its sickle-shaped leaves grew behind the big round lava chunk, and a variety of interesting foliage filled the hillside. She recognized palmettos and ti plants. Yes, she could make a nice drawing here.

Tim and Paco were examining the rock. Cory climbed down to join them.

"Here's an interesting design," Paco proclaimed, his hand tracing grooves the depth and width of a fingertip.

"Actually, petroglyphs look better as rubbings than they do on the stone," Tim said.

It was true. The lines were barely perceptible. And the carvings did look like doodles. Perhaps the markings represented the frustration of an artist whose culture had very little wood and no paper or canvas.

Tim brought their materials from the truck. They each chose a design and set to work.

What would Buck think if he saw her now? Would he ever come on such an expedition? She didn't know him well enough to guess. She thought of Paco's easel and roomful of canvases. Somebody certainly encouraged him. While she steadily rubbed Tim's black crayon over the rice paper, she wondered if Paco had told Buck where he was going. How many tabs did one keep on a fourteen-year-old? Whose responsibility was he?

"Paco, did you tell the aunts where you were going today?" she asked.

"We talked about it last night at dinner. They knew about this rock. Well, it's on their property. We also talked about where Buck was. You went out to dinner with him, didn't you?" Paco grinned at Cory's blank surprise.

She was acutely aware that Tim, on the other side of the boulder, was awaiting her reply.

"He took me out, yes," Cory replied levelly. "How did you know? Did he tell you?"

Paco made a face. "He never tells me anything anymore. Hazel told the aunts."

Tim said, "Paco's wise to most things that go on around here."

"He is?" Cory looked up from her work in time to see a meaningful grin pass between Tim and the boy. What was that about, she wondered.

So Hazel had told Irene and Mae. If she had gone to Buck's room last night, she supposed the whole town would have known it. In a way she was amused. On the other hand, she wasn't crazy about having everyone know Buck had asked her out once, then never called her again. What if the way Paul had dumped her had been common knowledge? She squirmed at the thought.

"Getting tired?" Tim asked. "You're almost finished."

"Getting cramped," Cory lied.

They were all pleased with their finished rubbings. Cory's was a stick figure about twelve inches high holding a smaller one by the hand.

Rolling up the sheets of rice paper, they put them in the truck, then began to sketch, eating chicken while they drew.

"This is such fun!" Cory exclaimed at the end of an hour. With a final flourish of her pencil she declared her drawing finished. No thought of Buck or Paul had intruded while she worked. She had concentrated completely and happily on what she was doing.

"Having a good time?" Tim asked low-voiced. Paco had finished and gone to fetch the water bottle from the truck. "It's not the Coco Palms, but my heart's in the right place."

"Don't—" Cory begged.

"How come Buck was driving you around the cane fields?" Tim questioned.

"He was showing me the mill," Cory explained, "and thought I ought to see the fields, too. Why were you driving through them?"

"Looking for this place."

"Why didn't you explain that to him?" Cory wondered.

Tim shrugged. "He didn't exactly give me a chance, did he?"

At that moment Paco returned. Tim held up his drawing for them to admire. "I guess that's it. Are we ready to go back?"

"I am," Cory said.

Their art materials stored carefully behind the seat, they climbed into the truck with sighs of relaxation, all three pleased with their day's work. It was midafternoon. White clouds hovered over the horizon as usual, but the sun was shining and the air was neither hot nor cool, but perfect, as usual. The truck sped along the haul cane roads until, at a crossroad, Tim slowed and coasted around a corner.

"What's the matter?" Paco asked sharply.

An old white stationwagon stood crosswise, blocking their way. Beside it two men in boots and cane workers' garb were holding rifles.

Tim braked with a jolt. Cory braced herself against the dashboard.

Tim thrust his head out the window. "What's happening?" he called.

One of the men stepped up to the car. He was young and brown skinned, with a well-fed look. His black eyes held no sparkle of friendliness as he surveyed the truck's occupants.

"Nothing's happening," he growled. "We're just doing a little checking."

"Checking what?"

"Checking who comes through here. I heard Mr. Bower ordered you not to come back."

"So you're checking for Bower, are you?" Tim laughed mirthlessly. "Well, I've got the boss's boy here."

"So I see," the man admitted sourly.

"So it's okay for us to be here."

"All the same," the man said, politely now, "I'd like to know what your business is."

"Sure, we've been making sketches of the petroglyphs back there." He opened his door and reached behind the seat. The pad he pulled out happened to be Cory's.

"Not bad," the man said. "You drew that?"

"This is the young lady's. Mine's in there, too, and Paco's. You want to see them all?"

The other man had come to look over the first one's shoulder. He was also in his twenties. He looked up at Cory and smiled.

"I suppose that's what you were doing the other day, too," the first one growled.

"Matter of fact, it was," Tim returned airily. "We were hunting for the rock."

"Sure you were! Well, now that you've got your pictures, you won't need to come in again." He stood back and motioned with his gun for them to drive on.

As soon as they were out of hearing, both Cory and Paco burst into speech.

"What was all that about?" she demanded.

"They're getting too big for their britches!" Paco cried. "I'm gonna tell Buck!"

"I wouldn't do that," Tim counseled.

"What was it about?" Cory repeated.

"They're guarding their crop," Tim stated with a grin. Beside her Paco giggled.

"Will you please tell me what's funny?" she demanded in exasperation. "I was frightened."

Tim said lightly, "Nothing to be scared of. This

is just part of the fun and games on Kauai.''

"I don't know about you—" Cory's voice dripped sarcasm "—but when someone points a gun at me, I'm scared.''

"Why shouldn't I tell Buck?" Paco interrupted.

Tim looked at Paco with one raised eyebrow.

"Do you think he knows?" Paco sounded shocked.

"Don't be naive." Tim returned his attention to the road. "This is Bower land. Do you think he doesn't know what's being grown?''

"Will you please tell *me*?" Cory begged, trying to keep her temper under control. "Crop of what? What is being grown?''

"Cory," Tim said languidly. "It's better not to know too much. The same goes for you, Paco. It's better not to let on how much you know.''

"I'll find out!" Cory vowed. "I'll ask Buck, if need be.''

"Don't do that." Tim sounded uneasy. "It's sugar workers keeping an eye on their crop, like I said.''

Cory didn't believe him for a minute, but her threat to ask Buck was meaningless. She might never have the occasion to speak to him again. But she could save her questions for someone who would give her straight answers.

That evening in the kitchen she was thoughtful. Why was everyone so touchy about cane fields?

"You seem pensive," Hazel remarked at dinner. "Did something unpleasant happen on your sketching trip?''

"Not exactly unpleasant. . . ." She told Hazel about the men who stopped them; the men who were supposedly guarding the cane.

Hazel looked a little worried. "Oh, dear, what are things coming to when a person's not safe driving around the Bowers' land? The crop those men were guarding wasn't sugarcane, my dear. It was *pakalolo*—marijuana."

And Tim had implied the crop was Buck's! Hadn't he?

After a second she said, "We were in the middle of the cane fields."

"That's right." Hazel nodded. "Cane takes two years, so at the stage when it's high enough to hide the marijuana, they go into the middle of the field, pull out the cane, and put in a little patch of marijuana. They get all the advantage of the cane field's drip irrigation—water and fertilizer."

"But those men were plantation workers. They knew Paco."

Hazel nodded again. "They're the ones with access to the fields."

Cory was silent, digesting the information. "Why didn't Tim tell me that?" she asked at last.

Hazel shrugged. "Who knows? He might think the less you know, the better."

"That's what he said," Cory recalled. "At least, he said it's better not to let on how much you know." She smiled. "I guess that's what he was doing. But why were those men so fussy about our driving through? You'd think they owned the place. Doesn't Buck object?"

"I'm sure he objects to having his cane pulled up, but once the deed is done it doesn't do any good to replant those spots. The cane would be way behind the rest of the field. Besides, there's no easy way of finding the patches until the cane's cut. Then it's too late. The *pakalolo* has already been harvested. All that's left is a bare place. If the police spot the patches by helicopter and go in and destroy them, they trample the cane, too."

It wasn't Buck's crop, then. If cane workers planted the stuff, why did Buck get angry at Tim and Johnny Komo that day, Cory wondered. She hadn't told Hazel about that. Was it only because they were trespassing? Who were those men guarding their crop *from*?

Before she could ask these questions Hazel bustled off to play bridge with the next-door neighbors. Cory thought uneasily that Tim was right: it was better not to know too much. But now she did. She didn't want to suspect Buck of doing anything illegal, like growing pot. Yet she would be a fool to close her eyes to the possibility.

She woke before daylight the next morning, having gone to bed early, weary from the day's confusing events. She leapt out of bed and decided to go for an early-morning swim. The temperature of the air scarcely varied from day to night; the temperature of the water not at all.

She was wearing one of the new bikinis and the lace overshirt when she stepped through the hedge onto the beach, expecting to find it completely empty. Instead, a figure was coming her way, running swiftly on the hard-packed sand at the water's edge. Buck!

Her first thought was to slip back through the hedge, but it was too late. He'd already seen her. Her heart beating fast, she walked hesitantly down to meet him.

Mopping his face and neck, he came to a springing halt, his running shoes making spurts of sand.

"You're up early." He was breathing hard, but by no means sounded out of breath. He was wearing red running shorts and a navy blue short-sleeved shirt, the cuffs of which curved around his muscular forearms. Cory raised her eyes to meet his smile. His blue eyes sparkled.

"Yes, I am," she responded.

"I can't stop," he panted, jogging up and down. "I still have five miles to go. Meet me at the hotel in an hour. I'll buy you coffee!" He was already starting on. "In the bar!" he called over his shoulder. Within seconds he was way down the beach.

Cory stood where she was, catching her breath as though she, too, had been exercising. The sudden tropic daylight had dawned. It must be about six-thirty. In an hour she would have time to swim, dry her hair and put on makeup. She ran joyously into the lapping waves.

Floating on her back in the gracious water, she realized with a thrill that she was actually meeting him where she had longed to the first day she saw him, when he had shouted to that other girl in pidgin. He had never talked pidgin to Cory. She was still an outsider. But not forever. Her small jaw set. It had occurred to her that Sondra wasn't getting half as much from her gift shop as she could. Cory wondered if she offered to work there mornings, for a percentage of what she took in, if Sondra would agree. She wouldn't lose anything, and Cory would have made a start. She'd find out what running a gift shop was really like.

"I'll talk to her today," Cory decided.

An hour later she entered the hotel. She was wearing her white shorts and a cotton knit sweater of blue-and-white horizontal stripes. On her way to the bar her eye fell on a small well-lit display window of the hotel's jewelry shop. Three exquisite necklaces of white shells lay on a dark silk scarf. They varied in length and number of strands. Cory drew closer. Shell Leis from Niihau, the Forbidden Island, said a discreet card. She had an instant desire to possess one and read the price tag. Five hundred dollars! She drew back, feeling foolish, and quickly consoled herself. She was meeting Buck for coffee. That was happiness enough.

She paused in the doorway of the bar. Her pale hair was several shades lighter than her skin by this time and seemed to glow in the unlighted room. Buck was waiting at a small table on the terrace.

When she was seated, he fetched the coffee himself from the kitchen, obviously quite at home in his uncle's hotel.

The terrace overlooked a leafy thicket of graceful bamboo. The heart-shaped leaves of variegated pothos covered the ground. Beyond the waving fronds, the trunks of coconut palms made curving lines against the deep blue horizon and the ever marching white lines of breaking surf.

"Sometimes I'm stunned to find myself here," she told Buck, her face glowing.

Buck sipped his coffee and sat back in his chair, frowning. "I heard you got stopped yesterday."

"We did," she admitted.

"Your friend Tim's pretty slow to get the message."

"What message?" She stared at him.

"To stay off the haul cane roads."

About to take a sip of coffee, Cory set her cup down quietly. "Are you the one who wants him off?"

"I told you the other day, those are private roads. Only cane workers are supposed to be on them."

"We had Paco with us. Don't the members of your family have any rights?"

"Not when they hang around with the wrong crowd." He might have been some hard-nosed judge giving a verdict.

"Are you including me in that?" she demanded.

"*Are* you included?"

What wrong crowd? Tim? Why was Tim wrong?

"I don't know what you're talking about!" Cory heard her voice rising.

"Don't you?" He stared into her eyes as if searching for some untruth. "Well, perhaps you don't. Don't you read the papers?"

"Not regularly," she admitted. Despite her rising anger at his vague accusations, she was sharply aware of his appearance. He had exchanged his running shorts for dark green pants of rugged material and a short-sleeved white oxford cloth shirt with button-down collar. She wondered if that was his working outfit. She caught a whiff of soap and men's cologne.

"If you did read the papers," he was saying, "you might have a better idea what goes on."

She tried to look suitably regretful and then changed the subject. "How far did you run?"

"Ten miles."

She wasn't surprised; he looked fit. Why had he invited her here, she wondered. She sipped her coffee in silence, waiting to hear what else he had to say.

"How's Hazel?" he asked lazily.

"She's all right." Cory's voice was short. Had he finished reprimanding her? Was she expected to leave now?

He sat forward, leaning his forearms on the table. "I'm invited to a baby luau Saturday night. I was wondering if you'd like to go? A baby luau is a party...dinner...to celebrate's a child's first birthday."

Something warm, beginning in Cory's toes, spread throughout her body. It was the same feeling she had about being in Hawaii, only more so. It was like a dream. He was asking her out again!

"If you're booked up we'll make it another time," he said coldly.

"No! Oh, no! I was just—" she paused and her smile lighted her face "—surprised. I thought you invited me here to bawl me out."

"I did! You've got no business running around back roads here unless you want to get into trouble. But—" he set his jaw and then his lips twisted "—I just remembered this luau. Some friends are celebrating their kid's first birthday."

"I'd like to go," said Cory. "Thank you."

He glanced at his watch and drained his cup. "Good. Wear that pretty muumuu again. I'll pick you up about six. I've got to get out of here. It doesn't do for the boss to be late."

A few of the hotel's guests had drifted onto the terrace. In front of them all he kissed Cory lightly on the lips. She was too astonished to react.

Her eyes followed him as he strode purposefully from the room. He was wearing the riding boots again.

I'm living in a fairy tale, she thought.

Again she went home in a daze, part of her bubbling with wild happiness, part of her afraid to rejoice, reminding her of what had happened the last time she was happy. To her surprise the usual pang at the thought of Paul didn't come. Almost with reluctance she realized that that era of her life was past. She really had left it behind in New Jersey. Never again, she promised herself, would she let her emotions get her into so much trouble, so much pain. She would go out with Buck; at least his attentions had soothed her wounds. And her reason for going out with him was to experience Hawaii. Thanks to him she had seen a sugar mill, the torch-lighting at the Coco Palms, and soon a luau, the traditional Hawaiian feast.

She walked on air all the way to the condo.

She planned to use the afternoon to go to the shop and talk to Sondra. That would be more businesslike than meeting her on the beach. Also, when she went to the library with Hazel's books this morning, she intended to go through the back files of the newspapers and see what Buck had been talking about. If she was going to live here, she ought to know the undercurrents.

Despite her rationalizing she had to work hard to keep from skipping. Buck wanted to take her out again! He hadn't minded her refusal to go to the hotel with him. If he was nursing some hopeless passion, that was his problem. She intended to have a good time and keep it casual. He had said he found her exciting, and certainly she found him— and Kauai—exciting. That ought to generate enough electricity to light up one evening together.

CHAPTER EIGHT

AFTER LUNCH CORY WENT to the gift shop to present her idea to Sondra.

"Missed you at the beach this morning," Sondra greeted her. She was barefoot and wearing shorts. Her sun-bleached brown hair frizzed in every direction.

"I was out early," Cory said, keeping her meeting with Buck a secret. There were no customers in the shop. Now was the time to talk to Sondra. She looked preoccupied, but Cory was eager to put forth her idea. She drew a deep breath and plunged.

"Sondra, what would you think of opening the shop mornings and letting me run it? I could work for a percentage, so you wouldn't lose anything. It looks like such a fun business."

"I thought it was fun, too, when I started," Sondra said with a wise smile, "but you get tired of answering the same questions over and over. Percentage, you say? I haven't really kept very good books."

"How do you figure your taxes?"

"The accountant does it. We could look at those papers. But it wouldn't do if we just spread the same customers over the whole day."

"Of course not," Cory agreed. "How about a certain percentage of the sales over what you make now?"

"I'll ask Johnny," Sondra said. "He has a good head for business. But he might not like being waked up if the shop's open earlier."

"You mean he sleeps here?"

"Sure. He lives here."

Cory felt awkward, but she said hastily, "I wouldn't have to go in the back. I was thinking that if things worked out...if your business improved...maybe you'd like to have me for a partner. I've got some money—" She hadn't meant to broach that part of her idea so soon, but she heard herself chattering into the silence.

"You don't know anything about running a gift shop," Sondra said bluntly. "How do you know you'll like it?"

"That's why I thought I could help out first... see how we got along."

Sondra seemed to make up her mind and smiled agreeably. "You're welcome to hang around. Start now if you like. I'll have to show you a few things before you can be on your own."

"Sure!" Cory exclaimed. "I'm so bored with doing nothing but Hazel's few errands and cooking dinner!"

"Lord knows, this shop could do better if it had more stock," Sondra said. Cory took it that her suggestion of a partnership had met with favor. If only Johnny Komo didn't object.

Sondra showed her how to ring up sales and then put her to work dusting shelves.

"After you've dusted every item a million times you know exactly what you have—and you pray someone will buy it."

Sondra talked while they worked. Obviously Cory's proposal had set her thinking. "I've got merchandise on order. With Christmas coming it *would* pay to stay open more hours, but it ought to be evenings instead of mornings. That might bring in local people. Would you want to work afternoons? I could go to the beach with Johnny and work evenings."

"That would be fine!"

"All right. Come in for a couple more afternoons and we'll try opening mornings till it gets closer to Christmas."

Cory was confident that her scheme would turn out well. Just hanging around the shop was satisfying. She had an excuse to advise the tourists according to her limited knowledge. She planned to study a guidebook on the island. People who asked for free advice would buy something in return. If only there was a wider selection! Her mind hummed as she dusted each item.

She would have to be careful how she made suggestions, she cautioned herself, or Sondra would think she wanted to take over.

She was fussing with a shelfful of perfume bottles when Johnny appeared from the back, yawning, his hair standing on end.

Sondra said, "Okay, Cory, you take over while I talk to him. He put up the money to get started here, so I have to see what he says."

"Sure." Cory was surprised. She wouldn't have thought Johnny would have cash to lend.

He and Sondra disappeared into the back and Cory perched on the stool behind the register. If the place were hers, she thought, she'd already have it decorated for Christmas.

But Sondra was right; there were long stretches when no one came in even to look. Sondra passed the time by reading. Cory found a row of lurid paperbacks beneath the cash register.

I'd rather pass the time by making something to sell, Cory thought, *but what?*

She was pondering the question when Tim wandered in. He looked surprised to see Cory in charge, and she was surprised to see him wearing long pants. He must have come directly from school.

"It's my new part-time job," was all she told him. "We're going to see whether business picks up."

"Is Johnny in back?"

"Yes. Sondra's asking him what he thinks of my working here."

"Oh, so do not disturb." Tim grinned.

"Yes, and besides, I want to ask you something." Cory's eyes narrowed. "Were you and Johnny looking for marijuana the other day when Buck almost rammed into you?"

Tim looked aghast. "Don't say that! I told you what we were doing—looking for that petroglyph stone."

"You told Buck you were searching for— You used some other word."

"Oh, a *heiau*—a Hawaiian temple. The stone

bases of some still remain and older Hawaiians still leave offerings there. A *heiau* sounded more impressive than a petroglyph stone.''

Cory narrowed her eyes. ''I read about 'rippers' this morning—people who go searching for marijuana that somebody else is growing. They climb telephone poles to survey the country or ride around on the roofs of trucks, as Johnny was doing. That's why those men were guarding their crop!''

Tim looked righteously angry. ''Are you accusing me, a high school teacher, of ripping off *pakalolo*?''

''I'm just asking you,'' Cory said levelly.

''No, we weren't! Let me tell you, it's not the kind of thing you accuse people of lightly. One or two people on this island have disappeared, and that may have been why. The big *pakalolo* growers are damn ruthless. Well, you saw for yourself.''

''Were they big growers?''

''What do you think?''

Cory didn't know what to think. A nagging doubt entered her mind. If Tim was telling the truth, why was Buck so belligerent? Could he be one of the big growers? The idea seemed fantastic.

At that moment some customers walked in. By the time she finished waiting on them Tim had gone. She hoped he wasn't angry with her.

Each afternoon during the rest of the week, Cory worked at the gift shop. Most of the people who came in wanted to browse. Cory needed something to occupy her hands while she waited for them to make up their minds. In one of Hazel's magazines she found instructions for making a pillow copied from Hawaiian appliquéd quilts. The magazine gave an exotic choice of patterns—breadfruit, tree fern, ginger, pineapple, hibiscus. Cory chose to make a yellow pineapple design appliquéd on a rust-colored background. Rows of quilting would outline the shapes.

"How did Hawaiian women get started making quilts this way?" she asked Hazel as she copied the pattern. "They're nothing like the pieced quilts of New England."

"Well, the missionaries came with whole bolts of material, and the Hawaiian women naturally saw no reason for cutting the cloth into little pieces and sewing it back together," Hazel said.

"But it doesn't get cold enough for quilts, does it?"

"Never. But the missionaries had rigid ideas. The Hawaiian women made an art of it, and everyone was happy." Hazel admired the appliqué Cory had cut out. "That's going to look very authentic."

That afternoon Cory sat in the shop and stitched.

Sondra was impressed. "What industry!"

The women shoppers who came in were also interested. Cory's sewing provided a subject for conversation and the atmosphere was friendly. Two women asked if the shop sold kits for making the pillows.

"I could make some kits," Cory told Sondra before she went home. "I could make several from

a few yards of material, and it would be something
with local color.''

"Great idea!'' Sondra said. ''You supply the kits
and we'll work out some arrangement.''

When Sondra learned that Buck was taking Cory
to a baby luau, her eyes widened.

"Buck Bower!'' she exclaimed a shade enviously.
"How did you meet him?''

"His aunts and Hazel are great friends. I told you
I spent Thanksgiving there.''

"Good for you, Cory!'' Sondra pulled her mouth
down in mocking respect. ''That almost puts you
out of our class!''

"Don't be ridiculous!'' Cory replied.

Sondra's eyes glittered. ''Buck Bower's the biggest catch on Kauai.''

"Don't expect me to catch him!'' Cory snapped.

"Why not?''

"I'm not interested in nabbing a man.''

"But aren't you glad you bought that muumuu?''
Sondra's voice was full of self-congratulation.

"Yes, but this date is no big deal,'' Cory muttered. She considered telling Sondra that Buck had
noticed her because she looked like his old flame.
She longed to confide in someone her own age. On
the other hand, she didn't want to talk about Buck.
How foolish she would have looked if she had told
Sondra about the ''beachcomber.''

"DON'T LET HIM talk you into anything,'' Sondra
said on Saturday when Cory left the shop at closing
time.

"Like what?" Cory's gentle brown eyes widened.

"I just meant—" Sondra hesitated "—Buck-o has something of a reputation. He goes for fast affairs. In fact—" she cocked her head to one side and looked Cory up and down "—I wouldn't have said you're his type. I mean that as a compliment."

"I'm *not* his type." Cory forced a laugh. "He just hasn't found out yet." She slid out of the shop before Sondra could comment further.

Opening the door to Buck that evening Cory experienced the same heart-stopping thrill she felt every time she saw him. His assured stance and his proud bearing gave her a surge of confidence. He smiled at her in a way that made her feel, rightly or wrongly, that he was attracted to Corinne Wells, not some long-ago love.

The lei he brought was made of creamy plumeria blossoms. He slipped it over her head and kissed her lightly on the lips. She felt his breath on her cheek. Her determination not to be overwhelmed melted. She knew she was the luckiest girl on the island tonight. His strong cool hands cupped her jaw, his fingers touched her neck, and she swayed toward him, her eyes drawn to his mobile, smiling mouth.

Hazel called for him to come in, and the moment was gone.

Hazel didn't offer him a drink; there would be enough eating and drinking where they were going. Tonight would be very different from the Coco Palms, where the crowd was mostly tourists. Tonight the people seeing her with Buck would be his friends.

"You look flustered," he said, discomposing her further.

She managed a stiff smile.

He was wearing black trousers and an aloha shirt of small white blossoms printed on a black background. He had slipped off black-thonged zoris, and his brown feet were planted confidently in Hazel's thick blond carpet. He looked like a successful, self-satisfied man. While he inquired about Hazel's progress, Cory tore her eyes from him and went to fetch her purse.

Daylight had faded when they arrived at the beach park where the festivities were being held. Buck pulled the car onto a strip of grassy sward.

"Hawaiian grass is special," he told her. "Nothing seems to harm it." He took her arm and steered her toward a group of people. "Come, we're in time to see them uncovering the *kalua* pig. *Kalua* means to bake underground. It's been steaming all day in a pit covered with taro leaves and heated lava rocks."

"Like a barbecue?"

"Not really. The pork isn't seasoned with any sauce. Only salt. The taro leaves give it a delicious smoked flavor. He laughed. "My mouth's watering."

He introduced Cory to the host and hostess—the baby's parents—and they joined the circle watching an old man removing rocks, wet burlap and leaves, followed by a layer of sweet potatoes, breadfruit and green bananas, which had been baking with the pig.

The guests were already convivial. Good-natured joshing flew back and forth between them and the old man.

"It sounds like they're speaking English," Cory whispered. "I mean the cadence, or whatever you call it, but I can't understand it."

"It's pidgin," Buck said, answering a friendly greeting in the same jargon.

Cory forced a smile and tried not to feel like an outsider. She thrilled at being with these kamaainas. The good-natured tone of Buck's incomprehensible speech brought back her initial impression of the carefree surfer.

"You'll hear pidgin everywhere tonight," Buck told her. "Nowadays it's spoken for fun, of course, to make us feel like insiders."

"As opposed to outsiders like me," Cory said wistfully.

"You're with me," he said, hugging her around the waist. "Muumuus are fun," he added, spreading his hand to locate her ribs and hipbone. He poked her ribs and she wriggled.

"Let's get something to drink," he said. "Beer goes well with the pork."

"Beer, then."

Buck took her to join two couples—men he had grown up with and their wives, whom he had also known forever. One man was the manager of another sugar mill; the other was in charge of the island's power plant. Cory felt even more like an outsider. She sipped her beer and pretended to be enjoying herself.

Buck's friends asked her how she happened to be on Kauai and she explained.

The wife of the power plant manager said, "Buck, she reminds me of that girl you used to date. Emma Somebody."

"I don't see any resemblance," Buck drawled, leaving Cory's pink lips agape.

The woman's husband said, "Hooray, they're starting to serve!"

Buck's intimate smile took Cory's breath away. "I hope you're hungry."

She returned his smile and was glad to join the line. The smells coming from the long serving table had been tempting her ever since she sat down.

The plates were large. Buck filled hers, telling her as he spooned up the food, "I'll give you a small piece of baked breadfruit...you may not like it. Here's the *lomilomi* salmon. You're bound to like that. It's salted salmon, shredded and rubbed with tomatoes and green onion...sort of a salad." He served her a heaping spoonful of something that looked like clear pasta. "Chicken long rice," he said. "Once Oriental but now Hawaiian. Ah, and here's squid luau—squid and creamed taro leaves."

Cory unconsciously drew her plate back. Buck laughed.

"Try some," he urged, and she allowed him to give her a spoonful. She did want to try everything Hawaiian, but she soon lost track of all the new and varied tastes. She ate *laulau*, pieces of pork, butterfish and herbs wrapped in ti leaves and steamed, and *poke*, raw fish sautéed in a hot sauce with chopped seaweed.

The small dish of poi was memorable because unexpectedly she liked it.

"I suppose you know poi is the Polynesian staple, like potatoes or rice," Buck said.

"I didn't," Cory said. "Do you like it?"

"Sure I do, but it's full of calories, not that you have to worry."

"Under a muumuu, how can you be sure?" she asked jokingly.

"I know what you look like in a bikini." His voice was again intimate.

The tremor that swept Cory from shoulder to toe jarred her out of her newly acquired ease.

"Forget what you've heard about poi," he directed, as though sensing he had made her uneasy. "The way to eat it is to dip your pork into it."

He was right. The smooth silky texture and subtle sourness of poi complemented the salty pork, and the new taste sensation took her mind off what Buck had implied: that he had memorized her body.

"The pork is the best I've ever tasted," she pronounced. He looked gratified.

They lined up again for dessert. The coconut milk pudding here was served with wedges of fresh pineapple. Cory had eaten too much to consider cake, but Buck returned to their table with samples of both chocolate and coconut cake, and a sticky coconut and taro concoction called *kulolo*.

"Try a bit," he urged Cory. "It's truly Hawaiian."

She could only shake her head regretfully.

With the ending of the meal the volume of friendly chatter had risen considerably, but it quieted and the crowd stirred when the master of ceremonies stepped onto the improvised stage where a piano and audio equipment were set up.

Amid applause he told jokes about the host and hostess and thanked them effusively. He called everyone to join in wishing the baby—a boy—long life and happiness. At last he announced a local singing group. Applause and cheerful catcalls conveyed the crowd's welcome.

Cory enjoyed every minute. Buck and his friends had secured places at the table nearest the makeshift stage. The entertainers, with straw hats, blue-flowered shirts and ukuleles, delivered their Hawaiian numbers with fine harmony and rollicking good humor.

Cory laughed and applauded and felt her heart catch at the blissful longing the music roused. The hour grew late and the party noisy. When the foursome returned from their break they were joined by a hula dancer. Cory watched with absorbed attention as the girl moved sinuously to the graceful rhythm. Her thick black hair swayed around her hips. She seemed to symbolize Polynesia. She also seemed to be dancing for Buck. Again and again her eyes rested on him, and Cory saw him raise his beer bottle in salute.

Conscious of undefined anger rising in her breast, Cory turned her head to stare directly at him. Buck met her stare and smiled blandly.

"Old school chum."

The woman did look thirtyish. She was dancing a faster hula now, the audience laughing at the words sung by the group. She undulated down the steps from the stage to the grass, her bare feet never missing a move, her arms held enticingly above her head.

The audience clapped and shouted, and Cory was not surprised when the girl...woman—she was as slim and supple as a girl—positioned herself in front of Buck.

She moved hypnotically, her smile seductive, the motion of her body, the beckoning of her arms provocative beyond words. No wonder the missionaries had banned this dance! Cory felt hot blood fan out over her tense body as she imagined herself in the dancer's place; luring, exciting the man of her choice with every sway of her supple willing hips, every twist of her shoulders.

Watching the rhythmic tread of the dancer's bare feet, the subtle play of knees hidden by the calf-length wraparound, Cory was enchanted by both the music and the dance. Every movement bespoke the dancer's knowledge of the lush night, of soft sand and darkness where two people would be alone to perform Nature's glorious demand. There was no doubt that the dance was meant to be the first erotic passage.

Blood pounded in Cory's loins. She knew a fierce longing to be the one dancing in front of Buck, to be the seductress offering him the joy of love in the shadows of pandanus fronds. The dancer's costume, a square of cloth knotted above her breasts, had only to be untied and spread on the ground.

Cory's breath quickened, responding to the heightened tension of the music. She wondered if everyone watching was as affected by the dance as she. The primitive response in her own muscles demanded that she, too, leap to her feet and perform the sensuous gyrations. If only she could! She forced control on her longing nerves. She felt the essence of Buck beside her. Her hands fought against her judgment and reached to touch him, only to feel the air of his movement. With a shout he leapt up to join the dance.

His entry was signaled by whistles and feminine voices raised in cries of encouragement. Cory heard them with a flood of pride and jealousy. He, too, was barefoot. He had left his zoris beside his chair.

The same scene might have taken place a century ago: beautiful maidens welcoming sailors from ships that had been months at sea, the sailors clumsily imitating the ancient hula.

Except that Buck was no clumsy imitator. To the cheers of the luau guests he was doing a male version that Cory found more seductive than the woman's. She had seen teams of male hula dancers on TV, clothed in nothing but ti-leaf skirts and circlets of leaves around heads and ankles, but she had not guessed that men did modern hulas.

Buck's movements held her attention to the exclusion of everything. She nearly forgot to breathe. She watched with fascination. His gestures were graceful yet entirely masculine, the strength of arms, legs and torso quite apparent. In the more stately dances the woman had kept her knees together. Now the dancers faced each other, slightly crouching, knees apart and hips thrust forward in gestures so suggestive that no one watching could fail to be stirred. Cory fought against the flush of warmth spreading through her.

It was too much! Buck was grace and power and the promise of never-tasted joy and fulfillment.

When the music ended, he laughingly hugged his partner and kissed her on both cheeks amid cheers and clapping.

He returned to his seat, his eyes sparkling, his chest heaving in a way that stirred Cory further. His friends laughed and admired.

The dance had been all make-believe; the woman wore a wedding ring and had given Cory a friendly smile. Regret overwhelmed her. In the same unreal way, Cory thought, Buck was merely amusing himself with her. All that aside, however, she knew she had succumbed to the island's lure. She had to find a way to stay here.

Bemused, she allowed him to lead her to the car. The party was breaking up.

"Have a good time?" he asked.

How could he doubt it? "Marvelous," she breathed. She had never felt so relaxed. The sensations roused by that final hula had drained her of all emotion and all tension, too. She knew only that she belonged in Hawaii.

She lay back in the car seat, remembering what she had seen, enjoying the feeling of satiety, answering his remarks with single syllables.

"Tired?" he inquired.

"Not at all. Just—" she searched for a word to describe her state of mind "—full of wonderful food and entertainment, and...oh, everything. Everything's so perfect here!"

"Does that include me?" She heard a smile in his voice.

"You were fantastic. Everyone thought so."

"I'm interested in what you thought." He reached for her hand.

She gave it to him easily enough. His sensuous dance had removed the wall around him. She understood how much he was a part of this island culture. She had seen him tonight in his public image—the wealthy scion of a family rich in land and sugar, his friends the elite of the community, his pursuits those of the island's aristocracy— sailing, surfing, probably polo, when the season opened in March. But she had also seen him stripped of all this worldly sophistication, performing a dance that was both primitive and passionate.

"Don't go to sleep!" he warned.

"I'm not. Just thinking. Thank you for a wonderful evening."

"You're welcome."

She opened her eyes to see him swinging the car off the highway.

"Where are we?"

"You're home. Did you want to go somewhere else?"

"No, but didn't we get here awfully fast?"

"You slept most of the way," he teased. "I shouldn't have fed you so well."

Despite the danger of such feelings, Cory felt disappointed at being brought tamely home. She pushed it out of her mind and held out her hand.

"Thank you for a wonderful evening," she repeated.

Buck held her hand to his lips. "It's not over yet," he intoned. "Doesn't the ocean lure you after a crowd like tonight's?"

She allowed him to lead her across the grass to the opening in the hedge. How white the charging lines of surf gleamed, even at night! She let him pull her down to sit on the warm dry sand. His supple hand gripped her shoulder and slid to encircle the back of her neck. The sound from his throat was a groan of desire. He drew her against him.

She went mindlessly into his embrace. Her body had been ready for this since she had watched the erotic motions of the hula. She had but to close her eyes to see herself as a dark-haired Polynesian, responding to a Hawaiian chief, his bare body crushing the petals of the lei he had adorned her with. The heavy tropical perfume rose around them.

His kiss carried her fantasy another step. He became the beachcomber again, bare thighed, bare chested, his arms as strong as they looked. She knew a wild delight at being enveloped in them. She could hardly believe she was in such surroundings— the clean sand, the lush greenery at their backs rustling in the soft breeze, the sound of the ocean like the breathing of the earth itself.

She didn't resist when he laid her back against the slope. The sand's coolness reached her skin through the lace yoke and then warmed to her body. Like everything in this paradise, it was welcoming, yielding. Everything might have been designed for her comfort and delight—Buck most of all.

She struggled feebly against this sense of perfection, wondering fleetingly if the plumeria fragrance was drugging her mind. If so, she rejoiced in the excuse to respond to the sweet, warm pressure of his lips. His tongue insinuated itself into her mouth, assured and demanding, like himself. A wisp of fear, of doubt, doubled her excitement. His body pressed against hers, warm, hard and oddly comforting, as though he would protect her from whatever fears or doubts the island offered.

Lassitude stole over her limbs. She was here to be made love to—in Hawaii, in this spot. She held him lightly, putting her whole thought into answering his kisses. The harsh increase of his breathing told her when his passion intensified, but before she could respond he sensed her unwillingness to be swept along so fast. He tore his lips from hers to press kisses over her eyes, the bridge of her nose, her cheeks. He bit playfully at her earlobe and held her against him with one arm while his free hand caressed her body—the curve of her hipbone, the saucy roundness of her derriere, her thigh, her small waist. His fingers traced her rib cage, cupped one breast, left one nipple tingling. She longed for the massage of his hand, but it moved on, along the tender underside of her arm, till every part of her body was alive and longing for his touch.

His lips sought hers again and the kiss drew her to

heights she had never dreamed possible. Every cell of her body responded. Desire flamed in her loins as she strained against him.

He ended the kiss and wrapped her in both arms, burying his face in the plumeria blossoms at her neck.

Suddenly his silence repelled her. She struggled to sit up, pushed her hair back and took great calming breaths.

"What is it?" He rolled onto his back and put his hands behind his head.

"This—" she faltered, "—this silent sex makes me feel like I don't exist as a person."

She heard his laugh rumble and felt safe again.

"I can't talk and kiss at the same time," he objected.

She gave her shoulders an impatient jerk.

"Oh, Cory, Cory.... All right, we'll talk."

Instead his fingers found the zipper at the back of her dress with what she deemed the ease of long practice, opened it, and pushed the lacy yoke aside to bare her tanned skin. She felt his lips warm and caressing at the nape of her neck, laying a line of kisses along her backbone while his hands clasped her upper arms, holding her motionless. Not that she wished to move. Her toes curled in the sand at the touch of his lips on her back.

"I don't express myself well," he muttered, "but I could lie here and kiss you till morning. And bite your pretty shoulders," he added, and she felt his strong teeth close on her flesh.

She squealed and wriggled. He laughed and pulled

her back against his chest. His heart thudded against her shoulder blade. She hadn't thought of him as having trouble expressing himself. Certainly he'd expressed himself well in that hula. At the memory of his movements there, the primitively erotic thrusts of his lean hips, the open crouch of his knees, her mind blurred and she thrust herself against him, wanting to feel his arousal, consciously inviting him to unfasten her bra and cup each breast in his firm hands. Her nipples tautened, tingling with pleasure. Again he buried his face in her neck.

"Cory, Cory," he groaned. "Don't disappoint me!"

"If you mean come to your hotel tonight—"

"Shhh!" With ease he turned her and cradled her in one arm while the other hand continued to fondle her breast and his forefinger teased its erect and pulsing tip.

"I didn't mean disappoint me that way, but now that you mention it, we'd be much more comfortable at the hotel. You could get out of this blasted muu-muu—"

Her mind whirled dizzily, but she managed to protest, "I thought you liked it!"

"I did like it—at the beginning of the evening. Slip it off. Nobody's going to come along." He began easing it down her arms. "Pretend you're a real Hawaiian. After all, I saw you in a bikini the other morning. I know what you feel like—"

Weakly she allowed him to remove her bra and slide the dress to her waist.

"Take it off," he whispered. "Keep it from getting wrinkled."

Her laugh at his false concern caught in her throat. She gasped at her daring, but she stood up and let the dress slide to the sand. Her dark half slip gleamed in the reflected light from the water. Fantasy turned it into a grass skirt. The crushed but still fragrant plumeria blossoms around her neck half covered, half revealed the rise and fall of her bare breasts. She stood before him shyly, proud that he wanted her.

"Beautiful!" Buck rasped, stepping forward, his hands cupped to hold her.

Like a flash of vengeance the thought of Paul came to her mind. Pain knifed through her like a narrow blade from throat to backbone. She stifled a moan and crossed her arms over her breasts. Then she crouched and began fumbling to find her dress.

"Cory! What's wrong?" Buck dropped to his knees, grasping her shoulders, forcing her to look at him.

"Nothing, nothing! I—" He must think her mad! She caught her breath and met his eyes, trying to smile. "A memory, that's all. Tonight was so fantastic and lovely that the memory, by comparison, seemed crueler than ever. I felt like I'd been stabbed." Two tears coursed down her cheeks. She turned her face away to keep him from seeing them.

Buck shook the sand from her muumuu and folded it around her bare shoulders like a cape. "I've noticed sadness in your eyes," he told her. "I wondered what caused it.'' He pulled her down to sit beside him in the sand. ''Does it hurt too much to talk about?''

Cory shook her head, afraid to trust her voice. She wanted to let him know she wasn't looking for a holiday affair; the experience with Paul was too recent. She needed to talk about it.

''I went with this man for almost two years,'' she said in a dead tone. ''I thought everything was fine. I thought we were perfectly happy. Then he dumped me.'' She shrugged.

''Just like that?''

''Just like that. He met a girl on his commuter train. The worst of it is, she lives in an apartment house right down the block. Every time I went anywhere I had to see his car parked there.'' The anguished words were wrung from her, but Buck had to be told. Her wound was too raw to cover up.

Buck was silent for so long Cory began to wish she hadn't told him anything. At last he said, ''Must I pretend to be sorry? If he'd been the answer to your dreams I'd never have met you. Obviously the guy wasn't worth much. You're better off without him.''

She was almost ready to agree.

With gentle fingers he removed the muumuu from her shoulders.

''Cory—'' He coaxed her to look at him by lifting her chin with one finger. ''Not all men are like that.''

''How can I be sure?''

''Oh, Cory, don't look so sad!'' He caught her

face in both hands and placed a kiss on her lips as though to cure her hurt. Then he sat back and studied her expression.

"What you need is to be loved. Tonight. You need to forget the past. It's over. You're here with me. There's only tonight and the future. Relax, Cory. Lie back. Like that." He pressed her against the slope of the beach. "I'll lie here beside you and we'll listen to the sea. It's been going on for a million years. Don't think, just listen."

"I'll fall asleep," she murmured, afraid to relax.

"No, you won't. You'll just lie still and feel my touch." He was stroking her arm. His firm warm hand slid over her bare ribs and down her slip.

She lay stiffly, willing to see if he could make her trust him. His hard male chest pressed against her arm. After a while she felt a slight impatience at the texture of cloth between them. If she was going to be bare to the waist, he should be, too. She reached to unbutton his shirt.

"That's it," he encouraged her. "Soon we'll be naked together, but not yet—"

His promise sent a sensation of desire running along her nerves. She should sit up now and end this, but the tracing of his hand over the curves and hollows of her body had brought on a languor that made her unwilling to move. She wished only to lie back and let him mesmerize her into forgetting everything but his hands, his lips, his husky voice saying, "How lovely you are! Lovely to look at, lovely to touch, lovely to know."

At the weight of his lips on hers, the languor in

her veins stirred, changing to excitement. Her breathing grew shallow; her blood began to race. She felt a flurry of impatience for more.

Their tongues met, caressed. Without interrupting the kiss he sat up, holding her against him with first one arm and then the other while he shucked off his shirt. Pushing Cory's lei aside he held her against him, breast to breast. Crisp hairs teased her tingling nipples. He bent his head to taste their firm peaks with his tongue and then his lips.

She knew then that she would give herself to him. The knowledge excited her. With a glad little cry she flung her arms around his neck and returned kiss for kiss. When his mouth left hers to kiss her breast, she ran her tongue down the taut cords of his neck and nibbled the smooth skin of his shoulder.

To undress while continuing to kiss became a fascinating challenge. Laughing a little with excitement, they managed. Then with a groan blended of accomplishment and desire Buck pulled her to lie full-length atop his hard-muscled body, his manhood hard and promising between her legs.

"My beautiful Cory," he murmured, burying his face in her hair, his lips tracing the crisp curve of her ear.

In unison, passion sparked them both.

"Cory!" he urged huskily and rolled her onto her back. "Cory?"

"Oh, yes, Buck. Yes—"

How sweet it was!

And how warm and satisfying to forget everything but the miracle of being alive, of sharing this act of love with this man she felt love for.

Cory's passionate response left no time for further thought. Buck swept her up on the tide of his fervor. When their desire peaked and was satisfied, they drifted back to earth, locked in each other's arms. Cory snuggled her face into his neck.

"Do you feel better now?" Buck asked softly.

Did he mean physically or mentally? He made it sound as if he'd given her some kind of treatment. Cory didn't try to answer his question.

He stirred. "I'd better get you home."

Her heart constricted. Was that all he was going to say? She swallowed the endearment that had risen to her lips. Buck sat up and fumbled for his shirt. He handed her her dress.

A band tightened across her chest. Already she was beginning to regret their lovemaking. She felt as though she had offered him her soul. She was no longer her own woman.

In silence he helped her to her feet. The evening was over. He led the way back through the hedge and together they crossed the lawn to the condo.

Approaching the stairs Buck said stiffly, "I hope you had a good time tonight."

"Yes, I did," Cory whispered. How stilted their words sounded.

"So did I," he affirmed. He kissed her lightly, dismissively, and turned toward his car.

With her head held high she ascended the stairs. His engine roared into life and he swung out of the driveway.

What had she done? She had given way to her true feelings for him. He was right about one thing: what had happened in New Jersey did indeed seem far in the past.

CHAPTER NINE

CORY WOKE WITH A HEADACHE. She lay in bed writhing at the memory of her behavior. She had bared her soul and then— She couldn't blame it on mai tais this time. She could only blame it on the tropic night, along with Buck's intoxicating company. His hula and his lovemaking on the beach had been enough to excite anyone. She had lost her head.

But he hadn't broken her heart! She had believed all along that nothing could come of their dating. At least he had helped her shove Paul into the past.

Determined not to think about Buck, she got out of bed, took an aspirin and slipped on the black bikini. Putting the long-sleeved lace shirt over it, she went to the kitchen to make coffee.

Hazel was there ahead of her.

"Well, how'd you like poi?" Hazel inquired.

"It was good! Everything was good. I won't need to eat for a week." Cory groaned and held her stomach, pretending that it, and not her head, was the cause of her discomfort. "I'm going to take my coffee and lie in the sun," she announced.

Hazel surprised her by saying, "I may join you after a bit. It's time I started going up and down stairs once a day."

Crossing the grass, Cory hoped the gentle air and sparkling water would soothe her thoughts.

She lay listening to the lapping waves and tried not to think at all. The aspirin or the coffee was helping her headache, and after a while her thoughts lulled. The soft breeze, the sun and the monotonous sound of the surf worked their magic. She exulted in being alive, in being in Hawaii.

She was in a state of suspension when footsteps brought her eyes lazily open. Hazel was spreading a mat beside hers.

"I got here," she announced, "and while I'm here I might as well swim. Probably be good for my hip."

"I'm sure it would," Cory recommended.

"First, I have something nice to tell you—two nice things," Hazel said calmly. "We're invited to sail to Honolulu."

Cory sat up so fast her head throbbed. "Sail to Honolulu?" she repeated blankly.

"That's right. With the Bowers. Irene called. Buck is running in the Honolulu Marathon, I suppose you know? So they've decided they'll all go and do Christmas shopping at the same time."

"Buck never said a word last night! How big a boat is it?" Cory pictured a small sailboat with everyone crowded into the cockpit.

"It's a yacht with staterooms." Hazel beamed, reading her mind. "Three staterooms, I think. You and I will share one."

A pleasant, warm sensation began to glow in the vicinity of Cory's midriff. She would see him again!

"When?" she breathed, a disbelieving smile widening the sweet expression of her mouth.

"Wednesday."

"This coming Wednesday?"

Hazel nodded. "You can get away from your gift shop commitment, can't you?"

"Oh. . . yes. How long does it take to get there?" Cory's mind was spinning furiously. Did Buck know she'd been invited? Maybe not, if the boat was Lester's and the invitation came from his aunts. Oh, Lord. She writhed with embarrassment. He probably had no idea she'd been invited.

"Irene thinks we'll leave here Wednesday afternoon and arrive in Honolulu about midday Thursday. The marathon is not until Sunday, so you'll have time to go sight-seeing."

"It sounds—" Cory gulped "—too good to be true." How would Buck react when he learned she'd been invited? Well, it might be uncomfortable around him, but she could put up with that for the chance to sail to Honolulu. "Just like in the old days!" she exclaimed.

"Very much so," Hazel agreed.

"Have you ever sailed there before?"

"Oh, yes. Some years ago you could get to all the islands by boat. If you mean on the Bowers' yacht, no. Lester uses it mostly to take special guests of the hotel for day cruises. I fancy this was Buck's idea."

"You do?" Cory's voice rose in surprise.

Hazel smiled knowingly. "You haven't asked me about the other nice thing. We're also invited to a Christmas party at the Bowers'—a buffet and dance. They hold it every year.'' She got awkwardly to her feet. "I'm off for a paddle.''

Cory sank back on her mat and closed her eyes. Did Buck know she'd been invited? The idea seemed hard to reconcile with his leave-taking last night, but why would Irene and Mae dream up the idea? They seemed to want him for the Vagos girl. He *must* have suggested it! Maybe he was sorry now.

Still...she allowed herself to slip into a lovely daydream, remembering the early part of last night. She imagined herself with Buck on an island of their own, swaying seductively before him, the gleaming white globes of her breasts browned by constant exposure to the sun. They were shipwrecked; only the two of them survived. The corners of her mouth turned up in a smile. Heartlessly her fantasy consigned Irene, Mae, Lester, Hazel and the yacht's crew to watery graves. She pictured Buck's happiness at seeing her battling to reach the shore. Despite his own fatigue he plunged in to her rescue the way he had actually done that day she was snorkeling. She lay quiescent on the sand, eyes closed, her breast softly rising and falling while his eyes roamed sensuously over her.

Try as she might, she couldn't continue the story, couldn't pretend to feel his arms around her, his mouth covering hers. For that she wanted reality.

What if he learned his aunts' plans and elected to fly to Honolulu instead? She made up her mind not to expect him on board. That way she wouldn't be disappointed.

CORY DID SUCH A GOOD job of convincing herself
Buck wouldn't be accompanying them that when
she arrived with the aunts and Hazel at Nawiliwili
marina and saw Buck shouting orders to two men
on the pier, she thought he must have come to see
them off. He came running down the gangplank to
help Hazel aboard. He greeted Cory with restraint.

Irene showed them their cabin—a snug affair on
the opposite side of the narrow corridor from the
one the sisters would occupy—and Buck set Hazel's
suitcase inside. Cory carried her own. She was so
conscious of Buck that she paid little attention to
the boat, though she couldn't help being aware of a
great deal of gleaming mahogany.

She noticed that Buck was wearing a blue officer's cap, shorts and a denim shirt. Maybe he *was*
going with them!

He took Cory's bag from her and placed it on the
bed.

"You okay, Aunt Hazel?" he inquired.

"Yes, but I'd like to sit down somewhere." The
compact stateroom had three portholes and twin
beds, but no chairs.

"Come in the saloon and have a drink." With a
glance that included Cory, he helped Hazel through
the narrow door to another door at the top of the
T-shaped corridor.

Cory followed and discovered she was in a spacious low-ceilinged cabin running the width of the
boat. It was equipped with a dining table, chairs,
lounges and coffee table. In one corner a small bar
boasted three stools.

"Are you all ready for the race, Buck?" Hazel asked as she sank onto a lounge.

"Ready as I'll ever be." He was behind the bar, fixing Hazel her favorite Scotch and water. "Anything for you, Cory? We'll get under way in a minute and then I'll show you around the boat. Lester's taking her out. He doesn't trust me." His lips twisted in a wry smile and Cory imagined him steering huge ships into exotic foreign ports. She couldn't believe he was really going with them.

Irene and Mae came in. They were dressed like Hazel in navy blue slacks and deck shoes, but Mae sported a white middy. Irene was wearing a denim shirt like Buck's. Cory had chosen pale blue shorts and a T-shirt. She had tied a navy blue sweat shirt around her waist in case the wind over the water grew cool.

Buck's eyes trapped hers. "Want to come to the wheelhouse?"

"If I won't be in the way—"

"There's plenty of room."

The yacht's engines had been throbbing since the women came aboard. Now the deck tilted slightly. As Cory reached to hold on she saw the dockside receding.

She followed Buck through the door by which they had entered the saloon and along the short corridor to a door at the end.

"That's the aunts' cabin, across from yours," he indicated as they passed. "This is the captain's cabin, which Lester shares with me." He ushered her in. Cory admired the built-in bunks and shipshape appearance as they crossed the cabin to another door, which led into the wheelhouse.

Lester was at the wheel, looking very nautical in a white captain's cap. Bright-eyed with excitement, Cory took in everything: Lester's navy blue shirt and shorts, his white boating shoes, the white paint and gleaming mahogany, the polished brass.

"How many people does it take to run this?" Cory asked, awed by the yacht's size.

"Four—" Buck told her "—in order to have two shifts. It takes one man to steer and one in the engine room or as lookout. One of the crew doubles as the cook. This is my mate's cap." He took it off and turned it in his hands. "It's been a lot of places."

Cory pictured him sauntering through a crowded street...in Singapore, perhaps, looking at the available women, and felt a stir of jealousy. Her face flamed. She turned away and stepped outside to catch the wind.

The sleek white yacht was sliding between green shores. Behind them rose a nearby ridge of steep green hills, their tops hidden in clouds at the moment. She realized Buck was standing behind her and her breath caught in her throat.

"That's Kalapaki Beach—" his hand clasped her shoulder and turned her "—and Ninini Point Lighthouse." Beyond the beach stretched an expanse of grass and the feathery tops of coconut palms among the other greenery.

The channel was tree lined except for a huge white building and a large ship anchored against the nearby dock.

"That's where we store our sugar until it's shipped to the refinery in California," Buck explained.

Cory heard his words, but her mind was questioning madly. His hand rested on her shoulder. Did that mean they were on good terms again? Did it mean he'd shrugged off her confidences of the other night? Had this trip been his idea?

They stood at the rail watching the banks on either hand grow farther apart as the yacht progressed down the channel, and then looked back to see the island recede into the distance.

Cory sighed with pure satisfaction. The unbelievably blue water caught at her heart. She turned to Buck, holding back her long hair to keep it from blowing in her face.

"If ever an island was set like a jewel, it's Kauai," she cried above the wind. "It must be wonderful to know that a lot of it really belongs to you!"

He gave her one of his rare smiles. "It's not the worst place in the world. It's getting pretty windy out here. Want to go back inside?"

In the saloon Buck poured sherry for Cory and Scotch for himself, and joined the ladies.

"Where's Paco?" Cory asked.

"School," Buck said succinctly.

"Doesn't he get to see you win?"

"He'll fly over for the weekend. Maybe I'll let him miss one day and sail back with us." He then went off on some business about the boat, promising to see them all at the evening meal.

They dressed for dinner. Cory chose to wear her second-best muumuu. In the narrow confines of the cabin she slipped into it and twisted her ash blond hair into a knot on the top of her head.

"My, I didn't know their boat was so comfortable," Hazel commented. "Do you like it, Cory?"

"It's fabulous!" Cory did not attempt to conceal her delight. "I'm so lucky you know the Bowers."

Hazel chuckled. "I think it's the other way around. I'm lucky Buck has taken a fancy to my guest. Irene says he bullied Lester for a week to get him to make this trip."

A week! Before the luau then! This afternoon Buck had behaved as though he had forgotten the uncomfortable end to that evening. Perhaps the sensible thing was for Cory to forget it, too.

At dinner Lester drew his sisters and Hazel into plans for an evening of cards, saying he would be free because Buck would take the wheel till midnight.

Buck leaned close to Cory to say in a coaxing undertone, "Come up and keep me company."

She promised with a smile, then tucked into the coconut pudding. She ate thoughtfully, listening to the elder Bowers' conversation and mentally pinching herself. Corinne Wells, on a yacht, sailing among the Hawaiian islands! It proved that good things could happen as well as bad. A shadow crossed her face as she remembered Paul's desertion. It was still a little painful, like a new scar, but she knew she was free at last. Free and cautious.

After dinner the older members moved outside to a card table on the well-lighted afterdeck. Cory saw that Hazel was settled, and went to her cabin to change back into shorts. The wind had died down and the evening was balmy. The sun had set while they were at dinner. A mauve afterglow streaked the horizon.

She pitter-pattered along the deck and stepped into the darkened wheelhouse. Buck glanced at her before turning his eyes back to scanning the sea.

"I thought you'd changed your mind," he drawled.

"I wanted to make sure Hazel had everything she needed," Cory explained. "And I didn't think a muumuu was quite the thing up here."

So he had engineered this trip! She studied him thoughtfully. What did he want of her? Did he see her as a person, or merely as a member of the opposite sex whose looks he happened to like? She perched on the stool by the chart table and admitted to herself that she liked his personality *and* his looks. While he kept his eyes staring forward she let her gaze feast on his beautifully tuned body. A night-light near the deck illumined his bare legs, turning the curling hairs golden. His body was so strong and powerful. She remembered what it felt like to have that naked power next to her—she brought her thoughts to a screeching halt and said quickly, "Doesn't steering get tiresome after a while when there's nothing to look at but water?"

He spared her a glance. "Why do you think I invited you to keep me company?"

"You didn't have company when you were a seaman, did you?" she inquired.

"I didn't steer, either. That's not the mate's job.

Want to take a turn at it? Come here." He held out his arm to coax her into the circle of it.

"Really? Would you trust me?"

"Sure! There's nothing to it."

She moved into the charmed circle. His arm went around her waist, pulling her against him. She felt his hard thighs against the yielding softness of her buttocks, the thrust of his maleness. His free hand continued to control the wheel.

"Our course is south-southeast." He indicated the point on the compass. "The black line represents the ship's bow. You have to keep it on the point. The ship steers like a car. Turn the wheel to the right to go right, and vice versa."

He loosed Cory but continued to stand behind her.

"Isn't the wheel awfully small?" she commented, thinking of the immense spoked and polished wooden circles one connected with ships sailing around the Pacific islands.

"You're talking about sailing ships," Buck said. "Sail— That's where the romance of the sea comes in, not this chugging along on diesel. You haven't seen my sailboat yet. . . ."

Would she be the next woman he took out on it?

"Steering's not as easy as it looks," she admitted after a while, breathless from his nearness.

"Let's put it on automatic and go outside."

"*Can you*?"

Buck burst out laughing at her astonishment. "Of course."

"Then why were you standing there doing it by hand?" she demanded, miffed by his laughter.

"To get the feel. It's fun for a little while. Someone has to stay on watch. It's easier to keep your wits about you if you're doing something."

His arm around her waist, he drew her out to stand beside the rail. The tropic night glittered overhead. Buck ran his hand deliciously up and down her backbone in such a way that she could barely keep her mind on what he was saying and answer appropriately. Did he know the effect he had on her? Did he understand that his hands were like the touch of a match—all she needed to burst into flame? She hadn't reacted like this to Paul, whom she had thought she loved. Determinedly she attributed her new, total awareness to the yacht and the starlight. It wasn't Buck; it mustn't be.

He pulled her against him and his lips found hers. Whatever the cause, her body responded with passionate willingness to the loving encirclement of his arms, the wonderful maleness of his body strained against hers, the tender give of her breasts against the bone and sinew of his chest.

In some corner of her mind she remembered gratefully that she and Hazel were sharing a cabin. Thanks to the proprieties, her feelings could not get out of hand.

His cool bare thighs touched hers and grew warm as their bodies drew heat from each other. The texture of his hair against her skin was wickedly exciting. She felt, as well as heard, someone's heart thudding. His or hers? The sound frightened her. That was too close, when you couldn't tell someone's heart from your own!

Buck ended the kiss and Cory stood trembling.

She racked her mind for a light remark that would protect her and keep him from knowing his effect on her.

"What a good thing you don't dress like an officer!" she managed. "All that white uniform and gold braid— You'd be totally devastating."

"And totally uncomfortable!" He laughed. "Would you like me better in a white shirt and pants?"

"I like your bare feet," she said playfully, and covered his instep with her toes. The gesture struck her crazily as more intimate than their kisses.

"I remember taking your little bare feet out of those flippers," Buck teased. "That was some introduction! You threw yourself against me."

"I did not!" Cory denied. "You ordered me to stand up and I tried."

He remembered! Her heart sang. He was running one fingertip up and down the side of her neck while dropping soft kisses beneath her ear.

"I wanted to pick you up and carry you the rest of the way," he murmured.

Cory sighed with satisfaction and curled into his arms without restraint. Nothing could mar the perfection of this moment. Buck was on duty, so boundaries were automatically placed on his behavior.

Nor did he try to rouse her passion. His strong warm hand found and cupped her breast, but he made no attempt to find his way beneath her T-shirt. She forced herself to face facts: this was casual flirting. It wasn't meant to be taken seriously.

As though to prove the facts, Buck said, "Cory, honey, this is the best watch I've ever kept, but I'm supposed to stop kissing you once in a while and look around the horizon. Let's take a stroll and cool off."

He was right, so why should she feel let down and rejected?

She followed him along the narrow walkway between cabin and rail to the afterdeck. The lamps there had been turned off; the ladies had disappeared. In the softly lit saloon Lester was perched on a bar stool having a last drink.

On the port side they passed one of the crew lounging against the rail smoking a cigarette. Buck clapped him warmly on the back. "Everything okay, Harry?"

"Everything's fine, sir."

Buck introduced him.

"Harry taught me to sail," he added. "He learned to navigate by the stars from his grandfather, who learned from his grandfather. His line of knowledge probably goes back to the first Hawaiians."

Back in the wheelhouse Buck made no move to continue their romantic interlude. He took over the wheel and suggested Cory sit on the stool. Ill at ease, she wondered if she should leave. She wanted to stay. His mere presence thrilled her, but she mustn't give the impression of hanging around. At last she yawned delicately.

"Bedtime?" he quizzed.

"Hardly," she denied. "Maybe it's the sea air."

"Want to go down to the galley and get us some coffee?"

She found her way to a shipshape cubicle, the smallness of which was impressive when she remembered the dinner for six that had come from it earlier. With the cups on a tray, she returned to the wheelhouse along the outside deck.

Something about setting a cup of coffee beside the bronzed hand resting lightly on the varnished mahogany counter hinted at a new intimacy in their relationship.

Buck's lazy smile and the glance from his sleepy blue eyes between thick black lashes warmed her heart. Something inside her melted like butter.

They drank the coffee in companionable silence. When she set aside her empty cup, he reached for her hand and pulled her to stand against him.

"This way I can hold you and the wheel, too," he told her, his breath fanning her cheek.

The crisp dark hair that feathered his thighs tickled the delicate skin on the backs of her legs. Above his encircling arms, her chest rose and fell with a disturbing lack of control. Did she still remind him of his erstwhile girl friend? Or did he like her for herself?

She sighed unthinkingly.

"You're tired," Buck said.

"A little," she admitted. Emotionally exhausted, if the truth were known.

"We have a calm sea and perfect weather," he told her, scanning the horizon, "but it's still tiring when the deck comes up to meet you at every step.

Go to bed. I'll be back on the wheel before daybreak. If you wake up early, come and watch the dawn.''

"I'll do that!"

He turned her around and kissed her with a thoroughness that left her gasping.

I've got to get hold of myself, she thought as she made her way to her cabin. *I've got to decide how far I want to go with this—how far I can go without getting hurt.*

She wondered about his relationship with Emma. It couldn't have been much, some stolen hours here and there. Their very unhappiness must have been a bond between them. She couldn't have been greatly in love with him or she wouldn't have been out with someone else. The worry about getting caught would have made their stolen moments tantalizing, though. And exciting.

Cory remembered that Buck had said she was the most exciting thing on Kauai. But men would say anything to get what they wanted; she had learned that. How would she feel if she did succeed in making her home on Kauai, and then Buck dumped her? She undressed thoughtfully and slid into bed, determined to keep him at arm's length for the rest of the trip. She had known all along that he spelled danger, and here she was, flirting with it. She deliberately failed to set her alarm clock. She was sorry not to keep her promise, but he had said, "If you wake up early..." so it wasn't exactly a promise.

However, when Cory woke before daybreak, she

decided sleepily that she could have early-morning coffee with Buck without compromising herself. Not to meet him would be rude. She dressed quietly in the dark to keep from disturbing Hazel, and scurried down the companionway to the galley. She brewed fresh coffee in the glass pot, racing the sun, though stars still studded the sky outside the porthole.

The pleasure she experienced when she saw Buck made her close her mind to all long-term consequences. Why not enjoy what was, in fact, the equivalent of a desert island while the opportunity existed?

Buck was leaning against the chart table, staring broodingly out to sea, the boat on automatic pilot. He was wearing white shorts and a nautical-looking white knit shirt.

"Good morning!" she caroled.

He brought his attention back from far away, his face lighted and he smiled.

Her heart lifted. She had been right to join him.

"You made it!" he exclaimed appreciatively. "And with coffee!" He set the tray aside and pulled her to him. "You can crew on my boat anytime."

"I don't know how," she reminded him.

"I'll teach you. All you need is the willingness to get up at odd hours."

She noted with concern that his eyes were red-rimmed.

"Don't you need to get regular sleep before you run?" she asked.

"Not if it interferes with my other pursuits." He

lowered one black-fringed eyelid in a provocative wink.

Cory's careful reasoning of the night before had no effect on the behavior of her emotions, which were doing a joyful dance. If he meant he was pursuing her, she welcomed the idea. They were safe on their desert island. She pressed against him and put her arms around his neck.

"Being on a boat's like being in another world," she said between his kisses.

"Sure is. Do you like this world?"

"Heavenly," she murmured against his collarbone.

His lips traced a line of burning kisses across the back of her neck.

"If I ever get you alone on my sailboat, I won't be so well behaved," he promised.

"So that's where you take your girl friends!"

Still holding her around the waist, he reared back to face her. "I wonder where you got that idea. Paco, by chance?"

He let her go and picked up his coffee cup. His blue eyes studied her over the brim.

"Maybe," she admitted.

"Paco has a great imagination, and so have you." He took her arm. "Bring your coffee. I want to point out some stars before they fade."

Outside he kept her shoulders in the circle of his arms, turning her where he wanted her to look. The black heavens glittered with the fierceness of the tropics.

"See those three stars almost in a row? We know

them as Orion's girdle, but the Polynesians called them the Three Little Eyes. That constellation was one of their main navigational guides when they set sail for Hawaii.''

Cory looked, but her mind was still questioning his remark about imagination. Again she had been the one to introduce a jarring note. Why couldn't she let things go at face value? Here she was, jealously accusing him of things that were none of her business.

But didn't a few sparks make for excitement?

With his arm still around her shoulders, he turned her toward the east. The horizon had begun to glow pearl gray. Nearby objects on the deck had become visible.

Cory watched for the green flash that was supposed to appear as the sun tipped the horizon. Buck refused to give credence to such a mysterious occurrence.

''The green flash was invented to give tourists something to look for while they wait for their early buses,'' he proclaimed.

Inevitably the sun rose. Gray brightened to blue above and below, and daylight arrived.

''Who needs a green flash?'' Buck scoffed. ''On a clear morning, the miracle of turning night to day is fantastic enough for me.''

Cory agreed. ''More coffee?'' she asked, wondering when breakfast was scheduled. She had become aware of a very healthy appetite.

Buck nodded, and she tripped along the deck, so alive she felt like dancing. What a miracle a sunrise was, and how wonderful to share it with Buck.

In the galley she found the other crewman cooking busily. He poured the coffee for her and told her that breakfast would be set out in due time and everyone could help themselves.

Lester took over the wheel and Buck and Cory breakfasted together. Then Buck went off to catch up on sleep. Cory put on the black bikini and lay in the sun. Later she sat with Hazel, Mae and Irene under the awning and watched the island of Oahu off the port bow grow larger and larger.

Buck appeared, looking well rested, his eyes no longer bloodshot, his white shorts and shirt a brilliant contrast against his dark golden skin.

The city of Honolulu became visible, a dazzling white between ocean and mountains. Hazel pointed out Diamond Head. Buck took the helm, and the two crew members moved smartly about their duties. The city grew larger, its buildings distinguishable, and the yacht's solitary existence became a thing of the past.

CHAPTER TEN

CORY WAS SECRETLY IMPRESSED by the skill with which Buck threaded the narrow waterways of the marina. He had every right to be pleased with himself and accepted his family's praise as his due. Cory couldn't help but notice that the Bower yacht was larger than most of the boats docked at the Ala Wai yacht harbor.

When the business of mooring was accomplished to Lester's satisfaction, Buck came strolling over to where the women lounged on the afterdeck.

Cory watched him with a catch in her throat. Would he now vanish into Waikiki? Irene had pointed out Waikiki Beach as they came in. The strip of sand was as thick with bodies as any watering place on the Jersey shore—though not at this time of year. The Jersey shore would be icy now.

To Cory's relief, Buck didn't disappear. He offered to escort the ladies wherever they wished to go. The big Ala Moana shopping center was within sight and walking distance.

"Shop or swim?" he asked Cory, pointing out the Ala Moana Park and beach on the other side of the boat channel.

She hadn't planned to buy anything. Her Christmas presents to the mainland had been sent two weeks ago, and she would finish the quilted pillow for Hazel, but she was looking forward to investigating the huge shopping plaza. She explained this somewhat hesitantly.

"That suits me," Buck said. "I have to buy presents sometime this weekend. You can come along and help choose something for the aunts. By the way," he announced to everyone "—Lester's taking us to the Kahala Hilton tonight."

Cory slipped her sandals on, took up her purse and was ready to go. They left Hazel comfortably bestowed on deck with a novel and a fine view of the waterway.

The shopping mall overwhelmed Cory.

"It's so beautiful!" she said again and again. "The palms and other greenery. It's so spacious... and...civilized!"

The aunts disappeared into Honolulu's largest department store, Liberty House. Cory loved the name. It sounded exotic and colonial...a place where one would find Oriental silks and rattan furniture...everything for elegant island living. She and Buck strolled along the upper level where Cory goggled at the enormous goldfish in pools along the promenade and enjoyed the passing scene—young men and women in the briefest of shorts, tourists in matching aloha shirts, stately island women in muumuus, all strolling, looking relaxed and unhurried.

"This is what civilization ought to be!" she exclaimed.

She enjoyed the afternoon to the hilt. She even

delighted in watching the women watch Buck. He was still wearing his white shirt, shorts, boat shoes and the navy cap, and he looked every bit the sailor.

Buck bought painting supplies and T-shirts for Paco. At a gem store he chose topaz earrings for Irene, garnets for Mae, and a pair of pearl earrings, for whom he did not say. Cory stayed as quiet as a mouse. She had never had occasion to visit such a specialized shop, where set and unset stones were displayed together in cases according to kind and color.

"I feel like a real tourist here," she said to Buck when he took her to a Japanese department store and made her choose among the Japanese versions of fast food. The plastic takeout containers were dark red stippled with black and gold and looked as beautifully Oriental as the food. Instead of plastic forks, short wooden Japanese chopsticks were supplied.

They sat outside to eat and were besieged by plump little doves looking for crumbs. When they returned to the yacht they were laden with packages—mostly Buck's, though Cory had not resisted buying a couple of paperback romances when they passed a bookstore. Buck stopped in the lounge to show his aunts the T-shirts for Paco. Cory went to her cabin to change for dinner. She had decided to wear the daytime muumuu.

"If I'd expected to have such a social life, I wouldn't have bought an everyday gown," she told Hazel, who was catching a few minutes' rest. "I'd have bought two dressier ones."

"Why don't you buy one while you're here?" Hazel suggested.

"It seems so extravagant," Cory protested.

"Don't forget we're invited to the Bowers' Christmas party," Hazel said.

Cory's everyday muumuu with blue forget-me-nots and blue ribbon looked a little unsophisticated for Honolulu's celebrated Kahala Hilton, but when the men turned up wearing aloha shirts, Cory felt suitably dressed.

Daylight still lingered when they arrived at the end of a twenty-minute taxi ride. Even Hazel undertook to stroll into the beautiful grounds, through which a saltwater lagoon wound. The lagoon was supposedly populated with turtles, surgeonfish and a quartet of dolphins, but Cory saw only a pair of black-footed penguins, not in their neatest plumage at that time of year.

The restaurant was at the bottom of a descending staircase resembling a lava grotto. Mossy walls sprouted lavender orchids so exquisitely beautiful that Cory could hardly believe they were real. The large dining area featured still pools of water in which more orchids were reflected along with masses of yellow heliconia. Cory's eyes widened when she saw the Belgian lace tablecloth. She stole a glance at Hazel, who winked to show she understood Cory's awe. The rest of the table appointments were spectacular, too, including plates decorated with gold rims and gold maile leaves—Hawaii's good luck symbol.

Lester ordered rum-based tropical penguins,

drinks christened in honor of the pair outside. The dinner started with papaya laced with port, followed by blue snapper soup, after which Cory had *mahimahi* again, strewn with julienne vegetables. For dessert she chose a cold, rum-flavored macadamia nut soufflé. Buck smiled at her choice, then ordered it himself, admitting that it sounded too tempting to pass up.

Back on the boat after the fabulous dinner, everyone gravitated to the afterdeck to sit and discuss the day. Cory was faintly disappointed that Buck made no attempt to be alone with her. Just as well, she told herself stoutly. Only last night she had decided not to let herself get serious, and here she was regretting that she hadn't been alone with him.

"What does everyone plan to do tomorrow?" Out of the darkness Buck's voice came deep, and to Cory's ears, sexy.

"Don't you have to work out or run or something?" Irene inquired.

"I'll get that over with while the rest of you are still in bed." Under cover of darkness he squeezed Cory's arm.

Mae said she and Irene had more shopping to do. Lester intended to play golf.

"I plan to watch the goings-on here as I did this afternoon," Hazel announced. "You'd be surprised how busy it is."

"I guess that leaves us to entertain each other, Cory." Buck's voice was filled with laughter.

"Wasn't that your idea?" Irene sounded snappish, Cory thought, but perhaps she was merely teasing. She went on to say, "Why don't you take her downtown to see the palace and hear the band concert? What time is Paco due?"

"After school lets out. He'll take the bus from the airport." Buck's chair creaked as he faced Cory. "All right? I think the concerts start at noon. Then we'll do the palace. I've never been inside, myself."

"Fine with me," Cory agreed.

"If you have time, walk over to the missionary houses," Irene directed. "They have a nice gift shop Cory might like to see."

"Okay." He stood up. "See you all in the morning."

He left, and it seemed as if a light had been turned off. Cory lingered for appearance's sake, anticipating the moment when she could lie in the dark and replay the day, beginning when she and Buck had shared the dawn.

The next morning Cory went swimming alone. While she lay on the beach drying off, she watched the friendly white pigeons that seemed to have made the beach their territory. How much more elegant they looked than ordinary pigeons! The park was filled with joggers, both male and female. She lay watching lazily, her chin propped on her elbows. Few of the men who passed were as well built as Buck, she thought, and then she saw him. His dark hair was plastered damply across his forehead. He had removed his T-shirt and it hung limply around his neck. He looked as though he had covered miles; he must have been doing laps around the park.

Cory did not attempt to draw his attention. She wanted to watch him when he wasn't aware of her scrutiny. He appeared to be moving easily, even lightly, but his wet locks and the way his muscles glistened with sweat told her of the grueling demands he was making on himself. She followed his bobbing head above the parked cars for as long as she could, remembering the first time she had seen him running, after he had paused to pull her out of the water and tell her she had to try snorkeling again. Her chest expanded with pride, and the simple thrill of knowing he was hers for the afternoon. She waited for him to go by once more before she headed back to the yacht to shower and dress.

I'm crazy, she thought, *lying here waiting to watch someone run by whom I've been seeing steadily for the past thirty-six hours.*

Her patience was rewarded. He bounded by, his strides apparently tireless. How long had he been at it? Two hours, maybe more. She let her eyes dwell on the tight buttocks, the sensuous curve of thigh into knee. He smiled and waved at someone near the concessions stand. Who? A friend. . . a new acquaintance? A woman? Hot jealousy flared.

Cory scrambled to her feet and stood on tiptoe, trying to see. Had he waved to that slim girl in the bikini who was now crossing the street? Buck had gone clear out of sight. All she had derived from her wait was a glimpse of him and a flood of jealousy so strong it turned her insides cold.

By the time he joined her on the afterdeck she was mistress of herself. He emerged from the cabin he shared with Lester looking crisp and clean in tan shorts and a matching knit shirt with white collar and placket. The contrast with his deep tan was breath catching.

Cory had elected to wear shorts, too, pale blue ones that set off her golden legs to perfection. Her white sleeveless blouse brought a quick reaction from Buck. He came to where she stood and took her shoulder in both hands as though it were a bone. Growling, he pretended to sink his teeth into it.

Cory's shriek of protest gave expression to the wildfire in her blood. She had the most dreadful urge to fall against him, entangle her legs in his and raise her mouth for his kiss. He hadn't kissed her for more than twenty-four hours.

"Ready to go?" His blue eyes gleamed impishly. "I could eat you up," he muttered, pulling her against him and giving her the kiss she'd been wanting.

Her blood stirred, but as it began to race Buck raised his head.

"Come away from here before I forget myself and carry you off to my cabin."

"It's Lester's cabin, too," Cory reminded him.

"He's gone golfing, remember?" He took her arm and unceremoniously escorted her off the yacht.

Did she really affect him like that...more than any of the other attractive women he must meet? She wished she could believe she did. Common sense warned her not to speculate, and she wisely put her mind on sight-seeing and enjoying the day.

They caught a bus that took them downtown. Cory could hardly believe it *was* downtown, it was so clean and there was so much open space and greenery. The air seemed every bit as clear as on Kauai. She remarked on the fact.

"It is clear," Buck agreed. "There's very little manufacturing, and the trade wind carries away the automobile exhaust."

The palace looked like an ornate Victorian mansion. The grounds were spacious, and Cory thought she had never seen such beautiful trees as the umbrella-shaped monkeypods. She noted the rows of royal palms lining the drives and admired the ornate iron fence encircling the grounds.

Buck led her into the heart of the business district to a health food restaurant with an eye-opening selection.

"This is the California influence," he said while they waited for sandwiches of pinto bean curd and sprouts on whole grain bread.

With the sandwiches in a paper sack they returned to the palace grounds. The Royal Hawaiian Band, their uniforms green aloha shirts, had already begun their concert in the white bandstand. Cory looked at the people around her. "The guests, star-scattered on the grass," she said to herself, remembering a line from the Rubaiyat. Buck found them seats on the ridgelike roots of a towering tree. They munched their sandwiches while the band played classical music interspersed with marches and Hawaiian solos, duets and hulas.

By turning her head Cory had a breath-catching view of the mountains, their steep green slopes unspoiled by buildings. Only the graceful shapes of coconut palms broke the skyline. She felt forced to share her delight.

She said softly, unbelievingly, "It really is paradise here."

Buck smiled and hugged her.

After the concert, while they waited to take the tour through the palace, Cory admired the huge banyan tree that grew on that side of the building. Then they crossed a grassy mall to the bold and dramatic state capitol building.

"It's supposed to represent a volcano rising out of the sea—the reflecting pools," Buck explained, and Cory heard the pride behind his offhand summary. "The columns represent palm trees, and the open center gives the feeling of our climate."

They walked through the open court to see the statue of Father Damien, the hero of the leprosy colony on Molokai, and then returned to the palace.

Cory emerged from the tour much more knowledgeable about the history of the Hawaiian monarchy.

"The only royal palace in America," she mused. "It's a beautiful building, but I wouldn't want to be imprisoned there like Queen Liliuokalani. I suppose you think the United States was right in taking the islands?"

"If we hadn't, England or China or Japan would have."

"I suppose it was expedient," Cory agreed. "Too bad they couldn't have been left undiscovered."

They crossed the street to stand before the black and gold statue of Kamehameha I.

Squinting sourly at the statue, Buck said, "During his reign the population dropped from three hundred thousand to about a hundred and thirty-five thousand. One of his accomplishments was to drive most of the warriors of the King of Oahu off the thousand-foot cliff at the Pali lookout. His military conquests bloodied streams and beaches, and foreign ships brought foreign diseases. To satisfy his greed he drove his subjects to strip the islands of sandalwood trees."

Buck shrugged. "On to the missionary houses," he directed. "They, at least, came to do good. And by and large their descendants were a stabilizing force. Certainly they took more interest in the islanders' welfare than the adventurers who came here to make money."

"Which were your ancestors?"

"Adventurers, I'm afraid." Buck grinned, and Cory could imagine him giving orders on the deck of a sailing ship.

"So the sea is in your blood," she suggested.

"The sea is a natural part of island living," Buck told her.

The three white houses, looking like another bit of transplanted New England, appeared tiny in contrast to the great coral church that represented the result of missionary endeavors. Their guide-lecturer took them through the frame house prefabricated in

New England, shipped "around the Horn" and erected in 1821. Among the mementos of that period Cory was pleased to see a quilt of the same pattern as the pillow cushion she was working on, and happily pointed it out to Buck.

She walked around the gift shop with a professional eye and was impressed with their range of items, all in some way connected with Hawaii. *This is how Sondra's and my shop ought to be,* she thought. She wanted to tell Buck about her possible partnership with Sondra, but she would wait until it was definite. Nowhere had she seen rubbings of petroglyphs for sale, yet done on muslin they would make nice, authentic souvenirs. She must discuss that with Sondra.

"Didn't you buy anything in all that time?" Buck asked when she emerged to find him sitting on a bench in the shade.

"I was just looking." She noticed he looked drawn.

Before she could comment, he said, "I'm sorry, but I'm bushed. I lost count of the times I ran around that park this morning."

Cory dropped onto the bench beside him. "You shouldn't have agreed to drag me around to all these places!" she exclaimed contritely. "I could have gone alone!"

"I wanted to take you. I wanted to see the sights through your beautiful, interested eyes." His warm smile and intimate look were too much. Her heart beat harder and she caught herself thinking that he must be sincere. He wouldn't go to all that trouble if he weren't. The sterner part of her mind, made wise by experience, mocked such thoughts. Buck made a point of being charming.

Before she realized what he was about to do, he bent his head and placed a warm kiss on her lips. She blushed as she saw the broad smiles of two couples coming up the path.

"They'll think we're honeymooners," he whispered. He stood up with a groan and a laugh. "I'd hate like hell to feel like this on a honeymoon! On Sunday it'll all be over."

"Have you run in marathons before?" Cory asked on the way to the bus.

"Never. I began running last spring to keep in shape, and when I found I could run ten miles easily, I thought, why not? But there's a big difference between ten and twenty-six. I hope I'll make it to the finish."

Keep in shape! Cory couldn't imagine his magnificent physique out of shape. What a wonderfully created machine he was! When she thought of the beauty and strength contained in those bones and muscles, the way the elements combined to give sparkle to his blue eyes and flash to his smile, she thought it was no wonder that men had conceived gods in their own image.

"Penny for your thoughts."

Cory laughed. "They're worth more than a penny!" She glanced at him and tried to memorize the hard curve of his handsome jaw, the strength of his brown neck.

"I was trying to imagine you out of shape," she admitted. "It's impossible."

He took her upper arm, pressing his knuckles unnecessarily against her breast. "Why, thank you," he drawled. "That's the first nice thing you've ever told me."

Was that true? If he knew how her thoughts dwelt continually on his looks, his charm, the sound of his voice, he would think she was crazy. Her every thought of him was that he was wonderful.

That evening they dined at the Willows. Paco had arrived full of enthusiasm for his weekend in the capital city. Cory wore her lace-yoked muumuu and on arrival at the outdoor restaurant felt like an Oriental princess. The secluded setting was unexpected in the residential heart of the city. No wonder it was a famous landmark. From the moment she stepped from the street into the walkway banked on either side by greenery, she stepped into another world that was only incidentally a restaurant.

Their party sat at a table in a palm-thatched gazebo beside a pool where white and golden carp leapt from the water to gobble tidbits thrown by the diners. Ti plants and bamboo, crotons and fronds of banana trees created the illusion of a garden that stretched on and on. And indeed, it did, because a busload of tourists came in behind the Bower party and disappeared, presumably into another secluded dining area.

Cory selected the shrimp curry, one of the dishes on which the Willows had built its reputation, and she and Paco were easily talked into finishing the meal with towering pieces of lemon meringue pie. A trio strumming ukuleles and a bass viol sang old

Hawaiian songs, which fit perfectly with the setting.

Cory kept her eyes on Buck. When he seemed in danger of dozing, she reminded his family that he needed an early night.

"What do you plan to do tomorrow?" Irene asked him.

"I'm going to rent a car and take Cory and Paco to the Polynesian Cultural Center."

"That's a workout in itself!" his aunt exclaimed.

"I'll lie on the grass and let them sightsee," he promised.

THEY SET OUT AT MIDMORNING to drive to the other side of the island, which everyone referred to as "over the Pali." The highway whisked them through two tunnels and they emerged to find themselves on the windward side of a clifflike ridge that ran the whole length of the mountain chain. The cliff was seamed and wrinkled, like chocolate frosting poured down the side of a cake, but the almost daily rains kept the perpendicular sides green with bushes and plants. Cory had seen those cliffs in movies of the South Seas, but she had somehow assumed they were a fantasy of Hollywood.

"It's unbelievable," she breathed.

At the foot of the cliffs the land flattened out into pastures, banana and papaya plantations and stretches of suburbia along the highway.

The cultural center—an outdoor museum run by the Mormon church—was built around a winding lagoon, on the banks of which authentic replicas of Polynesian villages had been erected. Cory and

Paco set off to see them all. Buck found an out-of-the-way stretch of grass and instructed them to come back and find him when they grew hungry.

Walking the paths from village to village, Cory and Paco traveled through the cultures of ancient Hawaii, Tonga, Fiji, Tahiti, Samoa, the Marquesas and New Zealand. Natives of the islands and students from Brigham Young University–Hawaii demonstrated the arts and day-to-day concerns of these ancient cultures. They showed how to open and grate a coconut, and how to get the coconut in the first place. The young man who demonstrated this climbed the tree trunk so fast that Cory didn't get a picture snapped until he was on the way down.

Cory, Buck and Paco lunched on *kalua* pig and rice in the dining area that served native foods. They left Buck lazily watching a basket-making demonstration and continued their tour. The afternoon ended with the *Pageant of the Long Canoes*, in which each culture performed native dances in costume on the floating stages of the double canoes.

"What a marvelous place!" Cory sighed at the end of the day, collapsing gracefully into the car seat.

"Yeah, it was neat," Paco agreed from the back, and launched into a description of all he had seen.

"Thank you so much for bringing us," Cory said when she could get a word in.

Buck smiled sideways at her and reached for her hand.

"I thought you'd enjoy it," he said. "And I

figured it would be educational for you,'' he added, eyeing Paco in the rearview mirror.

Paco reacted instantly. ''In that case, Buck, can I skip school Monday and sail back with you? Please! Harry says we'll get back before time for school on Tuesday, so I'd only miss one day. *Please?*''

''We'll talk about it later.'' Buck sounded like a parent, Cory thought with amusement.

That evening they all dined at John Dominis at the end of a rocky, surf-splashed promontory by Kewalo Basin, where the commercial fishing fleet docked. Their party was seated beside a serpentine saltwater pool. Paco pointed out varieties of tropical fish Cory might see the next time she went snorkeling, plus improbable hammerhead sharks and spiny Hawaiian lobsters.

Buck urged her to order a steamed whole lobster. It came with black bean sauce and sprigs of coriander. A notation on the menu said that in ancient Hawaii a religious taboo forbade women to eat these same lobsters on pain of death.

''Now the pain's in the wallet,'' Buck quipped, quickly adding before Cory could reproach him, ''Only joking! I wanted you to have it.''

THE RUNNERS STARTED from Kapiolani Park well before daylight the next morning. Cory was surprised to find a huge crowd milling around at such an early hour. Buck wore green-and-white running shoes and shorts. His matching T-shirt would probably come off along the way as the morning advanced. A green sweatband failed to control his tumbled locks.

In the darkness, with so many runners lined up for the start, Cory lost sight of him. She had wished him well and had promised to be on hand to cheer him at the finish.

When the runners had departed in a herd of thudding feet, Lester took the party to a Waikiki hotel for a light breakfast. Cory's mind dwelt on Buck. While they relaxed and enjoyed their meal, he was pounding along the roadway toward Koko Head. At some point the road climbed. The temperature might be perfect for lolling on a beach, but for running uphill it must be sheer agony.

Two hours later they all returned to the park. They brought water, towels and everything else they could think of that Buck might want when he finished. An undercurrent of excitement rippled through the waiting crowd. Hazel, Mae and Irene sat in folding chairs taken from the boat. Lester, Cory and Paco stretched on the grass. The first runners arrived. To Cory's disappointment Buck was not among them to receive the cheers and tossed flowers.

"Did you really expect Buck to win?" Irene asked, noting the sorrow on Cory's face.

"No." Cory sighed.

Paco sniffed. "Do you know how many hours those guys who win marathons train? Buck's not into that. He's doing this for fun."

"Some fun!" Lester pronounced.

Cory remembered Buck had told her that all he wanted to do was finish the course.

The good-humored crowd applauded each panting, suffering, sweating runner who crossed the finish line. A television camera ground away and everywhere people were photographing friends. Cory had brought her camera and was pleased at the marvelous excuse to take pictures of Buck.

The finishers came in singly, in twos and threes, running together for encouragement. At last Cory spotted Buck.

"There he is!" she cried. She stood breathless, watching him. She could almost feel how he must be suffering.

But Buck still had the energy to grin and fling up his arms as he crossed the finish. Amid the hugs and kisses and congratulations, he managed to give Cory a deep kiss. She retired pink faced to put another roll of film in her camera while Buck did his cool-down exercises, made use of the water and towels and drank two cans of soda.

"Are you ready to come back to the boat?" Irene prompted him when his chest was no longer heaving. "Harry's preparing a hero's breakfast, and brunch for the rest of us."

They made it a champagne brunch. People came from all over the yacht basin to ask how Buck had done. He regained enough strength to recall all the details of the grueling course.

Cory sat back and watched him enjoying the attention of his family, the other yachtsmen and a few friends from Honolulu who had been invited to visit. The celebration gained momentum and looked as if it would go on most of the afternoon.

Buck made his way across the crowded deck to where Cory sat beside Hazel.

"I'm going to have another shower and stretch out for a few hours... maybe till morning." He laughed. "Paco seems to have disappeared. Anyhow, I've decided he can sail home with us. Tell him that if you see him. I'll probably sleep till dinnertime." He looked at Cory and his blue eyes softened. His hand came out to touch her shoulder. "She's something else, isn't she?" he said to Hazel.

"That she is," Hazel agreed. "If you're not up by dinnertime we won't wake you," she called after him.

Paco turned up late in the afternoon looking pleased with himself. Cory wondered if he thought he had put one over on Buck by keeping out of sight. She let him know that Buck's decision had been made at noon.

"Oh, good!" Paco grinned and ran off down the pier.

Buck wasn't up at dinnertime so they went without him, and he was still asleep when they returned. Cory felt slightly disappointed, but after such an exciting day she, too, was ready to retire. She left the older members of the party playing bridge.

Having gone to bed early, Cory woke before dawn. This would be her last chance to sketch the marina, something she had intended to do since her arrival. Quietly she collected her drawing materials and left the yacht. It was still almost dark, but the tropic sunrise would arrive swiftly.

She found a viewpoint she liked, an unobtrusive place to sit, and began to work, blocking in masses.

She was working happily when a movement aboard the *Iwa* caught her attention. She saw Buck spring over the side of the yacht and swiftly, light-footedly set off along the dock, a fully stuffed white seabag slung over one shoulder.

Cory's first wild thought was that he was going off to join some merchant ship, but she dismissed that idea quickly and watched with pleasure his determined stride, the relaxed sway of his broad shoulders. When he was lost from sight she turned her attention back to her drawing, pondering his actions while her pencil flew. She wondered if he had brought sails from his sailboat to be repaired in Honolulu.

Some time later she noticed Paco leaving the boat in a way that struck her as furtive. He scurried off, wearing his rucksack and gripping a white bag that looked like a pillowcase full of something bulky and not too heavy. The rucksack was full, too, much fuller than when he'd come on board Friday night. What was he carrying? Where was he going? By the time she thought of calling to him, he had disappeared.

She shrugged and went back to drawing. Buck gave him too much freedom, in her opinion. But then, what did she know about young teenage boys?

About an hour later Paco returned. The sun was well up. Cory had become absorbed in drawing and had almost forgotten him. She noted that his rucksack now sagged empty, and he no longer carried the pillowcase. Reluctantly she knew she ought to question him.

The drawing was finished. She gathered up her materials and followed him aboard. The hour was still early. None of the older people were up yet and Cory entered the saloon without warning. She surprised Paco in the act of counting a fistful of bills.

"Paco!" she exclaimed. "Where did you get all that money?"

Startled, the boy jumped to his feet, but he recovered quickly. "It's not a lot," he said, abruptly shoving it into his pocket. "It's just small bills. It's my Christmas money."

Cory thought she had glimpsed some bills of much higher denomination but she couldn't be sure. Despite his explanation, something about his behavior wasn't right.

"Why were you counting it?" she asked, thinking even as she said it that the question was dumb. Why did anybody count money?

"I wanted to be sure how much I had," Paco said.

If he was telling the truth, why were his eyes sparkling with excitement? Cory was trying to phrase a question about the empty rucksack when a quiet footfall sounded on deck and Buck peered into the saloon. His dark wavy locks fell in fascinating disarray over his broad forehead. He looked like a little boy up to mischief. At the sight of Cory and Paco he grinned and entered. With a laugh he dropped the heavy seabag at his feet.

"Would you believe I'm sneaking clean laundry aboard this tub?"

Relieved at the interruption, Cory asked hastily, "Is that where you went—to the Laundromat? I saw you set off. I thought maybe you were shipping out,'' she added in an attempt to lighten what she knew to be a tense atmosphere.

Nevertheless, he felt the tension because he looked from one to the other. "Why are you two up and fully dressed?"

Cory waited to hear what Paco would say.

"No reason," Paco began, and then seemed to realize that Cory knew otherwise. "I had something to do for Harry," he said at last.

"I've been sketching the marina," Cory said.

Buck grinned engagingly. "Aren't you going to ask why I'm smuggling laundry?"

"Why?" Paco and Cory both asked obligingly.

"Harry forgot to take the laundry ashore after the last trip," Buck said. "It's been moldering away all this time in one of the lockers. I offered to sneak it out this morning before Lester finds out about it and gives Harry a hard time."

Paco said indignantly, "Why didn't Harry send the galley stuff, too? He made me take it!" He threw Cory a saucy glance that seemed to say, *See? I haven't been doing anything wicked*.

Buck laughed at him. "I told Harry to put you to work. The stuff you took to be washed was legitimate. Where'd you take it? I didn't see you at the Laundromat."

"I left it with the attendant to do. I'll pick it up later. That's what you must have done," he accused. "You didn't do it yourself. You went running." He shot Cory another look, as though to see what she was thinking.

She was wondering whether he was leaving something out. Had that been laundry in his rucksack, or had he taken something off the yacht and sold it? Surely not! She didn't want to think so. Buck wasn't the sort to keep him short of pocket money.

Buck was saying, "I left the wash, I ran, I picked up the wash." He threw an arm around Paco's shoulders. "Come and help me put this stuff back where it belongs before Lester sees it and starts asking questions. I'll be back for coffee," he told Cory over Paco's head.

The pair disappeared down the companionway to the lower deck. A moment later Hazel came into the saloon, followed by Lester.

Cory usually considered breakfast her favorite meal, but this morning she paid little attention to what she ate. The picture of Paco counting that wad of money continued to trouble her.

CHAPTER ELEVEN

AFTER BREAKFAST Buck donned a suit. He was going off to keep a business appointment. He looked so handsome and so much a captain of commerce that he seemed a stranger when he came into the lounge. Cory couldn't take her eyes from him. He gave her a brief salute and departed. A few minutes later Paco announced he was going Christmas shopping, and he disappeared.

At four o'clock that afternoon Cory sat on deck with Hazel and the Bower ladies while the yacht got under way and Buck took it out to sea. Cory watched the green tops of Oahu drop below the horizon and told herself she should have asked Paco outright what he had carried off in his rucksack. Perhaps she should still ask him. And if he told her? How would she know he was speaking the truth?

In her mind she went over all the possibilities she could think of, and at the end of her meditation she still hadn't considered the thing she most feared. Marijuana. What an overactive imagination, she thought. But once started, her suspicions knew no limit. What an ideal opportunity it would be for Paco, and whoever put him up to it, to smuggle marijuana to Honolulu on a yacht belonging to such prestigious people as the Bowers. The newspaper article had said that many of the pushers were teenage boys. Who would have put him up to it? She allowed her imagination to run rampant. Could Buck be involved? He had grown up on Kauai and probably knew most of the island's longtime inhabitants. Hazel had charged him with knowing who the big operators were, and Buck had sidestepped the issue. *Pakalolo* was rumored to be one of the largest crops the islands produced. A lot of unsavory people must be growing it, and exporting it, too. Just how wealthy were the Bowers? Everyone said the sugar business was in trouble, and tourism had fallen off. What was to keep Buck from planting a row or two of *pakalolo* in every cane field?

She had thought Tim was merely sounding off when he hinted that Buck was involved, but maybe Tim knew what he was talking about. Buck was certainly zealous about keeping strangers off his field roads. Or possibly Paco had delivered the grass for someone else on the plantation. Surely a rucksack full didn't constitute big dealings. But how did she know how much might have been taken ashore on other mornings by Harry, by the other crewmen?

To still her suspicions she ought to confront Paco and ask him what he'd been carrying. If he refused to tell her, then she could go to Buck, who might think she was a busybody. On the other hand, if Paco said his rucksack had been full of laundry, too, she would look like a fool. She groaned. Why must she keep feeling he was up to mischief? She had nothing to go on. If Buck wasn't involved in growing marijuana, and Paco was innocent, Buck wouldn't thank her for suspecting him or his family. If he *was* involved, he sure wouldn't thank her!

Why did she think he wasn't involved? Because she didn't want him to be? Because he was a big landowner? Who did she think the big growers were—simple Hawaiian farmers? Could someone as marvelous as Buck be without one flaw? She had shut her ears to what Tim had said, yet she knew his words by heart: "Do you think Buck doesn't know what's being grown?"

At last, tired out with emotional reasoning, she decided to keep her own council for the time being. All she could do was promise to be alert.

She stood at the rail, watching the mountains of Oahu sink below the horizon and wishing Buck could join her. Overhead a pair of black frigate birds circled, their exotic forked tails and sharply pointed wings expressive of tropical waters.

She felt more and more unreasonable anger toward Paco. She ought to tell Buck. Yet what if the rucksack had contained only laundry? Buck might think her accusations stemmed from jealousy. Or what if it were true? Paco had carried marijuana, and Buck didn't care, or took it lightly? No, as Tim had cautioned her, the less said the better.

Buck hadn't suggested that Cory keep him company at the wheel. When she went to the wheelhouse anyway, Paco was perched on the stool telling Buck about some school happening.

Buck made Paco get up to let Cory sit, but conversation between the three of them was stilted. After a few minutes she excused herself. Buck's lazy blue eyes gave her a look that seemed charged with meaning, but she couldn't interpret it.

"It's past time for cocktails, isn't it?" he said. "Paco's going to take over the wheel."

The boy grinned happily.

Cory left and sat on the afterdeck, studying the sunset. The older people had moved into the saloon. Her confusion over what to think about this morning's occurrence proved how little she knew about Buck. Or perhaps how poor her judgment was about men in general, she amended, as the memory of Paul intruded. She decided the thing she had learned was to be on the safe side and think the worst. Buck should be assumed guilty until proven innocent. Maybe she was being cynical, but experience seemed to show that an overly trusting nature led to sorrow. Nevertheless, she felt depressed by the outcome of her reasoning.

She was still musing when Buck appeared in front of her holding two glasses clinking with ice.

"Wake up!" he teased, setting the glasses on the deck and pulling up a chair for himself. "I've been counting the minutes till I could join you, and I find you with your head in the clouds."

"Not in the clouds at all," she said seriously. "My thoughts were very down-to-earth. Is Paco steering?"

"Yep." One corner of Buck's mouth twisted. "We may wind up in California, but at least he's out from underfoot for a while.'' He lowered his voice. "I wanted to talk to you alone.''

Cory sipped the glass of white wine he had brought her and eyed him warily. He was looking serious, his blue eyes narrowed. Cory found herself thinking he'd be a hard man to do business with.

"Hazel tells me you're thinking about going into partnership with that woman Sondra,'' he said. "What's the idea?''

"What do you mean?'' His tone made Cory bristle.

"I mean, why are you doing it?''

It was on the tip of Cory's tongue to tell him it was none of his business, but she remembered she was his guest. "I'm doing it because I want to stay on Kauai,'' she said defiantly.

She had wondered how he would react when he learned she was planning to settle on the island. Now she would find out. If he only went in for romances with tourists, brief romances that didn't involve him in any responsibility or commitment, he'd begin to back off.

"You like the place that much?'' He looked disbelieving.

"Yes, I do. I love it.''

For an instant a blue flame seemed to leap in his eyes. Then it was gone, like a reflection from the sparkling sea.

"Can't you just get a job or something?'' he asked after a pause. "Why become involved with her?''

"I applied for some jobs. For your information,

they don't hire newcomers—malihinis. And anyway, what do you have against Sondra?'' she asked levelly.

Buck took a swallow of bourbon and Cory watched the movement of his Adam's apple as the drink slid down his throat. His neck was a strong brown column disappearing into the white of his long-sleeved sweat shirt.

"Nothing," he admitted. "But I don't think much of the company she keeps."

"What does her social life have to do with how she runs her business?" Cory inquired.

"A lot, if she spends more time socializing than on her business," he replied reasonably.

"I agree that she doesn't keep the shop open enough," Cory admitted. "That's where I'll come in. We're going to buy more stock and open either mornings or evenings."

"You're determined about this?"

"Yes." Cory forced her brown eyes to meet his hard blue ones.

Buck shrugged. "How much are you putting into it?"

"I don't think that's any of your business," she said belligerently, forgetting she was his guest.

"I just wondered how much you're prepared to lose—"

"Thanks a lot!"

"Well, you have to admit there's some risk," he reasoned. "No business venture is a sure thing. That's why it's called a venture."

Cory sprang to her feet. "I'm not going to listen

to you!'' She hated the frightened, worried feeling that had invaded the pit of her stomach. ''Why can't you wish me well?''

''Of course, I do! Why do you think I bother to caution you? I'm sure not getting any thanks for it,'' he added, looking up at her with a wry smile.

He'd upset her so much she had gulped her wine. As she walked away from him she found herself shaking, whether from anger or fear of taking a wrong step, or some other emotion, she had no idea. She stalked into the cabin she shared with Hazel and flopped onto her bed. He didn't want her to stay on Kauai, and that was his way of saying so.

''Well, thanks a lot, Mr. high-and-mighty, but you don't own the whole island!'' she muttered. She wished she were anywhere but on this boat with him. She felt trapped and at the same time unwanted. And after all her worrying over whether to tell him about Paco. Talk about minding one's own business, she'd done a lousy job of minding her own.

''I hate him!'' she choked, and then realized there was no private place to cry on the damn boat except the shower. She scurried to get to it before someone got in ahead of her.

''COME ON DECK and watch the stars come out,'' Buck invited later. Cory sat in one of the deck chairs, her long skirt blowing lightly around her bare legs. The white sweater she wore provided protection from the cool evening breeze. Paco had returned to the wheelhouse with Lester. The three older women were talking animatedly in the saloon.

"Want to dance?" Buck asked, his blue eyes sleepily irresistible. Switching on the tape recorder, he directed the sound outside and held out his arms.

Cory walked into them as though mesmerized. The waltz music and the pressure of Buck's strong arms guiding her around the deck made it easy to blank the day's events from her mind. She existed solely in the now. *Tomorrow I'll be reasonable,* she thought soothingly.

"You dance like a feather," Buck murmured.

"Thank you," she whispered back. "I knew you danced well from seeing you at the luau."

"That was hardly ballroom dancing," he disclaimed, but he sounded pleased.

He's not immune to compliments, Cory thought, even though he has every reason to be overflowing with confidence. Perhaps nobody was without self-doubt, no matter what mask they showed the world. Still, it was hard to think of Buck as anything but supremely confident. No doubt he was, much of the time.

The music ended and they leaned on the polished mahogany rail, watching the sun set.

"So you're going to stay on Kauai," Buck mused.

"Yes. Any objection?"

"None at all," he replied carelessly.

The music on the tape switched to a fast, modern beat.

"Shall we?" Buck challenged.

As it happened, Cory had taken modern dance lessons. She took his hand and swung into the rhythm with smiling assurance. Buck's lazy blue eyes widened.

"Say, you're good! You must think we're living in another world out here."

"Of course not," she said, but she was pleased to think he considered her sophisticated. It was strange to think they hadn't danced before. Their movements coordinated as though they'd been partners forever.

The quick tropical night soon made it too dark to see the objects on the deck. Then Irene put her head out the door of the saloon.

"We're all going to bed and read," she announced. "I'll leave you to turn out the saloon lights, Buchanan, dear."

"I should go, too," Cory began.

"Wouldn't you rather stay with me?" He took her face in his calloused masculine hands and his mouth touched hers, gently at first, then with an enthusiasm that made her breath quicken.

"Come in here," he said, turning down the lights in the saloon and guiding her firmly to the couch. "I'd like to kiss you in comfort once, instead of in the sand."

He pulled her down beside him on the couch and his lips captured hers. Cory felt dwarfed by his embrace—dwarfed and cuddled and protected. Nevertheless, something kept her from responding. She lay passively in his arms till he shook her gently.

"Kiss me," he muttered thickly.

"I—I can't," she objected.

He raised his head and looked deep into her eyes. "Why not?" His eyes seemed to be smouldering.

"I feel uncomfortable," she tried to explain.

"Some of your family may pop in. And this is where Paco sleeps. What if he comes along?"

"He's seen me kissing girls before." Buck's tone was amused.

That was just it! She couldn't be so casual. She wanted to mean something special to Buck, not be just another affair. The knowledge turned her cold. She struggled and would have slipped out of his arms but he refused to release her.

"What is it with you?" he asked. "You're perfectly safe. I'm not going to undress you. Nor will I let you undress yourself," he added wickedly.

Cory stiffened, overcome with embarrassment at the memory of the night on the beach and the way she had displayed herself.

"You were beautiful," he whispered. "I want to see you like that again, but not here—"

"I'm sorry I got off onto my stupid love affair that night." The words burst from her.

He seemed to taste her lips thoughtfully before at last replying. "Why be sorry? I made you listen to me talk about my affair with Emma." Suddenly he looked sad.

Clearly it still hurt him to think about her. Cory envied her. Imagine inspiring that kind of deep love in a man like Buck. A woman would have to be crazy not to prize it. Hazel had said that Emma *was* crazy.

Anyhow, Cory reminded herself, his past had nothing to do with her. If she was right, his future wasn't going to have anything to do with her, either. He should know by now that she was not like

Emma and wouldn't fill the void in his heart. She managed to tell herself this even while Buck was running his fingertips up and down the inside of her wrist and dropping kisses on her neck in a way that turned her will to water.

He kissed her temples while he ran his hands through her hair.

"Silver hair," he marveled, sliding his fingers through it on either side of her head and holding it out to let it fall shimmering around her shoulders. "The sun has bleached it—just a little—but enough to turn you into a fabulous blonde."

His mouth took hers with masterful assurance. He seemed to know how he affected her, how his mere presence made her think of intimacies she had never allowed herself to consider. She wanted to stroke the soft curling hair of his inner thighs below his shorts, and run her hands across the muscular hardness of his abdomen. He had been too warm when they finished dancing and had pulled off his shirt. She wanted to touch the place where the soft hair of his chest disappeared below his belt. She willed the kiss never to end. Her hands fluttered over his back, touching, withdrawing, unable to resist touching again.

His questing, purposeful mouth seemed to draw all the forces of her body, leaving her fingers drained and tingling. She was drowning in a marvelous tidal wave of sensation that went on and on. Desire rose in her, a passion far more intense than anything she had ever felt before. She hadn't known she possessed such depths of response.

She wanted to say, do what you will with me, and longed achingly for the touch of his hands, his lips, on her bare breasts. Her nipples felt like pink-tipped buds straining toward the warmth that was his chest.

"Cory, Cory," he whispered. "How do you do this to me? I want to strip you naked and make love to you right here, or out on the deck in the moon-light."

Stunned by her own wild response, she could find no words to answer him.

"I thought I could invite you on this trip and keep my cool and have a little light-hearted fooling around," he confessed, "but I was wrong! You af-fect me like some kind of crazy wine. My head seems perfectly clear, but I keep getting wild ideas, like taking you up on the cabin roof, or out in the rubber life raft. God!" He tore himself out of her arms and ran his fingers through his tumbled locks. He laughed shakily. "See what you do to me?" He glanced at his watch glowing in the darkness. "Look at the time! I have to take the helm at 2:00 A.M.." He yawned suddenly. "I hate to admit it, but I'm still tired from that damned race."

Cory hated to admit the fact that she couldn't come back to earth as easily as Buck. To her mind that betokened a lot of practice on his part. She caught her self questioning suspiciously whether his phrases sounded worn.

He pulled her to her feet. "Come, I'll see you to your door. If you get up in time we can watch the sunrise again."

She murmured a promise to wake early.

He took her in his arms at her door and his lips found hers. She returned the kiss hungrily. How she would long for him as soon as he left her! Her body and her emotions urged her to capitulate. But shouldn't she wait? Shouldn't she be sure first that he loved her? A shiver of foreboding trickled down her spine.

He raised his head and patted her cheek. "Imagine me slipping in beside you in the middle of the night. That's where my thoughts will be while I'm up at the wheel." He kissed her lingeringly and she made no attempt to break away.

"See you in the morning," he whispered.

She slept restlessly. At one point her drowsy mind blew the scene from this morning into dreadful proportions. Paco's rucksack and Buck's seabag were both stuffed with marijuana and she was to blame because she wanted to stay on Kauai and needed money.

She woke perspiring, the light blanket twisted around her legs, a knot of fear balled in her stomach. She lay awake for a long time, thinking she should have asked Paco what he had carried out in the rucksack. The truth was, she hadn't wanted to do anything to spoil her friendship with the boy. The problem lay heavily on her mind. She fell asleep at last and woke long after the sun had risen. Hazel's voice roused her.

"Cory, we're about to make landfall. You'll want to have some breakfast before they start putting everything away."

Cory sprang out of bed, regret washing over her.

"You didn't sleep well, did you?" Hazel's voice held concern. "I heard you tossing and groaning."

"I'm sorry! Something at dinner didn't agree with me," she explained lamely.

"Well, it certainly can't be seasickness," Hazel said. "I've never taken a smoother cruise."

Smooth sailing and stormy emotions, Cory thought while she dressed.

Buck had already breakfasted and was busy bringing the boat in. Cory had no chance to talk to him until everyone was ashore and shaking hands.

"Thank you for a wonderful trip," Cory told Lester. I enjoyed every minute. And it was a marvelous chance for Hazel to get out."

Buck and the two crewmen were making the *Iwa* fast. Cory feared she would have to limit her goodbye to a wave, but when Buck saw that all the passengers were on the pier, he leaped over the side and joined them, shaking hands and kissing Hazel's cheek. He turned to Cory, his broad shoulders screening her from the watchful eyes of his aunts.

Her heart thumped as she looked at him. The end of the voyage. All else aside, it had been thrilling to be in a private world with him day and night; to share his meals and hear him talk to his aunts and uncle, to the crewmen, to Paco; to watch him handle the yacht and have him all to herself at times. He was smiling lazily now, so handsome that her breath deserted her when she tried to speak. Clearly he had forgiven her for not appearing in time for sunrise. She wanted to apologize, but she bit her lip.

Let him think she wasn't jumping at the chance to be alone with him. Perhaps their "relationship" would be over now that the trip had ended and she hadn't turned out to be a lighthearted romp.

"Did you have a good time?" he asked seductively, or perhaps it was simply that his voice was seductive, or the way he was looking at her, as though he, too, regretted the leave-taking.

"You know I did," she managed, smiling straightforwardly. "It was unforgettable."

"So were you." His big hand came out to cup her shoulder. He shifted from one foot to the other as though his thoughts were uncomfortable.

"I promised Paco I'd give him a sailing lesson next Sunday," he said. "Want to come? My boat's not in the luxury class like Lester's, but it's fun. It's up at Hanalei right now, so it's quite a drive, but that's close to the Na Pali Coast. If you thought the Oahu *pali* was beautiful, wait till you see our cliffs."

Cory accepted with delight. He must want her for herself. He must know by now that she was no replica of his former love, and if Paco was coming along, he couldn't be planning any of the wild things he talked about last night.

"I'd love to," she replied.

A look of satisfaction flitted across his handsome face and was gone.

"Buchanan, dear!" He heard Irene call him and turned. "Are you going to drive Patrick to school? If so, you'd better go or he'll be late. We're taking Hazel and Cory home."

In front of them all Buck kissed Cory on the lips. "See you Sunday," he promised, "but I'll be talking to you before then. Come on, Paco!" He ran lightly down the pier to his car, Paco close behind.

Back at the condominium Cory helped Hazel unpack. It suddenly crossed her mind that Paco hadn't spent any of his Christmas money, but she dismissed the thought. Buck was perfectly capable of looking after the boy.

"It was quite a trip," Hazel mused. "You've certainly made an impression on Buck. As well you should have, being not only pretty but bright."

"It's sweet of you to say that," Cory told the older woman.

"Nothing but the truth," Hazel said. "By the way, you haven't forgotten the Bowers' Christmas party a week from Friday?"

Cory shook her head.

"That might be a good time to deliver any little gifts you have planned for them. We'll be invited for Christmas dinner, too—I usually am—but I always think gifts should be on hand Christmas morning."

Cory agreed. It would be a delicate way of thanking them for the trip.

CORY WAS GLAD to get back to the gift shop. She and Sondra decided that with Christmas so near they should begin staying open evenings, so for the rest of the week Cory took the afternoon hours. The money she intended to invest arrived at the local bank and sat in her account waiting for Sondra's decision.

Cory awaited Buck's phone call with trepidation. She longed to hear his voice. It was ridiculous to think she missed him, because for the most part she was relieved to be away from him, not to be conscious of his whereabouts every minute, or listening for his voice, or trying to keep her eyes from straying to his face or his body. At times she realized she was walking out on quicksand, but short of leaving Kauai, how could she retreat?

He didn't telephone till Friday, and then he called from his office at the mill. His voice sounded clipped and businesslike.

"Will seven o'clock be too early?" he queried briskly.

"No, seven would be fine. I was wondering if you want me to fix some lunch—potato salad and sandwiches, maybe?" Strange how she thought of fixing lunch for Buck when an excellent cook presided over the Bower kitchen. She had never offered to make sandwiches on her outings with Tim.

"All right," Buck was saying, "but don't go to any trouble. We can pick up whatever's missing. Bring your bathing suit, but bring a jacket, too. It can get cool out there. If you have any questions, call me." He hung up.

Cory felt a wash of disappointment. That had not been a conversation to savor. She was left feeling she'd made too big a deal of the invitation.

CHAPTER TWELVE

ON SUNDAY MORNING Cory waited at the end of the driveway. She had elected to wear white shorts and the white eyelet top, with her bikini underneath, and had put her long fair hair into a single braid to keep it from whipping in the wind. She had packed potato salad, a stack of roast beef sandwiches and chocolate brownies into a plastic carryall. Sweater and towel were squashed into her shoulder bag.

She had come downstairs five minutes early. Dependable Cory, complete with down-to-earth food. Emma would have been a little late. She would have let Buck worry about feeding her. But Cory really had no desire to be treated like a princess.

She stood gazing around at the fresh green foliage. Rain had fallen during the night and the deep green hibiscus hedge sparkled with red orange flowers, their yellow stamens still glittering with raindrops. On impulse she picked one and tucked it behind her right ear. Married women wore theirs over the left ear, if she remembered correctly.

Heavier clouds than usual swirled above the mountains and threatened to spill down across the cane fields, but the northeast trade wind promised fair weather, or at worst only showers.

Buck's red sports car came around the bend, a surfboard on the roof rack. It pulled up beside her. Cory's heart beat faster at the sight of Buck. What could be more glamorous than a handsome dark-haired man in a white knit shirt and shorts, driving a red sports car?

Paco was seated beside Buck, his brown eyes sparkling with anticipation. Buck stowed the food away and Paco made room for Cory by crouching on the console between the seats.

"Have you been to the north shore yet?" Buck asked, putting the car in motion.

Cory shook her head.

"You've got a treat in store, then. It's about forty miles up there. . . with paradise at the end."

"I think it's like paradise here, or close to it."

"It's more like paradise there. That's where they filmed *South Pacific.*"

"Big deal," Paco muttered.

Buck lightly cuffed the boy's jaw. "It *was* a big deal. You're just too young to know about it."

The two-lane highway ran through a wonderful stretch of coastal scenery before it turned inland through fields of papaya and guava. The road climbed, and Cory caught glimpses of the sea beyond pastures and cliffs. All at once they came over a hill to glimpse an azure crescent at the end of a wide valley.

"That's Hanalei Bay," Paco said with a bounce of impatience. "Buck, I think I see the boat!"

Buck pulled the car off the road onto a lookout.

"What are you stopping for?" Paco demanded.

"I want Cory to see this view of the Hanalei Valley."

They were looking down on a scene of pastoral contentment. Cradled by mountains, the level land, less than two miles wide, lay between two dark green ridges that were part of some ancient lava flow now covered with dark greenery, which contrasted sharply with the valley's light green pastures. A gleaming river reflected the skyful of broken clouds, as did the watery rectangles that Buck said were taro patches and rice paddies.

"A lot of the taro for the poi you see in supermarkets is grown here," he said. "Hawaiians were growing taro here when the missionaries first came. The valley probably looked the same then as now. Water for the fields finds its way down from Mount Waialeale, the world's wettest place, as you've probably heard. All right, let's go before Paco has a fit. Once we get out on the boat, he can sail and you and I can talk."

Maybe while they were sailing serenely she could talk to Buck about marijuana.

They boarded the boat and Cory was quickly shown around it. Buck had brought cold drinks. She carried them into the tiny galley and began putting them in the small icebox. Paco brought down the bag of food. Buck was busy on deck.

"Paco, what did you have in your rucksack that last morning in Honolulu?" The question sprang unplanned from her lips.

Paco looked startled, and then affronted, but his dark eyes shifted. She waited with fast-beating heart for his answer.

"That wasn't Christmas money you were counting," she pressed. "Did you take something from the boat?"

"Sure! Laundry." His smile was sickly.

"In the rucksack?"

"Yeah, I guess." He shrugged, still without looking at her.

"I don't believe you."

"What do you think I had?"

She was surprised at the speed with which a winning youngster could turn sullen.

"I think you had marijuana," she said, stating her worst fears, hoping he'd deny it.

Paco's eyes widened, as though he wondered how she had guessed. His laugh sounded forced. "What if I did?" he said with a spurt of defiance. "You can't prove it."

Cory's heart thudded. For a moment she was too dismayed to speak. At last she said lamely, "I think Buck will want to know."

Paco's face reddened angrily. "You think he'll be shocked? He's growing it!" His eyes turned fierce—disillusioned and accusing.

"Hey, what's taking you two so long?" Buck called from above. "Put on water for coffee and come up here. Paco, you can take her out."

The small inboard motor coughed and quit. Buck swore fluently.

"Go ahead, tell him! Give him a good laugh!"

Paco threw Cory a defiant look and dashed up to the deck.

Cory stowed the food and put a kettle to boil on the little burner while she tried to recover her equilibrium. Why had she asked the question? Why had she felt called upon to probe beneath the surface and spoil what had promised to be a lovely day? What should she do now—tell Buck and ruin the day, or force the problem to the back of her mind and make the most of this outing, as a sort of farewell? She'd be making a big mistake to let herself keep caring more and more for Buck with this in the background. Should she tell him? She wanted to think Paco was wrong, that Buck wasn't growing pot, but hadn't Tim jokingly said that Paco knew everything that was going on? Paco was certainly in a position to learn Buck's secrets if he put his mind to it. And what if Buck angrily denied it? What a mess she had stepped into!

By the time she came on deck, Buck had the engine going and they chugged out of the harbor. She had lost her nerve. She decided to drop the subject for the present.

The appalling knowledge was creating heartache, but the scenery lifted her spirits—a sprinkling of anchored sailboats, the white surf breaking on the sand, the clear green water changing to cobalt blue outside the bay. Behind the palm-shaded beaches other trees hid the village. From green slopes the mountains rose in jagged, verdure-covered ridges. One minute heavy wind-driven clouds rolled ominously over the sun and hid the mountaintops. The next minute the sun broke through, sparkling on the water and tossing a double rainbow onto the clouds ahead of the boat. Cory was silent, marveling at the beauty.

"Okay, Paco, you can take over," Buck said, and he came to sit beside Cory, his brown legs textured with dark hair, a breath-catching contrast to Cory's slim golden thighs. She hurried her gaze back to the dramatic coastline. The wind was perfect, brisk enough to speed them along.

"That's Haena up ahead. It's where the road ends." He gestured. "Right here in front of us— we're too low in the water to see it well—is Lumahai Beach. When travel photographers or moviemakers want a beautiful, untouched beach, they photograph Lumahai. It's untouched because it's often dangerous to swim there," he added wryly. "Beyond Haena, for the next fifteen miles, is the Na Pali Coast. It's inaccessible except on foot or by helicopter or by boat when the weather's good."

"Buck hiked the whole trail to Kalalau Valley," Paco put in. "I've been as far as Hanakapiai," he added with a giggle.

"Why is that funny?" Cory asked, forcing a smile. She loved the sound of the Hawaiian names, though to her untrained ear they sounded confusingly similar.

"Hanakapiai is the place to go swimming in the nude," Buck stated.

"Did you go nude?" Cory asked Paco.

"On a school day, I suppose," Buck said resignedly.

"It was a day when nothing was happening," Paco explained.

"Sure!" Buck mocked.

"It must be a great temptation to skip school here," Cory said, "with the beaches always beckoning."

Buck grinned. "That's where the truant officers look. But they probably figure that kids dumb enough to hike two miles over a rugged trail just to go swimming in the buff might as well be allowed to grow up stupid."

Paco jumped threateningly to his feet, but before he could fling a playful punch at his mentor, Buck roared, "Don't let go of the tiller!" and Paco sank back down.

Cory feasted her eyes on the view. The majestic green sea cliffs soared up to meet the black underbellies of the clouds. Looking at the unspoiled grandeur, Cory felt insignificant. She could imagine the same process going on millions of years ago when the lava flows were fresh, the constant rains washing away particles then as now, the unforgiving sea flinging wave after battering wave to diminish the rock.

She saw herself as a Polynesian newcomer stunned by the forces of Nature in their unremitting clash.

"It's magnificent," she breathed. "It must be the most beautiful place on earth."

"One of them," Buck agreed. "There are beaches

along here that can only be reached by boat, and the sloping valleys are virtually impenetrable. Some of the gorges haven't felt a footstep for centuries. They think some of them may never have been explored.''

"Except by the *menehune*." Paco inserted.

"Perhaps." Buck smiled.

"*Menehune?*" Cory echoed. "Oh, the little people who are supposed to have built the fish pond near Lihue."

"According to legend, they pulled up stakes one day and disappeared into one of these valleys. I know some native Hawaiians who sincerely believe they still live there."

"Do you think they really existed?" Cory questioned.

"Yes. They could cut and fit stone with a skill the Hawaiians never knew, or have possibly forgotten, though that seems unlikely. They may have been an early race of exceptionally small Polynesians. Commoners were never fed as well as the chiefs. No skeletons of a race of people two or three feet tall have ever been found, but Hawaiian legends tell of a race of white dwarfs, and Captain Cook's journals mention a servant class on Kauai who were shorter and light skinned."

"I believe they existed," Paco declared. "They're still up there somewhere." He looked wistfully toward the misty cliffs.

"At any rate, the early Hawaiians lived in these valleys," Buck said. "The Kalalau Valley was well terraced and irrigated."

"Which valley is that?" Cory asked, frowning in an effort to remember where she had heard about it.

"That's the one you look down on from Kokee State Park at the end of Waimea Canyon," Buck explained. "Haven't you been there, either?" he asked when her face did not clear.

"Not yet."

"That's another trip you must take. You can look down into the valley when it's not full of clouds and see the sea, but there's no way into it from there. The walls are too steep for a trail. One of the other valleys where those people grew taro had such steep walls the people who lived there came and went by a rope ladder. Archeologists have found carved fishhooks and stone tools, such as drills with stone bits. Each valley was self-sufficient."

The beauty and grandeur of the stark, vertical cliffs was overwhelming.

Buck began giving Paco serious sailing instructions, having him tack into the wind and tossing him various other orders that Cory only vaguely understood. She went up front and sat on the rail at the prow, legs dangling, watching the bow cut through the clear water, reveling in the swift, engineless movement. With nothing visible before her but her own legs and the stay she straddled, she could imagine herself to be an oceanic bird flying low over the waves. She looked for porpoises or flying fish. Time slipped by dreamily. She felt herself at one with the wind, the sea, the boat. Maybe Paco was lying about Buck.

At last she noticed they were heading in toward a tawny beach. She looked over her shoulder to see what the boat's crew was doing. Buck was coming forward unsmiling.

"Is something wrong?" she cried.

"Nothing in the world," he assured her. Standing behind her he cupped her shoulders with his hands and pulled her back against his knees. "We'll have a swim and then eat lunch."

They anchored close in, put the food in the rubber life raft and paddled ashore. Not one footstep marred the smooth sand.

"I wonder how I would feel if I didn't know the world was full of people," Cory said. "If I thought only my little group and a few other little groups in the neighboring valleys were all the people who existed."

"I'd feel lonesome," Paco said.

"I think it would tend to make me superstitious in such an overpowering world," Buck replied. "No wonder they invented powerful gods."

"To somehow humanize all this raw nature," Cory agreed, stripping off her shorts to the bikini underneath. "And now people fly over these cliffs as if they're nothing. I suppose you've taken one of the helicopter rides?"

"Oh, sure."

"It must be nice to be rich," Cory joked. "I hear they cost seventy-five dollars now."

Buck's eyes narrowed, and his sensuous lips tightened. "What makes you think I'm rich?"

Cory looked at him flabbergasted. "I was just

joking," she stammered, "but everybody seems to think you are." Her attention was drawn to Paco, making a dash for the water.

"People exaggerate," Buck said sourly.

Cory was glad to drop the subject and plunge into the surf.

They frolicked in the incredibly clear water for perhaps half an hour. At last, shouting, "I'm starving," Paco waded out.

"We'd better get out, too, if we want our share of the food," Buck called cheerfully.

They sat around a checkered tablecloth spread on the sand and ate and laughed and joked.

"The ideal picnic," Cory sighed when she finished eating. If only she hadn't put Paco on the spot. She lay back on one elbow looking up at the cliffs.

"I'm going to climb that one there," Paco announced. "I've been sitting here studying it. It looks easy."

"Don't get up someplace where you can't get down," Buck warned, "or we'll go off without you."

"You couldn't go off without me," Paco bragged. "Your conscience wouldn't let you. You couldn't even do it in Hong Kong." He glanced at Cory to see if she understood the depth of Buck's regard.

"I won't make the same mistake twice," Buck assured him lazily.

"What'll you bet I can get clear up to the top of that ridge?" Paco demanded.

"Why don't you saunter up the valley instead

and look for *menehune*? But don't forget how long it takes to sail back from here.''

Cory smiled watching the two of them. "You treat him more like a younger brother than a son,'' she said when Paco had set off whistling into the junglelike undergrowth.

''He's not my son,'' Buck said, ''although I know what the gossip is. He's fourteen. I'd have had to father him when I was twenty. Hell, I was in college then, not larking in foreign ports. Come over here—''

Cory moved willingly into the circle of his arm. She owed herself this day. They lay on the sand, warmed by the sun and fanned by the wind blowing down from the mountains.

''We might be the only people in the world right now,'' Buck said lightly.

''Adam and Eve,'' Cory murmured, snuggling against his side.

''What's Paco then?'' Buck asked.

''The serpent?'' Cory suggested wryly. He certainly had spoiled this paradise for her!

''He looked like a drowned rat the first time I saw him,'' Buck reminisced. ''Some tough Hong Kong kids had pushed him into the harbor. He seems to have been born aboard a ship of some kind. His father—the only relative he remembers—had abandoned him in the Philippines, and he'd stowed away on a Portuguese tramp steamer with the idea of becoming a sailor. He was eight. When the ship got to Hong Kong the captain sent him on an errand. Of course, he got lost. By the time he found his way

back, the ship had sailed. So he was kicking around
the docks and getting tossed into the water because
he wasn't a Chinese tough. Little sod couldn't
swim. I jumped in and hauled him out.'' Buck
laughed. ''Ruined a brand-new suit I'd just had
made.''

''You make it sound as though saving a child's
life was nothing,'' Cory objected.

''No, it was something, all right. I was first mate
on the bucket I was on, so I didn't have any trouble
getting him on board. For a while you'd have
thought I was God Almighty the way he followed
me around. But it wore off as he got older and got
more self-confidence.''

''Did you teach him to swim?''

She felt Buck laugh. ''I did, and he came close to
deciding I was the devil instead of God. It took patience, believe me, but he finally lost his fear. Well,
you've seen him surfing. He might have been born
in the water.''

''You must be proud,'' Cory said.

''Yeah, I am. It's like having a son without having to go to the trouble of having a wife.''

''You think of that as trouble?'' She felt him turn
his head to look at her.

His finger traced the outline of her lips, tickling
unbearably. Unthinking, she caught his hand and
moved it to her waist. As soon as she relaxed her
hold, he moved his hand to cup her breast.

''I don't know,'' he said moodily. ''I really don't
know.''

She didn't pursue the subject. Instead she lay

thinking that Paco wouldn't peddle marijuana unless he knew that Buck wouldn't disapprove.

Buck drew a deep breath and rolled over to face
her. Leaning on one elbow he kissed her, tentatively
at first. She tasted the salt on his lips and breathed
deep of the scent of sun-drenched skin.

"You smell so sweet," he murmured. "This is the
first time I've had you in a swimsuit since I hauled
you out of the water." He ran his hand lightly over
her body. His touch set her afire in an instant, and
she rolled against him. He locked her in his arms.

"I wish I knew how long that kid was gonna stay
up there—" Buck muttered thickly. His tongue
thrust hot and demanding into her mouth. Her
body flamed, despite the cautions of her mind. She
pressed against him, her skin tingling at the contact.
She felt herself riding on one mountainous wave,
going up and up and up, the rush of sound thunder-
ing in her ears until Buck ended the kiss. He jerked
free of her arms, muttering an imprecation. She
raised her lids to see him sitting up, shielding his
eyes with his hand, and she understood that the
thunderous roar came from a helicopter dropping
down into the valley.

"Doesn't he see us?" Buck exclaimed, jumping
to his feet and waving his arms in a shooing motion.

The pilot tilted the helicopter to look down at the
two people already occupying that particular bit of
paradise. Throwing them a salute he lifted the
machine and disappeared over a razored ridge.

Paco came running out of the lush greenery.
"What's happening?"

"Somebody coming in to picnic. He didn't see us. Can you imagine how you'd feel if you'd just broken your back to hike all the way in here and then a bunch of idiots from some hotel arrive by air? Oh, well, it's time we started back, anyway." Buck gripped Paco's neck with one long-fingered hand. "See any *menehune*?"

"Course not."

"Not enough *okolehao*," Buck laughed.

"What's that?" Cory asked.

"Da kine booze."

We might be a family, Cory thought as they gathered up everything they had brought from the boat, and then she stood stock-still as understanding washed over her. *I'm in love with him!* For a moment she tossed caution to the winds. She threw up her arms and twirled around in the sand.

"Oh, I love it here!" she cried. Her eyes came to rest on Buck. She ran to him and hugged him around the waist. "I love it!" she repeated. Seeing Paco nearby she threw her arm around his shoulders. "You, too!"

Paco's look sobered her. "You guys find some *pakalolo* while I was gone?"

How dare he mention that! Cory came down to earth with a thud.

"Nope," Buck said and marched off with the hamper.

Cory followed, still stunned by her revelation... too stunned to ask herself how she could justify feeling this way considering what she now suspected.

On board Buck took the tiller and Paco disappeared below for a nap. Cory sat beside Buck, his arm around her shoulders.

"This is the life," he said, leaning comfortably back against the coaming.

Cory made no reply. The wind and sun seemed to have stilled her thoughts. She allowed herself to enjoy a momentary contentment, simply being here on the boat with Buck, here in Hawaii. She glanced at him. His ruggedly handsome face was thoughtful, his eyes half-closed, thick lashes hiding blue irises.

"What made you decide you wanted to stay?" he asked after a while.

"I like it here!"

"What about your friends, your relatives back east?"

"There aren't any I care about." Her jaw jutted forward and a shadow crossed her face. "After my mother's accident they forgot about us. All those years she was in a wheelchair the relatives on both sides dropped out of sight."

"You must have friends back there."

Why was he sounding so critical?

"Of course, I have friends. They'll be delighted to know I'm settled here so they can come and visit."

Buck smiled. "That does become one of the hazards of living here."

"I wouldn't consider it a hazard. I'll be glad to have them visit."

He made no reply. It was on the tip of her tongue to ask him if he had something against her staying, but she saved her breath. He wouldn't level with her anyway. The truth was, he was very comfortable having brief affairs with women who would leave the island and provide a clean, final break at the end. Maybe so they wouldn't know too much about him.

"I suppose you don't want my advice," he said heavily, "but you're making a mistake getting involved with Sondra."

"Why?"

Buck shrugged. His well-muscled shoulders moved sensuously beneath the light T-shirt. "Call it a hunch."

"You think I should give up and go back to the mainland just on your hunch?" Cory straightened angrily.

"It's not entirely a hunch," he told her quietly. "The sugar industry here appears doomed, and the tourist business has been falling off due to inflation and the recession. It's not a good time to invest money in anything."

Cory narrowed her brown eyes. "Are you worrying about me or the Bower businesses?"

Buck gave a humorless laugh. "A bit of both, probably."

"You'll figure some way out," Cory said with a tinge of bitterness. According to Hazel the Bowers owned land in Honolulu as well as on Kauai. She had been in Hawaii long enough to learn that the people who owned large parcels of land were powerful as well as rich. Maybe even powerful enough to grow *pakalolo* and have the authorities look the other way.

Buck shrugged again. "Don't say you weren't warned."

How could he dismiss her hopes so callously? "What do you think I ought to do?" she demanded, feeling hurt and bewildered.

"Go back to New Jersey," he said roughly.

Cory's hurt turned to seething anger. How intolerably selfish of him! He didn't know anything about Sondra or the gift shop business. He simply didn't want ex-girl friends hanging around the island as embarrassing reminders. You'd think he owned the whole damn place, she thought fiercely. How could she have foolishly let herself fall in love with a high-handed tyrant?

In stubborn silence she feasted her eyes on the magic cliffs etched sharply in the golden glow of the westering sun. Buck didn't own *them*, thank goodness. She had as much right to enjoy them as he did.

In the sheer spellbinding enchantment of the scene her anger drained away, leaving a wistful sadness. What a shame to end such a lovely day with a quarrel. No, perhaps it was the best way to end it. The event should serve as a warning to her to put Buck out of her mind.

CHAPTER THIRTEEN

DURING THE NEXT FEW DAYS Cory put her heart into the shop. It was the last week before Christmas, strange as it seemed when she stepped outside to balmy air and flowering plants. Local people, frantic for last minute gifts, came to buy from the depleted stock, and more tourists than usual came to browse. The shelves grew ominously empty.

"They won't send any more merchandise till I pay what I owe them," Sondra said of one supplier after another.

Customer after customer came in to look, didn't find anything, and walked out again. Cory had fits of frustration. Nevertheless, she enjoyed shopkeeping. Most evenings she returned to the store to keep Sondra company. At last Sondra reluctantly agreed that she needed a partner.

Hazel didn't mind Cory's being out of the house; having lived alone for many years, she liked solitude. She also liked hearing what went on at the shop. Cory chose to ask her advice instead of listening to Buck's, and Hazel encouraged her.

The evening after Sondra agreed to the partnership, Cory said to Hazel, "I'm sure that by investing my couple of thousand in the business Sondra and I can make money. Of course, Christmas will be over, but everyone says that January and February are good tourist months. We simply need more stock. If you're going back to work after the New Year, I'll be out of a job here—'' She smiled.

"You can still be my guest," Hazel assured her.

"Thank you, but it's only right that I pay some rent," Cory said.

"We can talk about it when you've got your business going. Did you contact the lawyer I suggested?"

"Yes. We're meeting with him tomorrow."

The following morning Cory and Sondra visited the lawyer's office and he agreed to draw up partnership papers.

Cory sat on the beach that evening and watched the sun set, wondering if she dared believe she would soon really be part of the island life. The sky's red flush turned to pink and then mauve. The fading colors were a little depressing to watch alone. She returned to the condo and started supper, glad to occupy her thoughts.

CORY WAS LOOKING FORWARD to the Bowers' Christmas party with mixed feelings. Despite everything, she longed to see Buck again. She hadn't heard from him since they had more or less quarreled on the sailboat, and she hadn't seen him on the beach. She wondered if he had gone out of town. What would he say when he found out she had gone ahead and joined Sondra in the shop?

She spent a pleasant evening wrapping the small

gifts she had bought for Irene and Mae, Lester and
Paco. She wished she had gone back and finished
her drawing of the Bower sugar mill, but she
hadn't. Instead she was giving Buck another drawing he had admired—an old storefront in Hanalei,
one of the old sugar towns. She had had it framed
and felt sure he would like it.

A week later, on the night of the party, it was
strange to walk into the Bower house and be met
with the piney scent of a Christmas tree when the
evening was so warm.

The tree stood in one corner of the spacious living
room, beautifully decorated and lighted. The expensive wrappings of the presents beneath the tree
bespoke the costliness of their contents.

Buck was at the door. From the formality of the
occasion Cory might have expected him to be in
evening clothes, but this was Hawaii. Buck was
wearing an aloha shirt of red-and-green poinsettias,
which was incredibly handsome on someone so
brown skinned and dark haired. His blue eyes
sparkled like Christmas tree lights. Cory's fingers
itched to touch the bronze column of his neck. His
light gray trousers and leather thong sandals proclaimed the island style.

He kissed both women on the cheek, but his hand
gripped Cory's waist and he gave her a special look
from under his eyelids that meant—she hoped—
that he would come to her as soon as his welcoming
duties were over.

Seeing him, having him acknowledge her special-
ness, confused her. She had had every intention of

keeping him at a distance. Instead, as soon as she laid eyes on him, she forgot her firm decision. When she thought of the last time she had been in this house, at Thanksgiving, when she hadn't even known who he was, she could only shake her head bemusedly. What danger the future had held then.

Cory put her presents and Hazel's inconspicuously at the back of the tree. Excitement bubbled in her veins.

A bar had been set up on the lanai, and an aloha-shirted waiter was circulating with trays of champagne cocktails. Through the door to the dining room, Cory glimpsed the holiday buffet—silver chafing dishes against the dark green of pine boughs and ti leaves, and the glimmer of candle flame. The living-room rug had been taken up. The polished floor reflected lights from the Christmas tree and the chandeliers. Straight-backed chairs lined the wall. The six gracious floor-to-ceiling windows stood open to the balmy night and the view of the sun dropping into the quiet ocean.

How respectable these surroundings were! How could she connect anyone from this social stratum with anything underhanded or illegal? Yet she knew such contradictions existed.

She took a champagne cocktail and stood by the tree, pretending to be watching the arrivals, but in reality watching Buck, her heart swelling. No matter how she mistrusted his character, he was the handsomest, most charming man on Kauai.

The two couples she had met the night of the luau gave her friendly hellos but soon moved off to talk to older acquaintances. She dragged her eyes from Buck long enough to look around for Paco. He was nowhere in sight.

A bustle on the lanai drew Cory's attention. A cold weight filled her chest as a dark-haired, dark-skinned, laughing girl with flashing black eyes threw her arms around Buck's neck and unabashedly kissed him on the mouth. The promise of her red lips must have made every male onlooker tight with envy.

Julia Vagos! Cory didn't have to be told. The girl was so small, even in high heels, that Buck could tuck her under his left arm while he laughingly greeted the people she had come with—a silver-haired man who looked Portuguese and was probably Julia's father, two giggling teenagers with braces and a handful of dark, bejeweled women and small, wiry men.

They moved into the room in a body and Buck seemed to consider that all the guests had arrived. He deserted his post at the door, tugged along by Julia's possessive fingers.

"That's Julia Vagos," Hazel told her.

"I guessed that," Cory said dryly, adding with a twisted smile, "She seems to be in favor of the merger, doesn't she?"

"She always was!" Hazel hissed. A spasm of pain swept over her features.

"Are you all right?" Cory cried.

"I think so. I just got a twinge. Probably for speaking unkind words about poor Julia." This was Hazel's first outing without her walker, and Cory had promised herself to remember the reason she was here and be available in case Hazel needed her.

Hazel didn't try to cross the highly polished floor to the dining room. She stayed seated and Cory joined the crowd at the buffet. Everyone stood at attention and applauded when the chef brought in a flaming plum pudding on a silver platter. The maid behind him carried rum-laced pudding sauce in a silver boat. Cory had never seen so many silver serving dishes. She did her best to choose what Hazel would like from the elegant array—salmon mousse, quiche Lorraine, coquilles St. Jacques, crab-and-lobster salad.

The maid appeared at her elbow and relieved her of Hazel's plate so she could fill one for herself. Cory wondered who had sent her. Buck was in one corner, surrounded by the Vagos family. If he had lifted his head and smiled at Cory she would have been thrilled, but he appeared deeply involved in discussion. She hoped forlornly that he would continue to ignore her. In time she would recover from her enchantment.

She returned to Hazel, the maid following. Everyone within hearing proclaimed the food delicious. Cory ate because holding the fork gave her trembling fingers something to do.

She watched for Buck to come into the formally arranged living room, but he didn't. Nor was he at the buffet when she returned for slices of pudding. She took the route across the lanai on her way back to Hazel. Paco and the other teenagers had claimed that area. They were chattering together in a "hip" pidgin that seemed to consist of mainland slang and "da kine" this and "da kine" that, interspersed with cries of "Eh, brah!" to get each other's attention. Paco saw Cory and waved.

Her face relaxed into a genuine smile. She delivered the pudding to Hazel and took her seat. She glanced around the room from under her thick lashes. No Buck.

No Julia Vagos, either, she noticed. Where could they be? Had he taken her outside—to some hidden arbor or one of the disused guest cottages? The excellent food lay in her stomach like stone.

Strains of dinner music came over the stereo. Everyone in sight appeared to be having a delightful time. The waiter came around with after-dinner liqueurs. Cory chose crème de menthe. Then she watched the waiter disappear through a doorway into a side room. So people were in there, too! Perhaps that's where Buck was. She ought to welcome his behavior; it might help her distressed heart face reality.

His hug and greeting had been an intimate promise that he would join her soon. Or so she had thought. Now it seemed her anticipation had fallen around her like discarded tinsel. Julia Vagos hadn't arrived then.

Cory began to wish she hadn't come. How could she expect to get over Buck if she attended parties where he was host? The majority of the guests, she noted, were middle-aged married couples with teenage children.

To cap it off, when she moved to the bar to get a

glass of Perrier for the sake of having something to hold, an elegantly coiffed matron in an elaborate muumuu came up behind her and touched her elbow.

"Emma! What a surprise! I heard you were coming back, but I didn't expect...." Her voice trailed off and her jaw fell as Cory swung around.

"I'm not Emma." Cory smiled coolly.

"You're not, are you?" the woman babbled. "How stupid of me."

"No, it wasn't," Cory said, touched by the other's embarrassment. "A lot of people have made the same mistake."

"You *do* look just like her from the side."

"I'm Hazel McNab's friend," Cory introduced herself.

The woman's face cleared. "I remember hearing someone had come to stay with Hazel. Well, Emma's in for a surprise!" The woman smiled with peculiar satisfaction.

"Do you mean she's returning to Kauai?" Cory had the sensation of being in a swiftly falling elevator.

"I heard she was, but I was surprised to see her here, of all places. Oh, dear, I mean— Excuse me, my husband's looking for me."

She fled, leaving Cory shattered. Buck would certainly drop her now, and all her agonizing over his character and his intentions had been wasted effort. Now that it was too late, she realized she had probably been too hasty in judging him. She should have gone ahead and told him about Paco and let the chips fall. She'd been too timid, and after all, what had she had to go on? Suspicion based on Tim's hints and Paco's peculiar behavior.

She carried her Perrier water back to her seat beside Hazel.

"Where's Buck?" Hazel demanded. "Have you two quarreled?"

The idea that Hazel had noticed his behavior made Cory wish she could get up and leave. She shook her head, not trusting herself to speak.

"I expect Julia's got him cornered someplace," Hazel said comfortably. "She'll have to let him loose once the dancing starts. As one of the hosts, he'll have to circulate."

The musicians were rustling around in their corner, tightening guitar strings and blowing into mouthpieces, but Cory felt no ease from Hazel's words. Buck's onetime love was coming back, and whether or not he was growing marijuana, whether or not he approved of Sondra, no longer mattered. Cory had been a mere stand-in, someone to make him remember Emma, someone to whet his appetite. She felt sick with disappointment. Now he would never have occasion to prove to her that he was an upright citizen. And whether she and Sondra succeeded with the gift shop would be a matter of indifference to him.

Her soft brown eyes glazed with regret, but she held her head high and hoped her face didn't reveal her feelings. The evening would pass somehow. A few male guests had thrown her interested looks. One or two might ask her to dance. She tried to remember the names of Buck's friends and failed. They'd probably forgotten hers, too. She only hoped, with bitter humor, that they wouldn't call her Emma.

The musicians struck up a waltz. Guests filled the doorways, moving into the room in groups of two and three. Buck appeared from the side room where Cory had thought he might be. He was conversing seriously with the three men who accompanied him, but Julia Vagos was clinging to his arm. With some parting words to the men, he swung Julia onto the dance floor. Other couples joined them and the room became a kaleidoscope of color. The teenagers crowded to the door to look and giggle.

Cory carefully avoided looking in Buck's direction. She only hoped that her flushed face and overbright eyes would be attributed to high spirits instead of the bitterness that burned in her heart. A flood of gratitude put out some of the flames when a stranger—tall, lean, gray haired—invited her to dance.

He introduced himself as Jake Olmstead, a neighbor.

"You must be the next-door sugar plantation owner, then, since this side of the island is all cane fields." Cory laughed with the sheer relief of being rescued.

"Hardly." Her partner smiled. "I'm a developer. I've just built a row of condominiums between the cane fields and the beach."

Cory's brown eyes widened. "I thought developers on Kauai were treated like carpetbaggers in the South," she quipped.

The man's laugh rang out. "An apt comparison! But they could hardly snub me in this case. The Bowers leased me the land."

"You're joking!" Cory exclaimed.

"Cross my heart," the man said, smiling down at her. "Some development is inevitable. This way the Bowers have some say in what's built."

The music ended then, but instead of returning Cory to her seat, her partner said, "That was only half a dance. May I claim the next one, too?"

"Of course." She smiled up at him.

They danced together again, and when he was returning her to her chair she was gratified to come face to face with Buck.

"My dance next," he rasped.

Jake Olmstead gave Buck a cool nod. "He's our host, so I suppose we have to be courteous." He sounded amused.

"We can at least pretend," Cory sparkled.

"I'll find you again," he promised.

"You appear to be full of witticisms tonight," Buck growled as he swept her onto the floor.

"Wh-what do you mean?" Cory stammered, thrown off balance by his sudden attack.

"You had old Jake laughing his head off."

"He's not so old!" she objected. "I mean—" she stammered "—he looks in good shape."

"Checked him out, did you?" Buck's eyes glinted angrily.

Cory had spent the evening looking forward to when he could spare her some time, and now this. Why was he so cross?

"Are you trying to pick a quarrel?" she asked icily, thinking, *Why do I bother to ask? That's clearly what he's doing.* She looked up, surprised to see fury in his face.

"Are you like Emma after all?" he gritted, his eyes blue flames. "The minute a man's back was turned she was taking up with someone else. Are you like that?" His arm around her waist tightened cruelly, driving the breath from her lungs. She winced in protest.

"You really are trying to pick a quarrel!" she muttered with fierce certainty. "All right, consider it done! You won't have to dance with me again tonight. Mustn't make Miss Vagos jealous!"

"Don't be a fool!" Buck growled. "I was talking business."

"So was I," Cory said with a brittle laugh.

They finished the dance in silence and Buck returned her to Hazel. Before she had time to be miserable one of Buck's friends, the sugar mill manager, swept her onto the floor. The power plant manager danced with her next.

Buck danced every dance, doing his duty by his guests. Most of the men in the room danced with Julia. She had grown up among these people. Jake Olmstead danced with her, too.

Had Buck really been talking business? But she hadn't done anything wrong in dancing with Jake and making him laugh. Obviously Buck was still thinking about Emma. Did he know she was coming back? Poor Julia Vagos didn't have a chance. When? When would Emma return?

The waiter was serving champagne. Jake Olmstead took Cory onto the lanai and brought sparkling, long-stemmed glasses for the two of them. The evening became a blessed blur. She had danced with Lester and with Paco, who had been so formal she was amused. She drank more champagne with Jake, not worrying, because Hazel was driving these days. They were standing in the darkness beyond the edge of the lanai, screened from the other guests by vines and shadows. Suddenly something—a creature the size of a baseball—hopped from the bed of ferns into a shaft of light not three feet from Cory's sandaled toes.

Champagne splashed from her glass as she shrieked and flung herself at Jake. His strong masculine arms opened to receive her and clasp her against his chest. Her heart thumping wildly, she shrank against him. At the same time she looked over her shoulder to see what had frightened her. She felt laughter rumbling in Jake's chest. On the flagstone sat an enormous toad, its jeweled eyes gleaming in the light, its throat pulsing gently.

"Oh!" Cory shuddered and laughed at the same time. Like the toad's, her heart seemed to be beating in her throat.

"Bufos, they're called here. The cane growers imported them from South America to deal with some pest or other." Jake gathered her comfortingly against him and offered her a sip from his glass. "Not very pretty, but they're harmless."

"Oh, yes, I'm not afraid of toads," Cory disclaimed. "It was the way it suddenly leapt out."

She tried to pull discreetly away, but Jake's arm was unyielding. He was looking at her as if he were going to kiss her.

The instant his lips touched hers, she heard Mae's voice. She was talking as she came out to the lanai.

"Buchanan, dear, don't neglect to dance with Mrs. Vagos. If you're looking for Cory, she...." Her voice trailed off, and she didn't hear Buck's reply. She assumed that he, too, had passed by.

Jake's kiss was firm and pleasant. Cory sensed from the way he held her that he was skilled at lovemaking, but she felt absolutely no interest in his advances.

"I think I should go back," she murmured when he raised his head.

"Because Buck's looking for you? Let him look!"

"Not that, but—" She turned in his arms.

He released her reluctantly. "Want to find my car and go somewhere private?"

"No, thank you." The thought of shocking Hazel and the Bowers by such conduct made her laugh nervously.

"All right. It was worth a try. Ready to go back to the dance? If I'd known what a charming armful I was going to meet, I'd have arranged for a dozen toads to be let loose, one at a time, to keep you jumping at me."

Flushed and laughing, Cory preceded him through the archway to the lanai. To her consternation Buck was standing in the doorway talking to two of the Vagos men. He broke off as Cory and

Jake passed. Head high and face suddenly pale, Cory marched onto the floor. Jake took her in his arms and waltzed her away.

Party! she was thinking bitterly. Everything had gone wrong. How could they call this miserable travesty a party?

Buck surprised her by asking her for the last dance. He guided her around the room in tight-lipped silence. She wondered why he bothered to dance with her at all.

"I'll see you Christmas day," he said offhandedly when the music ceased. Guests were already making their departure and he went to join Lester at the door.

"Ready to go?" Hazel asked.

"Quite ready."

Buck's farewell was cool. Cory, already stricken, found she could still hurt more.

She woke the next morning feeling horrible. Hazel attributed it to too much champagne.

"My, Buck was in a temper," she remarked at breakfast. "Sugar must be in trouble again."

"Does it come and go, like something seasonal?" Cory asked.

"It goes from bad to worse, from what the paper says."

Had Buck really been talking business? Cory's head throbbed so cruelly she hardly cared what had happened, if only she could feel like herself again.

AT THE SHOP, the day before Christmas was hectic till toward the end of the afternoon. By the time Cory usually left, the whole mall was empty.

"I guess there's no point in staying open this evening," Sondra said. "Most of the other stores have already closed."

Despite their depleted stock they had done a good day's business, and Sondra began emptying the cash register.

"Are you invited to the big house?" she asked.

"I guess so," Cory said, reluctant to think about it. "What are you two doing tomorrow?"

"Johnny's taking me out somewhere."

Cory wished her a merry Christmas and was starting out the door when Tim and Johnny Komo arrived, obviously in high spirits.

"Good! I was afraid I'd miss you!" Tim greeted Cory. "Come on, I want to buy you a Christmas drink."

"Okay!" Cory felt unaccountably cheered at the prospect. Her world wouldn't fall apart no matter what happened with Buck, she told herself bravely.

"Listen," Tim said when they were seated at the hotel bar. "I have a great idea. Johnny just told me about some really good petroglyph stones up in the mountains. There's a trail that goes most of the way and there's a pool with a waterfall. What are your plans for tomorrow? How'd you like to go on a Christmas hike?"

"I can't," Cory said regretfully. I'm invited to the Bowers' for dinner."

"We can get back in time, if we start early."

Cory shook her head. "Hazel expects to go sometime after noon."

"Oh, too bad." Tim looked dejected. It occurred

to Cory that he probably didn't have any other plans for Christmas. She realized she'd like to go. Why did she have to go to the Bowers' just because Hazel was going? Hazel could drive herself now, and had been doing so for several days. Why should she make it so easy for Buck to ignore her? If she left him first, he would never know for sure, nor would anyone else, that she hadn't preferred Tim. At any rate she'd be saving herself a lot of heartache, because it wouldn't have worked out anyway. Not with Emma coming back. Again she wondered if Buck knew.

"I don't *have* to go to the Bowers'," she said at last.

"Hey, great! We could get you back in time for dinner, anyway."

"We? Who else is going?"

"Nobody. You and I."

"Okay." Making up her mind, she said defiantly, "What time do we start and what shall I bring?"

Tim looked so pleased that Cory's crushed ego began to expand. "I'll bring some fruitcake and a bottle of wine. If you want to put together a couple of Christmas-type sandwiches—"

Cory began to laugh. "What are Christmas-type sandwiches?"

Tim grinned back at her. "I don't know...sliced turkey, maybe?"

"With jingle bells?" All at once Cory felt a wisp of nostalgia for snow and crisp, cold weather, but she easily shrugged it away. "The turkey sandwiches usually come the day after." Not that it mattered, she was thinking. Customs here, like the plants, were such a strange mixture of the familiar and the unfamiliar. You couldn't really have Christmas without snow and cold weather. These people out here—herself included—were just pretending to have Christmas. The idea of going hiking seemed no odder than the idea of sitting down to a supposedly Christmas dinner with the windows open and everyone in summer clothing.

"We'll have to start early," Tim warned, "if you want to get back for dinner. Six-thirty?"

"Fine." She took belligerent satisfaction at the thought of confounding Buck when she didn't arrive with Hazel. If he thought he could take her for granted, he would soon realize his mistake.

CHAPTER FOURTEEN

THE MUDDY, ROCKY TRAIL up the narrow valley almost made Cory wish she'd gone to the Bowers' after all. Or stayed home! Her sneakers were quite inadequate footgear. Tim was wearing hiking boots and carrying their sandwiches, wine and small sketch pads in an enormous backpack.

For the first half hour Cory enjoyed herself. The only trip she had made into the mountains and valleys had been when she, Tim and Paco had driven up to draw the other petroglyph rock. Clouds hung above the mountains, and they had not walked far when a mistlike rain began falling, as warm as the air. Minutes later it stopped, leaving the underbrush and rocks only a little wetter. The path wound beside a rocky stream that unexpectedly reminded Cory of woodland streams in northern New Jersey. But here varieties of exotic ferns grew among the woody underbrush and ti plants and pandanus. They passed through a grove of *hau* trees, whose gnarled branches interlaced above the path. The valley narrowed and the path climbed steadily.

Overhead the trade wind harried clouds across the mountaintops, but surrounded by undergrowth,

Tim and Cory got no benefit from the cool breezes.
Cory huffed and puffed and followed doggedly.
She began to think wistfully of the comfort of the
Bowers' dining room. Of course it was still early
morning, but the family would have unwrapped
their presents around the Christmas tree. She
remembered the gifts Buck had bought for his family in Honolulu. He must have unwrapped Cory's
gift by now. She hoped he was pleased; he'd admired the unframed drawing. When she didn't
show up this afternoon, she wondered if he would
be sorry or relieved.

The hike went on and on along the side of a ridge.
At one point they walked along the edge of a rock
ledge that supported a hanging garden of ferns like
a picture from a book of fairy tales. Farther on they
skirted a tall thicket of bamboo, but always the
ground on one side of the faint path lay uphill and
the other side downhill. They reached the top of a
ridge that supported a short fernlike vegetation,
and paused to view the cane fields on the level
cultivated land far below and the rolling surf at the
island's edge. It was easy for Cory to believe she
was standing on the slope of an extinct volcano. In
spite of vegetation, the ridges still looked like
poured lava. Before she caught her breath Tim
pushed on.

The way plunged briefly into another valley, then
climbed out again. Cory's pant legs grew wet and
muddy. She slipped once on the wet rocks and mud-
died the seat of her jeans.

But whenever there was a break in the trees and

she could look down, the views were magical. From down below, the ridges appeared too steep and thickly grown to have room for trails, but now that she was up here she could see how it was possible for the ancient Hawaiians to live in the valleys.

They reached a narrow gorge filled with the sound of falling water. With a groan Cory dropped onto a rock beside the pool. A narrow waterfall poured into it from the height of a four- or five-story building, and a myriad of delicate plants grew out of the rock, close beside the streaming water, their leaflets bobbing in the spray.

Cory stared wordlessly at the unbelievable perfection of the scene. *This must truly have been what paradise looked like,* she was thinking.

"Fantastic, huh?" Tim said.

"Fantastic," she agreed, still short of breath. "It's so beautiful!" She didn't care how trite the words sounded.

She stole a sidewise look at Tim. He seemed to be in high spirits, almost reckless, the way he had been jumping from boulder to boulder and running up and down dips in the trail.

"I figured you'd like it," Tim said smiling. "Did you bring a swimsuit?"

Cory nodded, not taking her eyes from the lacy water cascading down the cracked layers of perpendicular rock.

"Is this where we're having dinner?"

Tim laughed. "Ten o'clock coffee. That's what we've stopped for, and to give you a chance to bathe in the pool."

"Are you going in?"

Tim shook his head. "I'd rather watch you."

Cory felt a little uncomfortable. Tim was behaving so differently today. "If more hiking's still to come, I think I'd rather rest," she told him. "Besides, it's too beautiful to swim in. I'd rather sit here and dream."

"I know what you mean," Tim said. But he didn't know, because Cory was dreaming about what bliss it would be to come here with Buck.

Don't think like that, she chided herself.

Tim brought Styrofoam cups and a large thermos from the backpack. They talked desultorily, but the scenery was overwhelming, so beautiful and magical that human voices intruded on the peaceful setting.

Cory removed her shoes and soaked her bruised feet in the rushing water. Is it much farther?" she asked quietly.

"Another hour," Tim said. "Tired?"

"My feet are," she quipped. "Am I such a tenderfoot?"

"I should have worn sneakers to keep you company," Tim said, putting his arm around her.

Cory had to fight against the urge to shrug his arm off, and a faint worry darted into her mind. It would be awkward if Tim chose this trip to become romantic.

The valley had ended at the waterfall. When they started onward Tim led her up a steep mountainside, zigzagging and choosing the way as he went, apparently following a path made by goats.

This is crazy, Cory thought despairingly, pausing to wipe sweat from her brow. But Tim was above her, almost lost from sight in the luxuriant bushes. She couldn't voice her opinion here. She had no choice but to follow as best she could, determined to make him call a halt as soon as she caught up with him.

At last he gained the peak of the ridge and squatted there waiting. By the time Cory climbed the last steps of the ascent she was too breathless to protest.

Tim was looking at his watch.

"Dinnertime?" Cory said hopefully.

"Just about."

"There's a perfect place to picnic!" Cory pointed to a bed of ferns in a tiny meadow below them.

Tim took binoculars from his pack and began to survey the valley. He paused to give Cory a speculative look.

"Johnny's supposed to meet us here," he said.

"Johnny!"

"Yeah, he's coming up a different way."

"Why? I thought he was taking Sondra out."

Tim lowered the binoculars again and gave her a twisted smile. "We've got a little business to do first."

"Up here? Are you crazy?" Cory's effort to be a good sport disintegrated. If she'd climbed all this way for some wild-goose chase— "What kind of 'business'?" she demanded suspiciously.

Tim was keeping a lookout over the bushes. "See that big patch over there that's all the same color?" He pointed.

"Yes—"

"That's *pakalolo*."

"Not yours!" she gasped.

"Not yet." His cocky grin produced cold fear in the pit of her stomach.

"What are you going to do?" she demanded.

"Nothing! Just watch it for a while. I thought you'd like to know what a patch of *pakalolo* looks like."

"Sure, you did," Cory agreed sarcastically. "Come on, tell me what's up. Are you here to buy it or rip it off?"

Tim laughed with apparent delight, but instead of answering her question he said, "Let's have some wine and eat. Johnny will turn up sooner or later."

Cory's first feeling was relief. Hunger gnawed at her stomach. For the moment, food and rest seemed more important than anything else. Silently she accepted a sandwich. Tim produced two plastic wine glasses and opened the wine.

He raised his glass. "Here's to a merry Christmas!"

"Cheers," Cory said with what she intended to be a noticeable lack of enthusiasm. She sipped the dry red wine, deliberately shutting a door in her head and focusing on the scene at her feet—the distant beach, the shimmering ocean. She wished she were there. Clouds came and went over the sun. Up here the trade wind gently fanned the air.

Between bites of his sandwich, Tim studied the valley through his binoculars. Cory munched her sandwich in dogged silence. If Tim wouldn't tell her what was going on, she was darned if she'd make small talk. However, food and wine weren't enough to combat the fear spreading through her stomach. She soon realized that Tim was in no mood for chit-chat, either.

"Would it be naive to ask if there really are any petroglyphs up here?" she asked.

Tim grinned. "How did you guess?"

"Then why did you drag me along?" she demanded furiously.

"So we'd look like a couple of innocent hikers out for a Christmas climb, in case anybody stopped us."

"Who would stop us?"

"Some of the people up here don't trust strangers."

"I take it they don't trust Johnny, either."

"I told you it's all part of the fun and games on Kauai."

Before Cory could choke down her anger he said, "There's Johnny!" He uttered a low whistle.

Below them on what might have been a trail, Johnny looked up, waved and began climbing toward them, wading through the ferns. He, too, was wearing an oversize backpack. When he reached the ridge where Tim and Cory crouched, he was laughing.

"Merry Christmas!" he greeted them.

Cory gave him a dirty look in reply.

"Hey, don't blame me," he expostulated, still grinning. "Bringing you was Tim's idea."

"I notice you didn't bring Sondra," Cory commented bitterly.

"Nah, she didn't want to come."

"I wouldn't have wanted to come, either, if I'd known I was being used!" Cory exploded. Turning her back on them she stared longingly at the distant shimmering sea.

Johnny grinned at Tim and shrugged. "Seen anybody around?" he inquired.

"You guys aren't actually going to steal this stuff, are you?" Cory quavered, growing more frightened.

"It isn't stealing!" Tim answered sharply. "The pot's growing illegally on government land—taxpayers' land. I have as much right to the use of that grass as the next guy. How do we know who planted it?" he added in a fierce tone that seemed entirely out of character with his unassertive ways. But was it out of character, Cory wondered uncomfortably. Perhaps Buck's advice about avoiding these people had been correct.

"If the police come and pull up the whole patch, nobody gets it," Johnny said carelessly.

Cory's heart jolted. "B-but isn't it dangerous?" she stammered. "I read in the papers—"

"Aw, you have to know what you're doing, that's all. Today they'll be home celebrating Christmas. Pigging out on Christmas pig."

Cory hoped he was right, because she didn't want to meet a bunch of pot growers—or even one—on her solitary way down the mountain.

She turned to Tim. "I'm going back right now."

"No, you're not! Cory—"

In no mood to argue, she brushed past him.

"No, you're not!" he hissed. He grabbed her arm and twisted it behind her back, not enough to hurt, only enough to feel the threat of pain if she refused to go in the right direction.

"They live down below here," he gritted. "Do you think they won't notice somebody like you marching past their houses? Why do you think we came such a roundabout way?"

Johnny watched the exchange impassively.

"Let's go," he said. "There's nobody up there now. We'd have heard them or seen them smoking."

Tim shrugged into his backpack. "Don't be such a spoilsport!" he growled at Cory. "This is a game, don't you understand?"

Filled with dismay, Cory doggedly followed Johnny. Today's misadventure was putting her business association with Sondra in a new light . . . a shocking light. If she got out of today's scrape, she would take a new look at her plans for the future. Her throat tightened, but she shoved the thought to the back of her mind.

Just let her get safely out of these magical valleys without spraining an ankle, and she would find some way to cope with the future. Her leg muscles were trembling with every step and it seemed certain her knees would give way. No wonder she couldn't think straight! She mustn't fly off and do something she'd regret.

They walked single file along a ledge shaded by gnarled old trees and came to the faint trail Johnny had followed.

"Koa trees," Tim said over his shoulder.

Cory nodded dully. How could he imagine she wanted to know the name of anything here? All she wanted was to get back to civilization.

The trees grew thick on one side of the path. On the other, beyond a stretch of grass, Cory saw the distinctive green leaves of marijuana.

"Don't look so miserable," Tim urged. "You're seeing Kauai!"

These guys are incredible, Cory thought. How could they be so casual about something so dangerous? She collapsed under a tree, intending to rest her trembling legs and have nothing to do with the rip-off, but Tim had other plans.

"Hold this bag," he ordered. "The sooner we get these full, the sooner we can leave."

She sat stubbornly silent.

"Look," Tim said, "the longer we hang around, the riskier it is. If you want to get home faster, hold this bag!"

She got painfully to her feet and unwillingly joined him. She held the rucksack open while Tim stripped the tender tips from the plants. At the other end of the patch Johnny was working rapidly.

"This is going to be great stuff," Tim enthused. "See, we're hardly ripping these guys off at all. We're only taking the buds. They'll still have most of the plant. They'll make plenty on this crop if the cops don't find it."

Cory didn't reply. She had made up her mind never to speak to Tim again. What right had they to involve her in this? Oh, if only she'd listened to

Buck! Of course, that meant she wouldn't have a job on Kauai. But now she wasn't going to have a job, anyway. Damn Sondra for not warning her! Her stomach cramped with a combination of fear and hunger. She had hardly eaten a bite of her sandwich once she realized the true object of this expedition.

She held the rucksack stiffly, moving only when Tim impatiently ordered her to. She stared fearfully at the trees edging the clearing, expecting each moment that something would happen.

That was how she was the first to see the three men. They burst from the woods with leveled guns.

"Oh, my God," she whispered. She dropped the rucksack and raised her hands almost in reflex.

Tim turned around to see what she was staring at and raised his hands, too.

"Oh-oh," he said under his breath.

From the corner of her eye Cory saw Johnny standing at attention.

Three massive Hawaiians confronted them, their round brown faces contorted with anger. They were wearing enormous aloha shirts, khaki shorts, and, to Cory's astonishment, nothing but zoris on their bare feet. How they climbed up and down these rocky trails with only a sole and thongs for support was something to puzzle over later. To her shattered senses the men looked as alike as triplets. No doubt they were related.

One man angrily snatched up Tim's backpack and looked inside. The other two loosed a string of curses in pidgin and English. "Rotten lousy hippy bastards!'' were the only words Cory understood. The half-full contents of the packs brought another tempest of curses.

Tim's and Johnny's faces were impassive. They had lowered their hands. Cory gratefully did likewise.

"I guess you wouldn't believe we were hiking— showing this young lady the country,'' Tim offered half heartedly. The Hawaiians ignored his remark.

"I've seen these guys up here before,'' the third man said loudly. "I warned them away then. Warning doesn't teach them anything. What they need is a beating—a few broken bones.''

"Damned rippers!'' the leader snarled. "Anybody too damned lazy to grow his own grass deserves to be shot! And that's what we're gonna do this time!''

Cory's heart stopped, as though a gigantic hand had clutched her chest.

"Come on, you guys. It's all in the game!'' Tim's raised voice sounded authoritative. "You win, we lose. You don't have to get nasty!''

"You think this is a damned game?'' the first man shouted. "You haole bastard! You're too damned cowardly to risk raising your own, so you let us take the risk and you skim the cream. No way! You—'' He used a Hawaiian word Cory had never heard.

"Eh, Brah!'' Johnny reeled off pidgin in a tone designed to placate.

"To hell with them, let's go!'' Tim blustered.

For an instant hope rose in Cory's chest. It was as

quickly quenched. The man nearest Tim blocked his way with a double-barreled gun.

The spokesman for the growers broke into a jumble of pidgin that Cory had no hope of understanding. She watched his face in frightened desperation.

"Come on, man," Tim coaxed. "You don't have to do anything to us. You haven't lost anything. You've still got all your grass. If you let us go," he said winningly, "we won't breathe a word to anyone. Not even the police!" He managed a cocky laugh.

Instead of placating their captors, his speech infuriated them and raised a storm of pidgin. Cory didn't need to follow the words to understand Tim had lit a fuse.

"You jerk, what did you mention the police for?" Johnny snarled.

The attention of everyone was suddenly drawn to two teenage boys who appeared on the trail. They were carrying plastic hampers of food. They halted, looking uneasy, but obviously they were expected. On orders from one of the Hawaiian men they put the hampers on the ground and briskly departed. Johnny stood staring straight ahead, his arms folded across his chest like a prisoner on trial. Tim angrily tore a weed stalk to bits. His boyishness no longer appeared attractive to Cory. Instead, she saw it as irresponsible and careless.

The conference ended. The man who seemed to be the leader said, "There's no way we're going to let you go back down and tell the cops, you stinking haole."

"Oh, yeah? Short of shooting me, how are you going to keep me here?" One thing, Cory admitted with grudging respect, the men didn't scare Tim. The situation might be a lot safer if they did.

"Tie you up, maybe, you and your girl friend, just to make sure you don't talk to anybody. In three or four days the crop will be harvested and you'll be free."

The trees started to spin. To halt the dizzying blur she focused on Tim's face. It was colorless; his jaw looked slack. He had begun to take their captors seriously.

"You're kidding!" he yelped. He cast an appalled look at Cory.

"You can go, Brah," the Hawaiians told Johnny. "We take your word you not tell the police, but we no trust these haoles. But don't come back," they added grimly, "or you'll find your friends dead."

Understanding sank into Cory's numbed mind. Johnny was to go free because he was Hawaiian, too, but they didn't trust her and Tim. And Tim had threatened them with the police. . . .

"You can't hold us—" he was arguing now. "We'll be missed. If we don't come home our friends will call the police."

"You better have him—" the biggest Hawaiian indicated Johnny "—tell your friends some story. No police!"

"What are you guys going to do with us?" Tim demanded loudly.

"If we get our crop harvested—" the man held up his hand "—we treat you okay."

Tim looked apologetically at Cory and shrugged slightly. "We'll be all right," he mumbled.

Her throat constricted. Her outraged mind refused to frame a protest. For crucial seconds fright made her incoherent. Somehow she managed to cry, "No! Please!"

She was ignored. Everything happened with incredible speed while she was still grasping the realization: she was a hostage.

She saw Johnny start off. Only then did her brain begin to work with frightened haste.

"Call Hazel!" she cried. "Tell her I'm camping out with Tim! Tell her we decided to stay a few days."

What would Buck think when he heard that? What would Hazel think? Would she believe it? That was more important.

"Yeah, that's good," Tim agreed. He turned to their captors, who had shrugged into the backpacks. "You guys want to keep those, go ahead," he said impudently.

"You pick the buds. What you think we carry them in?" one of the Hawaiians growled.

"Shut up!" Cory spat at Tim. "Just shut up! Can't you see you're making everything worse? I am *not* his girl friend," she told the Hawaiians, but they paid no attention.

"Stay cool," Tim advised. Looking the nearest Hawaiian in the eye, he said, "This woman is Buck Bower's girl friend. I don't have to tell you the clout he has. If anything happens to her, you'll never get away with it."

The youngest of the husky Hawaiians spared her a curious glance. "If you're Buck Bower's girl friend, what are you doing with these turkeys?"

Cory groaned and shook her head. "I don't know!" Her voice rose. "I was invited to go for a hike and eat Christmas dinner in the mountains. That's all I knew. I don't even smoke pot!"

The man shrugged his shoulders and grinned. His shirt was a brown-and-yellow Tahitian print. "You eat Christmas dinner with us. We got *kalua* pig— wild pig we shoot in the mountains—and poi. You like poi? You follow these guys, my brothers. I stay here and make sure your friend don't come back."

The two wearing the rucksacks motioned Tim to walk ahead of them and set off up the mountain, with barely a glance behind to see if Cory was following.

She was amazed at how quickly she adjusted to her new circumstances. Her sharpest regret was that the man who had spoken to her with sympathy was not coming along. If only Tim didn't do something crackbrained they still might get safely back to civilization. Her reputation with Buck would be ruined. She could have laughed, bitterly, if she wasn't still so scared. Gone camping with Tim. One sure way to convince Buck she didn't care about him.

They marched perhaps a quarter of a mile to a grove where the stream ran between beds of bracken. In the trees on the far side the *pakalolo* growers had set up a regular camp, in an idyllic spot near the waterfall where the valley ended. With a sigh Cory dropped onto a rock and tried to feel invisible. Tim did likewise. He was keeping quiet, thank goodness! She made up her mind not to spare him so much as a word or a glance. All this was his fault, and she would never, never forgive him. He had ruined any slim chance she might have had with Buck, and he had ruined the partnership with Sondra. Partnership with Sondra meant partnership with Johnny. She didn't need that, no matter how much she wanted to stay on Kauai.

The men put their guns in one of the three pup tents. The man in the green-and-white shirt fished a six-pack of beer from the clearest pool Cory had ever seen. Ignoring Tim, he offered her one. She disliked beer but she accepted it because she was afraid to refuse. Tim bravely helped himself.

The men sat on the tumbled rocks at the edge of the pool and conferred in pidgin. Tim whispered something, but Cory couldn't hear what he was saying over the sound of the waterfall, and didn't want to know. Deliberately she turned her back to him.

The men finished their beer and got to their feet, gesturing with their guns for Tim to do likewise.

"Get going, haole," one said.

Cory sprang up nervously, but he said, "Not you!" and she sank down again.

"What are you going to do?" Tim asked, his voice thin, his face white.

The other man picked up a coil of rope. "We didn't bring you on no picnic! We're gonna tie you up, out of trouble, where we don't have to look at you. Move!"

They marched him out of the clearing and on up the mountain. Cory's heart froze at seeing him go. Angry at him as she was, he had provided companionship of a sort, someone on whom to center her fury, someone who shared her distress. She swallowed her beer in convulsive sips and stared around the campsite. What if she heard a shot? What if they had taken Tim off to kill him? Was she a fool just to sit here? As soon as they left she should have run. But if they had taken Tim off only to tie him up, she'd do better not to rile them. They might return any minute and she certainly had no desire to share Tim's fate.

The men returned so soon she was glad she had stayed put. She had calmed down enough to tell them apart, if only by their shirts. They no longer carried the rope.

It wouldn't hurt Tim to be tied up, Cory thought.

The leader, in the blue-and-white shirt, came over to where she sat and spoke genially.

"I'm Kapono, that's Keolo, and our brother back at the patch, he's Alfred."

"I'm Cory." She managed a frozen smile. *Kapono, Keolo, Kapono, Keolo,* she said over and over to herself like a litany.

"You don't worry," Kapono said. "We not going to do nothing to you. But we gotta keep you here so that bastard won't go to the police." He swallowed the last of his beer and crumpled the can as though it were paper.

"Tell Alfred we gonna eat," he ordered Keolo. "I don't think no more rippers gonna come today."

Cory crouched tensely on her rock. Her comfort, perhaps her survival, depended on the whim of these men. She must not antagonize them; she had no wish to be tied up. She tried to think of some safe subject that would keep communication going, but her mouth was as dry as cotton and her mind might as well have been cotton for all the ideas it supplied her. She could think only of reiterating her innocence, and she thought it would be wiser to keep quiet.

After a few minutes, which seemed like an hour to Cory, Keolo and Alfred returned. Alfred was whistling, but he broke off when he came into camp and his eye fell on the hampers.

"Boy, am I hungry!" he exclaimed. "Some Christmas dinner this, eh?" He looked at Cory.

She smiled faintly.

One of the hampers was full of beer, but the other held a huge container of pork that smelled so heavenly Cory's dry mouth began to water. Someone had packed paper plates and plastic forks and spoons. Cory had a fleeting vision of these men living a modern life in houses that had automatic washers and color television.

Alfred had uncovered a steaming dish of rice and was busy filling a plate.

"Listen, you sure you like poi?" he asked, his spoon poised over the bowl of gray substance.

"Sure, give her some," Keolo advised with a gesture of his beer can. "Maybe she'll like it so much she'll come live with us."

Kapono, the eldest brother, said something

mocking in pidgin that made the other two laugh. Cory grew tense again, but Alfred grinned at her.

"He's telling Keolo that his wife might not like you to live with them no matter how much you like poi."

Keolo looked sheepish and Cory found to her surprise that she could join in their simple laughter. Laugh while you can, she thought. What if police helicopters spotted the patch on their own? These men might assume that Johnny had ratted. Would they retaliate? They didn't look like murderers, but who could be sure?

Perhaps that was why the *kalua* pig tasted so delicious. The chewy rice was also cooked to perfection. Cory found the lack of conversation during the meal soothing.

Alfred finished first. Disappearing among the trees, he returned with his big hands full of round pale yellow fruit the size of lemons.

"Guava," he said, tossing one in Cory's direction.

He offered her another beer, but she shook her head, a little more at ease now that her stomach was filled with her captors' good food.

Keolo finished his meal and lounged off in the direction of the *pakalolo* patch. Kapono went off with a plate of food for Tim. They weren't going to be cruel, then.

Cory felt more comfortable than she had all day. Her legs no longer trembled from continuous climbing. Her feet were sore, but as long as she didn't have to stand on them.... If only she could be sure that she and Tim were safe! Could she count on Johnny to contact Hazel? She felt real pain when she considered what Hazel would think of her, to go off like that with Tim. And what if Buck called? Would Hazel tell him? Cory consoled herself by thinking that Hazel would have the wrong impression for four days at most—please God. Her life might depend on the fact that Hazel did believe it, so Cory could only pray that Johnny would make the story good. And Buck wouldn't call; he'd be miffed that she hadn't come to Christmas dinner. Or he might be too busy with Emma. Or Julia.

She did her best to shrug off the danger and live in the moment. Kapono had said they wouldn't harm her. She had better try to believe that.

She wondered how Tim was making out, but found she didn't care much if he was uncomfortable. Now that she knew what he and Johnny did in their spare time, she understood why they had been driving in the cane fields. Petroglyphs be damned; they were hunting *pakalolo* then, too. That was why Johnny was standing on the truck. Tim had been so mealymouthed it was disgusting.

And no wonder Buck was angry, if it was his crop they were hoping to rip off. She sighed. If only she could have remained in ignorance of all this! Tim was right: it didn't pay to know too much. It seemed a good guess that Tim and Johnny were the ones who put Paco up to delivering marijuana in Honolulu. Paco hadn't denied her accusation. Using a child for such dirty work didn't fit Buck's character; she gave him that much credit.

She looked up to see Alfred bringing a ukulele from one of the tents. Perching on a thick tree root, he began to strum.

Had she strayed onto the set of a grade B movie? Cory choked down an urge to laugh and recognized it as hysteria. To hide her contorted face she bent her head over her knees and unlaced her sneakers. At least she could bathe her tired feet, and the cold water would help her regain her sanity.

The water was heavenly. Not to have to hike down out of the mountains was a blessing and made her feel almost friendly toward her captors. For a time she turned her mind off. She sat soaking up the tropical surroundings, the high, splashing waterfall, the gentle music. Everything combined to form a magical dream in which she was a bewitched princess condemned to spend her days in this make-believe scenery until rescued by the prince. The prince... Buck... who didn't know where she was, and if told would say, "Good riddance!" The fact that he would be at home celebrating Christmas, that today *was* Christmas, was as unreal as the rest of this fantasy.

She shook the water from her feet and waited for the air to dry them, slumping tiredly, her eyelids beginning to droop. Kapono had disappeared into one of the tents. Alfred waved the ukulele at an empty one.

"Go sleep," he advised. "No one will bother you."

Why not, she thought philosophically. *Heaven*

knows, I'm tired enough. It will be a way to pass the time and keep from thinking.

The little tent had a plastic floor which kept out the damp, and tatami mats to lie on. With a sigh Cory stretched full length and to her surprise felt herself drifting almost immediately. . . .

She woke knowing exactly where she was. Her stomach clenched with fear, even though she realized she had been allowed to sleep a long time without being disturbed. Should she stay in the tent, on the theory of out of sight, out of mind? Or should she appear and behave as though on a picnic? Picnic! That was ironic! She could hear the two men carrying on a long, unintelligible conversation, probably in pidgin. At last the need to stretch and walk around drove her out.

Alfred greeted her pleasantly. "Hi, Cory. You sleep long time. You had long walk this morning, eh?" He grinned.

"I sure did," she agreed.

"You want beer or water? The water here is okay to drink. Nothing up there—" he gestured at the brink of the waterfall high against the sky "—nothing but goats." He handed her a plastic tumbler when she signified her preference for water. She stepped close to the steady downpour and filled her cup from a rivulet falling to the side.

As she drank she became conscious of Kapono's— no, Keolo's—liquid brown eyes upon her. He had been regarding her steadily since she came out of the tent.

Despite herself Cory shivered. She walked self-consciously to her rock and sat on it, keeping her eyes lowered. The men took up their conversation, or rather Alfred did. Keolo's replies were mainly grunts, as though something else occupied his mind. Cory had a strong, uncomfortable fancy that his mind was on her. Glancing sidewise at him, she wondered whether Alfred would protest if his ominously watchful brother decided to make use of her. Her skin crawled, her heart constricted, and her hands felt clammy. She sat unmoving, like a rabbit hiding in the grass. She kept her eyes lowered. They must not see she was frightened.

Long minutes passed. Cramped muscles demanded action. She drew a deep breath and jumped to her feet. Her courage returned.

"Do you mind if I have a beer?" she cried, crossing to where the cans lay in the water.

"Sure, Cory," Alfred said.

It would give her something to do with her hands, and maybe she would be able to think more clearly. Not that she had anything to think about, except to wonder how she was going to pass the time for the next four days. The men seemed content to spend their time drinking beer and talking.

Alfred squinted at the sky and began laying out four platefuls of leftover meat and rice. The food tasted every bit as delicious the second time around. She and Alfred chatted desultorily over the meal. She told him she had grown up in New Jersey, which he seemed to consider as far away as the moon. For him it probably was.

Kapono appeared before they finished eating,

and Alfred went off to do guard duty. Silently Kapono closed up the almost empty hampers. Taking one in each hamlike hand, he nodded to Cory and set off down the trail. She was left with the staring Keolo. Her heartbeat increased.

"Where's he going?" she demanded shrilly.

"To his house and his bed," Keolo said, his voice tinged with resentment. To Cory's utter relief he picked up the ukulele and began to strum. Soon he was singing a Hawaiian song she'd never heard before. These men obviously made music their pastime. He played better and had a more melodic voice than Alfred. Perhaps he hadn't been lusting after her earlier. Perhaps he'd merely been wishing Alfred would relinquish the ukulele. Nevertheless, a tremendous worry was dispelled when a sudden downpour sent them scurrying to separate tents. Over the sound of raindrops thudding on the tent Cory could still hear Keolo singing. Poor Tim must be getting soaked.

She stretched full length and allowed herself to think about Buck. The Bowers and Hazel would be having dinner now. She would have been there, too, if it weren't for Tim. He deserved to get drenched.

Occupied by her thoughts, she didn't realize the rain had stopped until she saw Keolo's big round face in the tent opening. She gasped with fright.

"What do you want?" she demanded. Beyond his shoulders, which looked like a football player's, she saw that daylight had gone. Fear gripped her, holding her motionless. Where was Alfred? If she screamed, would he come? Kapono, their leader, had left.

"Come out," he ordered. "We want to talk to you."

We?

Her heart thudding, Cory squirmed warily out of the tent. Should she try to run? Her courage rose when she saw Alfred in the gathering gloom.

"Listen," Alfred said. "We gotta tie you up. Otherwise you might run away."

"I wouldn't! I promise!" Cory cried, but her protest made no impression. Alfred produced a rope, ordered her to put her hands behind her back, and began binding her wrists together.

"Boss's orders," he apologized.

In the face of his easygoing nature, Cory's fear left her. "I can't sleep like this!" she complained loudly.

"We let you loose in the morning," Alfred soothed. "We gotta sleep now."

"What about my friend?" she demanded, giving a reluctant thought to Tim's plight.

"He'll be all right," Alfred said from behind her. At least he wasn't pulling the cords terribly tight.

"What if something gets him?" She had visions of wild animals.

Neither man answered and she realized they probably had no idea what she meant. The only wild animals on Kauai were pigs and goats.

When they left her she sat on the ground and used her heels to scoot herself back into the tent. There she collapsed on her side, too overwrought to do anything but watch the gathering dark and worry. With the night her fear returned. What did she know about these men? What if...what if Alfred went to sleep and Keolo came after her then? She could scream loud enough to wake Alfred. But what if...they decided to share her? Oh, God, why hadn't she listened to Buck?

CHAPTER FIFTEEN

By the middle of the night she found herself sleepless, her stomach tight with fear. Even half asleep some part of her mind had gone on worrying and trembling. For a while she lay in intense discomfort, every muscle tense, every nerve on edge. The pattering on the tent she recognized as raindrops, and the weird sounds that had penetrated her sleep were snores!

Eventually she fell again into a doze. Freed of its daytime controls, her imagination unreeled a sequence of frightening dreams in which she was forever eluding her captors, only to have them spring out in front of her. At last she slid over a waterfall into a pool just big enough to catch her sprawling limbs, and woke with a start.

She lay waiting for her breathing to slow to normal. Aside from the cramps in her arms, nothing terrible had happened yet. The gentle patter on the tent had ceased. She peered out of the tent opening to see gray morning light filling the glade. A moment later she watched Alfred emerge yawning from his tent, his hair on end. As naturally as generations of his forebears had done, he squatted beside the pool, splashed his face and drank from his cupped hand. Seeing Cory peering out, he crossed over to her.

"I'll untie you now. You act nice?"

"I've never acted any other way," Cory said frigidly.

Moments later, her hands free, she was rubbing her wrists with relief. She bit her lip to keep from exclaiming at the pain of returning circulation in her fingers, but the stinging was nothing compared to the joy of free movement. A wave of gratitude for Alfred swept over her, even though he had been the one to tie her.

"Thank you!" she exclaimed.

Alfred grunted, picked up his shotgun and moved off through the glade toward where they were keeping Tim. Cory's chest tightened. Something might have happened to Tim—anything! Then she heard his voice. He was shouting angrily. He must be all right to be so furious.

Was she free now to get up and move around? The night was over; she was unharmed. How good a cup of coffee would taste!

Keolo crawled out, scowling sleepily. Cory was tempted to say brightly, "What's for breakfast?" but she didn't quite dare. Instead, she followed the men's example and washed her face at the pool. Then she hunted through her shoulder bag for a comb. She was sitting on her rock wondering what these men ate for breakfast, when Kapono arrived. He was wearing one of the confiscated rucksacks and carrying an insulated jug.

"Coffee," he announced for Cory's benefit.

From the rucksack he took plastic cups, papayas and bread. He deposited his burdens and moved off in the direction of the *pakalolo* patch.

Alfred came back grinning, no doubt at Tim's fury. He took bread and coffee and returned to Tim.

The hot, sweet liquid gave Cory new heart. One night had passed safely. But as her mind grew more alert she faced the brutal truth that the police would hardly have made raids on Christmas day. Why kid herself? She and Tim would be in danger until the *pakalolo* was harvested. She longed to talk to him. It would be a comfort to share their distress. Her anger no longer seemed relevant.

She sipped the coffee and tried to stop thinking, but it was impossible. Had Hazel believed Johnny's story? Would Johnny keep calling if he didn't get Hazel the first time, if Hazel wasn't back from the Bowers'?

Stop guessing, she commanded herself. Conjecturing could drive her mad. Already her stomach had knotted into a tight ball, and the excellent coffee had turned unpleasantly bitter in her mouth. Relax, relax, relax!

Keolo cut open a papaya and offered her half. It tasted delicious. She concentrated on enjoying the simple pleasure of fresh fruit.

"You like papaya," Keolo stated with a broad grin. "We grow them."

"You do?" Cory exclaimed. "You have a whole papaya orchard?"

The big man's smile faded. "Not so much land.

The land belong to big growers. We have trees by our house."

That was typical of conditions in Hawaii, Cory knew. The native islanders had lost out in the land grabs of the last century.

Breakfast over, Cory decided to attempt to wash the mud from the legs of her jeans. She waded into the pool and scrubbed at her pant legs with the edge of a flat stone. Then she wrung as much water from the cloth as she could and returned to sit in front of her tent and dry out. The thought of wearing these clothes for four days or more made her skin crawl. Her serious brown eyes studied the varied pattern of green leaves. She wondered what had happened to the sketch pads in Tim's rucksack.

Alfred passed through the camp and went down the path to join Kapono. Keolo produced the ukulele and began to strum, composing a tune of his own. The music faded to the background and Cory's thoughts took over. What if Buck telephoned to thank Cory for the drawing that had been his Christmas present? Would Hazel tell him she was camping with Tim?

She dozed, then woke to see Alfred returning. Her spirits rose. Of the three brothers, he was the most talkative.

He fished a beer from the pool and sat nearby with a carefree expression on his open face. Cory noticed that his bare arms and legs were as smooth as a boy's. She smiled at him.

"It's amazing that you can hike up and down these mountains in thongs," she said.

"I never wear nothing else," Alfred said. "Kids go barefoot until maybe twelve. We live in the sticks here—no water, no electricity, no shoes. I suppose you think we crazy to grow *pakalolo* when the police, the bugs, everybody try to rip us off."

"Ever think about getting a job in town?" Cory kept her tone conversational. She certainly didn't want to sound critical.

"If I go downtown I get paid maybe three dollars an hour," Alfred said, "to work in the hotels. How you gonna support kids on that? I got three kids. Keolo, he have four. Kapono, he got five. You no can wait for those guys to throw you food stamps and all that. You gotta go out and hustle for yourself. So what we do? We fish, we hunt, we grow *pakalolo*. We live pretty damn good."

Cory was silent, thinking over his words.

"What you do in Hala?" Alfred asked. "You a secretary?"

Cory explained about Hazel.

"She no think it a bad thing when the *kanaka* tell her you shack up with that boy?"

"Oh!" Cory made a rueful face. "She probably will think it's a bad thing."

"But you explain when you get back and she forgive you," Alfred suggested comfortingly.

"*When* I get back," she said pointedly.

She sat on her rock and half listened to a long tirade from Alfred about *pakalolo*. Calling it by that name made it sound exotic instead of illegal.

"Everybody is growing it," Alfred bragged. "*Pakalolo* grown in Hawaii is the finest in the world. Especially when people fertilize it and hoe around the plants. But it's no sure thing. If you plant a thousand, and your friends don't rip you off, and the police don't find your plants, you still maybe only come out with—'' he made a face ''—four hundred plants. Listen, it's hard work!''

"And it's still illegal," Cory boldly pointed out at last.

Alfred shrugged elaborately. "My kids gotta eat."

When the sun was high overhead, the two teenagers arrived with hampers as they had the day before. The hampers contained the same fare— beer, pork, poi and rice. Cory realized that their Christmas meal was special only because of the day. The people in these families would eat of the pig until it was gone.

Dinner over, she was contemplating withdrawing into her tent to catch up on the sleep she had missed, when raised voices not far down the valley brought her head up. Alfred and Keolo sprang to their feet. Alfred grabbed his shotgun. With a brief word to Keolo he ran down the path, immediately disappearing amid the lush growth.

"Get in the tent," Keolo ordered. "Keep out of sight."

Cory's heart pounded wildly. Her breathing seemed wholly suspended. Had the police found the crop? Should she try to run to them? What if they had stumbled on this crop accidentally and didn't know she was here? Kapono could hold her as a hostage against the police, as well!

Keolo exchanged the ukulele for a gun. The musical instrument had looked like a toy, held in his big, plump hands across his ample stomach. The gun didn't look like a toy. It looked wickedly efficient.

Cory moved obediently toward her tent, dragging her feet only a little. The loud voices had quieted. Could it be only—please God—another party of hikers? Perhaps they had been warned away. Dear heaven, don't let it be the police! How could she believe herself safe, no matter what these men said—these men who were already flouting the law, who saw themselves as providing for their families? Would they risk killing her and Tim? If they got caught—and Johnny knew who they were—how much worse off their families would be!

She sat inside the stuffy tent, breathing shallowly, her ears alert for any sound that would tell her what was happening.

After long minutes she heard a rustle of footsteps, the slap of a zori, the thud of a shoe striking a stone. At whatever risk she had to know what was going on. With two fingers she pulled the tent flap open the merest crack. She caught a glimpse of broad, familiar shoulders, the proud carriage of a dark head. With a gasp she pulled the flaps apart, her heart leaping with wild hope.

Striding into the clearing, his expression confident, was Buck Bower.

Cory had not an instant of doubt but that he had come to rescue her, and nothing, nothing, not even shotguns could keep her from throwing herself into his arms. With a heartfelt cry of "Oh, Buck!" she raced toward him.

He saw her coming. As always, the intense blue of his eyes surprised her. They blazed now with anger, and his face remained tautly serious. His welcome was grim, but his arms enfolded her. She felt herself crushed against his pounding heart, her face smothered in his damp, T-shirt-covered shoulder. Fiercely grateful, she inhaled the strong musky masculine scent of him, intensified by the long hike he must have made at top speed.

The Hawaiians were treating him with quiet respect. Guns had been laid aside. She heard a beer can pop and felt Buck reach to accept it.

"Are you all right?" he asked, his voice strained.

She nodded against his chest.

"Then for God's sake go sit down!" He pushed her from him almost with revulsion.

Cory retreated stunned. She sank to the ground in front of her tent and had to work hard to keep from bursting into tears. How could he speak to her like that? She could understand that he might be angry at her for coming up here with Tim, but he had shoved her away as though she repelled him.

The glade filled with fast and furious pidgin as the Hawaiians gave Buck their version of the events that had led to detaining Cory and Tim. It came to her that the men knew Buck. She guessed from the aggrieved anger of their voices that they had plenty to say about the low-down, cheating behavior of Tim and Johnny.

Buck might be angry, but he must have come here for the purpose of rescuing her, unless—Good God! Could he have come for some *other* reason, such as to buy the *pakalolo* harvest? The crop had to be sold to somebody...somebody who could ship if off the island. Buck was certainly in a position to arrange that. Perhaps he hadn't known she was there until they told him. That would explain his fury. Naturally he wouldn't want her to know about his dealings.

The pain of his rejection subsided as she began to watch and listen. Kapono and Alfred were doing most of the talking. From time to time Buck nodded his head or asked a question. Cory thought he had never looked so handsome, like a hero from some tale of South Seas adventure, yet he was dressed much like the other men, in a thin white T-shirt and well-worn khaki shorts. His bare feet were thrust into crepe-soled moccasinlike walking shoes. It occurred to her that he had dressed that way purposely.

She didn't want to believe he could be involved with marijuana, and yet...the men did know him. And how had he found out so easily where she and Tim were being held?

He was talking persuasively. She did her best to catch the meaning of his words. How perfectly crazy to listen to a conversation where the flow of syllables, the combination of vowels and consonants, made the speakers seem to be talking English, yet only stray words held meaning for her.

She could understand Buck better than she could Kapono, who was doing most of the negotiating. Buck appeared to be making a deal. He was offering money! For her? For the crop? What about Tim? Surely Buck knew they were holding Tim also.

The negotiations ended abruptly. Buck took out his wallet and handed bills to Kapono. Alfred went off to fetch Tim. Buck didn't so much as glance in her direction. He accepted another beer from Keolo and laughed at something he said. Cory got to her feet, but she hesitated to step forward.

In minutes Tim came stumbling through the bushes, rubbing his wrists and scowling. A day's growth of brown beard added to his disheveled appearance.

"So you're the one who's getting us out of this," he greeted Buck ungraciously. "I might have known."

"You don't know a damn thing!" Buck said tersely. "And you'd better continue not to know a damn thing. I had to promise that you'd keep your mouth shut. They want your word on that. You, too, Cory." He barely looked at her.

"Naturally, I'll keep quiet!" Tim exclaimed. "What do you think I am?" He looked aggrieved and slightly penitent.

"I know what you are," Buck told him. "Get going before we have second thoughts."

With an apologetic glance at Cory, Tim departed.

Buck shook hands with the men. He turned to Cory, his voice commanding.

"Give them your promise. Then you can go, too."

"Of course, I promise! But aren't you coming?" she cried, anxious to explain how she came to be there.

"I'll be along," Buck growled. "I thought you'd be in a hurry to catch up with your pal."

Cory lifted her chin, not deigning to answer his accusation. She moved to where the brothers stood and held out trembling fingers.

"Kapono, Keolo, Alfred— I want you to know I wasn't in on any of this."

The men said something meaningless and cheerful and she turned away, too proud to look at Buck again.

She marched along the path, wanting to break into a run at every step, but pride and the irregular footing kept her pace stately. She heard Buck behind her. How far must they walk before they could stop and converse? How much had he paid to get her released?

She recognized the part of the path that ran past the *pakalolo* patch. They strode briskly on the level stretch. Before plunging into the bamboo thicket that marked the next part of the descent, she glanced back. Alfred had followed them down to resume guard duty. Cory returned his final wave.

"Buck, I was never so glad to see anyone in my life!" she exclaimed over her shoulder, unable to keep from expressing her gratitude any longer.

"Watch where you're going!" he commanded sharply. "I've got plenty to say to you, but it can wait."

The downward slope of the trail through the thicket made it easy to bound along. Cory fairly flew.

"Take it easy you little fool!" Buck shouted. "You don't need to break your neck."

"Much you'd care!" she taunted.

"It would just make more trouble for me," he replied nastily.

The trail descended steeply, but not too fast for Cory. She couldn't get back to level ground soon enough. But she wanted to talk to Buck before they caught up with Tim. He might be waiting at Buck's car for a ride back to his own.

For a time they had to shoulder their way through tall fernlike fronds. Cory wanted to remark how marvelous it was that all Kauai's rampant growth appeared to be free from creepy crawly things like snakes and insects, but she held her tongue. Buck obviously wasn't in the mood to respond to her comments.

They emerged at last onto a visible trail. Buck caught Cory's arm none too gently and pulled her back to walk beside him. He was scowling blackly.

"All right, what do you have to say to me?" she asked quietly.

"Nothing you'll care to hear!"

She tossed her head and would have strode on in silence, but he pulled her back.

"Slow up! No doubt your friend Tim will be waiting at the car. He's got nerve enough."

"He is not my friend!" Cory cried. "I hope I never see him again!"

"Didn't you enjoy your little rip-off party?"

"Of course I didn't! I didn't know what he was planning to do!" Her voice rose aggrievedly.

"Then what's your story?" he asked, clearly prepared not to believe a word.

"We were hiking up to a petroglyph rock. I certainly didn't known Johnny was going to show up."

"Disappointed at the interruption?"

"No!" She snatched her arm from his clutch. An imp in the back of her mind whispered that Buck was jealous, but she feared it was only a wish.

He studied her, his blue eyes contemptuous. "You don't need to keep on with this pretense. Paco told me everything. You can be thankful he did. You must have wondered how I found you so fast."

"No, I didn't," Cory ground from between clenched teeth. "I didn't wonder at all! I figured you ran across us in the course of business."

"What business? What are you trying to say?" Buck's eyes narrowed.

Cory maintained a sullen silence. Let him figure it out!

"You don't have to tell me!" Buck snarled. "Thanks to Tim, Paco believes I'm growing the stuff! Is that what you're referring to?" He shook his head disgustedly.

"Aren't you?" Cory challenged.

He didn't answer the question. He was so angry Cory wasn't sure he heard.

"I wasted my breath telling you to stay away from those freaks, didn't I?" he raged. "You're birds of a feather. Low enough to rope in a high school kid."

Cory felt the blood drain from her cheeks. She might have known that matter would catch up with her.

Buck's eyes blazed. "Paco told me what he delivered in Honolulu. And you knew about it." His beautiful masculine mouth had thinned to a gash.

"I didn't know at the time!" Cory choked. "I guessed...later."

"Why in God's name didn't you tell me?" Buck thundered.

"Paco said you'd laugh it off," she replied lamely.

"You want to know what I think? I think you knew because Tim bragged to you that he'd got Paco dealing for him. He'd like nothing better than to ruin my reputation."

"Why, for heaven's sake?"

Buck shrugged. "Who knows? Jealousy, maybe."

Tim jealous of Buck's position in the community? Of his wealth? Cory gave a short laugh before she remembered that her wrong judgment of Tim's character had landed her in this mess. Maybe he was jealous.

"How much did you pay to get me free?" she asked abruptly. That obligation must be met as soon as she could get to the bank.

"Forget about it!" Buck said maddeningly.

"Certainly not!" she exclaimed. "Not after the accusations you've made!"

"It was nothing—a loan. I'll get it back after their crop's harvested.

Cory's eyes widened. "What exactly are you saying?"

"I'm saying, forget about it!"

Her heart thumped. He didn't want to explain, but his words incriminated him. He *was* dealing with the growers. That's why they had been friendly and obliging. She felt sick at the thought of the corruption going on in this paradise. It hardly mattered whether Buck linked her with Tim or not. She couldn't go on loving a scoundrel.

"How did you find out where we were?" she asked at last. Despite her suspicions of his underhanded dealings, despite his anger, she couldn't close off what was probably her last chance to communicate with him. Quarreling was better than silence.

"Hazel got a bit dizzy at dinner," he said. "I suspect she drank more than usual. Her hip may have been hurting. At any rate, she wasn't walking very well. So Paco and I drove her home and saw her into the house. The telephone was ringing when we opened the door. Your friend Sondra."

Cory stole a glance at him. His blue eyes were still stormy. Sondra! So Johnny had involved her, too!

"Hazel answered the phone and Paco and I started to leave, but she signaled us to stay. When she hung up, she told us that Sondra's call was to say you wouldn't be home. You were camping somewhere with Tim Cooper. I didn't see how that was my business, but Hazel is nobody's fool. She didn't believe Sondra. At first she was shocked. Not so much that you'd spend the night with your friend Tim, but not telling her, letting Sondra convey the message. 'It's not like Cory,' she kept saying. Finally she said, 'I don't believe it. Something's happened. I feel it in my bones.' So I offered to drop by Sondra's to see what I could find out, but she and Johnny weren't home. I checked some bars, but couldn't find them. As far as I was concerned, if you wanted to hang out with that creep Cooper, you had every right, so Paco and I went home to bed.''

He halted abruptly, then grabbed her by the shoulders and whirled her around to face him. ''Wasn't it enough for you to get involved with those people? Did you have to draw Paco in, too?'' For the first time he sounded more hurt than angry.

''I didn't,'' she repeated.

Buck gave a short, exasperated sigh. ''At any rate, Paco got scared. Whether you know it or not, a few grim things have happened to rippers. By morning he was ready to tell me the real reason you'd gone hiking.''

''He knew?'' Cory was incredulous.

''He knew,'' Buck affirmed.

''I sure wish he'd told me!''

''Are you going to keep pretending?'' he shouted.

She was trembling. Her knees threatened to sag. Why didn't he let her go home before she collapsed?

His attractive lips twisted. ''Paco found Johnny Komo still in bed this morning and got the truth out of him. That's when Paco got really scared and phoned me at the office. I dropped everything and dragged Johnny out of bed and into my car. He showed me which valley he'd left you in, and you know the rest.''

"I'm sorry we put you to so much trouble," Cory made herself say. "I *am* grateful."

"You have Paco to thank," Buck said, loosing her and starting on down the trail. "He did you a better turn than you did him."

She felt too limp to put one foot in front of the other, but she gritted her teeth and stumbled after him.

"If you think so badly of me, I'm surprised you came to my rescue," she said through stiff lips.

"I did it for Hazel's sake," he growled over his shoulder. "And because those men don't deserve to get in trouble for the likes of a bunch of trash from the mainland."

"Trash?" Cory's voice sounded shrill, but it no longer seemed to be under her control. "Do you mean me?"

Buck said irritatingly, "If the shoe fits—"

In a fury Cory ran up behind him and shoved him out of her path. "Go to hell, Buchanan Bower!" she shouted as she passed. She would have stormed on downhill at top speed but Buck caught her shoulders. He was breathing hard. For an instant she thought he was going to pull her against him.

After a rigid moment he gave her a little shove. "Get going, but don't try to run downhill! You've given me enough trouble today."

Tears of hurt and misery filled her eyes. She blinked them away and set off at a cautious pace. They finished the trip in silence. They had nothing more to say to each other.

CHAPTER SIXTEEN

BUCK PULLED INTO the parking lot of Hazel's condominium and stopped the car. Cory glanced at his
stern-lipped profile. They had dropped Tim at the
road where he'd left his truck. During the angry
silence of their drive home Cory had grown re-
morseful over their quarrel. She should have shown
more gratitude to him for coming to get her, but obviously he was still angry. He'd made it pretty clear
he didn't want her gratitude; he wanted her out of
his life. In response to his unbending attitude
Cory's temper flared again.

"Since I apparently don't owe you any thanks, or
any money, I'll simply say goodbye," she said with
cold dignity, and stepped out of the car.

Buck drove off while she was climbing the stairs.
Hazel met her at the door. At the sight of the
motherly concern in Hazel's gray eyes, Cory lost the
composure she'd kept so bravely all through her
ordeal and burst into tears.

"I'm all right," she assured Hazel through her
sobs. "But I was so scared...and Buck thinks I
went up there on purpose!"

"No, he doesn't. We've both been beside our-
selves with worry. Go and have a bath, and I'll

make you some breakfast," Hazel soothed. "What would you like?"

Cory wiped her tears with the back of her hand.

"Scrambled eggs and toast would taste heavenly," she confessed with a watery smile, and headed toward the bathroom.

Luxuriating in warm sudsy water scented with the fragrance of white ginger, she let her thoughts return to the clear pool where she and Tim had stopped... was it only yesterday? What a Garden of Eden this island could be for two people in love.

Hazel was waiting. Cory briskly finished her bath, donned clean shorts and T-shirt, and appeared in the kitchen feeling reasonably composed.

While she ate eggs scrambled with mushrooms and bean sprouts, she told Hazel the story from the beginning.

"Taking a woman on such a jaunt was outrageous," Hazel declared.

"I couldn't agree more," Cory said, a forkful of egg halfway to her mouth, "but, of course, Tim's idea was to make the trip look like a hike."

Hazel shook her head. "I never would have believed such a thing of Tim. It shows how wrong you can be about a person."

"Amen to that!" Cory agreed fervently, taking Hazel's words as a reminder that her suspicions of Buck were by no means unfounded.

"By the way," Hazel said, "there were some Christmas presents for you under the tree at the Bowers'. They're on the coffee table. I loved the quilted pillow and everyone admired it. Buck was pleased with his drawing, too.''

Cory was startled to remember that this was the day after Christmas. She forced herself to smile. The sight of the brightly wrapped packages kindled a spark of enthusiasm in what promised otherwise to be a day of unhappiness.

Irene and Mae had given her a lovely white silk scarf. Lester's present was a book of early accounts of the Sandwich islands, as the Hawaiian islands were first called, and Paco's gift was a sketch pad of the kind he knew she used.

She saved Buck's present till last, and when she opened it, her gasp was one of awe. Reposing on a black velvet background was a five-strand necklace of white shells. Cory recognized it instantly as a shell lei from Niihau, the Forbidden Island.

Cory's chest still ached with the memory of the morning's quarrel.

''I can't accept it!'' she blurted, remembering the things Buck had said. ''He's probably sorry by now that he gave it to me.'' Nevertheless, she took it from its case and slipped it over her head. Each white shell was perfection. The long loop curved below her breasts.

''These cost a fortune,'' she breathed, looking at Hazel for confirmation.

''He can afford it,'' Hazel replied. ''He probably considers he's helping the lei makers, as well.''

''The lei makers?'' Cory echoed.

''Yes. The families on Niihau. They're mostly pure Hawaiian, you know. The women and children sift the shells out of the sand when the winter surf washes them ashore. You must have seen the island on the horizon when you went to look at the Russian Fort.''

Cory nodded. ''I understand it's privately owned and there's no electricity or telephones. Have you ever been there?''

Hazel laughed. ''Hardly! The Robinson family who owns it doesn't allow outsiders to visit, and they don't grant interviews to the press. A few public officials and physicians have gone there in the course of their duties, but for everyone else it's *kapu*. The people who live there can leave, of course. Most of the children come to Kauai to high school.''

Cory fingered the necklace wistfully. ''He gave those growers money to get us free. He wouldn't tell me how much. How can I keep it when he thinks I led Paco astray?''

''That's up to you,'' Hazel said, adding with a smile, ''I'm glad no one has offered me such a temptation. Wait a few days and see how you feel. I hope you'll still go to their New Year's party. That's the reason I gave you a gift certificate. I thought you might want to buy a new dress.''

''How can I go?'' Cory cried. ''Buck not only thinks I'm a ripper, he blames me for getting Paco involved.''

Hazel looked thoughtful. ''I wouldn't worry about that,'' she advised at last. Buck's not so unreasonable. He'll get the truth out of Paco. You've told him you didn't know what Tim was after. It seems to me the only thing you can do now is go to the party with your head up and behave normally. If you stay away, he'll think you *are* guilty. Incidentally, guess what Irene told me? Emma Lassiter's coming back here.''

So it was true! Cory's hand flew to her mouth to hide her dismay. Did Buck know yet?

''How did you hear about it?'' she asked with as much nonchalance as she could muster.

''Irene told me. Buck received a letter from Emma. She wrote him she's divorced. Irene is terribly upset. Mae, too, of course. They're terrified he'll marry her.''

''Is she coming to the New Year's party?'' Cory asked in a hollow voice.

''Oh, I don't think she's arriving that soon!'' Hazel exclaimed. ''Lester told us she'd made a hotel reservation for mid-January.''

Good! Cory thought. *I'll be clear away from here by then.* She fingered the shell lei. She would return it to Buck at the party. Today he must be furious that he'd given her anything at all. She felt like keeping it as consolation for the names he had called her, but she didn't want a reminder.

''Hazel, I suppose you realize—'' Cory found the words hard to say ''—I can't go into partnership with Sondra now.''

''You think she's involved in the rip-offs, too?''

''I don't know for sure. Not directly, I guess. But Johnny has money invested in the gift shop.'' Cory laughed cynically. ''I was wondering where he got money to invest! Buck warned me all along not to get involved with Sondra.'' She wished she knew for sure that Buck's hands were clean.

''That's too bad. I know how much you were looking forward to going into business. Maybe something else will turn up.''

''Maybe,'' Cory agreed, but privately she determined to be well away from Kauai before Emma returned. She didn't want to be around for that when she wouldn't even have the gift shop business to distract her.

By the next morning Cory's anger at Sondra had cooled. She began to want to talk to the other woman, to find out how much she knew about Tim and Johnny's activities. Sondra probably felt that Cory was furious at her. The sooner they straightened things out the better. She had to tell Sondra she had changed her mind about the partnership.

After Cory had taken an early swim and sunbathed, her adventure seemed like a strange, unlikely dream. Later she telephoned Sondra.

Sondra's voice on the answering machine requested her to leave a message.

''I'm home,'' Cory reported to the tape. ''Call me when you get a chance.'' She hung up.

She waited all week for Sondra to call. She telephoned two more times, but the machine answered. She didn't see Sondra on the beach, so she wandered past the shop. It was closed. She hadn't heard from Tim, either, which suited her fine. It looked as if they were all lying low.

Cory missed Sondra when she went to buy her dress for the New Year's Eve party. Hazel had been

sweet to think of giving her a new one. She'd worn
the same dress to the Bowers' for Thanksgiving, in
Honolulu and at the Christmas party. Everyone
must be well acquainted with it by now.

The saleswoman showed her a deceptively simple
white dress, one of the new minis with a deep V neckline in back. Cory's bare brown shoulders looked
provocative beneath the latticework straps when she
tried it on. The white accented the contrast between
her soft brown eyes and her pale blond hair. Perfect!

When she put the dress on at home with high-
heeled backless shoes and pirouetted into the living
room, Hazel agreed that it was perfect.

"You'll have more use for it on the mainland
than you would a muumuu, if you insist on going
back," Hazel said. "I gather you're not going to
wear the Niihau necklace with it?"

Cory shook her head. "I really can't accept it. I
owe him so much for going to all the trouble of rescuing me—"

"I daresay he loved that," Hazel broke in.

"He didn't act like he loved it." Cory sniffed.
"Plus there's the money he said he 'loaned' them.
On top of that, he blames me for what Paco did."

Hazel smiled. "He's obviously very confused."

Cory couldn't think what there was to confuse
him, but she didn't pursue the subject. Hazel
seemed to know quite a different Buck Bower.

CORY AND HAZEL were the first guests to arrive at
the New Year's Eve party. All day she had hoped
Buck would call, but he hadn't. The day after her

rescue she had tried to call him at the office to explain why she couldn't accept the Niihau necklace. She was told he had gone to Honolulu.

In one hand she clutched the black velvet case that held the necklace and looked around for him, wanting to get the ordeal over with, not that she expected to enjoy the party after that, but the worst part would be off her mind. She was wearing a pink carnation lei that picked up the delicate pink flush of her cheeks. Her naturally dark brows and lashes contributed to making her eyes deep pools of mystery, and her usual air of quiet poise pricked the imagination.

She stood to one side, watching the stairs, intending to waylay Buck as soon as he came down.

Julia Vagos, wearing an all black muumuu, arrived with her family. A diamond bracelet glittered on her wrist and the sparkle of diamond earrings against her midnight hair made Cory think of stars. Buck might not have looked at her in the past, but he surely would tonight. The faint hope Cory had somehow nourished all day that he might look at her died like the foolishness it was.

When Buck appeared he did not come down the stairs, but from the lanai. He was wearing a black polo shirt that molded his muscular chest and gray chinos that fit his lean hips seductively. Cory's eyes feasted on him as he moved through the doorway. She loved the way his biceps swelled the short sleeves, the strong brown forearms, and the unconsciously seductive way he moved.

Her chest felt tight. She almost forgot to breathe as she approached him.

"Oh, hello, Cory," he said in a hearty tone that told her instantly he was still angry, even before she dared to meet his eyes. They looked as hard as blue glass.

"Cory, I want you to meet Emma Lassiter."

Too late Cory woke to the fact that he was hand in hand with the woman behind him. She was saying something over her shoulder to someone still on the lanai. Buck unceremoniously hauled her inside.

Emma's brown eyes coldly inspected Cory, who felt ready to faint. Her innate self-respect came to her rescue, stiffening her backbone, helping her return stare for stare.

Cory was quick to admit that she and Emma Lassiter indeed resembled each other. They were the same height and the same build. Some similarity existed in their features. They might easily have passed for sisters. According to Buck, Emma was three years older. Under the chandeliers her hair shone golden as opposed to Cory's pale silver. Emma's reddened lips and cheeks stood out attractively against white, untanned skin. The body-hugging silky folds and plunging neckline of her evening gown made Cory feel her smart new dress was too simple. She spared a fleeting thought for Julia Vagos. Three women, all wanting Buck. Already the evening was a disaster, as far as Cory was concerned. If only she could give him his damn necklace and leave!

One couldn't force one's way into another person's affection. Friendship—or love—had to come from both parties. Emma needn't think that Cory would enter into a competition, with Buck going as the prize to the most determined. She summoned a friendly smile.

"I see I should have been flattered when so many people mistook me for you," she said.

Emma leaned against Buck in a way that sickened Cory. "So Buck has been telling me." She laughed up at him. "Did she make a good substitute, darling?"

Cory looked up to find his eyes on her. "She got into as much trouble, if that's what you mean," he drawled.

Before Cory could think of a reply, Julia Vagos flounced into their midst and clutched Buck's other arm.

"Buck, honey, who are these girls?" she demanded in sugary accents. "They look like twins. No, that one's older." She indicated Emma.

Her remark instantly gained her Cory's favor. Indeed, Cory barely managed to keep from laughing until the anger that flashed in Emma's eyes sobered her.

"You met Cory at the Christmas party," Buck reminded her. "And you were away when Emma was here before." He introduced them.

Cory drew a deep breath. "Buck, could I speak to you alone for a moment?" She was darned if she'd carry that necklace around all night. He'd probably be relieved to get it back and know she wasn't expecting him to act as her escort this evening.

He excused himself to Julia and Emma and led Cory onto the lanai.

"I have to return this to you," she uttered hurriedly, keeping her voice low and thrusting the case at him. "I can't accept it."

He took the box with a scowl. Gripping her wrist with his other hand, he dragged her through an archway into the garden.

"What's wrong with it?"

"Nothing! It's beautiful, but it's too expensive," she said lamely, reluctant to bring up the fact that he had paid money for her release.

"I can afford it." She hated the imperious way he raised his chin.

"That's not the point," she insisted.

"You can call it a going-away present," he said casually.

His words struck her heart like a dagger, and like a sudden wound they left a numbing impact. "What makes you say that?" she asked, lips trembling.

"I think your *partner*—" his handsome mouth twisted cynically "—has disappeared. Lester tells me she's way behind in her rent, and she and that Komo fellow were seen at the airport."

"How does Lester know about her rent?"

"Those shops—the mall—belong to the hotel."

She might have known! The Bowers had a hand in everything. Her insides writhing with pain, she cried, "You want me to leave! That present was to clear your conscience!"

"Don't be silly," Buck said coolly. "I have nothing on my conscience. I meant it for a pleasant souvenir of your visit to Kauai."

Now that he had Emma he wanted to dismiss her! Blindly she turned away, but firm hands gripped her shoulders. His touch ran through her like liquid fire, but she stiffened. He must not feel how his nearness affected her.

He turned her to face him. His eyes were still hard and angry. "Listen, I had a long talk with Paco this morning. I went to Honolulu last week. I've enrolled him at Punahou School and he'll be living with my old high school coach."

Even on Kauai, Cory had heard of Punahou, a private high school that prepared the children of Hawaii's elite to enter the mainland's best universities.

"Did he—" She swallowed. "Did he tell you where he got the stuff he sold?"

"Oh, yes. You're exonerated."

"Much obliged!" Cory's brown eyes threw out red sparks. She gave him a scathing glance. "Now you can see why I can't accept your necklace!"

He continued as though he didn't hear her. "Of course, it was your friend Cooper. Cooper, it seems, is an artist." Buck emphasized the word sarcastically. "To be an artist you have to join the counterculture. I suppose that explains why you hang around Cooper, too." Buck's grip on her shoulders was becoming painful.

"I don't hang around him! Let go of me!" She wrenched herself free of the hands she most wanted to hold her, and stalked across the lanai to the living-room door. She could feel Buck behind her and half expected him to snatch her back, but he didn't try. She came upon Paco standing at the foot of the stairs, looking ill at ease.

"Hi, there!" Cory cried, genuinely glad to see him. "I have to thank you for the fact that I was rescued!"

"No, you don't," he acknowledged, eyeing Buck doubtfully.

Buck snapped open the black velvet case, confirmed the necklace was inside, closed it and handed it to Paco. "Take this up and put it in my room," he ordered.

Cory's face flamed. "Did you think the necklace wasn't in there?"

Cold desolation filled Buck's eyes. "I had to make sure before I gave it to Paco. You can't trust people who get mixed up with drugs."

He meant her, too. Cory turned blindly away and nearly collided with someone bearing a tray of drinks. She reached haphazardly for a glass and marched rigidly to the far side of the room. She stood there, sipping her drink—it seemed to be pure gin—and watched Emma Lassister fasten onto Buck. He didn't appear to mind.

Cory found her way to the TV room. A bar had been set up there. Let Emma and Julia have Buck. Cory spent the evening drinking seltzer water and watching television with two old men and two small children.

Shortly before midnight the dance band stopped for a break. The sounds of voices coming from the spacious living room ceased as the crowd moved out to the lanai. The children grabbed Cory's hands.

"Come on, they're getting ready for the fire-crackers!" Tugging her arm, they worked their way through the guests until they stood only a few feet from what Cory perceived to be strings of fire-crackers hung from the edge of the metal awning. Her eyes widened. She had seen short strings of fire-crackers as a child, but in New Jersey children care-fully unwound the wicks and lit the crackers one by one. The way these strands were hung, they were obviously going off all together in fast succession. With amazement she counted ten strings, each about six feet long. Buck stood at one end of the lineup. Uncle Lester took his place at the other end after telling Cory and the children to move back another two feet. Cory glimpsed Paco behind Buck. Evidently the setting off of firecrackers on New Year's Eve was a game for adults, too.

Gradually the talk and laughter ceased as the seconds to the New Year came closer.

"Four...three...two...one...*midnight*!" cried Irene.

Working from either end, the two men set off such an uproar of earsplitting pops and cracks that Cory could only think of one phrase to suit: all hell broke loose. Sparks flew everywhere, extinguishing themselves before they fell, and the air grew thick with smoke and sulfur fumes. Bits of faded red paper littered the flagstones of the lanai.

"Now for the rockets!" Paco shouted, appearing at Cory's side as the racket ceased. "Bring the kids. You'll have to come out on the lawn to see them properly. Buck's got them set up in the garden. I have to go help." He sped away.

Cory and the other guests stood around and cried out with delight as a series of rockets, Roman candles and catherine wheels burst against the black Kauai sky and fell like symbolic showers of blessings for the New Year. Cory feared her share would be as ethereal as the sparks.

Faint steady popping could be heard coming from all over that part of the island. Rockets burst above the skyline. Fourth of July fireworks were nothing compared to this.

She and Hazel left soon after the display ended. Hazel wanted to be in good shape to go to work on the day after New Year's. Cory thanked Mae and Irene. Buck was dancing with Emma and didn't even notice Cory leaving.

She and Hazel chatted desultorily on the way home, but once in her room, in bed, Cory couldn't keep from thinking about Buck...and Emma. She wasted no regrets for having fallen in love with him. Almost her first sight of him had foretold that. She'd been vulnerable even then, though she had believed her pain over Paul made her immune. Paul had merely been the one who filled the void left by her mother's death. Buck she loved for his own sake—for his personality, his looks, because her chemistry reacted with his.

Lying wakeful in the dark, she realized that the likelihood that he was involved with *pakalolo* at some level didn't matter. She loved him; it was as simple as that. Unfortunately he didn't love her. She reminded him of Emma. She had made a good substitute, as Emma put it.

Cory ground her teeth. At least he didn't know

she'd fallen in love with him. She dwelt longingly
on the times she'd been with him: dinner at the
Coco Palms, the luau, the trip to Honolulu—oh,
that had been lovely—the sail along the Na Pali
Coast. She lost her heart, she decided, while watching him dance the hula. At the time she thought it
was Hawaii she wanted. She wanted Hawaii, too,
but mostly she wanted Buck.

She turned and tossed with the discomfort of her
thoughts, and daylight arrived before she slept.

She woke eager to go for a swim, and then shrank
from the idea. Emma might be on the beach, possibly Emma and Buck. The thought of seeing them
together nauseated her. Mournfully she spent New
Year's Day hiding in the condominium, reading a
novel. For a time she was grateful to Hazel for not
talking about the party or Buck. In the end she was
driven to speak about it herself.

"I thought Emma wasn't supposed to arrive until
the middle of the month," she said, trying to sound
merely curious.

Hazel looked at Cory over her glasses. "I guess
she couldn't wait to get her hooks into Buck."

"She's welcome to him," Cory snapped.

ON MONDAY MORNING Hazel went cheerfully off to
work at the library. Cory read and waited for the
phone to ring. If Sondra or Johnny had gone off
the island for New Year's, they would be back today, and Sondra would call.

Noon came. Cory ate a solitary lunch. Buck
couldn't be right; Sondra wouldn't have gone for

good without telling her. Cory had given her money to pay the upcoming month's rent, though the partnership papers had yet to be signed. She made up her mind to risk meeting Emma and walk to the shop.

The mall, with its lavish use of wood and plantings, struck Cory as more charming and intimate than ever. She had pictured herself arriving each balmy morning in a crisply fresh everyday muumuu to open the gift shop... belonging here. Maybe Sondra wouldn't have been the ideal partner, but she and Cory got along all right. It was the men, Tim and Johnny, who made the trouble.

Again Cory admired the sign over the door, burnt into a slab of wood: Treasure-Trove. But the shop was dark. She tried the door. It was still locked. Sondra had never given her a key. Buck was right; they had gone for good. Sondra would have known that after what happened up in the mountains Cory would be too angry to invest money in any enterprise Johnny was connected with. At least Sondra had spared her some embarrassment.

Nevertheless, her legs felt like stilts as she dragged herself to a nearby bench and dropped onto it. Tourists passed in twos and threes, but no one glanced at the empty windows of Treasure-Trove. Almost everything in the displays had been sold before Christmas, and Cory had removed the pitiful remainder, planning to create a different arrangement when the new stock arrived. The corners of her pretty mouth turned down. To her consternation, her chin quivered and her eyes filled with

tears. This was it! She might as well go straight back
to Hazel's and call the airline. She didn't belong
here after all.

Tears were still clinging to her lashes when someone stopped in front of her. She dashed them away
and saw Buck Bower. They stared at each other,
Cory with eyes of reproach because he had been
right. Buck's handsome features showed sympathy,
an expression Cory hadn't seen cross his face in
weeks.

"So much for the gift shop," she gulped.

He dropped onto the bench beside her and took
her hand, regardless of the interest of passersby.

"Are you crying?" he asked in astonishment,
cocking his head to look into her face.

"Is that so strange?" she asked angrily. "You
know this means I have to leave here. Hazel's gone
back to work, so I'm out of a job there. I don't
stand a chance of getting a regular job because I'm
not a kamaaina."

Buck's brows drew together. "You want to stay
that much, do you?"

"Isn't that what I've been telling you?" she muttered resentfully.

He glanced at his watch. "Listen, I'm due at the
bank and then I've got to get back to the mill. Let's
talk about it tonight over dinner. Okay?"

"Oh!" Cory hastily hid her surprise. What
about Emma? "Tonight's all right," she said slowly.

He got up and stood looking down at her reflec-
tively. "I wonder when you'll accept the fact that I

know a few things about the people here that you don't.''

Irritated, she watched him walk away. She hugged her annoyance to her. A small feeling of dislike served to keep her hopeless love buried. Summoning her courage she stood up and started back to Hazel's, determined to make the flight reservation without more loss of time.

CHAPTER SEVENTEEN

AT THE END OF THE MALL Cory came face to face
with Tim. He was wearing paint-stained shorts. A
week's growth of whiskers darkened his face. Apparently he'd decided to let his beard grow.

"Hello, Cory! Happy New Year!" he greeted her
jauntily.

"Happy New Year to you," she said with irony.

"Are you mad, Cory?"

"Not anymore." She sniffed. "I've had a week
to get over it, which you were probably counting
on. Listen, did Sondra and Johnny say goodbye to
you?"

"Yeah. Did you see them?"

"No, but it's pretty obvious they're gone for
good."

"Johnny's kind of related to those guys we met,"
Tim said. "He figured they might make trouble for
his family if he hung around."

"What about you?" Cory asked.

"I'll stay clear of them, don't worry!" Tim
dropped his pretense of jauntiness and sat glumly
on a bench. "I'm going to miss Johnny and Sondra.
They were about the only interesting people around
here, unless you're into surfing or tourists. Oh,

well!'' He shrugged. ''What are you going to do? I suppose you can't take over the gift shop?''

Cory shook her head.

''What will you do, then?''

She groaned. ''Go back to New Jersey. In the middle of the winter.''

Tim gave her a sidewise look but said nothing. Cory sat in gloomy contemplation of the cold weather awaiting her.

''Cory—'' Tim recalled her attention. ''Listen, why don't you move in with me? We—we could even get married if you wanted to.''

Cory stared at him, stunned by the sheer insanity of the proposal.

''You'd have a place to live,'' he said hurriedly. ''And if you really worked on your sketches, you could probably sell them. You wouldn't have to be dependent on me, if that would bother you. We could have a real wild time—''

''Smoking pot in the evenings, I suppose,'' Cory said with sarcasm.

Tim thought she meant it. ''Sure, if you wanted to. We'd have to buy it, though. I'm through getting it the hard way. Maybe your friend Bower would supply us.''

Ignoring the rest of his words, Cory fastened on his final remark. Tim really believed Buck dealt in marijuana. Wouldn't Tim know, if anyone did?

''Hey, I think it would be neat to have you around all the time, Cory Wells,'' he urged. He laid his hand on the back of her neck and pulled her closer, gazing at her with interest. ''Don't you want to get married? We wouldn't need any swinging friends then. You and I could entertain each other. My salary could support two people."

A picture of a married Corinne Wells—Corinne Cooper—flashed into Cory's mind. She saw herself coming out of the supermarket pushing a grocery cart, looking up to watch Buck's car flash by, her heart dead inside her to realize she had put herself out of the reach forever of the man she truly loved. The picture had a nightmarish quality. She shuddered. She wasn't prepared to pay that price to stay on Kauai.

"Well?" Tim demanded.

"I couldn't, Tim."

"Why not?"

"I don't love you. Besides, you only just thought of the idea yourself. It would be crazy and you know it."

"No, I don't!" Tim said stubbornly. "It's a good idea. You're just chicken."

Cory laughed. "I guess I am!" But she felt a great relief. How could she think of marrying anyone but Buck?

"Look," Tim was saying, "you don't have to decide right away. Think it over. The offer will still be open."

"Will it? Thank you, Tim." She stood up. The dull heartache was still there. "I've got to get back," she said. The truth was, she was too upset to stay long in one place. Movement seemed to ease the heavy pain.

"I'll drop you off at Hazel's."

"No, thanks. I need to walk."

THAT EVENING HAZEL RETURNED from her first day back at work before Buck came to pick up Cory.

"I'm tired," Hazel admitted, "but I enjoyed it, and everyone welcomed me. Even some of the patrons had missed me. Did you hear from Sondra?"

In a steady voice Cory told her that Sondra's shop was closed, and she repeated what Tim and Buck had said. She did not, naturally, mention Tim's preposterous proposal. She wished she knew what to think about Buck. Was she totally wrong in believing he was growing *pakalolo*? She hated to think she was such a poor judge of people, but the evidence indicated otherwise. First Paul, then Tim, Johnny, Sondra.... Must Buck be added to the list?

"Hazel," she said slowly. "Do you think it's possible that Buck is growing marijuana?"

Hazel registered surprise, and then her gray eyes began to twinkle.

"Did you accuse him of it?"

Looking self-conscious, Cory nodded.

"When?"

"When he accused *me* of knowing what Tim planned to do up in the mountains."

"No wonder he hasn't been around!" Hazel said pointedly. "He must have been livid. Haven't you realized the Bowers consider themselves to be the island's aristocracy? They feel they have a tradition to uphold."

Cory looked a little ashamed. "I know Irene and Mae do, and Lester, but there's a gap of two generations between them and Buck."

"But they raised him. Don't think he doesn't

have the family pride. Besides, he's got plenty of money. Why ever should he dabble in anything crooked?''

Cory shrugged uncomfortably. ''Tim said Buck was growing *pakalolo* in the cane fields—''

''Never! His workers may grow it. I can't say as to that.''

''Tim claims that's why Buck chased him and Johnny out. Those growers up on the mountain seemed to know him.''

Hazel frowned. ''Very likely. They probably went to school together. However, you can believe me when I say Buck wouldn't dirty his hands. My goodness, he has a legitimate business to run. Sugarcane is still the number one crop. Buck's got all he can do to handle the mill.''

Cory drew a deep breath of relief. She could leave Kauai with her vision of Buck unimpaired.

Impulsively she kissed Hazel's cheek. ''Thank you!''

''So he's taking you to dinner,'' Hazel mused. ''What do you make of that?''

''Nothing,'' Cory said flatly. She had told herself that Buck felt guilty about turning from her to Emma, and maybe he felt sorry for her because the gift shop had collapsed. She didn't intend to look deeper. No doubt if he had some other motive, he'd tell her.

In her bedroom she put on the new white dress. After all, Buck had scarcely seen it on New Year's Eve.

When she opened the living-room door to his

knock half an hour later he held out a lei of deep red carnations. Hazel exclaimed at how stunning the red looked with the white dress, giving Cory a moment to recover from the kisses that accompanied the lei.

Tonight she had been offered one last evening with Buck. The knowledge heightened her response to his touch. The room tilted, then righted itself. She heard Hazel saying something like "Too bad Cory's insisting on leaving us," and Buck's noncommittal reply.

"That's a new dress," he stated as they left. "I like it."

Cory expanded under his words like an evening primrose opening at sundown. It was part of his charm to notice a woman's appearance. No doubt he remembered Emma's clothes, too. Where was Emma tonight—out with someone else? Would Buck talk about her?

"Where are we going?" Cory asked to break a silence that had gone on too long.

"To the hotel." He slanted a look at her from under black-fringed eyelashes. She pretended not to notice. What game was he playing? Did he want Emma to see them together?

"Have you eaten there?" he asked.

"No." She fingered her lei nervously.

"The food is good. Lester's chef is something to write home about."

"Which the chef at a hotel for tourists particularly should be," she quipped, "to give them something to put on their postcards."

What was making her so jittery? The answer was simple: she didn't know what Buck had in mind. Was he taking her out to prove something to Emma? To himself? In a secret corner of her mind she held a mad hope. Maybe he planned to offer her an answer to her problem. What if he offered to invest in the gift shop and hire her to run it? Would she agree? Yes, a hundred times!

They entered the hotel, her confidence rising. She knew she looked her best. What if he *had* squired dozens of females through this lobby? She had been the lucky woman ever since they met...until Emma. Cory's sense of well-being fizzled out as she wondered again why he wasn't with Emma tonight.

Instead of steering her into the dining-room, Buck led her through the crowded lobby to the elevator.

"Where are we going?" she asked.

"Upstairs." He grinned confidently and ushered her into the elevator. "You can't leave Kauai without seeing the Bower family suite."

"Why can't I?" she asked suspiciously, relieved at the same time to hear him refer to a suite, not just a bedroom.

"For one thing, we'll have a fine view of the sunset, and for another—" the elevator stopped, the door opened, and he ushered her out "—I've ordered dinner served up here."

Cory hardly heard him. She was enthralled by the apartment, the moss green carpet, the white couches and wicker chairs. Bouquets of fresh flowers gave it a lived-in appearance, and glass doors opened onto a lanai, which opened, it appeared, onto the world. The hotel was only a few stories high, and this was obviously the penthouse. She crossed the thick green carpet to stand at the lanai railing, absorbing the scene.

"This island is so incredibly beautiful!" she exclaimed. "Doesn't it tear your heart?"

"Only when I've been away for a long time," Buck replied seriously, coming to stand at her side.

"Just look at that water," Cory commanded, "the way it goes from pale green to deepest blue, and the incredible majesty of the white breakers, advancing one behind the other. You know they've been doing that for millions of years, yet one wants to believe they were put here for us—for human beings. The ocean itself seems like something living."

Buck turned away from the view. "What would you like to drink?" he asked, bringing her back to earth.

"White wine, please." She recalled his words as they had left the elevator. "Did you say we're going to eat here?"

"Yes. One of the waiters is bringing it up. I ordered coquilles St. Jacques; I hope you like scallops."

"Yes, I do. But—" Where was Emma tonight? Cory could find no way to ask the question with indifference.

Buck said, "I want you to know I don't make a habit of bringing women up here, but I wanted you to myself this evening. Let's have a drink and watch the sunset."

The lanai wrapped around three sides of the apartment. One could step out onto it from the two bedrooms as well as from the living room.

"It's a gorgeous place," Cory said. "Why doesn't Lester live here?"

"He prefers the family life at the house."

After their tour of the apartment, Buck led her back to the lanai to watch the sunset. They sat in wicker chairs with a table between them. *Like strangers sharing a hotel balcony,* Cory thought. She waited for him to disclose his reason for asking her here.

Their dinner arrived on a tea cart, and the waiter served it by the light of flickering candles, protected from the moving air by glass chimneys.

"What a heavenly place!" Cory sighed.

"This suite?" Buck laughed. "I wouldn't go so far as to say that."

"I meant...oh, I don't know...everything. The fact that there are no bugs, so you don't need screens. The—" She took a deep breath "—the whole island is a paradise. You know it!" She glanced at the waiter, who was looking pleased.

Buck shrugged. "One gets used to it."

She couldn't keep up this pretense; she had to ask. "Tell me something," she blurted. "Where's Emma tonight?"

Buck cocked a black eyebrow. "How should I know?"

He knew the question had meant far more than the mere physical location of Emma. Cory was asking for reassurance, for some explanation of Buck's invitation. She supposed he must be waiting until they were alone.

She drew a deep breath and pain smote her. To be dining here, just the two of them in their own suite, padding around barefoot...a honeymoon would be like this. She brushed the thought away and tried to memorize bits of him. His brown fingers handling the silverware, the gold signet ring on his left hand, his strong masculine wrists sprinkled with dark hair, the shine of his blue eyes in the candlelight. He was giving her another memory to add to her store. They talked about inconsequential things until the waiter cleared the table and departed.

"Come into the living room," Buck coaxed. He poured brandy into two snifters and set them on the glass-topped wicker chest that served as a coffee table. Then he lounged against the fat cushions of the couch and invited Cory to do likewise.

Instead she perched on the edge.

"Sit back," he urged. "Relax."

He reached for her shoulders. She let him pull her back against his chest. She could feel his heart beating steadily against her shoulder blades. Could he feel hers thumping with distrust? Keeping one arm around her he leisurely sipped his brandy.

"There's no need to rush it," he murmured, his lips against her hair.

"Rush what?"

"The evening. Tell me what you thought of the fireworks. Why did you and Hazel leave so early? I looked around and you were gone."

"Hazel didn't want to be too tired on her first day back at work."

"She had all New Year's Day to rest."

Cory agreed indifferently. She was allowing herself to experience what it would be like if she and Buck lived here. He would come home after a day at the sugar mill. She would have cooked the dinner they had just eaten. They would be relaxing, as now, talking, and presently they would go into the large elegant bedroom. While Buck showered she would undress before the wall of mirrors and put on a white lacy nightgown....

"I said, *you* didn't have to leave." Buck set down his brandy and smoothed her hair back from her neck. She felt his cool lips against her skin, tried to suppress a shiver of delight and failed.

"You seemed pretty busy with Emma," she told him.

"Were you jealous?" he asked, suddenly turning her to face him. "I believe you were! Cool Cory Wells was jealous!"

"Maybe." She tossed her head. "Or maybe I had other plans for New Year's Day."

He looked so shaken out of his arrogance that she almost laughed. At least, she congratulated herself, he didn't know that she loved him, that she had lowered all the barriers to her heart, regardless of consequences.

He swallowed the last of his brandy, took her glass from her unresisting fingers and set it on the coffee table.

She felt suddenly breathless, wondering what was

going to happen next. She should be making up her mind what she would allow to happen, but her body was betraying her. She quivered at his touch. Her sensitive skin seemed to be awaiting his fingers, his lips. Her body, cuddled under his arm, would refuse to obey any orders given it by her brain. It... she... wanted to stay right where she was, pressed against him.

"Darling Cory," he whispered, smoothing her hair back from her brow and kissing her temples. "I want to tell you something I learned about Emma in a very short time."

"What?" She turned suddenly rigid and pulled herself out of his arms.

"I learned in the space of a day and a night—a day and an evening, I should say—"

Cory suspected that 'night' was the correct word, but she let it go.

"I learned—" Buck said, kissing the corners of her mouth "—that she made a very poor substitute for you. What she and I had—if anything—ended a long time ago. Believe me! I learned I want you. I want you to stay."

He recaptured her and his lips descended on hers. He kissed her forcefully, as if to put his stamp on her mouth, but gradually the pressure eased. A fierce joy began to burn inside her. He wanted her! She had the power to affect him. Yet he hadn't said he loved her. When his kisses ceased, her curling dark lashes fluttered and she opened her eyes to find him looking at her intently.

"What are you thinking?" he demanded. "How

can you look so serene when all the while you're sitting there tearing my insides out?''

Her brown eyes widened. "What on earth do you mean?''

"I mean I want to lock us both in here and make love to you till the hotel falls down! How about if *I* hold you hostage?''

"Please, don't mention that! You were so angry.''

"Reaction. You gave me such a scare.''

He gathered her to him with a groan. Cradling her head in his arm against the back of the couch, he traced the inner line of her lips with the tip of his tongue until she writhed with the exquisite excitement of his touch.

"Beautiful, beautiful,'' he murmured, and she gave herself up to the total enjoyment of his lovemaking.

"How would you like it if I just stayed here and kissed you all night?'' he asked. "I could begin with the tips of your little pointed ears and keep going down one side to the tips of your toes.'' His fingertip played a tattoo over her left breast and along her hip. "And then back up and across and down the other side to the other toes, then up to this other pointed ear.''

"My ears aren't pointed,'' she sparkled, responding to his teasing while the promise of such kisses sent the blood racing hotly through her veins.

"You'd have to be undressed, of course,'' he added before peppering her neck and face with expert, warm kisses that made it easy to imagine what his lips would feel like on every part of her body.

She ached for him to do what he was promising. He slid an arm under her knees, turning her and raising her legs onto the couch. His other arm around her shoulders pulled her down with him as he stretched beside her. She lay breathing shallowly, totally helpless in his hands, not caring even whether the sun rose. Only tonight and Buck existed. And yet, some part of her brain reminded her he hadn't made any commitment, any offer.

His tongue trailed fire along her collarbone and she longed to slide out of her dress and stand naked in front of him...in a bedroom of their own. He would bury his face between her breasts and she would run her fingers lovingly over his brawny tanned shoulders and curve her hand around his strong-muscled neck.

Muttering an imprecation against back zippers, he raised her arms and undressed her like a doll.

"How do you know Lester won't come up here?" she protested.

"I locked the door."

He bared her quivering nipples and covered them with his warm rough palms. She felt faint with joy, with delight in the sensuality of the movement. Her fingertips were numb. All the blood seemed to have left her brain to flood to the parts of her body where she desired his touch. He could have taken her there—on the couch, on the floor, on the ceiling.

"Oh, Cory, I want you!" His voice was urgent and husky, his eyes a blue flame burning into hers. "Let's go into the bedroom...."

She struggled to sit up. "No—please." She reached for the brandy snifter, gulped a swallow and waited while the fiery liquid burned all the way down.

Buck watched her, his eyes angry. "You're a real tease, aren't you?"

"No, I'm not! But I'm not a one-night stand, either." Her voice rose on a note of hysteria as she furiously pulled her clothes back on. "I'm going back to New Jersey. We'll never see each other again."

Buck's eyes lost their angry blaze, his face became impassive.

"I have a suggestion," he said coolly. "How would you like to share an apartment with me? One just like this on the other side of the elevators?"

Cory gazed at him, her mind blank. "You mean...live with you?" she stammered.

"I'm not proposing marriage," he said sardonically.

She studied his handsome face as if it had been a sculpture. He stared back at her without blinking.

"You really don't know me at all, do you?" she said at last.

"I think it's a damned good offer," he barked. "If you're not too old-fashioned—"

"Oh, is it!" she cried, suddenly finding a safe outlet for her pent-up passion. "A damn good offer—to be the 'roommate' of the great Buchanan Bower. No, not a roommate, because roommates share the rent. 'Kept woman,' or is that too old-fashioned for you?" She jumped to her feet and stormed around the room, collecting her purse, picking up the carnation lei then flinging it down again. Buck watched her, his eyes hard.

"I wouldn't marry any woman I hadn't lived with," he said brutally. "I thought if you wanted to stay here so bad—"

"That I'd jump at anything? Well, thank you very much! If I was that desperate I'd take Tim's offer. He at least proposed marriage!"

Buck scowled. "Congratulations!"

"Oh, shut up! I'm not marrying him, and I'm certainly not going to be your mistress!" Her overwrought emotions gave way in a burst of tears.

Buck got to his feet and would have taken her in his arms but she fought him off.

"Take me home!" she demanded, searching for her shoes through tear-blinded eyes.

What an arrogant bastard he was! She clamped her teeth against her full lower lip to keep it from trembling.

They drove to the entire distance without speaking. At the condominium Cory flung herself out of the car and up the steps to Hazel's door without saying good-night, without saying goodbye.

CORY WOKE TO GRAY SKIES and rain, warm rain that made no change in the temperature, but effectively lowered her already damp spirits. Her chest swelled with misery when she remembered how she had turned Buck down in no uncertain terms. Maybe she shouldn't have been so self-righteous. Insisting on marriage first did seem rather old-fashioned, but when she thought about it, she knew she was old-fashioned. If she simply moved in with him, she would have to live with the knowledge that he didn't love her enough to commit himself, and might desert her any minute. Marriage was risky enough without multiplying the possibilities for trouble. Even if she eventually found a job, her share of the rent on an apartment like that would take everything she earned. No, it was better to return to New Jersey.

In the kitchen she poured herself a cup of coffee and brought it back to her bedroom to wait until Hazel left for work. She couldn't bear to face the older woman's kindly arguments urging her to stay.

When Hazel had gone, Cory telephoned the airline and made a reservation for the following day.

For an hour she lay on the couch, numb with pain. At last she realized the world hadn't come to an end. No matter that her heart was dead, she still had to move her physical body from Kauai to New Jersey. She went to her bedroom and began to pack.

At noon the mailman brought a postcard from Sondra. "Dear Cory," it read. "As you can see, we've split. Don't be disappointed. The shop wasn't making any money. Hope Buck rescued you all right. Lucky girl!" The picture on the card showed the Los Angeles skyline. There was no return address.

CHAPTER EIGHTEEN

NEW JERSEY IN JANUARY was unbearably cold and dreary. A few inches of new snow fell and almost immediately turned dirty and slushy. Cory went about the business of taking up her old life with a heavy heart. She hated everything—her old job, the heavy traffic, the noise, the ugliness.

"You've changed," Ann told her disapprovingly.

"I have," Cory agreed, adding with a forced smile, "but so have you! With your new executive position and plans for getting married. What's a bigger change than marriage?"

"Thanks to you!" Ann bubbled. "If you hadn't gone to Hawaii for me, I'd still be the low woman on the totem pole. And if I'd been in Hawaii, Dave couldn't have proposed, could he?"

Cory shook her head. She was glad to think she'd accomplished something in return for her broken heart.

One bitterly cold evening she ran into Paul in the parking lot of the supermarket. He was alone, not that she would have cared if she'd met him with his girl friend, she realized with vague surprise. He asked how she liked Hawaii; she told him she loved it.

"You should have stayed," he smirked.

"I'll be going back," she said.

"I'll have to work fast then." He grinned. "How about going out to dinner Saturday night?" he asked with aggravating confidence.

She replied with satisfying bluntness. "No."

Arriving home she took wicked delight in telephoning Ann to gloat.

"You told him you were going back?" Ann echoed.

"I believe I am," Cory answered slowly. "I spoke without thinking, but I guess I spoke from the heart. I do want to go back."

She hung up the telephone feeling the first spurt of interest in life that she had since she boarded the plane on Kauai. If she saved money like mad and perhaps asked for some overtime work at the bank, what was to stop her from returning to Kauai and opening her own gift shop? No, not Kauai...not where she would see Buck day after day and go on aching for him. One of the other islands...perhaps Maui. And while she was working and saving, she could take a course in running a small business.

She went to bed that night feeling almost happy. At least now she had an aim instead of drifting in a river of misery.

The weeks crept by...a time of going to work in the gray dawn and coming home after dark. But each week she had the satisfaction of making a hefty deposit in her savings account, and her business course at the local college turned out to be surprisingly interesting.

One evening she came home to find a letter from Hazel. Buck's name sprang out at her, and she read that paragraph first:

Irene says Buck is working harder than ever. Their hopes for Julia Vagos have fallen flat. I hear she's going back to the mainland. I believe I wrote you last time that Emma L. didn't stay long, either. Looks like Buck will be an old bachelor like Lester.

Your plan to open your gift shop sounds admirable, but I'm sorry you're thinking of Maui. Perhaps you'll change your mind.

Cory tossed the letter aside. Didn't Hazel realize why she had chosen Maui?

She had been hungry when she walked in the door, but Hazel's letter had turned that sensation into a burning ache. Paradise lost.

Cory sat at the kitchen table biting her lip and painfully contemplating how life continued regardless of one person's misery. She wondered if Buck was also thanking his stars that Cory hadn't taken up his proposition to live at the hotel. For once it was nice to know she had done the right thing. The knowledge made her so happy that she flung herself on her bed and cried bitterly for half an hour.

When she rose to wash her face and find something to eat, she had crossed some kind of time zone. She would never stop loving Buck; her emotions, her loyalties ran too deep. But clearly the time had come to try to forget him if she was ever to be happy again.

The next day she applied for, and got, a job as evening cashier at a local restaurant. It didn't pay much, but it was all extra cash and her dinner was free. Best of all, it filled up her evenings.

She worked out how many months it would take at the rate she was going to save enough money. Thanks to her business course, she had a pretty good idea how much cash one needed to finance a small enterprise. She hung one of the bank's calendars on the wall and began crossing off the days, like a prisoner.

A short while later she arrived home from the bank—the only night she didn't work at the restaurant—and was opening the refrigerator when the buzzer for the downstairs door sounded. She buzzed back. Some tenant had forgotten his key or had his hands full. She turned back to the refrigerator, forgetting that someone might actually be on the way up to her apartment until her doorbell suddenly sounded.

"Who is it?" she called.

"Cory?" The masculine voice froze her in her tracks. "It's Buck Bower."

"Buck?" She tore open the door, hardly believing her ears. Her heart thumping in her throat, she stared at him. He was wearing a gray suit, a necktie, black shoes and an overcoat. He was holding a paper cone that could only contain flowers.

"How about letting me in before I freeze to death?" he suggested.

"Of course!" Cory cried. Her joy at seeing him was shooting up like mercury in a thermometer.

"C-come in," she stammered, her round brown eyes scarcely taking in the sight.

He stepped into the living room and thrust the flowers into her hand.

"Here, take these damn things before they freeze. Do you have anything to drink in this house?"

"Yes—yes! Take your coat off. Sit down." Luckily the polite phrases came to her lips. She was too stunned, too overcome with delight to think.

"Not till I get warm, thanks." He shivered. "By God, they ought to have Saint Bernard dogs roaming the streets with little kegs of brandy."

She laughed out loud at that, remembering how hard it had been for her to adjust to the cold. She devoured him with her eyes, in her mind nothing but amazement that he was here, standing in front of her.

"I'm not a ghost, you know," he said with a funny half smile. "Here—to prove it I'll take off my overcoat. Oh, Cory, Cory, I've missed you!" He dropped his coat on the couch. She felt her face harden as he opened his arms and moved toward her. She realized she was still holding the flowers.

"Sit down. I'll put these in water and make you a drink." Her voice sounded high-pitched and flustered.

He stood in the kitchen doorway and watched her unwrap the flowers—red carnations. Their scent brought back that last night on Kauai, and fear suddenly overrode her excitement. Why had he come here just when she had begun to make a life for herself?

"You were lucky to find me at home," she babbled. "I—I have a class on Wednesday nights."

"What time?"

"It doesn't matter. I can skip it once...if you can stay awhile?" she added formally.

"I thought we might go out to dinner. I have a rented car downstairs."

Her hands trembled as she wrested ice from the trays, but somehow she got their drinks together—glasses, ice, Scotch.

He stopped her before she added water to his, saying, "Never mind, I'll take it neat."

She handed him his glass and they moved into the living room.

"Here's to you, Cory!" he toasted her. "Happy days...and warm weather!"

She laughed a little wildly and watched him sink back on the sofa with a mutter of satisfaction. She took a gulp of Scotch to steady her nerves and perched at the other end.

"So tell me what you're doing here," she said, unable to hide her happiness at the sight of him. "I had some business in Washington," he replied offhandedly. "To do with sugar support prices, you know." He gave a strange half laugh. "New Jersey didn't seem that much out of my way."

"Did you succeed in Washington?"

"What?" He was looking her over intently. "Oh, yes! That is, I hope so. I had a good talk with our senators."

He asked what she had been doing and she told him the bank had welcomed her back. He didn't ask what her class was about and she didn't tell him. She asked about his family. The elder Bowers were going on as usual and Paco was enjoying high school in Honolulu.

Despite Cory's careful emphasis on the people they knew, the conversation didn't go smoothly. Buck didn't seem to pay attention to what he was saying. Most of the time he stared fixedly at his drink, glancing up only now and then, sometimes with a look of such burning intensity that after he had withdrawn his gaze Cory thought she must have been mistaken.

While he studied his drink she feasted her eyes on him. His long brown hands fingered the glass. She recalled their touch on her skin and her flesh tingled. Her eyes flew elsewhere, then returned after a moment. His thick black hair was neatly combed instead of hanging in unruly locks across his forehead. She remembered the look of it plastered to his head as he rode the waves on his surfboard. How impossibly far away and long ago! The memory clutched at her throat.

He looked incredibly handsome in his gray suit, the shirt collar strikingly white against his tan, but at the same time he looked too covered up. She undressed him in her mind, picturing his hard brown thighs and muscular arms, the way the hair grew in whorls on his flat brown stomach, the strong, graceful arch of his feet, and most tantalizing of all, the seductive curve of his back, the fluid movement of his hips as he crossed the sand.

With a start she realized a silence had fallen. At the same time Buck looked up and their eyes collided.

"Cory! My God, I didn't come all this way to give you the local gossip!" He gathered her into his arms before she had time to protest. She saw his lips inches from her eyes and knew that when he kissed her she was going to cling to him, knew that whatever he asked of her she was going to give.

His kiss was more tender and loving than she remembered, perhaps because she had never expected to be kissed by him again. She willed it to go on and on. Too soon he drew a short sharp breath and raised his head.

"You want to know why I really came all this way? It was to tell you I love you!"

She pulled back a little to look at him wonderingly, her brown eyes soft with love for him. Speechless with amazement she pulled herself against him. The joy that already filled her somehow expanded.

He nudged her. "Say something!"

She shook her head. Crazily her eyes filled with tears. Roughened fingertips tilted her chin. His features swam in a blur.

"Don't cry!" he exclaimed, jolted.

"I'm just so happy to see you!" Sniffing, she flung herself against him.

Again his arms encircled her. Their hearts thudded in unison. He kissed her again. Her arms around his neck held him tightly. She hated the thick layers of clothing between them—his suit jacket, her wool sweater over a turtleneck pullover.

Apparently he did, too, because he said, his blue eyes sparkling, "Let me take off my coat. I'm warm enough now."

"Oh, Buck," she whispered, kissing him to her heart's content.

By unspoken agreement they paused to talk. Suddenly they had much to catch up on. Everything that had happened on Kauai in the past seven weeks became important to Cory.

"Hazel wrote me that your old girl friend didn't stay long," she challenged.

Buck's eyes laughed into hers. "So you've kept up with the gossip!"

"I'm sure I'm a little behind," Cory countered. "Hazel seems to think you're turning into a monk, which I find hard to believe."

"It's true." Buck's voice deepened. "I've lost interest in playing around. Cory, you remember when I first met you, how you reminded me of Emma?"

How well Cory remembered!

"Well, after you left I set out to forget you. I'm sorry, darling, but I've been a carefree bachelor, and the more I thought of what I'd have to do to get you—marry you—the more determined I was not to get caught. Emma was still around. She stayed for two weeks. Every time I saw her, my heart almost jumped out of my throat. I kept thinking you'd come back. When I finally got used to being disappointed, I still found myself thinking, Cory looks like that, but she's prettier...or, Cory wouldn't talk like that...she's sweet and gentle." He looked deep into Cory's eyes. "What an angel you are!

You will marry me, won't you . . . after I've come all this way?''

Marry him! The words exploded in her head like a shower of multicolored rockets while her mind fastened on a quite irrelevant phrase.

"You came all this way! You said you came about sugar subsidies!"

"I can talk to our senators when they're home in Hawaii, for Pete's sake!"

It took a second for his words to make sense, and then she wasn't completely sure. "You mean—" she faltered "—you mean you really came here . . . in February . . . for me?" She took a deep breath to make room in her heart for unbelievable happiness.

"It had to be February," Buck said seriously. "We start processing cane in March."

She laughed. "It wasn't eagerness then that made you brave the snow!"

"You think not? I'll show you how eager I am!" He crushed her against him and kissed her till she was breathless, until her fingers tingled. When at last he raised his head, he cupped her face in his hands.

"Say yes, Corinne Wells!"

"Yes, oh, yes," she whispered, and the thought came that she would be going home. "Oh, there's so much more I want to hear about," she told him.

"All right, let's sit and talk for a while," Buck agreed, cuddling her against his shoulder.

How comforting it was to think that Buck wanted her friendship, her companionship, as well as her passion. For the present it was heartwarming and satisfying to hold him and be held by him, to devour him with her eyes, to feel his solid flesh beneath her fingertips, to know pure happiness.

Between kisses Cory learned that nothing had been heard of Sondra and Johnny. Uncle Lester planned to sell the small amount of stock left in the shop to the next renter, if one turned up. Tim had asked the school board for a transfer to one of the other islands.

"Why did Emma come back to Kauai?" Cory probed. "You said once she hated it."

"For a vacation, I guess," Buck replied evasively. He looked so embarrassed that Cory knew her assumption had been correct. Emma Lassiter had come back to marry Buck. Instead, in a roundabout way, she had sent him to Cory. Cory felt grateful, but Emma wouldn't appreciate that. She decided to forget Emma Lassiter. When she returned to Kauai, she would look like no one but herself—Corinne Wells. No! Corinne Bower.

The next time she looked at her watch it was ten o'clock.

"We forgot to eat!" she exclaimed.

"So we did."

They both knew without anything being said that Buck was not going to leave Cory's apartment that night.

"I'll make Cheddar cheese omelets," she offered, and remembered a bottle of wine in the cupboard.

They dined by candlelight and then they carried the candles into the bedroom. Cory blessed her luck. The room was warmer than usual.

By candlelight they undressed each other, laughing a little despite the banked fires of their passion, at the amount of clothing they were wearing.

"And I thought muumuus were bad!" Buck exclaimed.

They stood facing each other, tantalizing each other until, as in a dream, Buck reached out to cup her shoulders and plant kisses on each.

"Prettiest shoulders in the world," he crooned.

Slowly he slid her bra straps down over her arms, baring her round, pink-tipped breasts.

"Beautiful," he whispered. Cupping them in his hands, he buried his brown face in the white valley between them, his warm breath searing her skin.

Cory stroked the thick springing hair that was so like his personality: stubborn, going its own way, yet under control.

"I've wanted to kiss you all over ever since I carried you out of the water that day," he muttered.

Shyly she let him slide off her lace panties. She made no protest as he bestowed hot kisses all up and down her body, arousing her to a pitch that became frightening, yet she wanted more and more. He let her go only when she reached such an exquisite height of pleasure that she could no longer passively endure his tantalizing touch. Through eyes glazed with desire she watched him slide out of his briefs, their whiteness against his hard brown thighs a contrast that made her exclaim lovingly and reach out to touch him. Pride flared within her at the sight of him standing by her bed, male and splendid. He posed for a moment, unabashedly displaying his perfect body and male prowess with primeval arrogance, and then spoiled the picture by shivering and diving beneath the blankets with a laugh.

"Come in here!" he cried, holding open the covers like a cave and dispelling any momentary awkwardness by making her laugh.

There was something so infinitely cozy and natural about being in a comfortable, warm double bed with Buck that she could not regret the faraway sunny sands of Kauai. The time would come to enjoy them, too, but for tonight...they cuddled beneath the bedclothes. For a while they enjoyed the infinite luxury of caressing, of running exploring fingertips over each other's bare skin.

"Oh! You feel so good!" Cory whispered.

Buck pulled her tighter against him. "I'm finally warm for the first time since I left Hawaii. And for the first time since *you* left Hawaii I feel like I'm all together again."

"Did you really miss me?" she inquired unguardedly.

"Every minute."

His mouth found hers and he rose on one elbow to hold her close against his chest. She thrilled in returning a kiss with nothing held back. When he flung his leg across her hip, she reveled in the weight of it, the way the crisp hair tickled the silky skin at the backs of her thighs.

In the dark breathlessness of their cave, he kissed her quivering nipples again and again and felt his way to the secret parts of her body like an explorer hunting for hidden treasure.

"I love you, Buck!" The words were wrenched from her.

Their movements became like the waves of the sea, surging, retreating, surging.

"I love you!" he cried just before the final wave exploded and rolled over them, leaving them gasping in its wake.

"Oh, baby!" Buck collapsed and pulled her against him. "Oh, my love."

Later, as they lay entwined, Buck gave a contented sigh.

"I hope you're prepared to come back to Kauai with me in a day or two," he said tentatively, "because I'll tell you one thing, Corinne Wells: I'm not prepared to sleep alone from here on out, and this cold weather may send me into a decline."

"A day or two!" she echoed.

"The mill starts up in two weeks. If we're to have a honeymoon—"

The idea that he wanted to marry her so soon brought a new exciting dimension to their intimacy. It was heaven to lie beside him, sated with love, and make plans for the future. Security...excitement...Buck offered everything.

"We could get married here before we go," she suggested, wondering if that would give her more time to rearrange her life and dispose of her belongings.

"Impossible!" He laughed and squeezed her. "I promised Hazel and the aunts that they could arrange a wedding in the Fern Grotto," he said quietly, "unless you insisted on being married here."

"No, I— You what?" Cory tried to rise up on one elbow but he pulled her back against him. "You told them you were going to propose to me?"

"Shouldn't I have?" he asked with feigned innocence.

"What if I'd said no?"

"Then I'd have used their wedding plans as a further inducement. . . that you mustn't disappoint the old ladies."

"You were too sure of me!" Cory tried to say with mock severity, but she spoiled it by letting him hear the delight in her voice.

Buck's arm tightened around her. "I didn't think you were the kind of woman to go around doing bare-breasted hulas for every sailor on the beach," he teased. "Besides, you're indebted to me. I demand some gratitude for rescuing you."

Cory snuggled against him. "I *was* grateful. I'm afraid I didn't show it very well. I shouldn't have quarreled with you."

"I shouldn't have quarreled with you," Buck countered. "We had both gone through some pretty tense moments." He grimaced. "Don't ask why I told you I'd rescued you to keep the growers out of trouble. You surely didn't believe that? I went racing up there because you'd become the most important thing in the world to me. I was worried that those *kanakas* might scare you, and I was terrified that I'd lost you to Tim Cooper."

Wrapped in Buck's arms, Cory knew he could

feel her shake her head. "Tim? Impossible," she breathed.

"The way he tricked you into going up there certainly wasn't very heroic," Buck agreed.

"*You* were heroic," Cory said proudly. "Tim never had a chance."

"Not even when he asked you to marry him?"

"Certainly not. How could I? I was in love with you. I realized I'd fallen madly in love with you the day we went sailing to the Na Pali Coast. I don't know how it happened...I think when I watched you dance at the luau."

"The trip to Honolulu was my undoing." Buck's low-toned confession gave Cory a new thrill. "But I was so determined that we were going to carry on a light affair that I simply couldn't admit you were having a deeper effect on me."

"You were so sweet on that trip," Cory crooned. "And I was so wrong not to tell you about Paco."

"It all worked out," Buck said comfortably. "I'm glad you're on good terms with him. He'll be happy to see you."

For a while they talked halfheartedly about plans for the future, but Cory's breathing soon grew quick and shallow. She lay stiffly beside him, enjoying the exquisite torture of pretending interest in their discussion while every sensitive nerve in her body longed for his touch. How long would it take Buck to guess that she was ready to burst into flame at his first caress?

He broke off in the middle of a sentence to slide his hand down the length of her body. She knew she had lost the game of pretense and rolled against him with a muffled, eager moan.

Their loving was even better the second time. The desperation of their first passionate clutches, desperation that expressed the fear and loneliness each had suffered, had spent itself. They were relaxed, sure of themselves, sure of each other.

CHAPTER NINETEEN

ON THE WAY to the Fern Grotto the boatload of laughing, chattering wedding guests chugged slowly up the three winding miles of the Wailua River. The bride, in a haze of happiness, sat in their midst. A coronet of red and white hibiscus blossoms rested on her brow, and a long open lei of maile leaves encircled her neck. A dusting of yellow pollen from the hibiscus flowers had fallen across the lap of her white lace muumuu. The boat crew, flower bedecked, were singing to the accompaniment of ukulele and guitar.

Cory could hardly accept the fact that she was the bride; all this was happening to her. The boat overflowed with Buck's friends, soon to be hers, too. Hazel, Irene and Mae, Lester and Paco were all seated nearby, looking satisfied. Back at the stern someone had already broken out the champagne and it was being poured into champagne glasses and handed around to the accompaniment of shrieks and laughter.

This is it! Cory told herself over and over. *This is the culmination of these last few hectic days.* Hectic, but fun. Buck had made short shrift of all her problems in New Jersey. With money no object she had no reason to agonize over what to take and what to leave. Whenever a question arose, Buck said, "Take it!" Her job resignations had been accepted without recrimination, and she and Buck had skipped aboard a plane the third day after his arrival, leaving without regret a new fall of snow and a wind-chill factor of minus five Celsius. Their hearts had been warmed by a promise from Ann and Dave to come to Kauai for their upcoming honeymoon.

Buck was not making the upriver trip on the same boat today. Cory experienced a moment's supersti-tion that bad luck would somehow overtake her be-fore the wedding could be accomplished and her bliss completed. She glanced at the guests. None of them appeared to have apprehensions of disaster.

"Cory, you're looking pale," Hazel worried. "Do you feel all right? Here—" she thrust a glass of bubbling champagne into Cory's stiff fingers "—drink this and get some color in your face."

Irene was digging through her purse. "Here's my rouge. Let me put some on your cheeks, for heav-en's sake. You look scared to death."

"I'm not scared." Cory managed a tight smile. She looked around at the noisy passengers. "No one else seems to be worried about Buck, er, Buchanan. What if—" she knew her worry would sound silly, but she had to voice it "—what if his friend's boat wouldn't start?"

"He'd commandeer another one." Irene raised her voice to make herself heard over the music. "He wouldn't let a little thing like that cause him to disappoint you and all of us."

Cory's mind came out of its fog to absorb the meaning of Irene's statement, but she wanted to make sure.

"You mean you'd be disappointed, too, if he didn't marry me?"

"Disappointed? Dismayed, distraught, dis-everything! You have no idea how long we've waited and prayed for him to marry. And now—such a lovely girl as you, Cory! I couldn't be more delighted! I speak for Mae and Lester, too." They nodded confirmation.

"There's Buck!" Paco shouted at that moment.

Cory saw him at the same time. The blood rushed back to her face and her cheeks grew pink without the aid of cosmetics. She forgot about everything except the solemnity of the moment. She felt herself begin to glow with love and excitement. He was wearing white trousers and a white short-sleeved shirt that set off his marvelous golden tan and the green maile leaf lei. He looked stunningly handsome.

Was all this a dream? No, it was better and more beautiful than anything her mind could have conjured up. She had never dared to imagine herself marrying Buck. And in such idyllic surroundings!

The boat docked at the edge of a lush glade. Lester, who was to give her away, took her arm in courtly fashion and helped her ashore. She would have liked to stand and stare at Buck, but his friends were already hustling him up the fern-lined path to the grotto.

While she waited, Cory noticed the sun sparkling

lacily through the green leaves overhead. Then, with the ukulele and guitar players leading the way, Cory's entourage started along the winding path. What a joyous occasion it seemed! They rounded a bend and ahead of them, up some stony steps, Buck stood waiting under the shelving stone of the hoary cave, his white suit standing out against the inner darkness. Beside him stood the minister and best man.

Cory had eyes only for Buck, but she did catch glimpses of their surroundings, the masses of ferns hanging from the stone ceiling, a fairyland waterfall that poured from the edge of the overhead cliff.

At last Cory was allowed to go to Buck's side. In the magic grotto they took their vows. "Do you, Buchanan Bower, take this woman.... Do you, Corinne Wells, take this man...." And then Buck was kissing her, his lips cool from the cave's dampness. They stood arm in arm while two of the musicians sang the "Hawaiian Wedding Song." Amid laughter and rejoicing they trooped back to the boat.

On the return trip champagne flowed freely. Buck and Cory drank from the same glass. At the end of the short cruise the party adjourned to the Coco Palms to celebrate with an elegant wedding luncheon.

At last she and Buck slipped away. The tin cans and old shoes they found tied to the rear bumper of his jaunty sports car looked out of place.

"Your car tells the truth at one glance," Cory laughed, her brown eyes shining with affection. "Fun-loving bachelor takes the pledge."

"Never mind them, let's get out of here!" Buck urged. "I'll stop down the road and remove the junk. Believe it or not, I remembered to carry a jackknife."

The string of cans made a terrible racket. Buck pulled into the first turnoff and proceeded to deal with them. Cory stayed in the car, admiring her ring—a plain circlet of platinum. Buck had not given her an engagement ring, since there had been no engagement, but he insisted he would buy her an emerald solitaire to go with the plain ring the next time they went to Honolulu.

"Mrs. Bower," she whispered to herself.

Buck and his aunts had arranged for the newly-weds to spend their honeymoon at the hotel—in the same apartment where Buck had once offered to instal her.

"You knew what you were doing by holding out, didn't you?" he had teased when they went up to inspect it.

"I just knew I couldn't bear to be a kept woman," she had told him seriously.

"Well, you won't be now," he had said laughing. "I plan to put you to work right after the honeymoon. I'm not taking any chances of a bored wife getting into trouble."

She had thought of Emma Lassiter—she hoped for the last time. Buck had learned a lesson from Emma's behavior.

"Doing what?" Cory had asked.

"Ah!" He had grinned. "That's still a secret. If I told you, you might not marry me."

She had laughed and flown into his arms.

Their suitcases were already at the hotel. They planned to make it their headquarters, but a few days were to be spent sailing along the Na Pali Coast, introducing Cory to the rudiments of boat handling.

Buck pulled into the hotel's parking lot. Instead of going directly to their suite, as she had thought they would, he led her toward the mall.

"Let's walk through here," he suggested. "Let me show you off a bit."

From across the mall Cory glimpsed the empty windows of Sondra's gift shop, still bravely bearing its name: Treasure-Trove. She glanced at it wistfully and then pulled Buck to a halt.

"Look! It's got a sign in the window! Opening April First. I wonder who?" Though she had no cause to feel regretful on this of all days, she meant to have no secrets from Buck. "I wish it could have been me!" she told him.

He led her closer, as though he, too, wanted to look at the smaller sign underneath. As they approached Cory read in neat, half-inch letters: UNDER NEW MANAGEMENT, Corinne Wells Bower.

She stared and whirled around toward Buck, her mouth a pink O of excitement. Her brown eyes searched his face unbelievingly, laughter beginning to bubble from her lips at the wonderful surprise.

"Did you do this?"

Buck's face appeared studiously blank.

"You must have!" She stared at him with shining eyes. The look he returned was solemn.

"You said you were going to put me to work!" she cried. "Is this it? Is it really mine?"

Buck's blue eyes gazed around the mall. "I don't see any other Corinne Bower." He was holding his sensuous lips stiff to keep from grinning. Now when he looked back at her his eyes held a loving twinkle. "Like it? I wanted to give you a wedding present. I decided you'd like this better than anything."

"I love it! You couldn't have given me anything I'd like better!" Cory could not refrain from flinging her arms around Buck's neck and hugging him mercilessly.

He looked pleased. She thought she had never seen him look so boyishly happy.

"Come!" He took her arm with a proprietary air. "Let's go up to our bedroom and you can thank me in any way you choose. But don't start thinking about stocking your shop," he warned. "I want your undivided attention, Mrs. Bower."

"Oh, yes," she agreed.

"I do think you'll make a success of the shop, however," he said, relenting. "You have such good taste."

As they strolled back toward the hotel, Cory realized with an overflowing heart that Buck must have forgotten that she had had the bad taste to get involved with Sondra and Tim and Johnny.

"I love you," she whispered, "my husband."

"And I love you. . . my wife."

Cory looked up into his handsome, loving face and knew that she had indeed found her heart's paradise.

ABOUT THE AUTHOR

Heart's Paradise is Lucy Lee's third Super-romance. The inspiration for the tropical setting came to her while she was caring for a friend's sister in Hawaii. During the five months she lived there she fell in love with the lush islands, and it was a thrill for her to weave her impressions of their beauty into her novel.

Lucy also discovered that tropical temperatures were much more to her liking—so much more that when she left Hawaii she made the decision to leave New York and move to the warmer climes of California, where she continues to write.

HARLEQUIN
PREMIERE AUTHOR EDITIONS

6 top Harlequin authors — 6 of their best books

1. JANET DAILEY Giant of Mesabi

2. CHARLOTTE LAMB Dark Master

3. ROBERTA LEIGH Heart of the Lion

4. ANNE MATHER Legacy of the Past

5. ANNE WEALE Stowaway

6. VIOLET WINSPEAR The Burning Sands

**Harlequin is proud to offer these 6 exciting romance novels by
6 of our most popular authors. In brand-new beautifully
designed covers, each Harlequin Premiere Author Edition
is a bestselling love story—a contemporary, compelling and
passionate read to remember!**

Available wherever paperback books are sold, or through
Harlequin Reader Service. Simply complete and mail the coupon below.

Harlequin Reader Service
In the U.S.   In Canada
P.O. Box 52040   649 Ontario Street
Phoenix, Ariz., 85072-9988   Stratford, Ontario N5A 6W2

Please send me the following editions of **Harlequin Premiere Author Editions**
I am enclosing my check or money order for $1.95 for each copy ordered,
plus 75¢ to cover postage and handling.

☐ 1   ☐ 2   ☐ 3   ☐ 4   ☐ 5   ☐ 6

Number of books checked_____ @ $1.95 each = $ _____

N.Y. state and Ariz. residents add appropriate sales tax $ _____

Postage and handling $ _____ .7⁵

I enclose $_____   TOTAL $ _____
(Please send check or money order. We cannot be responsible for cash sent
through the mail.) Price subject to change without notice.

NAME_____
                        (Please Print)
ADDRESS_____ APT. NO. _____

CITY_____

STATE/PROV._____ ZIP/POSTAL CODE_____

PA-W

Offer expires June 30, 1984   31256000000

Get this book FREE!

Mail to:

Harlequin Reader Service

In the U.S.
2504 West Southern Avenue
Tempe, AZ 85282

In Canada
649 Ontario Street
Stratford, Ontario N5A 6W2

YES! I want to be one of the first to discover **Harlequin American Romance.** Send me FREE and without obligation *Twice in a Lifetime.* If you do not hear from me after I have examined my FREE book, please send me the 4 new **Harlequin American Romances** each month as soon as they come off the presses. I understand that I will be billed only $2.25 for each book (total $9.00). There are no shipping or handling charges. There is no minimum number of books that I have to purchase. In fact, I may cancel this arrangement at any time. *Twice in a Lifetime* is mine to keep as a FREE gift, even if I do not buy any additional books.

_____

Name   (please print)

_____

Address   Apt. no.

_____

City   State/Prov.   Zip/Postal Code

_____

Signature (If under 18, parent or guardian must sign.)

AR-SUB-200

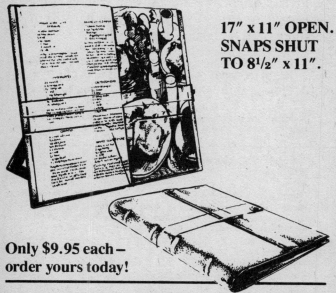

A Harlequin

ROBERTA LEIGH

Collector's Edition

A specially designed collection of six exciting love stories by one of the world's favorite romance writers—Roberta Leigh, author of more than 60 bestselling novels!

1 **Love in Store**   4 **The Savage Aristocrat**
2 **Night of Love**   5 **The Facts of Love**
3 **Flower of the Desert**   6 **Too Young to Love**

Available now wherever paperback books are sold, or available through Harlequin Reader Service. Simply complete and mail the coupon below.

Harlequin Reader Service

In the U.S.   In Canada
P.O. Box 52040   649 Ontario Street
Phoenix, AZ 85072-9988   Stratford, Ontario N5A 6W2

Please send me the following editions of the Harlequin Roberta Leigh Collector's Editions. I am enclosing my check or money order for $1.95 for each copy ordered, plus 75¢ to cover postage and handling.

☐ 1   ☐ 2   ☐ 3   ☐ 4   ☐ 5   ☐ 6

Number of books checked_____ @ $1.95 each = $_____

N.Y. state and Ariz. residents add appropriate sales tax $_____

Postage and handling $ .75

                                            TOTAL $_____

I enclose_____

(Please send check or money order. We cannot be responsible for cash sent through the mail.) Price subject to change without notice.

NAME_____
                        (Please Print)
ADDRESS_____ APT. NO._____

CITY_____

STATE/PROV._____ ZIP/POSTAL CODE_____
Offer expires June 30, 1984 ·   31256000000